SHATTERPOINT ALPHA

A NOVEL BY
LUKE TAYLOR

This is a work of imaginative fiction and features imaginatively fictitious characters, settings, and events.

ISBN 978-0-9906249-3-6

Also by Luke Taylor

Wolves and Leopards
Evening Wolves

Loeb and Cat Mysteries
The Quiet Kill

The Ageless Duel
The Muiread

Cover design by Laura Gordon

The events of this book take place approximately two months after *Evening Wolves*.

To René, who instigated this adventure

SHATTERPOINT ALPHA

ONE

Three seconds before the bone-jarring impact of the Fifteenth Street Metro, Henry Morell remembered why he had stopped taking Fifteenth Street altogether, but it was one of those days when he was later than late and nothing was going his way.

The sound of diesel fuel rushing through grimy pistons and cylinders below a morning-fogged window bored through his ears like a deep-water drill bit, and the thump of his own heartbeat cursed him for breaking one of his many rules.

He didn't want to die, a splat of peanut butter and jelly oozing from slivers of glass and crumpled steel on the evening news, and some skill of survival, carefully fabricated by the repetition of extreme training, buried way down within the simple muscle of his brain, snapped awake from the numbing repose of everyday life.

His reactions, made superlative by close calls with the US Army in Iraq and a storied stint with the Department of Homeland Security, saved him from severe neck damage as he twisted the wheel of his BMW Three Series sport coupe hard to the left.

The Metro bus squealed and shuddered through the intersection of Fifteenth and Parkway in an oblivious blitz of green and gold and the burdensome application of the brakes were an insult to the injury the Metro had dealt the rear end of the sport coupe.

Once sleek black paint sparked with metal on
metal contact and the framework it covered became
twisted and warped as the Metro bus clipped and nearly
destroyed the entire passenger side.

Morell's chosen speed of thirty five in a twenty
five didn't help his case and he clenched his jaw to
keep his hands in command of the wheel, though the
accumulative force of gravity tore at his shoulders and
lower back with a pain he wouldn't soon forget.

In that split second, the somehow relatable
images of full-sized homes being crushed and
obliterated to insignificant splinters in World War II
atomic test footage dashed across his mind and he was
powerless to stop what had befallen him, whether it was
his fault or not. It was the sheer strength of mass,
collision, and energy transfer, and the pain seizing his
body was unlike any he'd ever felt before because his
car was the bullet and the bus was the hammer of the
gun shooting him out across the street.

The path of destruction was far beyond Morell's
intrepid attempt at gaining control in the eye of
momentum's chaotic cyclone and the horror of striking
an innocent pedestrian or thoughtless bystander
swallowed him with a disorienting jacket of grief.
Landmarks of clarity were but zips of black and gray in
the blender of sight.

So Morell shut his eyes.

The car careened from the commuter lanes
toward the sidewalk with a hideous shriek, completing
a three hundred and sixty-degree turn at the popping of
the right rear tire. The eighteen inch smoked chrome
rim gnawed into the street with a storm shower of
orange-white sparks.

Morell's ultimate end came in a gash of
concrete two newspaper dispensers away from the
entrance to Capitol Station. Construction workers

shouted obscenities in scattering from the exposed water main, running for their lives. The whirlwind of German engineering hooked and tangled the plastic edge of barrier tape, dragging the ambivalently blinking safety barrels along behind like *just married* cowbells into the vein of concrete, and in doing so, scraped the exposed crown of the water main pipe in a furious slash of reckless speed.

A flashflood of cold blue liquid fizzled and splashed into the street.

Morell took stock of his body, just as he did when his Stryker vehicle had taken a thankfully ill-aimed Taliban RPG on the road to Fallujah so many years ago, and in the dull burn stiffening his body, he thought the wetness pooling at his feet was his own blood. Thankfully it was not, but it was another problem entirely, that torrent of water, and his nerves begged his muscles to act and act quickly.

Water.

God I hate water...

His eyesight was possessed by the colors of trauma, cracking and bubbling like an old Super Eight film to remind him of his near-death drowning some two months ago in the very moment when he needed to act. Unsnapping himself from the now unnecessary safety of the seatbelt was an involuntary and effortless action. Survival instincts were solar flares in his brain, short-circuiting the muscles of his body.

Go, go, go! Move it, soldier, move it!

Morell squeezed away the wash of nausea. He'd met it before, in combat, against the pneumatic repetition of machine gun fire and the sonic savagery of air-strike ordinance.

Nausea was weakness. Weakness was death.

Suck it up!

The passenger door of the coupe was crinkled

shut, sealed by the force of the collision as if it were a foil bag of corn chips. The soured scent of motor fluids floated through the claustrophobic cab and Morell squinted for some form of life beyond the jagged spider's web the windshield had become.

Hollers and calls of alarm swirled in his ears, diffused by the smacking of his brain against the wall of his own hard-headed skull, and considering what had happened to him as an Agent of Homeland Security back in November, a newly acquired fear of drowning was the only motivation he needed.

Morell shifted his weight to kick at the shattered windshield but the momentum of his first kick carried unforeseen consequences.

From its precarious angle, the BMW groaned and slid deeper in the grey slice of concrete. A sickening scrape across the glass of the driver's window, a dark and incoherent blur in Morell's thrashing, began gushing cold, metallic-tasting water all over the private security expert and the once pristine black leather interior of the sport coupe. Morell kicked and kicked, cursing with each thrust of his foot, until the window all but folded in half like a flimsy sheet of diamond fragments with a hollow plink.

Sore, disoriented, and syrup-limbed, Morell peeled himself from the recent purchase just thankful to be alive. Forty some thousand dollars of his money was, in a strange way, down the drain, but the monetary value of his own car was a lowly comparison to the mess of Fifteenth and Parkway.

He was thankful to be alive.

However, the flustered, steaming beehive of destruction jam-packed behind the brainless hulk of the green and gold Metro and the stunned passengers it carried reminded Morell, as he emerged from a foamy river of municipal water reeking of cadmium and copper, that being alive wasn't always easy, and he'd have one hell of a headache long after the day he was still late for was over.

TWO

After convincing the EMT he didn't need an icepack for his neck or any other part of his extremely fit body, despite his neck's gnawing *discomfort* and his complete inability to turn it to the left, Morell sat at an outdoor coffee shop table beyond the now soaked entrance to Capitol Station.

His face was morose, and not just because he had chosen to light a Marlboro Red and smoke it in three long drags considering his on again off again use of tobacco, but because he knew procedure and was well aware that his coming discussion with whomever was investigating the accident would completely and comprehensively ensure his firing from a job he was perfect for.

Competition in Crescent's private security market, with the slew of tech companies, fortune five-hundreds, billionaires and their arsenals of commercial properties and private estate, was something of a cutthroat business, and all of the *good* jobs, when available, were accustomed to quick hires and even quicker fires when met with any form of incompetency.

Just like the military, Morell thought as he became disgusted with himself for falling back on his cigarettes like a crutch, *it's so easy to replace you.*

He stared at the iconic pack for a few moments, wondering why he even had them in his jacket to begin with and stuffed them back in his pocket simply because there was no garbage vessel in sight.

Or so he told himself.

Morell then let his dark eyes wander across the proceedings; steam rising from his BMW as a crane gingerly lifted it from the snag of concrete, utilities men in rubber coveralls waiting to stop the hemorrhaging of the near-freezing wet, and the daze of the citizens surrounding the simple accident, still shell-shocked from the terrorist attacks of last November. After his cigarette stub flew despondently end over end to the sidewalk, Morell's breath still came in cloudy puffs considering the cloying overcast brightness of the chilly January morning in which he was supposed to be shaking hands with a woman for whom he had a great deal of respect.

Morell wished he could be holding a cup of coffee in his wait, for the warmth, at least, and his mind wandered from the woman who was about to employ him to a woman with jewel blue eyes he'd met for the first time just two months ago as his humbled gaze tried to catch the glance of anyone in a CPD uniform, hoping for the investigator to soon end the misery of his waiting. It was his meeting Sierra Marland during the Crescent Crisis that had changed his opinion of women forever, and since that meeting, and her subsequent departure into the shadows of anonymity, Morell's chronic issue of dating the opposite sex as if they were a new flavor of soda to be tried had, also, departed.

Furthermore it was as if an aggressive yet servile portion of his soul had died, and the charred remnants of the man that had risen from the frozen grave of the Targus River, as it ran parallel to the Crescent skyline, was just as much afraid of drowning in water as he was the crimson cage of his own personality and its rampant appetites. He had changed everything he could change, turned around from it all, walked the other direction and tried his hardest *not* to flinch in the face of its many flashbacks, distractions, and temptations.

And here he was, on the frostbitten dawn of a new life, smoking a cigarette because it had all gone south in the blink of an eye.

What was next?

Take it easy, Hank, it's just a car accident. Happens all the time. Your number just came up.

Just like Iraq.

You're alive, that's what matters.

Remember that.

Even though he forced his mind to accept the fact, it appeared to be far worse. Hundreds if not thousands of lives had been affected by the ripple effect of shutting down the street and who would pay for the damage? The state was forecasted to be in the critical throes of drought with a seven percent snowpack in the mountains, and Morell cursed under the white wisps of his breath. Taxpayers that had no part in it would take the hit once more, taxpayers who were already sacrificing to help clean up the aftermath of the Crisis because National disaster relief funding had fallen short.

All because he'd gassed on yellow instead of slowing and waiting for the light's change to red.

Morell stood with a bit of a wobble and corrected it quickly. His steps were tentative. He stretched to his full five feet seven and three quarters inches and knew the vexatious sensation of a needle protruding from the base of his spine would only spread till he had to get treatment.

Chuckling to himself, his thoughts were conciliatory and satirical.

You'll have plenty of time for the chiropractor now...

A flat voice interrupted his thoughts from behind.

"Something funny?"

Morell turned sharply and winced with an incapacitating spear of pain eating through his neck, shoulders and back.

The spiritless speech didn't fit the face he saw.

The woman was his height, to the centimeter, and her gray-green eyes sat unblinkingly in an angular face in a way that made her appear distant and detached, yet Morell could nearly feel the tangible nature of her intense focus because it was directed solely at him. She was a natural blonde and the odd glare of the January frost blanket, as the locals called it, a present from the northern winds, gave her a distinctly Scandinavian flair. Thoughts of such were cemented by tapered tan slacks and a form fitting purple turtleneck, the sleeves of which were scrunched up, making Morell look all the part of a desert-dweller in his gray woolen pea coat. She wore no jewelry, save the tiniest of genuine pearl earrings set in fourteen-karat gold and her only makeup was brownish-black mascara and shiny nude lip-gloss with the slightest tint of cinnamon.

"No, not at all." The former Army Sergeant said with a boyish smile that gave his cheeks dimples, even though the smile soon faded in a self-deprecating explanation. "It's just that I'm positive I'm gonna get fired from my new job, seeing as, not only can I *not* make my first day after being selected over thirteen other very qualified candidates but I've turned Fifteenth and Parkway into a warzone."

The woman's own smile was restricted to her eyes, which Morell adeptly noticed.

The rest of her face was a pleasant and attractive, albeit complexly unemotional mask.

She offered her hand for a shake. Her grip was practiced and firm. She'd been dealing with men for a while, and he knew it.

Army, maybe. Cop for sure.

"Lucy Radzewicz." She said. "Crescent PD, Precinct Three."

"Precinct Three?" Morell released her hand, noting the rhyming ring of her words. "You're a real hero, then."

She disregarded his comments for the moment and crossed her arms to view the restorative efforts.

Traffic was being diverted all the way down to Fourteenth and Brooks and one could nearly hear the curses spat over the inconveniences dealt to Crescent's white-collar army, rushing off to their digital capitalist battlegrounds up in the sky.

"It's not your fault, Mr. Morell." She said. "The driver had a blood alcohol content twice the legal limit. God knows how he even got past his supervisor this morning. No one was hurt, but I think you'll need to get a new car." She turned back to him with a smirk hidden across shiny lips, but it dissipated when she saw the pain locked in his face. "...Are you okay?"

"Yeah..." He said, stuffing his own hate of alcohol and drunk drivers further down into the bottomless hole in his psyche and then it clicked. "How'd you know my name?"

"I got down here when Officer Donovan ran your plates. *You're* the hero."

"You know about my Homeland Service during the Crisis?"

"I *am* a Lieutenant." She said, looking too young to be one.

Morell guessed she was in her mid-twenties, but could've been closer to her early thirties, not that he was very good about guessing women's ages.

It was just a number, after all.

"Forgive me if I salute you out of habit, then, Lieutenant." Morell smirked.

"I was up north during the time of the Crisis."
Lucy Radzewicz disregarded the former Army
Sergeant. "But I know you were at PierHouse. I've seen
your medical report. I know you were at the Arena.
Marvin Ross told me all about it before the shakeup,
before I got his old job at Precinct Three. Things
haven't been the same since the influx of new Officers
and leadership. They don't remember the way it was,
like you and I. We were born here. We remember."

Morell nodded as he rubbed his neck and
ascertained the cumbersome burden of her duties.
Crescent, especially Cherry and Eleventh, was still a
mess of construction and cleanup from the terrorist
attack that had downed the Pinnacle Building like a
leaning stack of cinder-block and plate glass cereal
boxes, and the general populace, having been alerted to
the gross understaffing of first responders and Law
Enforcement personnel in November's misfortunate
events, was caught in the tender limbo of a post-
traumatic state, much like the citizens of New York
City and Washington D.C. after the tragedies of
September Eleventh.

Morell tapped her on the shoulder with a friendly-
cupped hand.

"It'll be okay." He said, with warmth. "Don't take
it too hard."

Radzewicz agreed silently and nearly squinted at
him against the winter sky's bright and impermeable
coating.

"If you want I'll give you a ride, you can tell me
about the accident on the way."

The nod quickly nicking Morell's chin up and
down in acceptance was something of an autocratic
decision, seeing as a voice inside wanted to keep its
distance from pleasantly attractive blondes while
another voice most certainly did not.

Lieutenant Radzewicz owned a mid-millennium Chrysler Sebring coupe the color of gold dust and drove with the hybridized cautious, yet reckless abandonment of a cop who'd logged thousands of hours at the wheel, driving when no one else was on the road. Her accelerations up to exactly three over the speed limit were quick and Morell enjoyed the throaty growl of the sport coupe though it was a shade of what his BMW had to offer if they both took their rides to the track for a timed lap, and Morell mentally chastised himself for even thinking of doing something like that with the Lieutenant.

Thoughts had a way of presenting themselves as instant echoes, leaving him to deal with the consequences of whatever was left to reverberate around the canyon walls of his mind, and Morell had been reading psychology books to immediately dismiss the images associated with certain perfumes, hairstyles, gaits of walking, and the sound a black three-inch pump made on ceramic tile as it drew near.

Not that those books helped, much.

Sometimes, he felt like a vegetarian in a steakhouse, and other times, just miserably uncomfortable with his new way of life.

Morell's eyes were firm on the window, seeing as his neck still wouldn't let him look to the left, and he scowled as they slipped by the colorful trickle of human beings stressed and obsessed with the latest fads.

Lucy's thickly ring of keys rattled with a musical timbre against the steering column.

"So how much do you know about me?" Morell asked.

"Not as much as I'd like to, seeing as you're sitting on the answers to many of my questions surrounding November." She said, with the disembodied boldness that colored all of her words.

"You know, I haven't been able to talk to anyone who *really* knows what happened during the Crisis. Mike Erland disappeared as if he'd never lived here even though we worked the Granderson case together, seeing as Granderson caught the eyes of Vice long before he started killing people, and since Mayor Geffington is dragging his feet in appointing a new Police Chief, everybody's been in survival mode or damage control. Nobody, from *our* end, anyway, has been able to investigate what the Crisis was *really* all about, why it happened. All I know is that Homeland Security and the FBI somehow managed to get over their procedural differences to save the day, but I'm positive," the Lieutenant scoffed as she shook her head and took a peek at Morell to see he was silently agreeing with her. "I'm positive it's people like you and Mike that saved the day, not the *Bureau*."

Morell swallowed dryly as she continued. He got the feeling that she'd processed her line of reasoning in the matter over and over, having no one else to speak to about it, and was relieved to have finally let out what'd been brewing over the strangely passing season of greedy Christmas cheer and collective mourning.

"I've been secretly stockpiling data here and there and one of these days I'm going to take the guilty to court." Lucy signaled and punctually roared through a tentative space in traffic Morell was still just a bit squeamish about entering, considering. "I mean, look at these people. They deserve an answer. We protect and serve *them*, not the world's opinion of our nation. Someone at the highest level screwed up a dozen times over and these hardworking people are still picking through the avalanche. The suits and their over-analyzed handouts are all gone and what've we got? A bigger budget, yes, but still no *true* Police Chief, no firm, *dynamic* leadership. We've got more Officers than ever but they're never in the right place. Divisions are lopsided and Precincts are overcrowded. North Crescent has just about as many beat cops as South, even when per annum violent crime in South outweighs North four to one...poor admin and windfall don't equate long term success. And I don't think we're ready if something bad happens again."

Morell turned to the left as much as his neck would allow. Radzewicz's mental sharpness, almost like the old-school straight-edge razor Morell still shaved with, was impressive, but her critical views of the comeback regime everyone was praising with rallies, candlelight vigils, walks and other charity events, was near blasphemous.

He evaluated her caustic assessment: heavy-handed Federal involvement had spawned widespread ineptitude. Instead of two qualified, seasoned, partnered-up Officers responding to a call in a neighborhood they knew well, eight Officers piped in from out of state surpluses and inter-County transfers were ready to kick the door down if it wasn't answered on the first knock.

Trigger fingers were tenser and verbal commands carried a harsh and impatient undertone.

It was the recipe for a powder keg.

Worst of all, the hero complex, perhaps the very reason for Mike Erland's quitting the force and embracing anonymity, was on the rise, creeping into locker room discussions and code sevens.

Closed-door talk of the clouds rolling across Crescent's skyscrapers held a shadowed and existential threat: Crescent was still a fertile battlefield awaiting its next debacle.

Morell cleared his throat.

"Let's talk about the crash."

"Oh..." Lucy's smile was a secret in her eyes,

once again. "Sure."

"The light was yellow and I was going ten over and I gassed it." Morell said freely. He felt it was a practice run for the disappointment of his hopeful future employer. "The bus driver must've assumed since there was a gap in the traffic no one else was coming. I was late and I rolled the dice."

"The report will state your innocence in the matter." Radzewicz said, as though it didn't matter *what* Morell told her.

Her view on the incident was already as tight as the bun on the top of her head as it held an indeterminate length of hair up to the imagination.

"You're not playing favorites, are you, Lieutenant?" Morell jabbed playfully to hide his thoughts, twisting to read her.

Did she know what your duty was in the war on terror, overseas? Does she realize why Sierra Marland brought you into the fold of the operation that constituted what the public now knows as the Crisis, yet still knows nothing about the truth of what happened and why, just the aftermath?

Instead of divining her thoughts, Morell received a chiding glare.

"The bus driver was drunk, Mr. Morell. That's criminal where I come from. You of all people should know."

Well at least she confirmed cognizance of his brother, and why, since the night Robbie Morell died at the wheel of the rust-bitten nineteen seventy-six Ford Mustang they'd purchased and restored together in high school, Morell hadn't touched a drop of alcohol, and why he'd enlisted in the military the day after he graduated Griffin Park High School.

"Yeah..." Was all he could manage in lieu of the memory's stain.

"So this job you're late for…first day, you said?" Lucy sighed, pulling off of Millworth in favor of Tenth, as she thought about an undercover arrest she made two years ago in Vice on the corner near the Lucky Peacock Palace Chinese Restaurant and Banquet Hall and the look on the john's face when he found out she *wasn't* a prostitute.

"Yeah, it's, um…in the private sector."

"I don't blame you for getting out of Homeland Security, Mr. Morell, but why don't you join CPD? We don't have very many people that speak Arabic fluently and actually understand the ways and customs of those speaking it from first-hand experience."

So she did know.

"Besides, like I said, it's already so screwed up no one would blink an eye at you getting the position you wanted."

Morell couldn't test the fullness of her knowledge just yet but probed anyway, more or less because he was the instigatory kind and was learning to curb such tendencies.

"Is that why you rushed over?"

So Radzewicz was itching to bust Federal incompetence on a by-the-book methodology but keen to *use* that same chaos to install him in the roster as she saw fit, completely bypassing procedure and protocol put in place for a very definite reason.

"Precinct Three's a stone's throw away, Mr. Morell. And, like you said, it was a war zone. Where should I be?"

Morell scratched his ear and ran a hand through a trendy, quasi-paramilitary close crop of dark brown hair. He was a modern, urban figure, good looking in a cheeky sort of all-grown-up way, the kind of man that certain women said was charming and others said was too much of a pretty boy, too high maintenance, even

though his features were all God-given and he, with the
blessings and curses of a military soul, was as simple
and formulaic a man as there was.

"...The job's with Tidebender International."
Morell said, as if he was confessing to have just been
dumped by a supermodel.

Lucy Radzewicz whistled.

"Prestigious. You'd be making, what, twice as
much as me? And I'm a *Lieutenant*."

"I know, right?"

"You won't lose the job."

"Pardon?"

"I know Callie. Not personally, but, I'm very
aware of her...tendencies. She's a visionary, an
idealist." The Lieutenant said, slowing the Sebring to an
idling halt at Victory Park; a verdant, broadly sloping
rest area for the overworked corporate raiders of North
Crescent, guarded by the tall parental units of modern
office high rises and austere business structures. "I bet
she wanted you from the moment you applied, perhaps
even for a personal reason. The rest was a formality."

Morell was about to say something but twisted
too quickly to the left and snarled at the result, being
forced to rub away the discomfort with squeezes of his
right hand.

Lucy switched off the Sebring and exited.

The former Army Sergeant exited the car as well
and watched her walk two steps before she paused,
turned, and pointed all the way across the three square
miles of the winter stripped park to a circular seven-
story building of golden brown glass.

"Tidebender's just right over there, right?"

Morell's eyesight narrowed, having fully
recovered from the car crash in his brain but not his
bones and stuffed his hands in the pockets of his gray
woolen pea coat to lean against the sloping windows

and roofline of the Sebring.

Victory Park was quiet save a few ambling crows, lost pigeons, emaciated joggers and food truck vendors preparing their tasty ingredients for the rapacious fingers of the foodie-crazed lunch rush.

"So, you're going to do…what, exactly?"

Radzewicz crossed her arms as if he should know. Her expression was blank but the odd glare from above lit her professionally sharp platinum blonde hair and her bun appeared to be some kind of halo.

"I'm going to, as a representative of CPD, explain why you were late the first day of a job that's kind of a big deal and if Callie doesn't buy that and thinks you're some devil-may-care ex-military hotshot, then I'll call *my* office from *her* office and prepare the paperwork to see what we can do about getting you some sort of provisional status at Precinct Three."

It was then Lucy Radzewicz smiled and continued her purposeful stride, knowing full well Henry Morell was rushing to follow.

THREE

Maksimillian Andreyich Lenkov, all of six foot six and two hundred and forty-five pounds, left his wife of twenty years sleeping in the king-sized platform bed of their penthouse condominium as it sat high above the corner of Schwartz and Ninth like some sort of dictator's balcony.

He rubbed his eyes on the way to the bathroom, a serpentine marble-armored space as large as the homes of the less fortunate, and ran water in a gold-plated dual-touch faucet sink, waiting for the few seconds it took to heat up before splashing it on his face. Behind the mirror and above the sink, a bevy of prescription pills and their fine print awaited him and he swallowed his morning dosage, though it was nearly eleven o'clock, with cupped handfuls of warm water.

Still in the clutches of sleep, he waddled around the immovable object of his stomach with the habit of an arthritic Red Army march, towards his study, the entrance of which was but two yards from his bedroom, despite the floor plan's thirty-two hundred square foot layout. Once in his study he shut the door, locked it, and reached into the false bottom of a custom-made shelf as it sat in a custom-made granite-topped desk.

Maks Lenkov loved stone. It made him feel powerful. His psychiatrist said he *craved its stillness and strength*, not that he believed all that, just that it

was as pleasurable to touch as it was to look at. Glossy
and smooth, yet hard and deadly, a perfect metaphor for
the way a businessman had to be. Someday, perhaps, in
the medicinal side effects of his dreams, there would be
a life-sized limestone likeness of him somewhere, in
some broad municipal square or city park back home.

Flanking the back wall of the dining room rested
the marble busts made of his grandfathers, those of his
original, *deceased* parents and his adoptive parents, the
latter being decorated World War II military
commanders. He knew his wife didn't care for them,
staring at her with an arrogant vacancy as she ate her
meals, often alone, but Elena never married him for his
looks or his taste in home decor, both of which were
negligent.

Maks Lenkov was a multi-billionaire who'd sunk
all of his money in the failing and falling of the late
Soviet empire, amounting to his becoming one of the
ruling elite in the subsequent circus of capitalist
Moscow.

And nearly twenty-five years later, he was on the
cusp of yet another great failing and falling and was
looking for his lone lifeline to escape the black hole his
market was about to be, his businesses crushed within
the centrifugal collapse of economic dominos.

The smartphone and manila envelope he procured
from the false bottom were both irregular and his broad
and pallid mouth cracked with dehydration as he
followed the orders he had be given to the letter.

Stout hands worked quickly, knowing his wife
would naturally rise in another thirty minutes, and the
Russian billionaire double-checked the instructions
written in code on the single sheet of paper occupying
the manila envelope before powering up the phone and
entering a sequence of seemingly random characters
and sending them to the only number logged in the

phonebook.

Once he had sent his message, Maks Lenkov eased back in the chair he'd had specially made for his tall frame feeling no more secure about the future than an unfaithful man who'd cheated on his wife and had to face her interrogation.

Lenkov checked his watch as it sat next to his computer, just where he'd left it the night before. It was a Rolex Deepsea, custom made for him; platinum with prehistoric woolly mammoth tusk ticks and numbers in a ruby-inlaid bezel and a blue-tinted sapphire crystal face form-fitted for his generously-sized wrist. It was one of a kind in the whole wide world and it was a subliminally chromatic homage to the Motherland.

Something about its position on the desk caught his eye and he picked it up to dumbly stare at it in his overfed grip.

Was it where he had left it? Or was it placed there to make him *think* he had left it there? He had put it back in its case near the wet bar, hadn't he?

Instead of throwing a glance thirty feet behind him to the inset area of the wet bar and the chess set sitting next to it, the billionaire bowed his head in thought, glaring intently into the watery blue face of the priceless watch.

Maks Lenkov's age began to dance hand in hand with the collection of prescription drugs he'd swallowed only minutes ago. He couldn't remember last night, not just yet. Sometimes it took him a while to get going, like an old iron steam train after the whistle was blown, just a few huffs and puffs to leave the station and get up to speed.

Lenkov frowned and stood, completely unconscious in his self-involved haze of the flash of a man who'd been hiding in the alcove of the wet bar near the heavy cluster of bookshelves opposite the chess board.

The shorter man leapt to grab Lenkov around the throat, thankful that the element of surprise had been worth the tedium of entering the building the previous night under the nose of former military private security guards.

With Lenkov's carotid artery snug against the curved steel plate sewn into the fabric of the man's sleeve, the man's thumb deftly found the temporal artery just above Lenkov's ear and the receding hairline of salt and pepper. Age had a way of exposing the circulatory system, making a squiggly line of the tubes running past the man's temples to his brain.

Applying as much pressure as he possibly could on both crucial spots, so much so that his thumb ached with pain, the man felt Lenkov's pulse rate decrease beat by beat until it had stopped entirely.

Lenkov then fell to the parquet floor with a muffled thunk, lifeless and dead.

The man then ran into the nearby bedroom as quickly as possible, pulling a suppressed H&K Forty-Five caliber pistol from the holster in his jacket on the way. In the clinical recesses of his mind, the reverberating tick of a stopwatch echoed like some tinny thunder. If he wasn't lightning quick and ruthlessly efficient, it would all be for naught.

Lenkov's wife was sleeping soundly on her right side on the left half of the bed, facing the doorway, lost in a vast expanse of silk sheets and the assassin stood in the empty space of the door and shot her once, center mass. At her age, it would be enough.

The killer then rushed back to Lenkov and set the gun on the granite desk top, straining to get the giant into his favorite chair.

Haste was condemning him, cursing him of his failures and he threw a glance to the Rolex he'd placed there for the dual purpose of distracting Lenkov and acting as some form of timer.

Taking one appraising snapshot of the paperwork and the smartphone and the angle of Lenkov and the wall his tissue would hit when put to the pistol, the man reached within his jacket for an identical smartphone and a very different piece of paper. Using one of Lenkov's meaty fingers, the killer placed a three-digit call on the smartphone.

Convinced that his masterpiece was flawless in every which way but the time, a factor he could do nothing about, and had moved as fast as humanly possible considering, the man placed the silenced H&K in Lenkov's hand and stood back to avoid the damage as he pulled the trigger.

Lenkov's head jerked to receive the bullet, which was little more than a click with the attached silencer in the hushed office and at such close range, the madness of the Forty-Five caliber bullet made a mess of the left side of the billionaire's head

The exit wound, a perfectly aimed shot to the crossroads of the temporal, parietal, frontal, and sphenoid bone plates that formed the skull like a puzzle, had cracked and blown Lenkov's head apart as if it were an eggshell, and the result was grisly soup of splattered blood and brain matter, unbearable to look at.

The assassin took one final assessment of his handiwork and moved to the doorframe as the recipient of his call, or rather, *Lenkov's* call, gurgled over the small dots of the smartphone speaker with no answer.

"Hello? Nine-One-One, hello?"

And soundlessly returning to his alcove in the wet bar for a black rip-stop bag, the killer paused at the chess board and moved two pieces to the middle of the board; one black, one white, and knocked one over, leaving the other proud and tall before leaving to unlock the front door.

Officers Farwell and Coyle, having completed
their code seven at Millard's on Schwartz and Tenth,
where Farwell was all but badgering Coyle that their
double bacon cheese sliders *had* to be the best in town,
if not the most reasonably priced for the size, fired their
cruiser to respond to the aborted emergency call from
the high rise condo a block away at the intersection of
Ninth. It was well known that the clientele of the high
rise, the penthouse of which was valued at thirteen and
a half million, were an affluent bunch, albeit those that
were never home, and time and time again their calls
were the comical requests of those who were well
acclimated to silver-spoon service.

Coyle was still in his formative years as a
policeman, having just transferred from Chicago with
Crescent's new out-of-state signing bonus packages
being gobbled up left and right and was learning the
ropes with a man fifteen years his senior.

"Probably that one cat again." Coyle said.

"Which guy, the musician?"

"Yeah, but, the *cat*, not the guy."

"Gotcha." Farwell nodded. "See, when I was your
age, cat was the equivalent today's dude."

"Dude's on its way out, bro." Coyle smiled.

"Yeah, well, I'm not calling the ladder truck if
that *person* can't wrangle his own pet. You think the
guy'd get the message the thing keeps running away."

"What kind of cat was it?"

Farwell shrugged, running a hand over his nearly
bald head as he shut the car off and glared up the length
of the high-rise. He was slated to retire but the
Department had suspended the date of his departure to
help school newer transfers as Farwell had been a North
Crescent patrolman for thirty years.

"One who doesn't like jazz, I guess…but the call came from the penthouse."

"Oh…" Coyle's moustache-covered upper lip wriggled. "That's the Russian, isn't it?"

"Yeah." Farwell said, calling it in on his radio. "And he doesn't own a cat."

The elevator of gold leaf and taupe marble, home to an itinerant string melody wandering from hidden speakers, pinged open to release Farwell and Coyle to the small entrance hall of the penthouse.

Farwell buzzed the ringer at the heavy brownish-red door flanked by two hand-carved black granite eagles in mid-flight as if they were MiG fighter jets and cast Coyle a sideways shrug about them. They cost as much a piece as the Police cruiser, at least. Sitting above the left eagle was a multi-axis HD security camera, and Farwell made sure to throw a perfunctory smile to its glossy dark eye.

On the second buzz, Farwell stifled a belch from his hurried eating and careless digestion and moved to leave but Coyle zealously tried the door to see it was unlocked.

"Come on," He said. "I don't want to be ready to clear day watch and have to come back *here* again. That elevator ride took at *least* three minutes."

Farwell rolled his eyes and locked his hands on his utility belt, following Coyle, who knocked on the heavy door twice.

"CPD." Coyle raised his chin and called out over his moustache, holding his position in the open doorway not to disrupt the privacy of the rich inhabitants.

When no voice responded, Coyle peered into the empty sitting room that greeted him. High wainscoting, painted stark white, bent around a generous space the walls of which were regal and red. The dark hardwood floor, as an overtly plush sectional of brown was bracketed around it, was covered by a hand-knotted Afghan rug depicting a scene of conquest much like a medieval tapestry.

"After you." Farwell insisted, and Coyle's adoptive leer bent into a smile.

"CPD." He called again, stepping into the penthouse, unable to deny the fact that he was, for all intents and purposes, in a Russian embassy.

When voices refused to answer he squinted and turned to Farwell whose balding head glinted with morning light spilling down from the upstairs hall, where bedrooms and offices were sure to hold the homeowners and the chance that they were rapt in the sonic delights of Tchaikovsky on headphones.

Coyle nodded and Farwell walked with intentionally heavy steps as Coyle drifted to the right where the dining room and kitchen would be.

He didn't get far before Farwell hollered, his voice ringing throughout the deadened space.

"Greg, in here!"

Coyle ran and reached the door just as Farwell was calling in the gruesome death and destruction of the late Maks Lenkov, multi-billionaire.

Coyle cursed with Chicagoan bluntness and Farwell covered his mouth with his sleeve to keep his double bacon sliders down.

Thirty years on the force and Farwell'd never seen the contents of a man's skull so displayed across the space of such classy surfaces. He turned away and his eyes darted across the bookshelves, the globe, the wet bar.

The chess board.

And so taken by the horrifying muck of tissue, blood, bone, and the physical division of a small set of stairs and several dozen feet of linear space, neither Officer saw the killer silently leave the butler's pantry adjacent to the kitchen and reach up, with his right hand, still in the safety of the doorway, to disable the security camera before taking the elevator to another floor.

FOUR

Subtly twisting the contemporary aesthetic, Tidebender International took modern architecture's graphic coldness and uninterrupted geometrics and subverted them, thus all but declaring their thematic opposition to the world they inhabited.

The shell of the building was made of warm brown glass where tradition would call for it to be blue, and was nearly amber in tone with hints of gold as the January sunlight took to it, making one think they were entering a giant mint julep. The floors of the building were covered with a thick, deadening Berber carpet and many of the walls were eggshell, leaving any exposed beam work and structural columns, as well as accent pieces, such as lamps and furniture, to be variant shades of black.

Morell surveyed the breadth of the lobby space and couldn't help but think of an airport he'd been to back east. Clocks of every nation and time zone lined the wall to his far right, and following the list of cities to see which he'd been to and which he hadn't, his eyes jumped across the shoulders of busybodies caught in their routines. Razors of light, diffused by the soaring sheets of warm glass, cast a pleasant, yet transitory glow upon the bodies walking the highway of stairs and elevators to the bank of doors at the front and back up to their workspaces and Morell turned to Lucy

Radzewicz, feeling her gray-green eyes upon him.

Strange it was, in that split second of a moment, when their pupils touched each other in silence, she seemed, in her purple turtleneck and platinum blonde halo, that she belonged in the golden brown and sandy neutral scheme, as if it was her own building, and she was to be his tour guide of the premises.

But her irises cut a startling contrast. Their unsentimental Baltic forest color claimed no home in the expansive warmth of the airport-styled lobby. They were the eyes of one who'd lived her whole life in the evergreen cobwebs of Crescent, had seen its ups and downs, and was caught in the holding pattern of doing a job fueled by the hope of the human spirit with not much left but fumes in her gas tank.

"Could you imagine working here?" Morell said, just because no more than two or three comments about the delicious smells of a falafel truck on the walk through the park had passed between them because she'd tried to ask him about Iraq and he'd tightened up.

"No." Lucy said, crossing her arms. "I'd get lost."

"Precinct Three isn't too small." Morell said, remembering his time there before assisting SWAT with PierHouse.

The Waterfront was still under renovation. Mayor Geffington was shooting for mid summer, just in time for Crescent's tourist season, given its northern longitude, but the damage had already been done to the weak North Crescent psyche.

"It's still just one story, not counting the parking garage. What's this place, seven or eight?"

"Seven." Morell's hand unconsciously returned to his left shoulder near the neck to rid himself of the restrictive tightness eating it alive. His back was tense, too. Perhaps a pinched nerve. "But apparently three of them are just the lobby. Callie's private office must take up the other four…"

His eyes worked up the glass wall to the left and
the hanging hand-written script of *Tidebender
International* spanning the width of the lobby above the
reception desk. Maybe it was the *International* caveat
that sold it in his mind as an airport. It certainly was
one of the reasons he'd taken the job.

Henry Morell wanted out of Crescent.

He had unfinished business in Iraq.

Allowing his eyes to fall back to the flatness of
the endless lobby floor, Morell saw the Lieutenant had
soundlessly walked the twenty some feet to the free-
flowing wooden reception desk and seating area beside
it. A quick appraisal of the ones taking the best seats
spoke to Morell of the tech industry Tidebender was
perhaps better known for in public consciousness. They
were one of the nation's leading providers of digital
security for the corporate workspace, such as anti-virus
software, customized firewalls, personal data signatures
and company-specific PIN numbers, as well as mobile
IT support groups to help maintain the major players of
North Crescent's capitalist bourgeois. In addition to
that, they provided *boots on the ground* private
contractors, all former military.

For Morell's type, it was like getting into
coaching a sport just after retiring from it. He was
extremely interested in the CEO's *concept of conduct*,
as she called it, and was eager to see what he could
learn from her before researching what he was sure
would be his final destination in life.

Baghdad.

"She should be down in a minute." The
receptionist smiled to Lieutenant Radzewicz, who only
nodded with a blank expectancy. Morell knew what it
was like to wait. Patience was harder to teach some
soldiers than physical endurance, and while coming

pre-loaded with the one, Morell had been born with a severe deficiency of the other.

"So, are you married?" He brushed the bridge of his nose before asking her, as to appear breezy, though he definitely *was* curious about her, seeing as she was aware of so much about him.

"No." She said, flatly. "Know anyone?"

Morell laughed, genuinely, and his dimples deepened.

"I've heard that one before."

"Just cold leftovers from Vice." The Lieutenant crossed her arms as was her habit and he noticed in that moment as his eyes took a quick peek at her leanness that she wasn't carrying a gun and her badge wasn't proudly displayed as was the habit with most. "It's about right now most men usually change the subject on me."

"You a football fan?" Morell frowned in following the humor of her joke as his assumptions of her grew. Sure she was more than likely a swimmer, lacking both gym-membership bulk and the bouncy feet of an addicted runner.

"No, not at all. I was in the marching band in college, though. Never missed a game." Her smile was contained in her eyes again, how it gave her the slightest hint of crow's feet and the rest of her remained a still, nearly sullen mask. "Would you believe that I got a full-ride scholarship playing the clarinet?"

"No, really? Which college?"

"Mountain County State. They were hard up for woodwinds."

"Oh…what's that, like…seventy miles past Mount Turbus? Division One double A?" Morell squinted. "I think they've got a decent basketball team, if I remember right. Have to wait till March to see just how decent, I guess. But, uh…you must've got on with

Mike Erland really well, he was born somewhere out there in the sticks and hops fields where everyone hunts white tail and elk and lies about what they've killed down at the local watering hole…"

"Yeah, we talked about it. He went there for boxing. I went there for clarinet. Different times, of course, him being older than me. Somehow we both ended up back here. And now he's gone and I'm still here."

Lucy's eyes drifted down the length of her crossed arms to the floor, hovering around the visually unbroken desert of carpet.

Morell sensed she was referring to her own Iraq War-experience and didn't want to push it, but Detective Erland's quitting the force after the Crisis had done a number on her, and Morell couldn't decipher whether it was guilt or animosity, but she was sore about him, or something that had happened between them, or maybe even *to* him.

Morell spotted Callie rushing from one of the nearby elevators with the stiff stride of one who was desperately late and caught Lieutenant Radzewicz on the elbow before closing the distance to Tidebender's CEO.

"Ms. Calabrese?" Morell called out, having caught up to her.

Rachel Calabrese, whom everyone called *Callie*, even her political enemies, stopped dead where she stood at the sound of his smoker's voice and her crisp blue eyes darted between Morell and the door, some form of terror stretched on her face before she washed it away with the practiced smile of a network news anchor.

Her handshake was quick and tentative.

"Henry Morell." She said with a soft and soothing though in no way artificial voice through a generous smile of white teeth, directly matched with the slightest under bite. Her heart-shaped face was framed in a shoulder-length flip of light brown hair, colored so by her travels to sunnier climates and her smile quickly faded as she shook Morell's hand.

"I'm very sorry I'm late," He began. "I got in a…"

"It's quite alright." She cut him off politely. "Don't worry about it. If you'll excuse me, there's another matter I have to attend to and I'll catch up with you later."

Lucy's brows attempted to pinch together and her speaking nearly startled Tidebender's CEO. Perhaps, given Lucy's visual anonymity in the lobby, Calabrese assumed, in her flustered state, well managed though it was, that Lucy was just another employee the ex-military man had managed to flirt with in his short wait.

"Is everything alright, Ms. Calabrese?" Lucy asked.

Callie's pointy chin nicked to the left and her eyesight slimmed, trying to place Radzewicz. The pensive bent of her face highlighted the fact that she had two subtle scars just above her brow; two opposing, slightly ajar curves that formed an odd skewed *H*-shape.

"Excuse me, and you are?"

"Lieutenant Lucy Radzewicz, CPD." Lucy said with the dullness of having said it a thousand times before and reached within the back pocket of her slacks for her ID.

Callie's face washed itself of its stress and she nodded ever so slowly and sighed.

"Well then, you'd better ride with me. One of the men under our guard killed his wife before committing suicide."

Callie's limousine was chauffeured by a man
Morell swore to himself up and down he'd seen before
but couldn't place; a real Jarhead-type, bearing no
uniqueness outside of the strong cowlick his tight fade
still couldn't hide. The squareness of his head, just
visible beyond the glass partition window, failed to
move but twice as he drove the short distance to the
condominium high rise on the corner of Schwartz and
Ninth.

After getting over the initial shock of hearing
Maksimillian Andreyich Lenkov of textile and footwear
fame had shot his wife before committing suicide,
Morell and Radzewicz listened to Callie flesh out the
rest of the story before beginning whatever
investigation would ensue.

Her gentility, while coming across as polished
and erudite, was entirely sincere and naturally
indivisible within the very core of her soul, which made
her an anomaly in the world in which she worked and
waged her own private psychological war. She
respectfully wore her heart on her sleeve, and her rarity
lived in the fact that she truly was as sensitive as she
was intelligent, and as honest as she was tactful.

Morell noticed Lucy relax as Callie explained the
situation, and more than that, it was as if Lucy was in
the presence of a mentor and she hung on Callie's every
soft and well-chosen word. Callie sat across from them
both but directly opposite Lucy Radzewicz on the left
side, as Morell was alone on the right. It'd just
happened that way on the count of politeness, but
Morell wished he had wedged himself on the left side
because his neck was nearly frozen stiff and was
refusing to turn at all.

"For about a month, Maksimillian Lenkov has
been employing our Tier One service."

"That's their custom package, variable schedule,

hand-picked roster." Morell added, having done as much research as possible about Tidebender before applying in order to supplement the great detail he was already aware of during his time in Homeland.

Lucy didn't break her focus on Calabrese though Callie did shoot Morell a graciously winding smile.

"Did he explain his reason for hiring you?" Lucy asked, reaching into her back pocket for a palm-sized notebook and pen.

"Yes, he said, and I quote, 'I'm afraid for my life.' I record every contractual business transaction concerning private security…it's like saving receipts for tax-time. I'm very aware of both the oversight *and* the negligence concerning PMC's and PSS's at home and abroad and I want to do my part in changing the culture, as I'm sure you both well know."

"You can send it to my office…" Lucy wrote, nearly mumbling. Morell noticed how fast her hand was moving and that the scrawls and scribbles of her white-knuckled fingers were impossible for him to decipher, even from two feet away. "Was that *all* he said?"

"No, he gave me a good dose of paranoia; a litany of possible enemies all clearly stated on the recording. Understandably, most of them were old crime families in Moscow. The fact that he moved to Crescent all the way from New York City just this past year to retire caught my attention, and when I pressed him about it, he said he was working on a complicated baton-pass to his children, Sergei and Alexis. The transition would constitute the bulk of his wealth, which hovers, for the record, somewhere around three billion. Off the record I would guess that number to be *much* greater. I tried to fish for something to investigate on his behalf but he wasn't going to trust me on first contact alone. I was very careful to explain how a Tier One service was designed to remove the psychological threat of death, but…" Callie sat back, crossing legs made visually longer in high-waisted black dress slacks. "It was his schedule that ruined him."

"How so?"

Callie frowned, the duality of her opposing scars amplified.

"The Officers *just* found him…isn't that why you're here?"

Morell sat up in his seat, the plushness of which was easing the needle-like pain in his back but Lucy was too quick.

"Mr. Morell's BMW was totaled by a drunk driving the Fifteenth Street Metro."

Callie's chin dropped and tipped to the right and her features saddened. Morell was instantly touched by her concern. It hit him in that moment how he would have to triple cross her and spit on all she stood for to be fired, and that the job really meant something to him or else he would've never taken Fifteenth or gassed on yellow or been so eager to make a good first impression.

"My God, that's horrible. Are you okay?"

"Yeah."

"I'll give you the number to my chiropractor when we get back to Tidebender. I don't want you working till you're felling better." Callie reached across the space of carpet between the seats and held a cupped hand on his knee for a moment and the stilling peace of her touch made him draw a slower breath and ease lower into the seat so that the comfort of the headrest applied a soft pressure to his injured neck.

"He was worried you were going to fire him." Lucy said, without embellishment, but Morell did spot the hints of crows feet around her eyes to betray the fact that she was enjoying what she was about to do.

Callie made a clicking noise back in her throat

and shook her head.

"That's just like him to take responsibility."

"It gave me a chance to talk to him."

"Oh? About joining CPD instead?"

"Something like that."

Callie placed the index finger of her right hand to her lips and tapped it as she thought. There was a glow in her face and she folded her hands and rested them on her knee.

"Give me your best pitch."

"There's no way he's coming to Precinct Three at forty-eight K base salary in hopes of me plowing some provisional status into the *unofficially* official duty of his choice with a ceiling of sixty-five under the new budget. Not that it's all about money, but, we both know you've already doubled those numbers."

"...I wouldn't say that."

"Do you know something I don't?"

"How many times have you met him?"

"Once. Today. You?"

"Once. Christmas Eve."

"But you know?"

"About the Crisis? Of course."

"Do you know how he cleaned out RepMax before he quit Homeland? RepMax was the largest Private Security Service in Crescent before he led the audit team and ripped through their hard drives like piles of wrapping paper."

"Are you saying he doesn't like the private sector?"

"Ladies…" Morell interrupted. "You know I'm sitting right here, don't you?"

Two sets of eyes drifted his way and their friendly glares forbade him from speaking further.

Callie ran her hands down the lapels of a chocolate leather jacket in consideration of her words.

The rich color of the Italian-cut jacket somehow made her blue eyes brighter. She wore her nearly fifty years attractively and had the bankroll to take care of herself via the strict dieting of a private chef as well as the help of a fitness trainer, a bevy of itinerary assistants and a personal stylist with good taste.

But it was her graceful diction and her feminine manner that spoke for her even when she did not, a *je ne se quoi* that money could not *ever* buy.

"Let's say he does want, in a perfect world, the comfort of procedure and the gratification of the justice system, not that that perfect world exists." Callie smiled. "We both know CPD's work is *far* more valuable to the community, and ultimately the world in the wake of the Crisis, but…let's be honest, Tidebender is an *international* firm. Based on *my* assessment of his long-term goals, he won't be staying in Crescent for ever. It would be unperceptive of me to believe Mr. Morell's desire is to…shield politicians in suits and ties from the rants of picketers and protestors or loaf around some gated castle of an estate while the trophy wife of a CEO who's never home suns herself by the pool."

Again both eyes drifted toward Morell who said nothing because his thoughts were contained in the hint of a sideways smile that gave him dimples about the way he used to be.

"Point taken." Lucy said and jotted a string of words in her notebook. "I think it would be in both of our best interests if you allow Mr. Morell to be your company's liaison with CPD's investigation on this case."

The car slowed and dipped into a parking garage, all but facilitating a close to their bargaining.

"Mr. Morell is uninformed on the case."

"Then I suggest you get him up to speed." Lucy's eyebrows rose and she unbuckled her seatbelt as the car

came to a halt. "You know as well as I do he's already
more informed in the short time we've been together of
the situation than the lead of your Tier One team. I take
it you were about to tell us why they weren't protecting
Lenkov at the time, something about his choice of
scheduling?"

Callie's nod was slow as she processed.

"You're quite well informed, yourself,
Lieutenant…and an astute listener. I admire someone
who listens. It's a trait that denotes the presence of
other good qualities." Callie unbuckled her seatbelt and
sat forward on the long bench of black leather, its
croaking sound a preamble to her offered contract's
final clause. "Perhaps Mr. Morell can use this
experience as a primer to the procedures and practices
of *both* sides of the same coin, thus determining
through the course of the process which best suits his
unique set of skills. Would you agree?"

Lucy chewed on her lip and looked past Callie's
light brown shoulder-length flip of hair to see the
chauffeur was exiting his seat to open the doors for
them, the destination having been realized.

"I would."

Callie's hand reached across the carpeted space
and Lucy shook it firmly, as if a pact had been made.
With double doors spread wide for them both, the CPD
Lieutenant and jet-setting CEO left Morell for a brief
moment of silence to contemplate his immediate future.

After the whirlwind of throwing his rage over
Crescent's damages and the loss of friends and
colleagues and other unspeakable atrocities into a
dismantling audit of RepMax's corruption and his
abrupt quitting of Homeland Security's fractured
splinters in the wake of the FBI's congressional case
against them, Henry Morell had a clear-cut choice in
the matter but he was afraid, understandably so, of

rushing through one of life's intersections on a yellow light.

FiVE

The moment Henry Morell spotted the sentinel pair of black granite eagles frozen in mid-flight; regal, hostile, and as hard and vigilant as the fallen night of a Russian winter, his hands balled into fists in the pockets of his gray pea coat. He knew they were the proud mark of an ancient way of life now relegated to the ranks of a secret society and the presence of them, flanking the heavy door to the penthouse, spoke of a deep darkness Morell wasn't sure he would bring to light just yet, but would wait and see if such was addressed during the course of the conversation on the count of the billionaire having chosen to end his own life, whether allegedly or apparently, though not factually.

The elevator's lengthy silence had been accompanied by classical music Morell knew next to nothing about, but hearing the music made him think of Lucy Radzewicz in full marching band regalia, complete with epaulettes and shiny shoes. She'd used something people scoffed at and turned a disinterested eye to as they left their seats to go get a hot dog at halftime to gain a full ride scholarship to a small college no one cared about. Now she was a CPD Lieutenant, in Precinct Three of all places, the left ventricle of downtown Crescent. It highlighted other qualities, as Callie had wisely noticed and grazed over, and her emotional reservation struck Morell as yet another practiced skill and his respect for her increased because of it. He was sure she *had* emotions and experienced their often-crushing weight and dealt with their birthday balloon-like desires as they conflicted with the consuming labors of her judicial duties, but when she took up the office and shield she was able to *control* them, not be *controlled by* them.

Morell scratched at his ear, last in line of those being led by a nearly bald CPD Officer who, judging by the lines on his face, especially around the eyes, had seen his fair share of crimes. The Officer, whose name was Farwell, had passed him a glower during the brief introduction of last names only, unable to hide a snarl at Morell's gelled swoop of hair and the upturned collar of his pea coat as it sat above black slim-taper pants, calfskin zip boots, a fitted white shirt and a sixties-style skinny tie, patterned blue, pink, and gray. The Officer's nearly detestable assumption of Morell was something of another pretty boy who thought he was a pro because he had a concealed carry permit and waltzed around the private sector playing secret agent.

Their movement whisked them past a sitting room, the Medieval rug of which was a dead giveaway like the eagles and Morell tried to throw a glance to the kitchen beyond but supposed he'd have plenty of time to look around and was, in no small way, excited by the fact that he was going to be some strange squeaky third wheel, because *leading* the team that annihilated RepMax, the gang of mercenaries wearing tight smiles and tailored suits, had been a stressful experience.

As a soldier, he knew his role well, and knew he was better in support than at the tip of the spear.

"We found him just like this." Farwell said, his face a bit pale.

Morell entered the room last and held in the space of the doorway. Callie looked away. Lucy winced but refused to let it get to her.

The left side of the sixty-two year old man's generously-sized noggin was a jagged shell of bone, a splintered concave coconut, cracked to a point of cataclysmal devastation by the sheer force of terminal velocity. The soupy contents of his skull were splattered on the unyielding surfaces of desk, wall, and floor, respectively. Bits and fragments of bone looked like slices and slivers of garlic in a morbid and runny tomato sauce.

The slug, the caliber of which would be determined by forensics, even though Morell knew it was a Forty or a Forty-Five from the silenced H&K gun on the floor, was embedded in a crumpled implosion of insulated plaster and drywall.

"He *just* did it." Radzewicz said. The scent of death and decay would only increase as time shuffled its feet, and it was undeniable though still faint in each of their noses.

"Yeah. Couldnt've been more than thirty minutes. Blood was still moving when we called it in." Officer Farwell pointed to the wall and the stains and streaks of the aforementioned.

"And his wife is in the next room?" Lucy's mind was already shifting to lower gears and Morell felt concern for Callie, as her head was still bent toward the chessboard and wet bar, unable to give the suicide a second look.

Officer Farwell's booted steps led Lucy to the bedroom and their voices were audible mumbles, with Lucy no doubt writing up a storm about anything and everything she saw, heard, smelled, and thought, putting sparks of fire to her palm-sized scratch pad with the friction of her rapid and dexterous penmanship.

"You okay?" Morell asked Callie, carefully. She was attempting to control her stomach.

"Yes…it's just…well, you know I don't approve of violence." She said, with her back to the scene.

"I know. Why do you think I wanted to work with you? I'm just as sick as you are of 'justice' being two squeezes of the trigger and people dying pointless, meaningless deaths…the human condition, after all, is an expiring contract the moment it's drawn up."

Callie nodded, almost to herself about why she'd been so eager to accept Morell into her prestigious firm.

"Did you just quote one of my books?" She asked, to which he gave no response. He was adept at hiding a perceptive, nearly scholarly sense of aptitude, as he called it, *the human condition*, behind a dashing soldier-gone-privateer image, and he was capable of playing the front with the panache it deserved. The Tidebender CEO knew it was an easy façade for a much deeper man carrying a yet to be manifested personal agenda. Constantly in the presence of retired military, she saw through his guise with ease, but was still unsure of his ultimate goals.

After all, he wasn't like the others.

Considering his military expertise in the area of Interrogation, his flawless fluency in Arabic and his six years in the Middle East, Rachel Calabrese knew his time in Crescent was a means to an end, and she was somehow his last civil stop before setting out into the lawless desert of a modern wild west.

Callie spun on her heel and squinted at the mess of the Russian billionaire she'd had in her office on the seventh floor of the Tidebender building only a month and a half ago. The gurgling sound of his accented voice bubbled in her ears in memorandum.

Her blue eyes scurried between Morell's face and the still warm body of Lenkov, slumped in his favorite chair, the gun on the floor a few inches from a curled and lifeless hand.

"What?" Callie asked, as Morell stared at her.

"It's *not* a suicide." Morell said and put a finger to his lips as Officer Farwell's thick stride announced Lucy's return. Morell opened his posture at the frame of the door like a hinge, still leaning against the woodwork and Lucy brushed his chest with her shoulder and allowed her eyes to stab his way before moving across the brown palette of the study to stand next to Callie.

"It's probable he shot his wife from just outside the bedroom given the wound to her abdomen and the blood pooling on the mattress and came in here directly after. With the unusually warm temperature in this place the blood of each shooting is in the same condition, so the shots were sequential, well within a minute, I'd say."

Morell hadn't noticed, but just as Lucy said it, he felt a slight scratchiness in his armpits. He'd have to remove his woolen pea coat but waited as Callie spoke.

"Mr. Morell doesn't think it's a suicide."

He turned to her with a flat mouth and she tipped her eyebrows, placing her hands on her hips. A smile that would've been conceited was on her lips had it not been for the fact that she was aware he had tested her, saying what he'd said to see how she was going to treat it.

Morell opened his mouth to prove he'd spoken out of professional opinion and not made something up *just* to see how his new boss would handle it, given his Homeland reputation of being cheeky, offhanded, and hard to manage. Callie wanted to see what he had to offer; if he was a diamond in the rough or just an instinctual protector who'd never been developed *beyond* the training he'd been given, having survived the extreme circumstances of combat and the Crescent Crisis as a Homeland Security Agent caught in the eye of the storm.

"Did you see those two eagles outside? Or the rug in the sitting room?"

Lucy's hand held her pen in dead space above her notebook.

"...Yes?"

"Long before the reign of the Czars, Russia wasn't Russia yet, and was inadvertently involved in a brutal power struggle. The Knights of the Teutonic Order had been displaced from the Holy Land by the end of the Crusades and with their plunder, they relocated to Transylvania and later parts of Poland and Germany and as far north as modern Estonia and Latvia. It's my belief this billionaire was *not* Russian and is actually of a very, *very* old family and was assassinated for some reason that may be virtually impossible to discover given the age of the bad blood I'm speaking of."

Lucy Radzewicz bit her top lip with her lower central incisors and zipped a probing glance to Callie, who was trying to hide an even broader smile of satisfaction.

"You think it's a murder because of a rug and two sculptures?" Officer Farwell asked, having walked the concrete beat of North Crescent Morell's entire life. "How can you be so sure?"

"How far out is the ME?"

"Four or five minutes."

"And the Detective handling the case?"

"*I'm* handling the case." Lucy said. "But there'll be one coming with the ME."

"Okay, I'll try to be quick." He removed his coat, handing it to Farwell who begrudgingly took it. "The call to Nine-One-One was made on the cell phone after the fact, the suicide letter conveniently placed as to scatter it with blood and brains and create a great big *distraction,* when the message was clearly sent over here."

Morell walked toward Callie who stepped back as Morell gestured toward the chessboard.

"The Black King has been defeated at the hand of the White Pawn."

Four pairs of eyes examined the lone duel between the two. It *was* a message, a static emblem of defiance. With Morell's explanation, it seemed obvious.

"The Teutonic Order was an atypical religious order, a bit like the Freemasons, and the much more hyped-up Knights Templar, only they were first and foremost fearsome professional soldiers and mercenaries. They were loosely affiliated with the Catholic Church and as a warring group of super religious…doctors, scholars, bankers, and what have you, they had a very strict code of conduct and harsh penalties if their rules and mandates were not followed. Once they settled in the Baltic, they waged war on the Lithuanians, because they were the only pagans in the region, but later they fought with the Polish and the Russians of Novgorod. To them, the war was black and white, considering themselves righteous in the sight of God, killing these pagans who stood in their way and worshipped…nature and what have you."

Morell left the significance of the pieces and moved back to the body.

"A simple bullet in the head at the hand of a depressive suicidal wouldnt've done so much damage, I mean, seriously, I've seen more bullet wounds than any one in this room, agreed? He was assassinated point blank."

"And his wife?" Lucy asked. "Same shooter?"

"Sure. There's no way this stiff old codger could've got between the rooms that fast."

"He's got a big stride." Farwell muttered.

"Then check his system for prescription meds."

Morell fired back over Lucy's shoulder with a
defensive edge, and lowered his tone to her. "When you
do the autopsy, I'm sure you'll find his cognitive
function at the time of death was quite low with all
those different meds floating around in his bloodstream.
Suicide's not improbable. It's *impossible*."

"The silencer definitely lends to an assassin."
Lucy nodded and asked for a pair of nitrile gloves,
which Officer Farwell stepped away for a moment to
get.

Rachael Calabrese surveyed the wet bar and the
neat old parchment globe until Farwell returned and
Lucy slapped on a pair of blue gloves to snag and study
the first thing that caught her eye.

"I'm quite the watch aficionado and I have never,
in my life, seen this Rolex…have you?" She asked
Calabrese, the richest of them all. Combined.

"No." She replied. Then, "Russian, much?"

"Yeah." Lucy considered the not so subtle red,
silver and blue color scheme and didn't see the critical
thread that it incited within Morell's face as he took his
jacket from Farwell and excused himself from the sour-
smelling study. She set the watch back and her eyes
jerked toward the door at the gargle rolling over
Farwell's radio and he excused himself, leaving the two
women alone.

"Quite the history buff." Lucy stated with an
intentionally dull ambivalence, squatting to examine
Lenkov from the right side. The entry wound was
consistent with the angle of a suicide, as if he had been
sitting in the chair, holding the gun, the whole nine
yards. Very careful, very deliberate, if not actually true.

It was plain flat suicide, no questions asked.

Or it very much was not.

"He has *many* hidden talents." Callie drifted to
the wet bar, taking an inventory of Lenkov's taste in

alcoholic beverages to see if it lined up with her own.

"You're talking about the fact that he can speak Arabic?" Lucy stood and was careful as she braced her one hundred and twenty pounds of weight on the desk to lean past Lenkov and browse the bloodied suicide note as she didn't even want to stand *near* the area of the splatter. The consideration of assassination had already tainted her thoughts and she was eager to see what the assigned Homicide Detective would surmise when he arrived, any minute, with the ME.

"You already knew that?"

"Yes, of course." Lucy said. "And I don't want him to go back to war." Lucy left the violence and walked to the chess table, scanning the spines of books along the way. "I would assume you agree?"

"He's paid the soldier's debt…a Commendation Medal *and* a Purple Heart." Callie said as Lucy stood shoulder to shoulder with her and a bottle of vodka occupied half of their thoughts because its label contained eagle iconography and it was displayed in a place of prominence, centered within a line of generic brands not associated with such a rich man.

"So his duty's done."

"Yes…" Callie nodded once slowly, as if Lucy was failing to see her point. "But if something that happened over there is keeping him up at night, you know how it'll play out. Do you think making him a cop'll change that? It'll eat at him for the rest of his life. Or did you have a more…*personal* relationship in mind?"

Lucy took the bottle from the shelf and squinted at it. Callie accepted that she wasn't going to respond.

"What?"

"Something's wrong with the label on this one."

"How so?"

"Well…the name's Polish. I know that because

I'm half Polish and my eyes naturally gravitate to c's, z's, and k's, especially if they're all together in a row...but this isn't the Polish eagle here." Lucy brushed her thumb across an unreasonably black, nearly luminescent eagle as it eerily soared above a distinctively styled castle, something in the vein of an embellished photograph, nothing like those of English design or the oft copy pasted fairy-tale castle of Bavaria. It was blunt and militaristic in its stylings but the mixed media treatment had given it an ominous sense of power as it was slightly rimmed by an eventide horizon of deep crimson red and a bordering void of black, the same going for the black eagle guarding the castle more like a dragon than a bird, when juxtaposing the scale of the two.

"What about it's different?" Callie asked.

"The Polish eagle is a white, two-dimensional sort of thing with a crown and goes on stamps and soccer jerseys...and vodka labels. This one's a lot like the two in the foyer. Someone's trying to preserve its existence by keeping it alive instead of honoring its place in history by leaving it alone and moving on with life."

Callie steered clear of the sharp double-edge of Lucy's words and their relation to Henry Morell but applauded the CPD Lieutenant's tenacity concerning him. She was obviously keen on making sure he would be at her side for the reconstruction of Crescent's fractured senses of safety, civility, and community. Whether that hope bordered intimacy or not was not yet clear to Callie.

But the choice did not belong to her.

Or Lucy.

Officer Farwell was dabbing a handkerchief on his forehead due to the stuffiness as he poked back in the doorway.

"Coyle's downstairs with the ME, his assistant,

the photographer and Detective Romero."

"Okay, thank you." Lucy said and twitched her head toward the doorway. Callie followed under the pretense that Lucy had something further to say but she only shut the door to the study behind her and left Callie, arms crossed, in the hall as she departed for the lengthy elevator ride down to bring Detective Romero up to speed before he saw the room.

Callie let a meandering smile crease her lips.

"Hey."

She turned to see Morell half leaning from a doorway near the bedroom.

"I don't want to see Mrs. Lenkov." The CEO spread her hands at her hips.

He only shook his head and beckoned with two fingers in a hurried, military gesture of waning patience.

Callie wondered, as she walked, if he was upset that she hadn't kept his opinion to herself, even though she was delighted at the quickness in which he assessed the situation, as the vodka bottle she was positive he *didn't* see only corroborated his hypothesis with the cryptic omen of ancient blood ties and whatever talisman or totem such was to Lenkov.

Morell was standing at the door of the bathroom and simply threw his eyes to the half-open medicine cabinet. Once Callie got past the dense crypt of green marble and unending gold plating, she saw the organized arrangement of prescription pill bottles as if they were a mirror of the wet bar.

"Do you think he was poisoned?" Callie asked, her voice hushed from normalcy, even though Lucy was several floors away by now and couldn't hear them.

"No."

Morell dipped his head and sighed.

Callie's brows tightened and her opposing scars were made noticeable as Morell took his time in choosing his words, waiting till his pea coat was back on his shoulders and properly adjusted to look dashing, which he checked for in the mirror.

"I know exactly who did this." He said, his smoker's voice nearly as plain and unadorned as Lucy's static face. "They're the very reason why I quit Homeland…"

They?

Homeland Security?

Callie's bottom lip pulled down at the corners and she held his gaze for more information, but his dark eyes were unyielding.

"Not here." He said, and his calfskin zip boots were muffled clip clops as he walked down the hall.

Attaching a special and highly illegal device to the receiver of the payphone outside the halal deli in Griffin Park, the man who'd so easily killed Maks Lenkov and his wife counted the seconds of the dial tone after entering an international number. The sprawling indivisibility of eighties one and two story cul-de-sac neighborhoods, nineties apartment complexes, and early millennium condominium blocks of Griffin Park, edged North Crescent by sitting to the northwest of the metropolis' jagged teeth of steel and glass. The killer's eyes were metallic broad brushes, noticing the variants of dress among those walking around the two-mile long grounds and the shoddy par three golf course that paralleled the edge of the Targus River and the waters of the Bay. Griffin Park housed Crescent's Arabic-speaking community, and though most were Pakistani and did not speak Arabic, but rather Urdu, the killer could tell who was of which nationality based on their wardrobe alone.

"Hello?" The voice on the other end asked before coughing once harshly.

Sounds like the flu, the killer surmised, a man in the constant state of human study as the clock inside of his mind clicked and ticked with automatic movement.

"One down." He said, his speech heavy with London, because it was a replica of someone else's voice, someone who had many of the same vocal qualities as the killer and was instantly recognizable to the ear. The killer used the artificial voice at all times to conceal his true identity, not as worried about his face as so many in his business were, and strived to create within those who could burn him the rock-solid deception that he was honest and up-front about who he was even though it was all an act.

"Three to go, then." The man halfway around the world coughed again.

"What's wrong, mate?" The killer asked, catching the man off guard.

"Foreign food." The man, who was American, lied, and the killer squinted as plastic clicked, followed by the swishing of cloth, and finally a guzzling of water.

"I'll call you soon, then. Cheers" The killer said, hanging up the phone, smiling to himself about a number of things, such as the time of the call, the oddly musical sound his quarters had made inside the machine, and finally, just how easy the man who'd hired him would be to kill when the billionaires selected for liquidation were out of the way.

SiX

Having taken the stairs to avoid CPD and any initial questions Lucy may've had about his comments, Morell waited till they were in the parking garage.

"Being the world's premier expert on nonviolent defense, what's your view of conspiracy theories?"

Rachael Calabrese let her eyes roll around the parking garage.

"Are we talking about aliens or...the Zapruder film?"

"Secret societies."

"Is there buried treasure involved?"

Callie shook her head at her own stabs of humor considering the paleness of Morell's boyish face.

"You know, that *would be* funny if it weren't so close to the truth." He said, digging into his pea coat for his pack of Marlboro Reds only to remember he'd impulsively thrown it away behind Lucy's back as they'd entered the Tidebender building. "You don't have any cigarettes, do you?"

Callie rubbed her lips together since she'd recently applied some chap stick to combat the cold and her eyebrows twisted together. Her scars became a question mark above her nose.

"Treasure?"

"Lenkov's a billionaire," Morell's hands spread wide. "And I bet you my job another just like him will be dead by the end of the week. I quit Homeland because I discovered RepMax was little more than just another private army for the super rich; not the Hollywood A-listers, but the ones pulling the strings in the World Bank, International Monetary Fund, and the swamp of corporate capitalism stronger here in Crescent than anywhere else in the United States. I quit because the Crisis would just be the tip of the iceberg if things don't go their way. God knows it's academic to say the hand controlling the cradle of you, me, and everyone else underneath the almighty pyramid is sitting next to a *very* large bank of computer screens, crunching the numbers and watching the gages like some cross between a stock trader and an interstellar astronaut."

Callie was adept at reading faces and body language on behalf of her pioneering research into non-combative psychological profiling and saw his concern was far from the cavaliering levity she'd come to expect.

He was just as startled by the discovery of Teutonic iconography as Callie was by distraught the grisly mess of Lenkov's demise.

But it was as if the discovery had uncapped an endless well of personal opinion no doubt influenced by the traumas and stresses of his line of work.

Especially when considering vociferations of such lofty conspiracies.

Her hand clasped around his wrist to still him and her voice was a calming influence.

"Okay Mr. Morell, don't jump to conclusions. I'll do what I can. If it's that bad we'll handle the situation accordingly. I'm not above asking for a *great* deal of help." She said. "…If you want to be a cop I understand. Lieutenant Radzewicz has already stepped up to bat for you but if you want to work for me, then you have to *work for me*, okay? I'm a moral free agent and I don't give a damn who the Pope is or what the interest rate is and how many suits it takes to change a light bulb at the oldest bank in Zurich, or if Kennedy was killed by agents of the Federal Reserve or not." Callie leaned in, her voice still soothing and controlled. "I was put on this planet to *stop* violence and to educate a culture so obsessed with it that five year old children are killing scores of ultra-realistic renditions of *human beings* on video games in their own homes but don't even know what a great many vegetables are, where they come from, what they taste like, how to plant them, when to plant them, or how to spell and add and subtract and form intelligent responses and requests and grow up to be college graduates that don't know who the fifth President was and think that life has a pause button."

Morell's cautious assessment of her was capped by the fact that she was, first of all, protecting *him*.

Or was she first protecting herself and her company?

He nodded weightily in complete agreement.

"Good, so you get it...I'm going to take a walk. We've both got enough to think about, considering."

Callie smiled and gave him a small bow of her heart-shaped face.

"I'll call you if anything comes up."

Morell shoved his hands in his pockets and walked past her, toward the cold glare of the January frost blanket visible from the broad rectangle of the parking garage's release to Ninth.

"One more thing." Callie said and Morell spun, still walking backwards. He saw her like another column in the garage, unbreakable and solid, yet comfortable enough to lean on for a rest, to slouch against while waiting for someone.

"Yeah?"

"I know you have your own methods…always have, always will. Tidebender's not the Police. We don't have the red tape. We have ways of getting what we want. Don't forget that."

Morell accepted the tidbit with a wise grin and considered as much.

Tidebender didn't have the authority, either.

And who would an army of shadows and secrets, a group of power-hungry capitalists so possessed for accumulation of wealth they were liable to commit any sin on the path of doing so respond to?

Who did they answer to? Whom did they fear?

They were a faceless sea void of morality, save when it saw them a profit.

Morell detested them, and felt powerless against them; powerless for Tidebender *and* for CPD.

Hell, for the very city he'd been born in and seen fall to its knees with the leveling of one of their tallest buildings.

The first law. *For every action there is an equal and opposite reaction.*

Even if the action was invisible, the reaction sure as hell wasn't.

And he, the decorated former soldier and Crisis survivor was merely a speck of dust floating in the sprawling darkness of shade their omnipotent monolith cast across the world.

To hell with Baghdad and what had returned after so many years to chew on his dreams as he slept, reminding him over and over of how he had been wrong, of how things could've been different.

Evil was roaming free in Crescent and was about to strike again. Surely he would curse himself if he were in position to do something about it, whoever's name he was operating on behalf of, whoever took the credit.

It didn't matter. Something had to be done.

And as the frigid light of midday welcomed him to the rumbling automotive fumes of Ninth and Schwartz, Henry Morell placed a call on his smart phone to requisition some first-class help as would any well-trained soldier worth his salt.

Safe in the comfort of the Italian-motif café in which she had a regular corner spot along the bar top window facing Page Avenue, Kelly Barnett nursed a cup of coffee of its final remnants of warmth as fat raindrops fell to earth. She removed her squarish black vanity frames in anticipation of walking back to her apartment and took ten dollars from the wallet in her purse, placing it beside an empty plate.

She was about to leave when her phone began to vibrate across the Formica and she combed her short brown hair behind her ears before answering with anticipation.

"Hank?"

"Hey Kelly, how are you?"

"Hank, this better be friendly. I just ate."

Morell chuckled with a pair of breathy sounds and held his silence for a second to communicate that he had called her in haste without knowing exactly what he was going to say once she had answered. In the space of her waiting, Kelly heard the blips and zips of North Crescent's quagmire of traffic, so different from the peaceful and historical postage stamp community known as The Zoo, named for the underfunded Crescent Municipal Zoo and the tight huddle of trivial shops and quaint dwellings offhandedly reminding people Crescent used to be an unimportant and hardworking little place back in the day. Kelly secretly resented the outsiders and imports clogging the streets and rushing to stuff themselves in the bank towers and corporate offices, and knew how the calloused hands of the South, still caught in the job shortages of the Targus River docklands and the space spreading from the water those in the North called either *Rusty Lung*, *Cancer Corner*, or *Welfare Way*, had cleared the path for the North and their flagrant luxuries, though the North'd just as soon delete the squatty red and tan brick structures and failing small businesses of South from their mental hard drives with a single click.

"Are you free today?"

"Like…you want to take me out to dinner *free* or you have some more work for me to do for you *free*?"

"…the latter."

Kelly released a comical sigh, spinning in the bar stool to lean against the corner as dots and spots of wet slapped and blurred the window viewing Page Avenue and the antique movie theater across the street.

"…Okay, *I guess*."

"It'll be worth it."

Kelly Barnett smiled slowly to herself, her intelligent brown eyes heavy with contemplation. Her features were modest and pleasant, unobtrusive and amiable. She had been at her life's lowest pit following the Crisis, and Henry Morell had saved her from self-pity and apathy by secretly enlisting her help against RepMax. Many a night they had spent together in her apartment, and his, in the strictly platonic company of two people working their asses off to find the truth.

Kelly knew Morell trusted her and had a thought that he didn't want to talk about it over the phone.

"Your place or mine?"

"I'm on foot, Ninth and Schwartz."

"Mine, then…" Kelly kicked from the bar stool and snagged her purse. "Oh hey, how'd it go? First day and all?"

Morell's chuckle of two light breaths returned.
"It...*didn't* go. It's a long story, Kel."

"Oh well, then you'd better save it for that dinner you owe me." Barnett said, standing in the vestibule of the cracker box-sized café, peering into the indistinguishable muddle of shiny gray above in hopes there would be a break in the windy spittle for her to run across the street.

Jasmine Keelan returned a broad smile of pristine, overly white teeth as she received her weekly indulgence, La Casita Solana's number nine platter, from an equally as friendly waitress. The sandy earth tones of the restaurant's décor, set off by the bright murals of sunshine and seashore, reminded her of her college days, though she had to keep herself very slim working for Channel Two News, and was so rapt in the tangy spices of their special sauce and the gooey orange blanket of greasy cheese that covered a splat of marinated grilled chicken, rice and refried beans, she failed to see Jessica Birchall rush into the restaurant and scan the booths for her co-worker.

Jasmine had taken far too big of a first bite as Birchall found her and sat gingerly across from her.

"So this is the place you always talk about."

Keelan was quick with a napkin to her mouth, not wanting to have droplets of salsa on her nose, or a brown smudge of beans dirtying the corners of her wide mouth.

"To what do I owe the honor?" Keelan asked, after a sip of ice water though the large bite was not yet in her stomach. They contrasted each other in every way, and the Channel Two News intern was shocked to have been pursued at lunch by the Network's premier investigative reporter. Birchall had earned national recognition for her journalistic bravery during the Crisis

and one heck of a status lift in the Channel Two
building, having become some kind of celebrity where
she used to, just months before, chase down house fires
and car crashes. Keelan looked up to her, as all of the
younger women did, but where the brunette Birchall
was small of stature and delicate, naturally critical and
serious, Keelan was five-foot ten, bright and cocky, and
her flaunted her artificially curly blonde tresses.
Though she was raised in the lower-class suburb of
Wayilow, ten miles outside of Crescent, she appeared,
to the casual eye one offered a newswoman, to be a
sunny yet spoiled Californian transplant, avaricious and
athletic, and she always played those cards to her
advantage.

 "I just wanted to let you know that I'm off to
Boston for two weeks and I came to see if you're
ready."

 A knot inconveniently lodged itself in the young
journalist's long and slender neck, halfway between her
oversized first bite of the number nine platter and an
appropriate response.

 After another sip of ice water, she cleared her
throat.

 "You know I am." She said, with nervous
veracity. "I've been preparing…uh, memorizing
entrance and exit lines; varying them, practicing in the
mirror…"

 Birchall's delicate features were docile and
sorrow slipped from her dark eyes. She felt bad for the
woman as other, more experienced women had once
felt bad for her. Their game was laced with greed,
political scheming, jockeying, and in far too many
cases, pure deceit. Take Jasmine Keelan, for example, a
woman who'd taken a volleyball scholarship to a small
Californian coastal college, used her four years of
absence to their fullest, and returned to Crescent with a

skillful plan of attack as, visually and figuratively, a brand new person so that no trace of the old Jazz Keelan remained. The skin she'd chosen to sell to the network and subsequently the American people had been carefully fabricated to inhabit the vibrantly aggressive soul of a woman who wanted what she wanted and was willing to do anything possible to get it.

She's too ready. Birchall thought, trying to remove some stress buildup from her system by wringing her hands. *She wants it too bad.*

"Todd'll take care of technical when you air, but remember, for two weeks, you get two night-cast live camera spots, one at five and the other at eleven. Concentrate on saying *what you want* to say, not trying *not* to mess up."

"Who's filling in for you?" Keelan inquired.

"Nobody. Nobody else really wants to get their hands dirty these days."

"Yeah…" Keelan stared at the frozen cubes ambivalently floating in her drink and weighed their metaphorical nature. Nearly everyone she met in the business, especially in the Channel Two building, carried the stringers of shell-shocked speech, cringing at the very thought of enduring the emotional struggle of consuming themselves once again, for weeks on end, with the bitter diet of destruction and loss.

"And…uh…" Birchall's thin eyebrows pinched together with a conciliatory offer marking her face before she spoke. "I want to give you a leg up over the others, so…if you sacrifice your lunch you could secure an exclusive with the possible suicide of Maks Lenkov on Ninth and Schwartz."

Suicide?

The billionaire?

My first story is the suicide of a billionaire?

Jasmine's eyes, a murky and muddled shade of blue, swelled in their cloak of jet-black eyeliner and mascara. She wiped her mouth hastily with a napkin, knowing she'd be able to apply a fresh coat of bright pink lipstick at a later time.

"God, thank you *so* much Jessie…I'll leave right now." She said, grabbing the satchel she'd learned to adopt as an essential part of her repertoire from watching Birchall's every move like a small toddler. She paused as Birchall hadn't moved an inch, looking sickly and frail across from her in the orange juice and seafoam surroundings of La Casita Solana. "You sound like I'll never see you again."

Birchall shrugged and the smile on her face was weak.

"You might not. But I'll see *you* on TV, quite a lot, I'm sure." Birchall stood and hugged her understudy as if Keelan had a terminal disease and didn't want to admit it yet.

Maybe she's not going to Boston for two weeks. Keelan surmised, smelling Birchall's shampoo, and how it wasn't the kind she usually used, the kind Jasmine had begun to buy, just because. *Maybe she's going and not coming back. Ever.*

Channel Two news with no Jessica Birchall?

The regret of losing the one she admired was quickly tainted by the prospect of getting a sudden rise up the food chain because of it.

"You're going to be a star." Birchall confessed, hollowed out by the stress of overwork following the Crisis; of being forced to wear a genuine-looking smile for the sake of thousands when there was nothing to smile about and dress in designer overcoats and boots when those she interviewed were either homeless, jobless, or tangled in the throes of life-threatening injuries.

"One more thing." She added, eyeing the number nine platter and smiling ruefully. "Don't forget the relationships. I'm telling you something the Police haven't told the press yet because a good friend inside the case *just* passed it along to me. Don't mess that up. Be nice. Be courteous. Don't let ten years from now get in the way of today. Treat this like it's the only story you'll ever get and you'll do a really good job with it. Everything else will follow."

Jasmine nodded tightly, her curls bouncing, staring down at Birchall with a sober grimace. She was trapped between the finality of Birchall's departure and her own bottled-up eagerness to dive head-first into her inaugural report behind the camera and the sensational satisfaction such contained.

She'd thought about it, cried about it, dreamed about it, and now, here it was. Whereas some girls wanted the ideal wedding or their own palace of tchotchkes and kitsch, Jasmine Keelan wanted the camera.

She wanted to hear *you're on in five, four, three, two, one...*

Smiling her goodbye to the woman four years older than her with theoretically twice as many years of experience as she slapped twenty dollars on the table, Jasmine ran to her red late nineties Ford Taurus station wagon to grab an interview before the Police broke the story to the circling vultures of the fourth estate she'd been given a strict warning *not* to be a part of.

Only time would tell if such was possible for Jasmine Keelan and her desperate ambition or not.

SEVEN

Steve Romero, CPD Homicide Detective First Grade, popped an Ibuprofen from the stash occupying the left pocket of his tweed sport coat and swallowed it dry as the elevator doors pinged open to welcome him to the penthouse. Assisting the Medical Examiner with the gurney was no small feat and Romero pawed at his head and the pulse rushing through it, ignoring the security camera above the heavy penthouse entrance door for the moment.

Lucy was in the kitchen speaking in a hushed tone on her phone, wrapped in a cage of buttery yellow cabinetry with gold filigree handles and white marble countertops. Romero noted the fact that she ended her call with the deft swipe of a thumb the moment she saw him and had a hunch it was a personal call.

What did he care? She was a Lieutenant. He did what she said to, went where she told him to go, even if he didn't believe in her, as had been the case more than once since mid-November, but again, what problem was it of his that Lucy Radzewicz didn't agree with the interim Police Chief or Mayor Geffington's inability to make a decision for the future that wasn't somehow political and was purely for the purpose of maintaining order and giving Crescent the backbone it was lacking?

It wasn't her place to question those above her, to speak against them.

Especially considering her age.

Who did she think she was, anyway?

"Good afternoon." Romero said, the words barely escaping his dour features. His skin was reddened and unhealthy and the coarse tuft of black hair, the crown of which was gray and slowly receding to nothingness on his head, spoke of a dissociation with the times, aging him nearly a decade. After twenty years of being a Detective he was used to the grind and wasn't in the running for *miss congeniality*.

"In here." Lucy said, and he followed her to the study. Lucy watched the Detective's face as he surveyed the cracked skull and the mess the bullet had made of it.

Romero didn't even nod, and didn't seem to notice the putrid stench of the billionaire's passing.

"Suicide." He said, looking past the grisly splatter to the blood-soaked paper on the desk next to the smart phone. "Can't wait to read that."

Lucy pursed her lips and squinted, stepping back for the photographer, the ME, and her assistant, to begin their work with Lenkov, having already processed the less controversial fate of Mrs. Lenkov in the bed at Lucy's go-ahead.

"Would you like to see the bedroom?"

Romero shook his head, his arms hanging limply at his sides. He hid the fact that he was miffed Lucy had removed the body of Mrs. Lenkov before he'd been able to see it. Was he on the case or not? She may've been a Lieutenant, God knew how, but her experience was in Vice, *not* Homicide.

But he wasn't about to speak out of turn, not like she was doing in quietly criticizing the Mayor; no, one did *not* disregard the chain of command. It was sovereign for a reason.

Lucy studied Romero as he pretended to examine

the soupy mess of the wound and was nearly saddened by the incredible contrast he cut with Henry Morell. Romero was tall and thick, something of a gym rat still in his fifty-fifth year of life. His output was low; sometimes she forgot he was there in squad room briefings, always in the corner, but he was consistent, and never shirked his duties, even if he did perform them at a snail's pace.

"Did you find anything else?" He asked.

"Haven't really looked." Lucy said, leaning against the wall near the wet bar. She was still giving him time to say something or show some spark, not to put him in competition with Morell, but, Lenkov had no apparent reason to commit suicide, and Romero didn't know about Tidebender and what Lenkov had said *in confidence* to Rachael Calabrese about fearing for his life.

Lucy passed a quiet sigh of patience, bothered that Steve Romero hadn't even moved from his stoic position near the door as the ME and her assistant worked their magic with photographing, sketching, and the most tedious of all, collecting the grisly bits of evidence and preserving the corpse for an autopsy.

As Romero left the study, Lucy continued to stare into the parquet floor in thought. Perhaps his cold read was suicide because the assassin, or the *alleged* assassin, had done a wonderful job of staging such, with the angle of the bullet's entry and the blood-stained note, all of it, and Romero was only waiting, as was *his* natural process, till the evidence could be compiled, laid before him, and analyzed to make a decision one way or another.

Logic. But what about the silencer?

Had Morell flexed a muscle, false though it could've been, to impress...*her*? Or Callie? Was he just charismatic enough to make sense out of two and two, getting twenty-two instead of four?

No, Lucy thought, turning to the wet bar to fix her gray green eyes on the ominous black eagle spreading its wings over a castle she knew was familiar for some strange reason and the Polish name that sat above them both.

There's no way it was suicide.
No way in hell.

She found Romero in the kitchen, perusing the drawers with a pair of blue nitrile gloves that complimented his perfunctory brown tweed jacket and tan slacks in an unconscious way.

"Are you sure it's suicide?" She asked, with a flatness she didn't have to apply, though she was thinking about prodding Romero to see if he was going through the motions or not.

"Looks that way." He said, not breaking eye contact with the space beneath the sink, obviously more interested in the cleaning products the Lenkov's used than his Lieutenant.

"Not a mafia hit?"

"Nope."

"I'm sure Lenkov had enemies."

"I'm sure he did."

"Back in Russia…"

"Yup…"

"So why are you certain he pulled the trigger?"

Romero stood up from his half-bend and moved his attention to one of the cupboards.

"You'll know why when you get *your* first gray hair, Lieutenant." Romero said with the dryness of his disdain for her having been so consciously removed he only amplified the fact with his insincerity.

He was poking at the point that she was younger than him by nearly twenty years and if it hadn't been for the Crisis, there's no way, in anybody's hell, she would've been nominated *and* selected for Lieutenant.

And Precinct Three of all places.

Back in the day they used to call it the Lion's Den. But she was too young to know other than by having it passed down to her, overhearing the war stories of CPD's old guard, those who were banking on Mayor Geffington hiring an outside man, an old school Policeman from the east coast who they could count on making some major roster changes; a man who valued experience over who looked better on camera.

Romero turned slowly to Lucy and tilted his head in the slightest.

"If you don't mind, I'm going to take a day of vacation until all the evidence is processed."

Lucy succeeding in keeping her face impartial, and though she felt her stomach burning, her nearly severe, clean half Polish half Swedish features offered the twenty-year veteran a visage of professional compliance.

"Sure."

Romero nodded, throwing a shaving of a glance toward the four bust sculptures in the dining room as if they interested him before sticking his hands in his pockets and walking to the elevator.

His vulture's posture disappeared in the closing of the elevator doors and Lucy was left with an empty feeling curling around the slimness of her stomach and her eyes cast themselves down to the parquet floor, searching for something to take her mind off the disappointment welling up within her.

It was then the Medieval scene on the rug spoke to her and her eyes danced around with a beady surge of excitement and she nearly ran to the study for the bottle of vodka and the name written in block and scrollwork above the castle and the black eagle belonging to a dark and ominous power.

Kelly Barnett's walk up, above and to the right of the historical Page Avenue Theater and its unlit marquee of giant light bulbs, was accessed by a narrow-shouldered set of stairs that spoke with each step as if they were aching to break underfoot. Once past the pedestrian convenience store door, plastered with the ads of a monthly playhouse troupe that had since lost their funding, cigarette smoke-glazed walls ended in an abrupt left hook.

Henry Morell knocked twice on the door, hidden in the body-sized alcove, and stared down the length of the stairs at the back of the colored adds blocking the street till the door opened. A passing spritz of rain was visible in his appearance but had since dried and evidence of walking eight blocks in the cold pinched at the tips of his ears and nose.

"Hey." Kelly smiled, pushed her glasses further up her petite nose and stepped back to welcome him in.

It was a poor man's studio, with a detached closet of a bedroom partitioned by a blue and white Japanese-themed silk curtain some twenty-five feet from the door, patterned with a quaint hillside scene of farmers at harvest time; some caught in back-breaking toil, others hauling their goods toward a town of pagodas while a misty mountain loomed high above them all in ancient observance and casual indifference.

Hardwood floors the color of tar and bitten by the nicks and scrapes of age were a neat contrast to wallpaper the shade of white pearl that had dulled over time and was beginning to peel along the ceiling. A shrunken dark green couch was half-draped with a brown hand-crocheted blanket. Two plaid orange pillows awaited bodies in an inviting manner. A giant flat screen TV was bracketed by towers of uninteresting books and a bicycle was hiding along the wall behind a wicker rocking chair.

"Been busy?" Morell asked, removing his coat to place it on the back of a kitchenette chair in which rested a heavy stack of books. Morell twisted to read the spine of them. They were textbooks.

"I'd still like to go to the Hill someday."

"It's a *long* way from Crescent." Morell said, following her to the couch. The kitchenette was covered in papers and the smell of coffee was strong in the air in an inviting manner. In the quirky catacomb-like environment of leather-bound spines and research papers she'd carved out, which he remembered being much cleaner the last time he'd been up, she seemed perfectly at home while being just as equally stressed out.

"Coffee?" She said, holding a University mug as if it were a wood-burning stove.

"No thanks…so you decided to go back to school after all?" Morell took to the couch where a plain notepad and ballpoint pen were awaiting their conversation on the free space of a low coffee table. He sat carefully next to her, as the couch wasn't exactly new, and he weighed nearly fifty pounds more than Kelly. She was paying next to nothing renting the place from the family who owned the theater and were struggling to keep it open. The place had an odd and confident charm to it, as she did, now that she was free of the Crescent Modern Journal and its dismal attempts at old school political print publications.

"What's on your mind?" Kelly said, crossing her legs in front of her, away from the table, so that her right foot was twisting like the tail of a cat sitting on the kitchen countertop while the owners were away. She was wearing an oversized crochet sweater and leggings and pulled the sweater down her blocky slimness. As Morell spoke, beginning with the car crash and finishing with Lenkov, her pleasant face was a neutral palette, colored by journalistic skepticism and genuine interest.

"Okay." She set her coffee on the table and adjusted her posture to sit crisscross, facing him at an angle. "First things first, what about your wheels?"

Morell shrugged.

"I'll get another car. I might rent something. It's just a tool to get me here or there, and I like to walk, as it is...I'm never taking the bus again, that's for sure."

"That could cost you a lot of money."

"The city'll work it out with the insurance company. Besides, a lot of people in my position would've sued their butts off, getting t-boned by a drunk like that. I'll be fine, especially with Tidebender's signing bonus."

"New car then?" Kelly's shoulder shrug was flirtatious.

"Kel, I just told you about Maks Lenkov and you want to talk cars?" Then it clicked with Morell. "You want to sell me the GTO, don't you?"

"What am *I* going to do with it?" She leaned against the sagging crown of the couch with her left elbow, her right hand gesticulating. "And I mean, look at you, all you need's a muscle car and the ladies'll..."

"Stop right there." Morell squinted. "If you need some money to get out of here and move to Washington D.C., I'll buy it from you...but if you need to offload it because of its sentimental value then you have to make sure you'll never see it again."

Kelly removed her glasses and folded them up, placing them down the middle of her sweater, their weight pulling at the collar. Henry Morell was a damn good friend, never having tried to take advantage of her throughout their long nights alone together over computer screens and take away containers. He knew she'd kept the GTO in honor of a dear friend who'd died in the Crisis and since the Crisis, Kelly'd lost weight, quit her job, moved across town, gone back to school, and worked her ass off for a friend she'd never thought she'd have on a job she never got paid for.

"I'll give you a good price." Kelly tossed back the remainder of her coffee like a shot of rum.

"I'll make you a good *offer*." Morell showed dimples and slouched in his seat, wiggling the stiffness of his neck. "What do you think about Lenkov?"

"And the whole secret society thing?"

"Yeah. I could be wrong but I don't have the time to research anything beyond my own limited knowledge of it."

"Impressive though it is." Kelly barbed. "I'll use the University's library and talk to any faculty who might know about it. The place is loaded with experts. Do you have any pictures?"

"Unfortunately not, that's part of the trickiness of what I'm asking you to do." Morell sat up and winced.

"What's wrong?"

"Oh, it's nothing. Just my neck…"

"Just your neck and a four ton Metro bus. Come on." Kelly bounced up and motioned to the free chair at the kitchenette where her laptop was in sleep mode.

Morell took one of the pillows and sat in the chair and she began to squeeze his shoulders.

"Relax." She said and he did so, staring at the spread of notebook paper not yet collated into a three ring binder.

"I forgot how good your handwriting is."

"I forgot how tight your shoulders get."

Morell tipped his head up to smile at her and she pushed it back down.

"Relax, Hank. Just keep talking. I know there's no shortage of words once you get going. Something about an occupational hazard from your days of

Interrogation."

Her hands were strong and skilled by thousands of hours of handwritten notes and keyboard strokes.

"You think I'm nuts?"

"No, not at all. I mean, when a billionaire gets shot it's cause for alarm. You said he had Tier One service with Tidebender? Has anyone ever died under their watch? I mean…they're the best of the best."

"Yeah. That's like…half a million a year…for the service." Morell let his eyes close at the comforting sensation Kelly was working through him.

"Well, the assassin knew Lenkov's schedule and exploited it. You should interview the Tier One team and check the security cameras on every floor."

Morell chuckled at her. Her journalistic mind was sharper than ever by going back to school and attacking dense subjects with renewed tenacity. By the time it was all said and done, she'd have two Masters' degrees as well as the Bachelor's she already had and be academically prepared for the Hill's politics, *on top* of her faithful tenure covering Crescent's legislative ups and downs, as well as those further south in the State Capitol rotunda.

"What?"

"You're such a natural, Kel. You would've made a great Interrogator."

"Heh…"

"In all fairness, though, I don't want you to go overboard."

"I shall research the middle ages for you with great cheer." Kelly enunciated perfectly as if she were a cross between a college professor and a renaissance fair maiden.

"How you holding up over here?" Morell asked, his tone changing, and his smile fading. She knew what he meant.

"I'm okay. I'm just trying to push through it, you know. One degree online keeps me here in my academic rat nest, the other degree gives me three days at University, mostly in the new off-campus library. And that thing's massive. It's like an airport terminal. I still get all kid-in-a-candy-store when I go in there. It'll be fun to browse for something dusty on your behalf."

"You haven't met anyone at University?"

"Nah…" Kelly kept squeezing, and began rolling small circles with her thumbs, her eyes drifting to the silk partition screen and how, whenever she did get lonely late at night, she sulked into the kitchen for an aspirin and clicked on the TV to drift off till she was brought to life again by the cold sun of a new winter day. "Damaged goods only get second chances in the movies."

"Then you qualify, living above an old theater."

"No *Hank*, I haven't met anyone."

"Well if you do, let me vet him first, okay? You know, with all my connections and stuff."

She tapped his shoulders and moved to the refrigerator, not saying yes or no or anything further on the matter as it was a sore subject.

"Hungry?"

"Not really…" Morell twisted his neck, still irritated by the stiffness in his back. "I feel like a million bucks, thanks."

"Speaking of money," Kelly took a piece of German chocolate cake from the refrigerator and removed the cling wrap. "What's your offer on the GTO? Whatever it is I'll take it."

"Ten thousand cash."

The former journalist had opened a silverware drawer and paused.

Ten thousand dollars?

Kelly took her store-bought cake back to the

couch and sat down with some uneasiness.

Morell was browsing one of her class papers and caught the sullen mien that had taken her over.

"What's wrong, Kel?"

Kelly carved off a fork of cake and stared at it before metal clinked on ceramic and her fists were balled in the sleeves of her oversized crochet sweater.

She turned toward the blackness of the television set as tears burned through her eyelashes. Morell knew not to move. It was something Kelly dealt with off and on, something any citizen of Crescent who'd lost someone in the Crisis dealt with, and even though it was a new calendar year it was the same, icy season of rebuilding in which hope kept charging itself like a credit card.

"I'm sorry." She said.

"Don't be…you know what," Morell stood, "I should go."

"No, no, please don't..." Kelly wiped her face in a crochet-covered bicep. "I mean, I was thinking like two or three…your offer's very generous. You know…with what the car represents…it just seems wrong to make money off of it…"

"It's nothing Kelly. I'm going to be making a hundred and twenty two a year for peanuts compared to what I was doing and you never got paid a dime for helping me when I was at Homeland."

"I got a citation." Her smile was feeble. "And I made a friend. That's priceless…the citation, I mean."

Morell moved to the couch, grabbing his jacket along the way, his dimples enjoying her deflecting attempt at humor.

"You know what I mean. Besides, I know what it's like to lose someone close, okay? I lost my older brother in a car accident when I was eighteen and I lost plenty of good friends in Iraq, not to mention my whole damn squad in the Crisis."

"I know…" Kelly sniffed. "You've got me ten to one. I'm just being selfish."

"Hey…it's alright." Morell held her from the side. She smelled like coffee, chocolate, and office supplies and he squeezed her to himself imparting his best wishes, thanking God he didn't know *how* to take advantage of women any more. In retrospect he didn't know who that guy was, just that he was more like the neighbor's dog than a man and if it took a near death experience to make him a better human being, then it was a damn good tradeoff. "How about this?" He said. "Tonight I'm going to take you up on that dinner I owe you, okay? But you're going to have to drive."

Kelly laughed and he could feel it reverberate in her bones. He stood to throw on his jacket.

"Remember." He pointed. "School's first. Call me whenever you're ready…I have no idea where I'll be."

"You're going out to dinner dressed like that?"

Morell frowned, considering his modern urban uniform was, to him, the perfect harmony of his boyish good looks and his unconscious military vanity in which a man's personal appearance and the precision of its cleanliness and sharpness spoke a lot about his character, unless he was in the field. Then it was all about becoming one with the surroundings. Somehow, the two had fused in Morell's mind and he had become one with the monochromatic gloss and gel of North Crescent, looking as if he'd fallen off a Fifth Avenue billboard ad and yet was still somehow *Mil Spec* about it.

"Your sarcasm is, as always," Morell smirked with sarcasm itself, carrying six year's worth of military jokes in his mind. "Wasted on me."

The door held a hollow sound in shutting and Kelly sighed what remained of her grief out of her

lungs and smiled at his offer of ten thousand dollars. It
would go a long way with tuition. Her future was as
clear as the sky itself and knowing that Henry Morell
was on her side, even though her selfish desire to
become a part of Washington D.C. politics would mean
that *Morell* would be losing the proximity of a friend,
she felt like the road before her was less murky. In
considering dinner, she took the store-bought German
chocolate cake and scraped it in the garbage and viewed
the solitary bite she'd taken on her fork with scorn and
scraped it against the edge of the garbage under the
kitchen sink as well.

Then she dialed a number on her phone and
padded into her bedroom to find something nice to
wear.

EiGHT

By some magic of architectural alchemy, Callie's private office at the domed zenith of the Tidebender building took the cruel haze of frigid weather and transformed it into a golden brown luminescence that reminded Henry Morell of the glasses he used to drink fresh river water out of at his grandfather's place just north of Katonah National Park. There was nothing like that water, cold as ice and endlessly refreshing; so clear he could see the steelhead trout swimming through it for miles up ahead and still never catch one. It was that spectrum of light, he found, that brought him comfort the way certain smells could pull the strings of the brain and work instant consolation in a troubled soul, and Morell drifted from the entrance door, caught off guard as he was, by the sound of water and the small rockery pond that recalled his vacationing childhood with a gentle trickle of liquid, smooth stones, and bamboo, under the arched dome of brown glass.

"Welcome to my retreat." Callie said, stepping down from an elevated platform, which, separated by a flowing Zen balustrade of woven bamboo slats, evaded Morell's scrutiny because Callie was an eye-catching woman in any sort of room, empty *or* full. It must've been a quaint psychiatrist-style setup with a great view of all the little self-important busy bodies milling about the park below, like ants in a colony, a place where

Callie could sit and reflect on the change she was
fabricating within the world, if, in her mind, any at all.

"It's so peaceful." Morell said and his finger
whirled around inquisitively. "Is it soundproofed?"

Callie clasped her hands together. The Italian cut
leather jacket had been removed and her sleeveless
blouse was a soft shade of true pink.

"Do you like water?" She asked.

Morell was quick with a tight frown.

"No. I hate it. Why?"

"Because…" Callie was careful in choosing her
words, though her natural demeanor was always
considerate and attentive; present in the moment to who
she was looking in the eye and what she was saying to
them.

"You weren't profiling me just now, were you?"
Morell asked, removing his jacket. Her private office,
basically a quarter of the top floor, was hovering around
a comfortable seventy degrees and the gray pea coat
would be unnecessary in its coziness.

"Occupational hazard." She said, coming to stand
next to him and her feet made no sound on lush carpet
the color of whipped cream. She smelled like fresh cut
flowers, though Morell didn't see any around. "I see
you gravitated toward the fountain."

"It's right out here in front of the elevator, isn't
it?"

"Kind of." Callie offered a smile, and Morell
knew she was stowing the fact that she *had been*
profiling him for the moment because an explanation
was on the way. "Most people notice that."

"What?"

Callie pointed to a modern art painting hanging to
the right of the fountain, some forty feet by forty feet.
Elevated nearly twenty feet in the air, the fountain was
just an afterthought in contrast to its wild streaks of

vibrant color, the brushstrokes all but dripping down to the floor in the warm neutrality of the angular brown glass dome at the top of the building.

"You honestly didn't see it?"

Morell's nose and forehead wrinkled.

"No, thank God. It's hideous." He chuckled. "Guess I hate water less than modern art."

Morell looked back to Callie and the winding curl of her lips, much like he'd seen in the limousine and again when she'd divulged his theory to Lieutenant Radzewicz.

"What?"

"You're the only candidate I interviewed who failed to notice the painting. In fact, *everybody* notices the painting except for me…and my daughter."

Callie held out her hands for his jacket and motioned for him to join her on the elevated platform. She took his outerwear carefully as if it were a baby. As they walked, Morell noticed several desks of computers and a spread of cabinetry and a kidney-shaped table far off to the right hiding a door to the rest of the top floor. Why had he not noticed any of it before? Why the fountain? *Just* the fountain?

Callie continued once seated across from him on the edge of a white chaise and he found a seat on the broad sectional. A low coffee table, also made of bamboo, sat between them with a single file folder on it and Morell wondered why he didn't remember anything about the office when he'd met her for their initial interview.

Was he *that* nervous about getting the job?

Was he *that* nervous about…working for *her*?

Or was it that thick file folder, tannish and unobtrusive in shape, that spoke of her intimate knowledge of him and what kind of transformative restoration she was hoping to work in him as if he were a patient in a mental institution.

"Only those coded as *Cereberally Atypical Peacemakers* notice the fountain. It's called CAP Syndrome."

Morell had no snappy comebacks and didn't want them. A swallow slowly worked down his throat and he was becoming numb in the womb of golden brown glass. Callie's soft and sensitive focus was for him and him alone, no one else. It felt as if there were no one else in the whole building, and the tiny blips of people in the park below were juxtapositions of the distance Callie gave everyone else in someone's mind when they were across from her, in her presence. It was why she hired him, why she wanted him; something that held permanency far beyond the case of Maks Lenkov. Even from dozens of feet away, he could hear the freedom of the water, its trickling ploinks and plinks, and no certain emotion began to bubble down in his belly.

"Do I have it?" He asked skeptically, nearly whispering, as if he didn't want anyone else to hear he was even entertaining the idea of such weakness.

"I've reviewed your military records and your Homeland Security psychological profile, even though I owe somebody over there a favor now, but…we play tennis that way, so it'll all wash out in the end…and it struck me, reading this file, that you've never taken a life."

"No. I haven't."

"Do you know why?"

"I never could…I mean, I never had the chance to."

"That's not true."

"What are you saying, then? I have this Syndrome?"

"It may be obvious to me as many things are to an objective third party but the inherent problem with

someone who has CAP Syndrome is that they are a
liability to themselves when confronted with life or
death situations. For example, you would instinctively
take a bullet rather than fire one."

Morell idly tapped his fingers on the arm of the
couch and let his eyes fall to Victory Park. Hours ago,
he had been walking across the grey veins cutting
through the rolling green expanse, dodging Lucy's
questions about his service in Iraq.

Well, Callie knew.

She crossed the distance, sitting next to him
gently. Her voice was soothing, the sound of the mother
he never had, as his mother's voice was laced with
Camel non-filters and McNaughton's and Callie's touch
was even more so on his shoulder.

"It's okay, Henry. I'm here to help you."

He chanced a glance at her and the segregated
subject of Iraq in the charred remains of his soul
couldn't handle her proximity.

He took a deep breath in, still managing himself
as if he were resisting temptation. He was a soldier. His
father was in the service, too. Crying wasn't something
Morell men did. They just didn't.

He hadn't cried at Robbie Morell's funeral.

So he wasn't going to now.

Even so, he spoke honestly. It didn't seem as if
there was another option with Callie, whom he simply
wanted to say nothing to, give a hug, and leave.

"Look…this isn't going to help us find out what
happened to Lenkov, who's after him and all, if they'll
strike again, or what the endgame is." Morell stared at
her. "I don't know what it is about you or this place, but
I feel like I could talk to you for hours about stuff that
I've just decided to live with and you'd actually give a
damn…" Morell turned back to Victory Park and the
tiny figures parading around it, living in their cages and

their walls, as was the curse of the human condition. "And wouldn't be judging me."

"Henry," Callie left to pour him a glass of water, elaborating as she did. Again, the splashing of water worked hand in hand with the golden brown shell of a psychologically *safe* sanctuary and began to release the pins and clips that had been holding him together like ill-manufactured papier-mâché. "The first symptoms of the Syndrome began with your father and your mother and only compounded itself with the death of your brother. By going into the military shortly after that, you only made it an irreversible fact."

"I don't plan on doing anything dangerous, if that's what you're getting at."

"I know you don't, but you couldn't avoid danger working for CPD." Callie nearly winked as she gave him the glass. "And if you go back to Baghdad, it's a guarantee. What happened over there that makes you so desperate to leave Crescent?"

Morell's forehead wrinkled like a pug's as he bit his lip and searched for a joke.

There's no way in hell I'm letting that out.

Not yet, anyway...

"I'd rather talk about my childhood."

"Was it *that* traumatic?"

"Listen..." Morell held his tie flat to his chest, reaching forward to place the water on the bamboo table. "I've been in conflict all of my life and I've been able to deal with it really well. I used to bunk with guys that turned into basket cases because their threshold had been broken. One of the Doc's called it a *shatterpoint*. A man can take his share of bumps and bruises but once that little glass box inside of him breaks into a million pieces, there's no putting it back together-it has to be replaced wholesale with a new one. Some of these guys we're talking about have three kids, mind you, so when daddy finally does come home to the little ones, they don't understand why he's not the same and are too young to comprehend the full effects of what's happened to him...not that the wife really does, either."

Callie nodded with pain edging her kind blue eyes.

"I never hit the shatterpoint." Morell said. "I was shot, blown up...I was even briefly captured and beaten to a pulp, not to mention the insanity constantly at work around me, and God knows what happened in the Crisis changed me forever, but I've *never* hit the shatterpoint. It's like there just isn't one."

Callie opened her mouth to say something and searched for the right words before placing her hand on his knee and looking him in the eye.

"Maybe the only shatterpoint there is for you is taking a life. Maybe you're just holding on by a thread. If that moment comes, by luck *or* design, I don't want you to be sabotaged in that split-second reaction."

Morell sighed heavily, though not knowing exactly why, and held his examination of the window for a moment.

"So why are you doing this?" He asked.

"CAP Syndrome is one in a million, Henry. Look at me. Everybody who knows my work knows how much I hate violence and how I've dedicated my life to stopping it but in the same token they know I'd sacrifice myself on behalf of a stranger in the blink of an eye. I wish there wasn't a single gun on planet earth, that we could live in the cave man days as far as weapons are concerned; that withstanding, CAP Syndrome has side effects, namely relationships. It warps your understanding of perspective, communication, and most of all, intimacy. I've been married twice and ruined both of them, and my daughter doesn't want much to do with me." Callie stood and drifted toward the window, hands in her pockets. "I know the reputation you had in the military and later with Homeland as a skirt-chasing party animal and I'll be the first to chalk up your paper chain of relationship failures to CAP Syndrome." Callie turned, her face critical. "I could explain the whole thing in psychology terms with a whiteboard, but you know good and well what I'm talking about, and it's a feeling that gnaws in your gut like an autoimmune disease.

Morell licked dry lips but only stared at the water in the glass.

That was the feeling he hated, and once he felt it, burrowing around like some alien creature waiting to split his belly wide open from the inside out, he knew the relationship he had hopes for was finished.

That damn numbing ache down in his belly.

"None of that was in the file."

"It didn't have to be." Callie said. "I'm not a registered psychologist just because I don't have a certification but you must understand that what motivates people constitutes my life's work. You want to protect and defend and you'd do *anything* to save someone. You're overly generous with money and you work yourself to the bone on behalf of other people. It's a good thing, Henry, but it's also a chronic flaw. If I didn't know what CAP Syndrome was, there'd be no Tidebender and I'd have no worldwide platform to study it, talk about it, and use it to help others." Her shrug was laced with some form of regret in even remotely considering her life having taken a different path. "I'd probably be just another social worker in South Crescent trying to restore broken families and taking the false responsibility to do so *so* deeply it'd drive my blood pressure higher than the Regency Tower."

The former US Army Sergeant blinked away the

remnants of regret in his eyes as the phone sitting on one of the desks some thirty feet away rang with a barely audible bleep.

"I'd better take that." Callie said, standing and smoothing her pants near the hips. Morell stood as well and she placed her hands on his shoulders, looking him in the eye.

"I care about you." She said with a small nod, eyebrows rising. "Not because we're both some scientific anomalies, but because you're a fractured human being that needs psychological treatment before something traumatic is allowed to injure you in a way that would facilitate little to no chance of recovery. I believe in you and I can tell in the blink of an eye when you're playing poker with me and when you're telling the God's honest truth. Whatever happened in Iraq, whatever you can't let go of, even though I can't find it in your file, *can't* be allowed to ruin you. You have no value to anyone you love or are trying to protect when you're *dead.* Remember that, okay?"

Callie skipped down the stairs and reached the phone before the caller had grown irrevocably impatient, leaving Morell to think about what she'd said as tiny bits and bobs of humanity walked their dogs, played with their cell phones, and huddled around food trucks below.

He also thought about what *he* had said, and the ease in which it came out, no ridiculous one-liners, military curses, or sarcastic knife-jabs involved. He took the water and drank it in one, refreshing gulp, relishing the chance to speak with her in such a manner again.

He felt safe in her office, unlike his childhood of overhearing shouts and bottles breaking as his dad returned home from deployment.

Morell found his jacket and Callie caught his eye,

calling him over to where she was seated, being
subjected to a dose of extreme unhappiness on the other
end of the phone. Morell thought he'd heard something
about the *FBI*, but was in no way alarmed, knowing
Callie dealt with the government on a daily basis due to
lucrative retainer contracts. He stood at ease and she
quickly wrote a note and threw her thumb back to one
of the file cabinets. Morell gave her a quick and lazy
salute and left Tidebender with Lenkov's file to call
Lucy Radzewicz.

     Jasmine Keelan checked the flip down vanity
mirror one last time, making kissing lips and other
slightly demonstrative facial gestures. She had been
subscribing to acting webinars for a few months as
supplementary training to what she was learning as an
intern and knew that if she could control her face and
use it to project what the person she was listening to
wanted or needed to see, she'd be able to get more
information from them. She couldn't disregard the
butterflies in her stomach with fidgety fingers fluffing
up her curls as she pressed out into the cold from her
humble Taurus station wagon to see that, across the
street, the high rise bore no signs of a Police
investigation.

     Not even a black and white patrol car on Ninth.

     Parking garage, I bet.

     Jasmine folded her cardigan across her body as
tight as possible and adjusted her belt strap so that she
could barely breath. Almost eighty percent of Crescent
Detectives were men, so…what was the harm? Keelan
also released another button of her white blouse, though
the cold forbade it.

     Jaywalking a space in the traffic, Jasmine nearly
skipped into the emptied lobby of the condominium
high rise and with an instant appraisal, found a woman

in a purple turtleneck and tan slacks speaking in a muted tone with a man who must've been walking the beat back when there *were* no women cops.

Exhaling the butterflies, Jasmine's heel-toe footsteps caused the Officer to throw a glance her way and the Officer did a double take and pretended not to see her as she approached a conversation she was not a part of.

"Excuse me, Officer, my name's Jasmine Keelan, I'm from Channel Two News, may I…"

"What?" The woman in the purple turtleneck eyed the taller blonde and when she didn't say anything further and her gray green eyes simply held the uncomfortable annoyance of being interrupted, Jasmine began again, her inquiries directed to the Officer.

"My name is Jasmine Keelan, I'm a reporter for Channel Two, I'm here to ask about Maks Lenkov."

The bald Officer's lips stretched as if busted by a higher power for something he was trying to hide and could no longer and Lucy simply passed him a gesture to say it was all going to work out.

"Ask whatever you want, it doesn't mean you'll get anywhere."

"Excuse me, who are you?" Jasmine scrunched up her face.

"CPD." Lucy offered no more and her face was flat and nonplussed.

"Your name?"

"Why?"

"For my report."

"What report? About what?"

Jasmine towered above Lucy in her heels as Lucy was wearing brown flats with an active tread.

"About…what happened in the penthouse."

Lucy only continued to stare, not giving anything to the reporter. Lucy had never seen her before and was deeply concerned with Morell's theory. Perhaps the nosy woman was related to the assassin, checking the work, so to speak, if even unconsciously, maybe paid to do so without knowing who was paying her-just a voice on the phone telling her where to go and what to say and a tidy sum in a bank account afterward.

"May I see your credentials?" Lucy asked, as if indulging the prospect of a conversation that would include the truth on behalf of Keelan's mention of the penthouse.

Jasmine handed a bi-fold wallet with her press registration and driver's license side by side.

Lucy simply took it and gave it to Officer Farwell without even looking at it.

"Run it." She said.

"*Excuse* me." Keelan's face was struck by a jagged bolt of outrage before she contained the unruly purity of such a sharp reaction with a contemptuous simper of defiance. "I came here on good faith that I would secure an exclusive with the senior investigator on the death of Maks Lenkov by a member of *your* Department…how am I going to explain this to my boss, or the American people? They have a right to know!"

"Know what?" Lucy frowned and Jasmine sighed over clenched teeth, turning the hardness of her gaze to the elevators and stairs. "Go outside there and see how many people give a damn. Do their cars just all of a sudden stop working? Do they drop their croissant sandwiches mid bite and have a heart-attack? No." Lucy took a step forward, a scolding finger hovering in the neutral space between them, demanding Keelan quit her pouting and look her in the eye. "Concerning Maks Lenkov, *for the record*, CPD will release a statement to the media, the *whole* media, and nothing but the media when we are *confident* with our findings. Until then, there's nothing for you to do here."

Jasmine stood obstinately on the same square of tile she had when she'd first began her unfortunate choice of words and now that she was speechless she could only wait out the few seconds of flaming embarrassment, burning her skin like a solar flare, till Officer Farwell trundled up to return her identification.

"Ike, who in our Department told this woman that Maks Lenkov was dead?" Lucy asked, gray-green eyes unblinking and fixated on the face of the young reporter.

"I'm not sure, ma'am."

"When you find out will you please put them on probation?"

"Yes ma'am."

"And would you do so expediently?"

"Yes ma'am." Officer Farwell trudged off as the elevator door pinged open.

Jasmine stood her tallest and clasped her hands behind her back, shoulder blades nearly pinched together in her yoga stance, though such was granting her no inner peace.

"So, are you confirming or denying that Maks Lenkov is no longer alive?"

The extra large gurney, draped with a white sheet, rattled with a hollow clatter in the vacated lobby as Keelan waited for an answer.

A smile was contained in Lucy's eyes and she threw her eyebrows to a sweaty Detective Romero, the ME and her assistant, struggling to push the heavy man to the middle of the empty lobby as he wouldn't fit in the elevator and they were waiting for the van to get to street level.

"If you want to know so bad, why don't you try the morgue? I can give you the address. I'm sure none of the other reporters would fight you for an *exclusive* with sanitarium white walls, ammonia, bleach and that giant bone saw they use to split open the ribcage and carve up all the vital organs to weigh them like vegetables in a supermarket."

Lucy only twisted her head and crossed her arms, watching the young reporter who more than likely had nothing to do with the death of Maks Lenkov sulk back through the door, hugging herself for the much needed consolation of crushed pride being her only companion in the bone-chilling cold.

NiNE

With a puffing lung of air fluffing up a fist of curls, Jasmine hit the second speed dial on her phone and rolled her eyes when the Midwestern-accented bleat of her boss' voicemail prompted her to leave a message.

"Cindy, it's me, Jasmine. Call me when you get this. I have some information about a possible death involving Maksimillian Lenkov at his condo on the corner of Schwartz and Ninth…um…it's time sensitive, so…yeah. Bye."

Then Jasmine let the phone flop to the seat next to her and contended with the growling sounds in her stomach. The morning had begun with hot yoga and a shower, then a smoothie with curlers in her hair while browsing the world news on her computer against the brash volume of a stock market television show. It struck her, in the dreary nothingness of waiting, how tired she was, and how, if she didn't have the adrenaline of *go go go* she felt, not only completely worthless as a human being, but as if she'd committed some kind of sin.

Her oversized smart phone began to vibrate and twisted in place as it did so.

"Hello?" Jasmine was quick to answer, her cheek hot against the touch screen.

"Hey Jazz, I just got your message." Cindy

Schiller honked with scratchy undertones. She'd recently left one of Minneapolis' premier fortune five hundred companies and was Channel Two's senior information analyst. Nothing was reported unless she laboriously cleared it, which, many times over, meant Channel Two was the *last* to say the same old thing, and it was only the neutrality of everyone's attitude toward it that provoked Jasmine to get out there and get as many exclusives as possible.

After all, Channel Two, without Birchall, was fast becoming the third choice in the city, much akin to saying one could have Coke, Pepsi, or the grocery chain's not-so-subtle copy.

"Yeah, I got stonewalled."

"What do you mean, what does that mean? Explain." Cindy said in her manner of self-elaborating. Often she gave three adjectives for the same sentiment, thus driving home the point she wished to make by beating a dead horse.

"The woman in charge of the case…"

"What woman? What's her name? What's her rank?"

"I didn't get that."

"Why not?"

"…" Keelan's mouth was open but no words came out. She only shrugged, releasing the smallest stream of frustration and surprise in a throaty squeak, as if she were a pot of boiling water puffing condensation from a rattling lid.

"Get back in there." Cindy Schiller nearly barked, and Jasmine could faintly hear the small refrigerator door in Cindy's office open and shut, more than likely for her daily nonfat yogurt. "Be tenacious, be stubborn and inflexible. Don't let them sleep till you get what you want."

"You haven't heard anything, have you?" Jasmine

asked, checking her face again in the flip down mirror. She was sure the cold was going to make her lips crack. Acclimatizing to California's year-round sun had been easy. The reverse was proving to be tedious.

"No, other than I know Birchall told you and she got it from an old friend in the Department, probably one of the forensic team. Cops respect consistency, Jazz, but more than that they like backbone. Once they realize you're their mouthpiece they'll give you anything you want to hear. But you have to tell it like they give it to you."

Jasmine flipped up the mirror and stared across the street as the gurney was leaving the front door for the some ten feet it took to stuff it in the back of a nondescript van.

"I'll do what I can." She said, firing her car.

At two o'clock sharp, just as she'd said, Lucy's gold Sebring found a spot on the edge of Victory Park.

The rain's coming back, Morell thought, leaving the welcoming smells of the falafel truck where he'd been passing the time speaking Arabic to the Turkish man who owned it, asking him about his recipes and what part of Turkey he came from and, once finding it was the gateway city of Istanbul, if he favored Galatasaray, Fenerbahçe, only to learn the man hated soccer.

"Hungry?" Lucy called out, shutting the door and splitting the distance between her car and the food truck. She was wearing a khaki trench, cinched up tight, and her hands were buried in its deep pockets.

"Yeah." Morell cast his vision behind him and his nostrils were flared. "But I'm saving myself for a big ol' fancy dinner tonight. I owe a friend."

"Oh." Lucy said and Morell gave her the file on Lenkov, clearly marked with Tidebender's script logo.

"How'd you get this?" She asked.

"Callie gave it to me on your behalf."

"You're a good liaison." Lucy said with the plainness of someone stating the facts of the weather, and they took to a reasonably dry bench nearby. "I'm used to getting hell from suits and ties. If I had a dime for every minute capitalists and politicians stole from this Department with their stall tactics and procedural runarounds I wouldn't be sitting next to you right now."

"Lucky me." Morell crossed his leg, having already read the file during his wait for Lucy. He wasn't about to ask for the Detective's opinion, though he felt confident she was leaning his direction.

It was hard to know *what* she was thinking because her exterior was such an emotionless mask.

She has nice bones, he thought, as he placed his arm across the back of the bench and rolled his neck in circles, *maybe she looks so young because she doesn't laugh or smile or run any of the other histrionics that women so often rely on to push a man's buttons...*

"Anything stick out to you?" She asked, flipping the second page.

"I don't like his kids, that's for sure." Morell said, recalling the surprise that'd captured the falafel truck owner's face with his perfect Arabic, even though Turks spoke Turkish, the man knew flawless Arabic when he heard it and more than that, Morell's consciousness of culture and customs, and his respectfulness of them despite his nearly arrogant urban North Crescent appearance, looking much like the kind of person the truck owner cursed for their blistering impatience.

"What about them?"

"When there's that much to gain there's got to be some kind of temptation."

"Temptation is temptation." Lucy flipped another

page, her reading intent and steady. "No matter what the stakes."

"Right, but if they could get rid of him *before* he finalized whatever checks and balances he was putting in place, they'd have a free hand in company policy, regardless of the board and what not. If I understand right, he wanted to split the company in half, giving the less profitable portion solely to his children, taking the other half public with a board of directors to run it. It was an extremely generous gesture in some ways, in others, quite insulting. I don't know the dynamic between them, but I've seen a lot more done for less."

"Me too." Lucy said. "And I'd like you there when we interview them. You *are* the expert."

Lucy finished the file and closed it, shaking her head. The manner in which she held the edges of the folder, fingers broad and linear despite their small size, struck Morell as muscle memory from holding a clarinet.

"There's something missing, isn't there?" Morell asked.

"Yeah. Nothing about…what you said."

"Maybe it's not true."

"No." Lucy shook her head with a tight movement and fell forward to lean on her knees. She craned her neck and peered at him, the harsh gray light obviously hurting her eyes.

"My…help on this case is fading out." She said. "I'm sure you've seen older guys do it in the service. He doesn't care *what* happened to Lenkov…" Lucy squinted at the sky and scratched her ear with a manicured nail. Morell wondered in that split second of a moment, with her choice of pearl earrings, the smallest possible, what she'd look like with her hair down, relaxed and able to release all of the professional pretenses she was forced to walk in as if they were a tightrope act without a net below.

"Burn out? Sure, I've seen it."

"And it never happened to you?" Lucy asked and then backed off. "Sorry. I have to stop asking you about Iraq. I know you don't want to talk about it."

"It's okay." Morell stuffed his hands in the pockets of his gray pea coat, crossing his leg and sitting back in the bench to watch the man in the food truck slice off shards of pressed kabab meat as it spun beside the glow of a heat lamp.

"What's next then? The waiting game?"

"I'll call the kids and we'll speak with them tomorrow, but it's the media I'm worried about."

"How?"

"They're sensationalist leeches, every damn one of them."

"Lucy," Morell frowned and his forehead crumpled. "Do you have a positive opinion about *anybody*?"

Her eyebrows made an effort to come together and the smallest semblances of crows feet winked around her gray-green eyes.

"You."

"I walked into that one."

"It's true." She said. "I trust you. You're the kind of guy I wish there were a lot more of…and just between you and me, I don't think I'm doing any good as a Lieutenant, as badly as I wanted the job."

Morell's lips were flat and he stared at the falafel man, wiping down a plastic cutting board. There was no lie in her, and he remembered their first conversation in her car when she all but unloaded to him about doubting the Feds and the Mayor.

Don't jump to conclusions, he wanted to say, *but I guess we're both pretty good judges of character with time-in-grade abuses on our collective conscience, aren't we?*

Then he swallowed, dryly, hoping to share a cup of Callie's cool, fresh water between them because he'd misinterpreted many of her signs of emotional control when they were really products of *loneliness.*

"It must be hard, being a Lieutenant post-Crisis."

Lucy stood, rolling up the file and peering up into the heavy haze of gray.

"I'm not going to force you to give me information Callie doesn't want to on behalf of client privilege, even though I'd have every right to subpoena if I wanted to." She said. "If she's found negligent in his protection it'll hurt her and I don't want that. I'm happy she's the top dog in town after RepMax got torn apart because frankly, they scared me, every one of them packing a Glock or a Sig Sauer, and with all the cops running around this place looking to be the next hero, and the crazy CRT plan I hope never sees the light of day, I'm worried that more innocent people are going to pay the price, whether it's a pack of journalists or a Mayor who refuses to commit...I just feel stuck in it all. Tell Callie I'm on *her* side and I'm on *your* side, Mr. Morell. My Detective is going to call it a suicide and that's what the press are going to get, open and shut. Anything else would jeopardize whatever modicum of security we've worked *so* hard to develop within these people's souls." Lucy Radzewicz shook her head in disbelief of the words that were coming out of her own mouth. "I know it's not right but it's what I'm going to do. Enjoy your dinner. I'm going to research a lead."

Morell stood with the natural reaction of CAP Syndrome rushing over him, *begging* him to ask her to come to dinner. Kelly would enjoy it, and it would loosen the Lieutenant up and give her a chance to let her hair down.

But instead, he shook her hand and its coldness, and saw, as she crossed the space of grass back to her car, how fractured her walk was, and how the burden of responsibility, of an *entire city* had fallen to her shoulders.

She didn't deserve that.

Morell checked the time on his cell phone and walked a half a block to catch a cab back to his place. Before he knew it, night would fall and the story of Maks Lenkov would be on everyone's lips, albeit, not in the way it could've been.

But if he was right about what he'd seen in the thirteen and a half million-dollar penthouse, then Lenkov wasn't about to be the last billionaire who'd conveniently committed suicide within the fragile walls of Crescent's corporate cage.

TEN

Sergei Petrovich Lenkov was detachedly staring into the odd glare of the low sky, the gray streak of it scraping the spires of the pines and firs surrounding the expansive acreage of horse stables and private gardens he called home, stealing the sun from him and every other citizen of greater Crescent for yet another cold January day.

"Sergei Petrovich, were you listening?" A female voice spoke in Russian. Sergei had been nursing a glass of Pinot Gris, the only alcohol he was allowed to have before dinner, as it was fast approaching.

"Hmm?" Sergei turned from the window.

The large emerald eyes of his sister Alexis Maksimillia refused to remove their reprimanding undertone until he apologized and returned to the broad French-polished crotch mahogany table in the grand dining room of their private estate just three miles south of Bay County Airport.

"I know we have a lot to do," She soothed, "but it will only be done *once*, and never again."

Sergei drained his wine and winced with hidden pain. Alexis reached out to him and ran a hand through his jet black slick of hair. The oversized and multi-faceted green oval chrysoberyl ring dominating the middle finger of her right hand instantly betrayed her wealth and only paired, in the strange marriage of instantly acceptable perfection, with the long, billowing tapestry of auburn waves falling from a high forehead to exemplify the fact that she was a royal princess.

"I was just thinking about Papa…" Sergei confessed. "I know I…"

"Shh…" The princess soothed, her hand tracing the hard, granite-like edges of his face down to his chin to lean in for a gentle peck on the thinness of his bloodless lips, still tasting of tart pear and grass from the Pinot Gris.

"I know you are. But Papa made his choice. He will live with it, as we will live with ours."

Sergei nodded and stared down the length of the table and its opulent endlessness.

Its gloss…its emptiness.

Soon it would be full of diamond-laden hands and monogrammed cufflinks, its polish refracting nervous smiles until the Lenkov siblings made their announcements about the empire's future, allowing a new way of life to flower from the seeds of ancient roots.

"Live with it?" He shook his head. "Sister, you *are* cold."

"I know." She kissed him again, and he was captivated, as always, by her gem-tone green eyes and their ability to steal the breath out of a person's lungs in one long, cool, scrutinizing gaze.

A faint smile curled Sergei's lips, provoked by the glass of Pinot Gris he'd just finished.

"Will they ever find out?" Sergei asked, considering the fact that Alexis Maksimillia looked nothing like him and the only blood that linked them was as old and distant as the vow of revenge it harbored.

"That is not your concern, brother." Alexis tipped her head to the left and reached out for Sergei's hand, squeezing it. "You can only do what you must. Remember that. Our enemies must not be allowed another day in power."

Sergei nodded, looking longingly to his glass and its vacancy.

"Not yet, brother…there is much to be done."

It was then the ivory and gold antique telephone rang in the hall and the look that passed between brother and sister over the call regarding the death of their father could've only been construed, by an objective third party, as positively devious.

The two men waiting patiently in the comfort of their brand new black Chevrolet Suburban across from the eighty nine-year old Page Avenue Theater cast forlorn disgust to the heaviness of the passing shower coinciding with Kelly Barnett's shutting and locking of the ad-covered door to her walk-up. It was nearly four thirty.

Somehow the way the rain pelted the weathered plum colored paint and the dated orange script of the sign above the marquee gave the water a sense of power, as if it was acidic and had been instantaneously responsible for the years of wear and tear sitting before the two men. In the prospects of falling evening, the Suburban was a toasty paradise.

"That's her." The beefy man hogging the driver's seat and most of the center console said, despite the fact that inherently obvious statements bothered the man in the passenger seat. He only nodded, opening his door to silently peer into the intransigent wall of wet, darkened though it was, still weighing options further down the road as it stung his eyes.

The driver, nearly six foot two, appeared dense and heavy in his choice of waterproof jacket and tan slacks, and his naturally sunned face of half-Puerto-

Rican, half-Italian descent was tainted by a haughty glaze, the conception of which began in his shiny black eyes and ended in his stridently over-confident strut.

The passenger searched both directions for traffic as he buttoned his suit, and his choice of a black-three button with a watery blue shirt, no tie, only compounded his blocky and naturally squinting face to indicate he was a man of protocol.

Kelly had reached the safety of the marquee a few feet from her door when the two men accosted her, the passenger taking the lead, as he was an inch above her eye level.

"Pardon me, Miss Barnett." He said with a reserved quietness as Kelly was adjusting her purse strap.

Kelly's astute brown eyes, free of the thick black vanity frames and honored with an artistically heavy application of kohl, passed quickly between the two men and the threatening nature of the taller man and the pride emanating from him was immediately offset by the shorter and classily-dressed man who was courteous with the presentation of his badge so that Kelly could see she was dealing with the Federal Bureau of Investigation. The man in the suit reminded Kelly a bit of Henry Morell in the fact that his hair was intentionally short, though not in the stylish way of Morell's, more of an even-keel and low maintenance choice of cut, and the man's three day growth gave him a sense of domestic uniformity, as if he were another soldier in off-the-rack urban armor.

"I'm Special Agent Blake Fosnick, this is my partner, Junior Special Agent Ricky DiMocco." Fosnick said with an arid and clipped speech, hiding an impediment that'd taken years to control and left him with a slow and discreet diction.

Kelly's brows crept together and she hitched up

her purse. The uneasy trio were protected from the rushing deluge of water pounding the street beneath the awning of the theater marquee.

"How can I help you?" Kelly raised her voice, the rain demanding it.

"We're here on behalf of the Department of Justice," Fosnick began, removing a leather-bound notebook from his inner pocket, much like the kind Kelly used, and flipped to a marked page before continuing. "And we're running a preliminary investigation into what may or may not amount to multiple counts of the obstruction and miscarriage of justice toward RepMax Security Contractors, LLC. Do you understand this as I have read it to you?"

"…Yes, but…"

"Ms. Barnett," Fosnick stuffed the notebook back inside his suit jacket. "It is my understanding that you assisted then Homeland Security Agent Henry Morell in his audit of RepMax as a private citizen given provisional clearances and allowances?"

Kelly's misanthropic frown deepened, and not on the count of Blake Fosnick's considerate and naturally peaceful demeanor.

Kelly made a few quick calculations.

"If you're asking the question you'd know I got a citation for that…what's the problem?" Her spine stiffened, though both men were still taller than her.

"The Department of Justice has been probing the facts of the case and are contemplating the possibility of Mr. Morell having acted unfairly, considering the circumstances."

"What circumstances?" Kelly's tone was sharp.

"Easy, Barnett." DiMocco chided with a sideways evil eye, as he'd been a smarmy-faced pillar gawking at the rain the whole time.

"I used to be a *political* journalist, you know,

don't try and muscle me." Kelly glared at him and
Fosnick passed a nearly saddened gaze to DiMocco and
knocked his chin toward the car, to which DiMocco
sighed and flipped the hood of his waterproof jacket
back up to lope across the sheets of raindrops as they
nearly bounced off the pavement.

"I'm sorry, Ms. Barnett." Blake Fosnick bowed
his head in the slightest and his right palm was up as his
left hand pulled at his suit jacket to rest on his firearm.
"The Department of Justice believes, as is the purpose
of this *preliminary* investigation, that Henry Morell was
acting under the interests of Tidebender International
during Homeland Security's audit on the count of his
findings reducing RepMax to ashes, whereupon he
subsequently *quit* Homeland Security to pursue a job
with Tidebender International, the first-year salary of
which would amount to, after taxes, one hundred and
seventy-two thousand dollars."

Kelly received Fosnick's mild-mannered and
reasonable delivery and seeing that she was attempting
to hide her surprise on what could be construed as
coincidence and more than likely was not, Fosnick
blazed on as if he was driving an unassumingly
mundane station wagon just a hair below the speed
limit.

"My goal is not to intimidate you into false
testimony or to badger you in any way into cooperating
against your will, and I apologize on behalf of Agent
DiMocco, but if you *were* privy to the knowledge, at
any time, that Mr. Morell was conducting the audit as
an abuse of Homeland Security's authority for the sake
of destroying a future competitor, then you *must* come
forward and have your statements sworn into a
deposition."

"For the sake of the truth or to save myself from
prosecution?"

"...Both."

The heavy sizzle of the rain and its scathing assault on Page Avenue drilled a wet tunnel through Kelly Barnett's mind, and all she could think about was that one night before the story of RepMax's bankruptcy broke the news.

Kelly could still hear Jessica Birchall's voice on the lead-in story like it was yesterday.

How on earth...

Kelly would *never* tell them what Hank told her that night, jabbing his chopsticks into a carton of Peking Pork and glowering with a vicious intent at the flickering images of the television.

Kelly sighed and swallowed with difficulty.

"Have you spoken with Henry, yet?" She asked, and then cursed herself for using his first name, perhaps appearing too intimate.

At least she didn't call him *Hank*.

"No, ma'am, I have not. Tidebender International has not been too...cordial with us and his cell phone appears to be switched off at the moment."

"Well," Kelly shrugged. "I'd like to help you but he's really the man you need to talk to."

Though nothing changed in Fosnick's blocky features a hardness subtly slid into his throat.

"Are you sure about that?"

"Excuse me?"

The hardness drifted up into Fosnick's eyes, and they began to burn as would a hunter who'd waited and waited in his hide to get the killshot of a rare and elusive game animal.

"You spent a great deal of time with Mr. Morell during this audit, Ms. Barnett. I'm quite sure you were aware of the circumstances."

Kelly flattened her lips and ran a finger along the edge of her purse strap till her elbow was locked and stiff.

It was an unconscious gesture, Fosnick noted, much like one shifting their weight to their heels. Considering her emerald green wool overcoat and all the semblances of a dress poking at its warm fringes, Fosnick decided to take a stab. Dark was falling and he would be speaking with Kelly Barnett again, in the future.

He was sure of it.

"Have a good night." Special Agent Fosnick nearly whispered, offering a trivial smile. "And if you see Mr. Morell, would you please tell him to turn on his phone, the FBI wants to have a word with him; or better yet…" The polite Agent reached into his inner pocket for a business card. "If you see him give him this. Especially if you're seeing him for dinner tonight. The Grand Ballroom of the Continental Plaza Suites, perhaps? Or maybe…Washington Centre on Fourth? He likes his steaks black and blue, New York strips, with a glass of Merlot, doesn't he? Oh, that's right…he won't drink a drop of alcohol. Kind of makes it hard to toast your…*friendship* without something to take away the bittersweet taste of the future from your palate, doesn't it?"

Kelly swallowed with even greater difficulty, averting her eyes from Fosnick's oddly passive sense of confrontation.

How did he know?

"Would you like a ride to Second Avenue, Ms. Barnett?"

"Goodbye, Special Agent Fosnick." Kelly said, with a plea edging her lips. She was and always had been afraid of Law Enforcement. Perhaps that was the deep psychological flaw in her friendship with Henry Morell; she was convinced he would protect her.

Even when he could not protect himself.

"Good evening, Ms. Barnett, thank you very much for your time."

Fosnick watched Kelly's figure shrink along the covered sidewalk till a two-story parking garage pulled her to the right and she disappeared altogether. Then DiMocco fired the engine and the lights of the Suburban cut through the falling tint of the rain-soaked evening.

Special Agent Blake Fosnick stared into the darkening sheets of rain in suspicious meditation before crossing the street to shelter from the dense weather.

"Do we need to follow her?" DiMocco asked.

"Nah..." Fosnick leaned back in his seat and reached for his phone. "She's going to the Grand Ballroom on Second. Morell lives like...four hundred feet away."

"Wanna make a bet she spends the night at his place?" DiMocco buzzed with confidence.

"Shut up." Fosnick stared out the window and DiMocco chuckled in between unsheathing a stick of peppermint chewing gum from the foil and his snapping chews of the gum as they competed with the slaps of the windshield wipers.

Regardless of Barnett's relationship with Morell, the bait was set.

ELEVEN

Rachael Calabrese was idly swirling a tumbler of Kahlua and half and half, letting the tinkling of the ice cubes work their own sonic therapy when the intercom chirped for her response.

"Go."

"It's Aimee…" Callie's assistant Meg Herman said with a strain of hesitation.

"The door's always open." Callie said and continued to run through Henry Morell's file, wondering why the FBI was calling her directly, asking to speak to him.

What have you done? She asked him silently, knowing there was only one way to get to the bottom of it. *And why isn't it in your file?*

Did you kill someone?

Callie's visitor had taken the door hidden in the arms and elbows of office necessities instead of the more cinematic entrance everybody else used. Callie pushed the folder aside and stood.

"What is it now?"

"Hello to you too."

Callie's head fell, chin nearly tucked in her neck.

"Did your dad send you?"

Aimee Jaziri, having taken her father's last name instead of her mother's and having chosen the college of her father thousands of miles from Crescent instead of her mother's alma mater *in* Crescent, was *still* her mother's child, despite the differences in their skin tone and whatever regret remained about a childhood spent questioning why her mother wasn't home. The night, in its dampened darkness, only solidified such memories, yet Aimee had come to the office by herself, for her own purpose.

Aimee was nearly the same size as Callie, so much so they could've shared clothes, and Callie deposited yet another passing thought in the wish bank about how life could've been different had it not been for the manifestation of CAP Syndrome, a psychological phenomenon not *one* accredited Doctor or Psychologist was willing to stake their reputation on the validity of.

Yet.

Which left Callie and Morell and those who had it to just...*deal* with the fruit of their actions and the personal pain it often caused for the greater good.

Aimee stifled a yawn. She was a striking young woman, with her mother's heart shaped face and blue eyes and her strawberry blonde mane of flirtatiously kinked curls were only partially embellished by the hairdresser. Despite the edge of attitude it gave her, her attire was conservative, albeit, a bit affluent.

"Remember what we were talking about last time I came here?"

Callie nodded, even though the event in question was late summer before her daughter's sophomore year had begun, and Callie snagged her drink on the way to the elevated seating platform. Five o'clock was smeared and smattered with dark rain making the seating area that much more cozy.

"About going to college?"

"Yes."

"What about it?" Callie shrugged. "I told you

there were a lot better colleges for you, but…your
father is a part-time faculty member there, and most of
his connections are back east. I understand."

It was then Aimee began to bite on a thumbnail
and stopped herself, sitting next to her mother on the
creamy chaise lounge.

"I had a fight with dad…about the future. He said
he won't pay for college anymore if I don't want to
work with him once I graduate."

Callie's lips pinched in an expression of shared
guilt. Blue-collar families often thought it was easier to
raise children if one had more money but with more
money came more responsibilities in the form of more
complications, and Aimee was caught in the middle of a
power-struggle for loyalty.

Since their divorce some ten years ago, Callie'd
done everything she could on Aimee's behalf, finding it
never to be enough and the most recent Christmas had
not been easy with the strain the Crisis was placing on
Tidebender. RepMax was getting lambasted in the news
and Callie was trying to smile and tell her college-age
daughter that mommy wasn't corrupt, a daughter that
was seeking to become a social reformer as her father
was and was equally as challenging by nature.

"Aims, we've made our mistakes, your father and
I, but at the end of the day, whatever you do is your
choice. We've always trusted you to do the right thing
because we've been upfront with you. I mean…you're
pro-life and you're saving yourself for marriage in a
culture that sneers at you and condemns you for doing
so as if you're brain dead…how is that not the perfect
environment for a social reformer?"

"Not to mention the racism."

Callie frowned, due to the nature of the Ivy
League school Aimee was attending and was still on
winter break from.

"Really?"

"Yeah. Last month I got called the *N* word after class." Aimee laughed, looking down at her mom's choice of Kahlua and cream, nearly the same color as the skin in question. "I told the girl my father was *Egyptian*…even though she's so dense I should've given her a point for knowing Egypt's in Africa…and Dad's got a bit of Sudanese in him."

"More than a bit. And your mother?" Callie smiled as Aimee poured herself some water.

"You didn't help." Aimee sipped and kicked back on the sectional. "I told her you were Miss Wonderbread. Then she thought I was making fun of whites. I mean, seriously, how come the most intolerant people in the world are those who claim to tolerate everything? She's a part of like, every club. She's anti-violence like you are but I thought she was going to claw my eyes out. Kinda scared me…"

Callie sensed a thread running though the conversation.

"This wasn't in *Ethical Consciousness and the Legal System*, was it?"

"Yeah."

"Were you grandstanding about pro-life?"

"…Maybe. It *was* a debate…but I just called her on her facts and she made it personal." Aimee kicked up to sit straight and her hands were curled as if holding an imaginary globe between them, a gesture she'd learned from her father when his words became impassioned with the prospect of making a difference.

"She tried to reference a Supreme Court case that never existed…I mean, that girl'd do *anything* to get her view out there."

"Politics are a dirty game, Aims." Callie sipped at her drink. "But social reform is a *way of life* and I don't want you to get the two confused." Callie's hands fell to her lap. "You've got a job here if you don't want to go work for your dad, you know that. There are always bathrooms that need cleaning."

Aimee rolled her eyes and shrugged, just her left shoulder.

"It's just that…I don't know. I don't want to be pressured. I've got two years left, and he wants me to declare a certain way so that he can *set things up*, as he said…I was wondering if you could talk to him."

"And say what?"

The intercom interrupted them and Callie pressed herself up, suddenly feeling her age as she crossed the distance to the splat of empty desks for the one that belonged to her.

"Go."

"Two men from the FBI are here to see you. I put them in ConFour, downstairs."

Callie's eyes drifted around the room.

Dammit, Henry. Why do they want you so bad they're putting pressure on me? What did you do to them?

Or was it something you didn't do? Something you should've done?

You've got to tell me, before they drag you through the mud.

Or drag me through the mud.

You can handle the mud.

I can't.

"Should I go?" Aimee asked, standing.

"No, no…it'd be better if I get them on neutral turf, I just have to think of something…"

"What about the SAAP Convention at the Continental Plaza?"

Callie hid a proud smile.

"Figures you would know about that."

"I was going to go."

"Well you can stay here for a bit, too, if you
want…it's a quiet place to make hard decisions, trust
me. Just stay away from my Kahlua. If you want,
though, there's a nice little sushi place hardly anyone
knows about within walking distance, maybe we could
meet up for a dragon roll or two after the Convention."

Aimee nodded with a winding twist curling her
lips as Callie rushed out of the office and Aimee saw
her mother's face shift to the difficulties of business in
the closing of the door as Meg helped her with the file
on the FBI Agents.

In the rushed conversation that passed between
them before the door wheezed shut, Aimee Jaziri
wished she could just wad up all of the bad memories
and open up one of those blurry brown glass panels and
let it fall to the ground.

Callie was a remarkable woman, and the older
Aimee got, the more it became an unavoidable truth.
Sure she had been home once for every six days a week
she was not, not to mention the foreign travels and
dad's constant assumptions that she hadn't been faithful
to him, but for some reason, seeing how she'd handled
the Crisis by taking on *more* work in the face of her
main competitor falling to a scandal of corruption
impressed Aimee to no end, considering not one of her
employees carried a gun or were allowed to use one in a
city overloaded with cops on edge. Her father always
spoke of change and this and that, but he'd chosen a
classroom, *part time* and Ivy League at that to get his
point across, whereas her mother was breaking her back
every single day to make the change happen.

The trickling sound of the fountain called to her
and before she could contemplate what she would say
to her father when it was time to go back to New
England for that strange push through to Spring Break
that every student felt so hard, Aimee noticed the file

her mother had been so intensely pouring over upon her daughter's entrance.

It was a thick one, seemingly divided between two subjects, and left open, either intentionally or unintentionally.

Did it matter?

Aimee checked the slim fashion watch at her wrist, knowing she still had a few hours till the Convention was to begin, and sat in the chair, still warm from her mother's presence, to read about a man she'd never met.

The details of the documents, once she began, were classified and illegal for her to be in the very vicinity of, making them all the more desirable to her spear-point attitude about what was truth, what was not, and what the public was allowed to know and not know.

Again, another heated debate in *Ethical Consciousness and the Legal System* class, this time with the teacher.

Aimee's blue eyes darted through line after line and she felt her pulse jump as if she'd mainlined caffeine after reading the harrowing account of Henry Morell's condition for his Commendation Medal and Purple Heart.

Not to mention what'd happened to him during the Crisis.

Was he one of her mother's employees?

On the very last page Aimee squinted and craned her neck to read her mother's wiggly cursive shorthand.

He was the one she'd opted to meet Christmas Eve. *He* was the one she'd turned down Professor Jaziri's ritzy shindig in Boston for.

She had to meet him.

The killer, all of five foot six without his platform

boots, opened the door for room service with a hasty
smile poking from beneath a scruffy, reddish beard. The
waiter was a lanky man, twenty-three or so, and didn't
notice the killer steal the security pass from his own
back pocket. The entire right wing of the Continental
Plaza was locked down on behalf of the State's
Awareness And Procedure Convention concerning the
Crisis, even though it was a not-so-subtle front for a
meeting of monetary policy and the diceyness thereof.

And, though it had nothing to do with the next
three billionaires on his list, the killer relished the
thought of panic sweeping the city at his shadowed
hand.

After all, it was anxiety that forced error, never
tranquility, and a true assassin operated in silence and
secrecy by the very notion that chaos was *his*
tranquility. The killer had been studying videotape of
the press conferences, first at some smaller levels and
then consecutively up the food chain as they lead to the
unorthodox tri-state confluence of elected officials, and
Law Enforcement, determined not to let something like
the Crisis happen again.

As if they had a choice.

The killer laughed inside. At their pride, their
vanity, their foolishness. At his age, one knew what life
was about, how to push all the buttons, and how to see
past the ridiculous pretenses people insisted on living
by.

And dying by.

"Just leave it there, will you?" The killer pointed
to a spot near the television across from the bed and the
young waiter complied with slow precision as if the
tray was carrying a soufflé.

The five o'clock news was limping through itself
at far too loud of a volume and it seemed to rattle the
young waiter. The killer knew he'd commit the fact to

memory and counted on it. Channel Two's newest entry-from-commercial graphic whipped across the screen, accompanied by a catchy and somehow at the same time irritating jingle, and the aged face of Don Cramer who relayed breaking news in his deep and resonant voice abruptly followed.

He set up the story as if those listening had never heard it even though every station in the city and even those at a national level were including it in their feeds.

News was an instant occurrence now, like a scratch ticket. Just pay for it up front, with your time or your money, give it a scratch, and wear the sullen face of a loser because you've been had.

The killer laughed to himself that his was an honest profession.

Sort of.

The picture shifted to a young blonde, whom the killer thought was quite pretty and was probably wasting her talents being a member of the fourth estate when she very well could've been an actress with a face like she had.

And those teeth, they practically glowed as she stood under her umbrella rambling on about how Maks Lenkov had committed suicide just after shooting his wife. No further details were known, though this particularly fine-looking woman hinted at both foul play and a cover up and the killer smirked that she was so bold. Did the cops know all that? He hoped she had some pretty good facts. It was a shame she'd probably lose her job, he didn't remember having seen her before, but being so glamorous for the camera and all had its benefits.

Oh well…

There wasn't much upside for reporters, their jobs *constantly* on the line with the caveat of truth and all, since truth was harder to appropriate than clean air, and the killer laughed inwardly at the joke of it all, considering his falsified press credentials on the bed and the camera equipment next to them he was no where near adept at using.

"Will that be all, Sir?" The waiter asked as the killer stood on the balls of his feet, the remote in his hand like a knife.

The waiter repeated himself and the killer turned, squinted, and held a cupped hand to his ear. His eyes were hidden by thick false glasses so the waiter couldn't read the color of them.

"Will that be all?" The waiter offered a shrug and pointed to the food and the killer shook his head and threw his hand to the door, urging the man to shove off without a tip. The young man cursed under his breath at the middle-aged press photographer as he left, completely unconscious of the fact that he was a killer of extreme savvy and was actually ten years older than the waiter assumed and the moment the waiter left, the killer began the painstaking work of cutting up the burger he'd ordered as if to make it look like he'd bitten into it once or twice and gotten bored, going as far as to apply a quick drying clear gel from a small bottle with a swab.

Then he shifted his focus to the bathroom, the place an assassin spent nearly as much time as anywhere else, and flushed the portion of the burger that he was supposed to have eaten and removed his beard and slipped in his contact lenses, preparing himself to commit murder, as he was so adept and well-trained at doing.

TWELVE

Morell found a half-empty pack of Camels in a leather jacket draped over the edge of his bed and contemplated smoking one, standing near the drizzle of rain spilling from the gutters of the businesses; coffee and tapas bar, misses boutique, and art dealer, respectively, that sat below his cottage-style apartment complex, rated one of the hippest in town. To Henry, it was more of a cover than anything, seeing as he was hardly home, and Kelly seemed to come alive when visiting, something about the vibrancy of the well-to-do youngsters chewing through gigs of Wi-Fi data over foamy tops of their chai lattes and the buzz of the conversation snipping and snapping between them.

Morell was glad he hadn't smoked the cigarette, because Kelly smacked him on the arm whenever he even *thought* about it, and the Nineteen Seventy Verdoro Green Pontiac GTO was a sight for sore eyes, glugging through gas with its rumbling resonance in a hot zone of bus passes, bikes, and toy-like electric cars.

Kelly rolled down the window at the same time Morell was stuffing the pack in his inner jacket pocket.

"Those aren't Marlboros, are they?" Kelly's astute brown eyes were narrowed and looking particularly pretty without the thickness of black plastic and clear class to cover them up.

"Your coat matches the car." Morell said, rushing

around the front and the fizzling of raindrops dancing in front of the yellowed glow of the headlamps.

"Does that make it a car coat?"

"You avoided the question." Kelly said, putting the car in gear to complete the short drive to their destination. She had to wait for a space in traffic since the heaviness of the sky's dirty blankets had put a damper on everyone's day and slowed life to a crawl. "And you would know what a car coat is better than I. You *do* live above a boutique."

Morell shrugged with a *c'est la vie* sort of energy he knew Kelly needed, in lieu of her on again off again bouts with sobbing and winter sadness.

"Am I acceptable?" Morell pinched the lapels of his gray Burberry suit he knew was Kelly's favorite because of its sixties mod flavor.

"Just barely." Kelly signaled to hop over a lane and ease the muscle car into the Continental Plaza's grand pillared entrance, looking all the more regal and Georgian in the dampness and the glow of the inset spotlights cutting up the fences of green hedges to wash the five story block in an ethereal sense of pomp and circumstance.

"I'm starving." Morell said, rubbing his hands together.

"Do you think it'll be better than the Jade combo at the Lucky Peacock? I got kinda hooked on the sweet and sour."

"You know I turned down a lunch date with a CPD Lieutenant today?"

"Really?" Kelly said, exiting the car as the valet tried to hide a smile at being able to putter vintage muscle around the parking lot. One became weary of high dollar German imports and similarly styled luxury vehicles.

Morell waited for Kelly to link arms as they

passed the towering pillars of the golden, nearly royal
block letters ushering them inside.

"What's her name?" Kelly curled her hair behind
her right ear, her eyes lingering over the massive
bouquet of Arabian jasmine, Turkish tulips, and Indian
lotus, once inside the spacious lobby.

"Her? Am I that obvious?"

"I *was* a very good journalist in my day."

"Was? Tell that to RepMax."

Kelly swallowed and bit her lip, pretending to
examine the ruddy hematite tiles flowing through thick
blocks of chalky Carrara marble creating an intricate
rose pattern. Her reticence was not on behalf of a
woman asking Morell out to lunch, no doubt one who
was professional and competent and was very aware of
her offer, but of the FBI's accosting of only minutes
ago, joggled from a place of avoidance by mention of
that company's accursed name.

I have to tell him, she thought, but hated the idea
of ruining the moment, and whatever the moment had
to offer.

*God, he's so happy...I'm so happy, or at least I
was.*

I'll tell him later.

The Grand Ballroom, the restaurant and not truly
the destination thereof, as was the location of the State
Awareness And Procedures Convention, was *the* place
in town for the way food used to be, rich and decadent,
as if the Continental Plaza was a time warp in the fact
that it occupied the most *progressive* district in all of
Crescent. The booths were deep and high backed in a
broad space of forest green, claret red, dark wood and
gilt trim with pristine white table cloths and the lounge
was dominated by a Steinway older than the one that
had been burned to a crisp at the Fircrest Mansion in
November.

"Blonde or brunette?"

"Oh the cop?" Morell smirked, enjoying the fact
that he didn't know if Kelly was jealous or as eager to
see him paired up with someone as compatible as he
was with her. His eyes went to the calligraphy of the
menu, set in the wall behind glass, pretending to study
it, even though he wanted a steak with mushroom
cream sauce, whether it was on the menu or not.
"Would you like to meet her?"

"I'd rather meet Callie." Kelly confessed as they
were lead to their seat, an intimate two-person model in
the core of the restaurant floor. Morell's view two
hundred feet past Kelly was of a stainless steel bar and
a muddle of white chef's jackets and tall hats behind it,
one of them managing the licking flames of an order of
Bananas Foster, whereas Kelly's view, two hundred
feet past her date was of those slowly milling into the
lobby for the Convention, many of them constituents of
the middle class.

Morell whistled as Kelly removed her green
overcoat, and she blushed, having been unconscious
about his eyes on her. She'd chosen a sleeveless form-
fitting white dress of pink and red cherry blossoms with
a peter pan collar. Gold bangles clinked at each wrist
and a gold band was on her engaged finger.

"I've been saving it for a rainy day."

Morell laughed with two easy exhales.

"You're amazing."

Kelly Barnett's smile was sallow on her cute face
because the thought of two FBI Agents ruining their
evening would *not* leave her mind.

Callie had taken a quick detour to her private top
floor restroom to change, having several sets of clothes
on hand for the various scenarios she often found
herself in, such as a foreign climate or a black tie event.

Choosing a black silk kimono dress, stockings and shrug boots of the same color and an opera-length eight millimeter Akoya pearl necklace, she put her hair in a bun, stuck a pair of lacquered chopsticks in it, and affixed a pair of silver wire-framed reading glasses on the bridge of her nose. To complete the ruse, she took a stack of meaningless folders Meg had given her under her arm and used the long elevator ride to the lobby to mentally prepare herself to deal with the FBI. Meg had informed her of the FBI Agents' impatience and their inability to wait in one of the Conference rooms, which ended up being for the better, as Callie felt more comfortable in the spaciousness of the lobby she had designed to give those in it a sense of transition.

Callie just about reached the concierge desk when one of the Agents made eye contact.

Let the games begin, she thought.

"Hello." She said, nearly squinting. "Have we met before?"

Blake Fosnick stood and buttoned his suit jacket, crossing the distance to Callie as she handed one of her classy minions the stack of folders. Agent DiMocco sat dozens of feet away, tapping on his smart phone.

"I don't think so."

"No," Callie tipped her chin to the left. "It was the Pentagon, wasn't it? You were on the Secretary of the Navy's staff."

"No." Fosnick lied, stopping once he was standing just a bit too close for Callie's comfort, though Callie wouldn't budge, fully ensconced in her mantle of civility. "You must be thinking of someone else."

"Well I'm Rachael Calabrese."

"Blake Fosnick." They shook hands. "Special Agent, FBI."

"And my assistant was telling me your were anxiously awaiting my arrival, so, here I am." Callie smiled warmly, trusting in her patented psychological tactic of cycling subtle attacks and backhanded compliments, hoping Fosnick would get confused as to what Callie knew and what she was bluffing about, and most importantly, what she was hiding and why. In Callie's opinion, Fosnick *had* to assume she would be protecting Morell and his actions, even though they predated his *official* contractual employment with Tidebender International. Perhaps Fosnick would be sly and try to convince her that if Morell was negligent in his prosecution of RepMax, and if she supported the FBI's investigation with full disclosure, then Morell would burn *independently* of Tidebender and Callie would be free of him, especially since it was his first day on the job.

What a coincidence…

"Does Henry Morell work here?" Fosnick asked in a near whisper.

"You know he does." Callie said. "Or else you wouldn't be here."

"Is he available?"

"No, he's off for today."

"Well, we might have to be subtracting him from your roster for awhile."

"Oh? Why's that?" Callie removed her glasses, folding them slowly. Her face was a genial veneer disguising extreme disgust. The fact that RepMax was a collection of mercenaries hidden in plain sight, stealing contracts from a woman who was determined to *remove* violence from third party security groups frustrated her to no end. In that regard, Callie was Morell's ally, regardless of the way he'd destroyed her rival.

"The DOJ is interested in him."

"Is that a subpoena I hear in your voice?"

"Does it have to be?"

Callie pursed her lips and brought her hands

together as if praying, pointing them at Fosnick's chest.

"Let's not stand on ceremony here, Mr. Fosnick." Her words were clear and delicate. "We both know what you want."

Fosnick's blocky face was unimpressed, no need to hide it. She wanted him to spell it out, to come out and say it. But from his point of view, he held all the cards on the matter and wasn't playing a single one till he was sitting opposite Henry Morell at FBI headquarters in Washington D.C.

"Then we both know I'm going to get it."

"If only these things worked like that."

Fosnick sighed with a long and laborious inhale, letting his eyes drift around the busy airport concourse-styled lobby as many of Tidebender's employees were leaving for the night. The carpet danced with the dots and splotches of rain as if they were amoebic shadow puppets.

"And you know how these things work?"

"More than you know, Mr. Fosnick."

"Agent."

"It doesn't change the fact that I can't help you if he's not here."

Fosnick seemed to be distracted for the smallest second by Callie's lacquered chopsticks but when he did speak his eyes were dead in their sockets.

"Before you take your daughter Aimee to the SAAP Convention at the Continental Plaza where Henry Morell is more than likely having dinner with a former political journalist by the name of Kelly Barnett, I just want you to know that there's no reason to ruin your outstanding and...*morally* venerable career over a soldier of fortune type like Hank Morell. He's not worth it, never will be. If you know what's good for you *and* your company, Ms. Calabrese, you'll find the time to pass my message along to him. Good evening to you, ma'am."

Fosnick wouldn't let Callie respond, leaving the bitter taste of his words in her mouth as he skulked towards the couch DiMocco was slouching out his stint of nonverbal support on and collected his partner to press back into the rain for the next phase of their plan.

The disturbing detail of his comments and the stiff, cold manner of their delivery chilled Callie's spine like the night breeze coming straight off the shipping lanes of the Targus River and she was left standing in the broad lobby to contemplate what to do about it.

After a shared starter of crab cakes with corn whipped cream and watercress foam, Morell moved his water glass aside to lean on the table.

"So, Kelly…" He said, hiding a smile. "What did you find?"

"Your history lesson?" She shook her head. "No way. Not here. That's not right."

Morell's hands were wide.

"Come on, seriously Kel, what do you think all these people are talking about?"

"I don't know…" She shrugged and cleansed her palette in anticipation of something she couldn't afford to eat every day and her eyes swelled comically. "Work?"

"You are particularly funny tonight, Kel, any reason for that?"

"Yeah…" Kelly curled her hair behind her ear. "I've been hanging around this one guy a lot."

"Oh?"

"Yeah, he's kind of annoying, but he's alright. He makes me laugh, so…I try to return the favor. Or I should say *tries* to make be laugh…but, you know, recycling is good for the planet and all."

"He sounds…tolerable?"

"Yeah, he's not one for sarcasm, which is like my second favorite thing in life behind coffee and cat memes."

Morell mashed his lips together not to laugh as she flexed her sarcastic muscles and her eyebrows were twisted together with an incredulous cuteness all her own.

"Yeah, well...I've been meaning to ask you about something..." Morell moved his chair a hint to the right and crossing his leg high at the knee, and a small knot wriggled around in her stomach at the thought of him saying something deep and meaningful considering their relationship. She'd avoided it as if it were wildfire to even think it, and wondered if Henry ever knew she'd reciprocate in a heartbeat if he wanted to marry her.

Above anything, she *respected* Henry Morell and was ever-conscious that he *respected* her.

"Excuse me, Sir." The waiter lisped, ducking his head in some form of embarrassment. "We just ran out of morel mushrooms, would you be okay with chanterelles?"

Morell stared at the man blankly for a second before nodding.

"Imagine that?" He said. "The nerve of this place to run out when I show up. Do they know who I am? There goes his tip."

Kelly could tell he wasn't going to say what he wanted to, the train of it having left with the waiter's untimely interruption and Henry's jovial spin of it, and he certainly wasn't going to say what she *hoped* he was.

Not now.

It wasn't fair to him. Especially if he did desire to deepen their relationship.

She had to tell him.

"Two FBI Agents accosted me as I left my place

to come get you."

The man's boyish features solidified as his eyes snapped to lock on hers, losing the dimples that had become permanent since entering the car.

"What were their names?" He nearly growled, and it was obvious he knew what they were leaning on her for.

The notion sickened him.

"Fosnick and..."

"DiMocco?"

"Yeah, how'd you know?"

"On behalf of the DOJ, they said?"

"Yeah." Kelly's breath was tight in her chest and she took a sip of ice water to still herself, finding it was *no* placebo.

Morell stifled a string of military-style curses for the sake of the wining and dining surrounding him and balled his fists. His dark eyes were boring holes in the carpet as he weighed his options, now that they'd tempted to drag Kelly into the mud pit.

She was petrified; the sinister intention tinting Morell's face in the mood lighting only sealed such insecurities.

If the FBI ever found out why and more importantly *how* Henry Morell had destroyed Tidebender's competitor in the confusion following the Crisis, Kelly would not only lose proximity's promise with her close friend for good, but be restricted to seeing him once a month, in the visitor's wing of Supermax as he shuffled from his cell in an orange jumpsuit.

Because she *did* know, for better or worse.

THiRTEEN

After Jessica Birchall had cast a weary brown-eyed glance to the digital readerboard to see her flight had been delayed for the second time on the count of a storm front stretching diagonally from Kansas City to the tip of Maine, she drug her small carry on and satchel of nearly the same weight to a sports-themed bar in the departure terminal to wait it out. Boston was suffering under a heavy dose of snow and the already beleaguered Channel Two News reporter was staring down the straw of a Long Island Iced Tea when a man's voice broke her self-centered concentration.

"Is this seat taken?"

Birchall pushed her drink aside and removed her wallet from the satchel.

"No, but I was just about to leave."

The man, whom she hadn't really got a good look at in her state of depression, checked the bent elbows and muddled voices of travellers sporadically dusted across the sports bar to see their involvement stretched no further than the bottlenecks of their beers, the noise of flats screen TV's, and the company they kept.

No one was listening.

"It'd be better if you stayed…Ms. Birchall."

Her eyes leapt to him and froze on the business card cupped in his hand.

"I take it…" The reporter eased her wallet back in

the satchel. "You don't show that to a lot of people?"

The man only affirmed her question with a shake of his head and sat down. He was tall, with a tight reddish goatee and frameless prescription glasses. She noticed he was wearing the hat of a football team from some other city, though she honestly didn't know enough about football to remember where from, or if it was collegiate or professional. His drab and heavy choice of clothing completed a certain amorphous disguise and it wasn't until he removed his hat that she saw his hair was short, brown, widow-peaked and spiky.

"Is that your real name on that card?" She asked further, the pilot light of her investigative consciousness flickering to life.

The man only offered her an expression, saying *it is if you think it is, it's not if you think it's not.*

"It is my understanding that you've been fired from Channel Two." He said.

"I bet that's not *all* you know." Birchall's Iced Tea suddenly became more appealing, and then it occurred to her to offer him a drink, which he declined, stating that he *couldn't*, and that he'd be glad to take a rain check, no pun intended.

"So you want to become a whistleblower?" He asked.

"You're blunt."

"I don't have a lot of time."

"Whereas I have five hours…" Birchall frowned at him. "Are you sure you won't have that drink?"

"I know you've been offered an anchor position in Boston, which…" The man shrugged and cast his eyes quickly to his hat, and the coincidence of the symbiotic location thereof. "I mean, that's cool, but, don't you think it's kind of a dead end job?"

"It's not dangerous, that's for sure." Birchall said,

implying that she was well aware of where he was leading her, considering the acronym spelled out on his business card.

"You don't know what I'm about to ask you."

"I don't have to." Birchall removed her cell phone from her jacket pocket, placing it on the table, to which the man gave no reaction. "I worked with Homeland Security during the Crisis and we both know what happened there. I wasn't exactly protected from the fallout. I was nearly forced to testify against someone I knew was a hero and was only saved by the bell, so to speak."

"You seem to be doing alright."

"I just got *fired*."

"You can't have your cake and eat it too, Ms. Birchall. If you want to know the truth, you're going to have to get your hands dirty."

Strangely she'd used a similar tone with Jasmine Keelan. But their conversation seemed so distant now.

Perhaps it was the man's honesty, and the lack of the old butter-up process she was so used to dealing and being dealt, but Birchall felt like he was appealing to a segmented portion of her psyche, buried deep beneath the many necessities and processes so vital to make it in the business and climb the proverbial rope ladder without hanging oneself in the rat race or being hung by someone else. In essence, the man was saying, *if you want to shine a light on the truth, stop caring about everything else. It doesn't matter. If you agree to what I'm about to ask you, you won't have to worry about make-up sessions, Teleprompters, and a corporate bureaucracy that says what you can and cannot report. You get the truth and whatever comes along with it, all or nothing.*

"Okay." She said. "What is it?"

"War crimes. Iraq."

"Would you mind if I record this?" She asked, eyesight tightened.

"No one's going to dump you this time."

"So that's a no."

"Yes, it is."

Birchall cast a *to hell with it* gesture to the man, and perhaps the Long Island Iced Tea was to blame.

"Okay, just lay it out. I'm not going anywhere."

"War crimes, Iraq." The man reiterated, with a slow nod. "Two-thousand three, a JSOC mission code-named *Wolf Stone*." The man waited till a romantic couple stumbled past, obviously about to return from a honeymoon and caught in the throes of each other's intoxicated proximity. "A CIA operative lead a hand-picked team in Baghdad to a spice market in Karkh for the purpose of securing a man named Abu Abd-Al Safah for interrogation. The Intel was that he knew the exact location of roughly seven hundred biological ICMB's." Jessica Birchall leaned forward, clasping her hands and the man's face betrayed the pain of a difficult situation, cultivated by the insanity of demanded retribution, the truculent nature of which only brought out the worst humankind had to offer.

"I'm listening." She said, encouraging the man with a softer tone. Judging his face, it was apparent that he was coming to Birchall not on *behalf* of the CIA, but on behalf of a man who more than likely still worked for the CIA and was sick and tired of carrying the burden of what had transpired in his conscience.

"It turned out to be a trap, but…the problem was not the trap itself, but what happened after."

"War crimes."

He nodded gravely.

"Forty eight people died."

Birchall's eyebrows jumped and she craned her neck.

"Forty-eight?" The pitch of her voice spiked. "How many were combatants?"

"None, if you discount the fifteen that ambushed the JSOC team and, eventually, Abu Abd-Al Safah."

"Eventually?"

"Yes, the…lead operative cut off both of his feet, leaving him alive to expire in agony and ordered the execution of a nearby boarding house *with* the ambushing soldier's weapons." The man swallowed with difficulty. "Furthermore, this operative planted evidence to insinuate that it was the Taliban who performed the massacre. Joint Command took this *evidence* further up the chain till it got to the President, leading to the passing of much harsher policies concerning the treatment of indigenous personnel."

Birchall's critical and penetrating brown eyes hovered in the space above the man's head as the puzzle pieces slipped together.

"Waterboarding?"

"Not just that," The man shook his head, his right hand stilling her thoughts as they began to run away with themselves. "General policy, rules of engagement, command decisions and the like; infecting everything from black ops to daily street sweeps to the humanitarian relief budget. What I'm saying is that the President was lied to and everything that happened *from* that date was directly influenced by this little secret in the back of his mind that the US Government was acting on behalf of innocent people, granted, this falsified report gets lumped onto a great many sins of *true* account and dirties the water. That's the difficulty of the predicament. I've just been waiting for the fog of war to fade and can't wait any longer."

Jessica Birchall finished her drink, welcoming the slight numbness in her throat. She'd have to get over her fear of imprisonment if she wanted to expose the darkest secrets of humanity, and the despondency she'd succumb to was on the count of her dying to that desire by verbally committing to the anchor job in Boston where she'd glam it up and smile and sit with her hands neatly folded on the news desk like some trained house cat.

"What do you need me for?" She asked.

"Isn't it obvious? You're a member of the media."

"But what do I need to do?"

The man reached inside of his jacket for a folded piece of paper Birchall couldn't read and checked it.

"How long till your flight leaves, Ms. Birchall?"

"Five hours, give or take…if ever." She said with a hollow smile and decided to stand, thus declaring herself in as if she were a poker player who'd pushed all of their chips to the center of the table. "But I'm going to get thirsty if we're going to be talking the entire time."

The man reciprocated, grabbing his red, white, and blue hat.

"You're right, and I'll tell you what, I'll take you up on that drink but not here. There's a lounge further down the concourse where no one will bother us."

"Sounds good." Birchall nodded and shook hands. Hers were cold and delicate in his grip. "I'll be there in ten minutes."

The man departed with quick strides and left Birchall to pay for her Iced Tea and decide whether she really was all in or not.

Because, once she'd fallen into the deep end of the pool, she'd find the water was dark, thick with sharks and short on lifeguards.

Lucy Radzewicz set her keys in the earthenware dish on the kitchen counter, lit a scented candle, poured herself a glass of Rioja, threw her badge next to the gun in the safe in her office and bent at the waist while unbuttoning her trench to scan through her alphabetized CD collection. Feeling like Olga Kern's devastating gold medal performance of *Rachmaninov's Third Concerto* from the Van Cliburn competition, Lucy set it in her stereo system and took to a small white couch, knowing she had all of forty-two minutes to stare into the relative sparseness of her mid-century modern one-story retreat in Eavesdale and let the perfect combination of masterly performed music and thirty-five dollar red wine work their magic within her soul. As if on cue, the moment the pianist's fingers made contact with the weighty keys of the glossy black Steinway, Lucy's right hand released the bun holding captive her straight blonde hair, spilling it down the back of the white couch. As the piece progressed, its melodies weaving with the smell of lemon peel, her face betrayed, if only in the corners of her eyes, extreme satisfaction, akin to a baby in its mother's arms.

The applause at the recording's completion provoked her to rise from the light slumber she'd surrendered to and, wine in hand, Lucy found a bit of smooth reed-driven jazz for a dinner of boxed grilled chicken Caesar salad from the refrigerator, which she ate in a civilized manner, on a glazed earthenware plate with a fork and knife, staring out the generous squareness of the full-sized window to the boundless backyard of gently sloping communal property classified as protected wetlands. Eavesdale was one of those forgotten about middle-class neighborhoods, set up on a knoll beside which ran a pathetic yet somehow beautiful creek in which deer were known to loiter, and most of the mid-century modern homes were owned, as

once was hers, by those who'd purchased them some
seventy years ago. Some of the homes had a view of the
distant skyline, others did not, and the evergreen of
pines and firs bracketed a small shopping center two
miles' walk from the seemingly random spread of
houses, tucked up on top of the knoll that appeared
inadequate next to the riches of Fircrest and the
looming mountain of a hill it was. Eavesdale never
materialized into the Palm Springs of greater Crescent,
as the developer had hoped back in the Rat Pack era,
but the result was a nice hideaway for those who were
still keeping the peace of the place a secret. Lucy had
received the home in her father's will and there were
times, such as the moment, when she wouldn't know
what she'd be like, what *life* would be like if she
couldn't, at the end of the day, come back *home.*

After all, she'd taken her first steps only ten feet
away from the small white couch, waddling across the
walnut-toned wood floor, and not much time after that,
she'd tripped on the corner of the horizontal-striped rug
in which slept every color the crayon box had to offer
and hit her head on the broad lip of the low fireplace,
thus sustaining the injury that would follow her for the
rest of her time on earth.

She was a miracle, the doctors said, with near
total facial paralysis being the only permanent side
effect to the extreme head trauma that had hospitalized
her for the entire month of January, all of thirty-eight
Januaries ago.

Henry Morell had looked at her like she was too
young, well, paralysis had its side effects but it had its
bonuses, too. Her VikingPole baby face and God-given
straight blonde hair had made her a real man-killer so to
speak in Vice, having more arrests of solicitation for
prostitution on undercover operations than any other
Detective in the *history* of Crescent Vice.

Had she changed? Well, everybody changed with the Crisis, the city of Crescent itself included.

But had she?

In Vice, she was one of the guys; getting a laugh with the beat cops when they slapped the cuffs on yet another john after she walked out of the bathroom with her badge and gun and the john thought it was all a part of what he'd paid for, in a manner of speaking, only to find the permanency of the mistake was no joke.

Somehow those seemed like the good old days, just as it did after her mother died, as terrible as that would sound to most people, and her father would give music lessons all day at the old upright piano in what was now Lucy's office. It was still there, dusty and unused, more of a decoration than anything, but Lucy could never play the piano as he dreamed she would, and he could never teach her as a man who, himself, was incapable of perfection.

Now, she just didn't have the time, and the dream of being such a skilled pianist was out of reach.

And she had been prepared to give her precious time to the Department and take on more responsibility even with the new salary cap, as she'd promised the interim Police Chief following the chaos of November, but it was as if those around her resented her for being a Lieutenant, *despite* all that she'd done in Vice, they resented her skipping a few spaces on the proverbial game board, and she couldn't for the life of her figure out why.

Once her glass of wine was finished, Lucy poured herself another and switched off the music in an effort to track down the castle she knew she'd seen before via the internet on the workhorse of a desktop in her office.

The thought of calling Henry Morell flashed through her mind and she pursed her lips as he'd be eating dinner somewhere, having a good time, completely relaxed and removed from the contained environment of the investigation. To think of Morell's upside, his humor and what sort of outrageous stories he had stuffed up his sleeve, embellished though they held the possibility of being, bothered her all the more because she couldn't change. Lucy in the office was Lucy at home. There was no phone booth for her to transform in, no switch to flip, and her environment only sealed that. She'd lived in no other home her whole life, no other city.

She'd been in no other skin nor made any attempt to transform the one she'd been given, flaws and all.

Maybe that was the very reason for the eyes of judgment she's seen over the rims of Styrofoam cups of bitter coffee, and the emotional distance everyone seemed to take with her.

No one wanted to be her friend because she wouldn't play the game.

Wouldn't and *couldn't*.

She didn't have the capacity to scrunch up her face and coo over the cuteness of a co-worker's new baby as they flicked through dozens of pictures on a cell phone, driving their point in the dirt.

But some were called to be alone, weren't they? Olga Kern had played *Rachmaninoff's Third* with a full orchestra before an audience *yearning* for the very best she had to offer, but had they been there every time she sat down at the piano to practice?

Day in? Day out?

Lucy decided not to call Morell but sent him a text about coming to pick him up at the Tidebender building at eight o'clock sharp and changed it to ten, on the prospects of his wining and dining turning into a much longer night.

Only time would tell if he really was different than the rest, or if her judgment had been tainted by the

fact that she was a loner in plain-sight, anachronistic in
a society so driven by the motivation of human emotion
that being a woman cop who simply did a damn fine
job and not much else just wasn't good enough
anymore.

FOURTEEN

The man known in the circles of international
terrorism and paid killings as *The Lynx* threw the
photography bag over his shoulder and walked with a
jaunty strut down the hall, conscious of the cameras,
their blind spots, and what fun he'd have in retrospect
with the cops trying to piece together the disappearing
act he was about to perform right under their pedantic
little noses. Security was heightened for the
Convention, obviously, as the very nature of the whole
proceeding was to placate the public with a policy of
transparency on their safety as citizens.

Bollocks, the killer thought, and laughed at
himself as he took the stairwell, all the while the clock
inside of him tick-tocking away. He'd acted British for
so long he was unconsciously *thinking* British. What
was next, driving on the left?

The Lynx hated politics and hated politicians
even more. To them, lying was all a part of the game,
and though the killer known as The Lynx wasn't the
foolish and sentimental type, his blood boiled over the
injustice of governments and the idea of bottle-feeding
the citizens of Crescent about security and safety
following the mayhem of the Crisis was the other side
of the coin from running a hush-hush cover-up, and the
Convention might as well have been passing around
blotter acid like it was Woodstock, seeing as it would

create the same hallucinogenic parameter of protection when weighed against the harsh facts of truth.

Better keep it far from the public, then. The truth always had a way of stinging like frostbite.

Crescent was balancing on a tender tiptoe, walking the psychological tightrope, and he was about to bring out the pruning shears and watch Crescent free-fall into the void.

It would make the next three billionaire assassinations as easy as palming a candy bar in a convenience store.

At least to him.

It was nearly seven thirty when The Lynx re-entered the Continental Plaza, having spent the time outside in his rental car wiring an explosive to the door remote lock and placing a suppressed one-shot Twenty-Two-caliber marksman's pistol into a hollow camera with a telephoto lens. Clearly labeling himself as a member of the press with his baggy cargo pants and scruffy mop of greasy blonde hair, fake though it was, and multiple cameras slung around his body, he was nowhere near the man registered to room Seven-Eighty-One or the man who'd left Seven-Eighty-One and traipsed around the halls with canvas bags over his shoulder.

Instead, his vest, branded *AP*, coordinated with his timed entrance, stuffed him in the middle of a great many other photojournalists and news media eager to check in their credentials with the grim-faced suits of the plainclothes Officers and the jump-suited, nearly tactically-armed CPD beat cops funneling the fourth estate through the airport-borrowed full body scanner.

Once in the throng of seventy-some media lemmings, overeager to sell the same shot as the one next to them, The Lynx noted the placement of the security cameras in the left wing of the Continental Plaza as it worked its way, with a broad and nearly palatial sense of unnecessary opulence, toward the Grand Ballroom.

He waited till he'd hit the blind spot of one and stole the credentials from the man in front of him as they dangled at his side on a lanyard.

Then he started to cough, lightly at first and then more violently, holding his breath as he bent over and worked his way to the back of the line, conscious of the cops' location.

A flash of black, white, and ruby red struck his fancy and he nearly ran into it.

"Sir, are you okay?" One of the caterers asked.

"Waadah…" He said with an exaggerated New Yorker's drawl, his voice dry and scratchy. The flesh of his face was tomato red, and his eyes were nearly bulging from holding his breath to the point of light-headedness.

In the curtness of the caterer's nod, The Lynx committed to the hope that he lived by, that the man saw the color of his eyes, and noted they were brown, as was the color of the contacts he'd placed in them, instead of their being the strange shade of yellowy-green they truly were.

"Please, follow me to the kitchen."

The gears of his inward clock ticking, The Lynx followed the caterer to the kitchen, which took five minutes of walking and in its furious clangor and chaos he took a seat on an overturned vegetable box near the corner of the walk in freezer and weakly awaited his promised glass of water.

"Thanks." He said, and the caterer rushed off, the headless chicken that he was, not knowing that the man he'd given water to was a deadly assassin and was in no way going to leave his DNA so blatantly at the scene of

such imminent mayhem, insanity, anarchy, and
instinctually primal self-preservation.

Kelly dabbed her napkin at the right corner of her
mouth, thus completing the splendiferous event of
never having eaten so much food in her life, save that
one Thanksgiving in her youth where it all came back
up again. Chemically, the opus of fats, oils, sweets and
other negligent members of the food pyramid were
slouching her a bit further down in her seat and
loosening the cuteness of her bookish features.

"Better than sweet and sour?" Morell smirked,
still working on a cup of coffee.

Kelly leaned on the table with both elbows tight
in front of her.

"Yeah…"

"I can see it in your face, Kel. You need a couch."

"You can carry me."

"You can sleep it off in the car, Kel, but if you
want to meet Callie you'd better finish this coffee."

Kelly's eyes regained their intelligent snap and
she took Morell's cup and threw it back like a shot, all
but gargling it.

"Thatagirl." He said and stood, having already
paid and got Kelly's chair for her and gave her a side
hug, which he held more for her stability as they
walked to the sumptuous lobby of white Italian marble.

"Thanks for dinner, Hank, I mean…"

"Hey, you had it coming."

Kelly waited till they had crossed the lobby and
were approaching one of the heavily guarded entrances
to the Grand Ballroom. Walking helped straighten her
posture and it occurred to her how comfortable the
restaurant chairs had been, now that she'd left the
coziness they'd worked hand in hand with the Beef
Wellington and demi glace to fabricate.

"Hank, there was something you were going to say."

"Hmm?" He was scanning the group of faces waiting to get in the Convention and take their place. The back of the spacious Ballroom was open for a reasonably priced, stand-only general admission; and seats, arranged in comfort and proximity to the elevated stage, were purchasable by reservation with all monies going to the city's dwindling relief funds.

Charitable donations and favorable appearances by the city's corporate ruling elite had been privately encouraged, but were yet to be realized.

"You were going to tell me something earlier and you never did."

Thoughts passed across Morell's dark eyes as if he was viewing a kaleidoscope and then it came to him.

"Oh yeah, I…"

"Mr. Morell?"

Henry turned, both surprised and delighted to see the gracious loveliness of Rachael Calabrese, looking every bit the international traveler she truly was. He wouldnt've put it past her to know conversational Japanese with as much as she crossed the Pacific in her private jet and the chopsticks in her hair only convinced him of such.

"Hey Callie."

Callie unleashed her soft smile on Kelly Barnett, who was star struck, if only a bit.

"And who might this adorable young woman be?"

"This is my friend Kelly." Morell laughed with two small breaths of air. "Kelly meet Callie; Callie, Kelly. Don't get confused."

"It's an honor, Ms. Calabrese."

"It's an honor to meet you too, Ms.?"

"Barnett." Kelly said, curling her short brown hair behind her ears the moment the handshake had ended.

"Barnett…" Callie squinted and her posture shifted to lean on her left leg. "You work for the CMJ, right?"

Kelly's genuine surprise brought a great deal of pleasure to Morell's face, which he tried to hide and Callie saw his doing so in a wry and wise glance.

"Y…yes, yes that's right."

"I read your work in the election special, covering the Libertarian Party. I can't say I voted for any of the people you covered, but, are you still with the paper?"

"No, no…I'm going back to school at the moment, kinda in the middle of two Masters programs." Kelly admitted sheepishly. "Political Science and Economics. I have a BA in Journalism already from University of King's College in Halifax."

Callie's smile broadened.

"I *knew* you were Canadian. I *love* Canadians."

Morell excused himself on the prospect of getting tickets knowing quite well Callie would probably have it covered. Her appearance would be the stamp of approval the ruling power's nearly insecure gesture of the Convention itself so desperately needed. Callie's scars were visible in the understanding smirk she passed Morell as he left, as it would give Kelly an unfiltered chance to speak with someone she'd wanted very badly to meet and for Callie to ask an unfettered question or two about Henry Morell, or even Kelly's relationship with him for that matter, with the surety that in her star struck state, she would gladly volunteer an honest answer. In some ways, it bore a resemblance to their mutual test of each other in Maks Lenkov's office.

Morell passed a few fearful faces, waiting to be searched and enter the Ballroom to take their seats, dressed in their finest though it couldn't cover the honest and simplistic morality of citizens who needed the truth but would settle for a double shot of hope in the mean time.

Morell was about to have a word with the concierge when a woman's voice stretched from his left shoulder.

"You don't strike me as a political man."

The voice bore a strange relation in his mind to one he was familiar with, that was to say, *comfortable* with or that it was *comforting* for him to hear.

The face the voice belonged to bore an equally as unexpected similarity to someone he'd allowed past the outer shell of the personal armor any soldier bore as a result of losing those in direct proximity to themselves.

But it wasn't an old girlfriend.

Dark skin contrasted pure blue eyes like the rich soil of country earth and the dawn of a brand new sky, and the freedom of her strawberry blonde curls were ready to catch the passing breeze of such a beautiful day, as only the spirit of a young woman could.

She was one of those rare and matchless women that a man had to stop and think about, even if just for a second. What was her name? Where did she come from? Did she have an accent? She was the kind of woman that could cross a man's wires because she had the potential to be one thing and more than likely was something far different, and for a man like Henry Morell who'd only further developed the art of Interrogation by the many hours he'd spent playing verbal tennis with a host of manipulative women over the glossy top of some nightclub bar, she was a challenge waiting to be addressed.

Or not.

Something about her voice soothed him like the trickling water of the Zen fountain in Callie's private office. What was it?

"That's because I don't strike women." He said,

with a smile, before offering his hand. "Henry Morell."

"Are all your jokes that bad?" She asked, not giving her name, but her handshake was quick, as if she'd waited for the moment to do so and had thought about what she'd wanted to say and a handshake wasn't a part of it. Perhaps she'd been watching him from a distance. Thinking about being observed and studied ticked Morell's comprehensive military and security training and brought tremendous clarity to the fact that the room could've been full of serial killers and his world had been, since the moment he'd decided not to smoke that cigarette under the rainy porch of his cottage apartments, consumed by Kelly Barnett and the pearl that she was.

Everything else in life had capitulated to the vanishing act of having a great time and not giving a damn, of laughing and enjoying good food and not worrying about where the car was parked, how much gas was in the tank, or if the rent check was in the mail.

Even after that small hiccup about Kelly being accosted by Fosnick and DiMocco.

"No, I have worse." Morell said, suddenly frustrated with the woman and whatever game she was running, though he flushed it with a winsome smile.

"Try me."

"Uh…what has four legs and no teeth?" His eyes darted around the space to find Kelly or Callie but the size of the place was far too big and too busy with the milling of Crescent's citizens filling its grandeur for him to locate them with such a cursory effort.

"I don't know, what?"

"A coffee table."

"That *is* bad."

"Howabout two arms and no eyes?"

"I can't wait."

"A sofa."

"That's even worse."

Morell squinted.

"I'm not sure I caught your name."

"Aimee Jaziri."

Morell frowned and did some cultural math. *Arabic.*

"Then you would know," He said, sliding his hands into his pants pockets, his chest and back gaining a little stiffness because he was about to show off in order to see if she was who or *what* he thought she was, and if not, it was fun *and* true, regardless. "Imši fi ganaaza walla timši fi gawaaza."

"Ya me'aammin lir-ragaal ya me'aammin il-mayya fil-gurbaal." She responded, then, "Your Arabic is better than your jokes."

"Hold up now, those are Egyptian proverbs."

"Yes, and you could've learned them from the Internet to impress people like me."

"Assif, fahma."

"Kalam Fady."

Morell smiled again.

"You just proved to me you're Egyptian. At least *half* Egyptian, that is. And I roughed up my Arabic a bit so you could show me yours was better. Or so you thought."

A cunning smile fell from her eyes to her lips.

"It *is* true that a funeral is better than an arranged marriage, but what exactly are you implying, Mr. Morell?"

"What are *you* implying about men being as trusty as water in a sieve? Guess I deserve to be hit with sixty shoes if I fall into that category."

"Match point," She said, arms crossing themselves, and despite her conservative use of affluent albeit muted colors and size-appropriate though in no way form-fitting attire of a skirt, a ruffled blouse, and calf-length boots, the spark inside of her was capable of setting Fircrest Hill and all the evergreens on it to flame. "Who do you think I am?"

"Well, apparently you know who *I* am, Miss Subtlety."

The slightly defiant and antagonistic smile on the woman's heart-shaped face was interrupted by Callie, who had her arm linked with Kelly, and they both approached from Morell's right so that he had to nearly turn his back to the striking woman named Aimee Jaziri.

"Ah," Callie's face held an unreasonably satisfied glow. "I see you've met my daughter."

Morell turned with broad hands and falsified surprise.

"Wow, I could've sworn..."

Aimee's clear blue eyes were chiding, especially considering his comment on arranged marriages, and that he'd chosen to speak Egyptian Arabic and not the Iraqi dialect he was used to, even though his facility in both was stunning.

Callie's kind blue eyes, so much like her daughter's, only exceedingly artful in their ingenious knowledge of human dynamism, bounced between Morell and Aimee and the uneasy silence that was broken by the extending of Kelly's hand, bright in her sleeveless dress of springtime cherry blossoms.

"I'm Kelly."

"My girlfriend." Morell added.

Aimee's smile was forced and obligatory, too much so to see Kelly's pupils dilate but Callie did, and with the rigidity of Morell's back and more than likely the balling of his hands in his pockets he was standing strong in his words though it was the first time Kelly'd ever heard such.

He hadn't introduced Kelly to *her* that way, and

she even asked when Morell had left, and Kelly said they were just friends and went on to say how Hank was really a solid and dependable kind of guy but that he kind of had a tendency to show off. Kelly had also told Callie how they'd met after the Crisis and how he'd helped her through a tough time.

Kelly's expression had lost color, as if she'd received the answer to the question she'd asked earlier but not, in any way, in the manner in which she expected.

Aimee's striking face was cut with courtesy, and if Callie'd offered Morell the same look, he would've taken it as genuine, even if Callie was lying through her teeth, because she simply was *that* authentic and hospitable.

But Aimee, well, it was as if that same conviviality had been usurped by the desire to poke and prod and get answers to questions that were hard to ask. Was it their motives, their way of thinking that made them different? Only time would tell.

Callie stepped across the scant space between them to place her arm around her daughter. The resemblance was obvious, and yet, so were the differences.

Morell unconsciously put his arm around Kelly and the polite standoff worked its oddity in the midst of the buzzing mill of Convention attendees.

"Well then, shall we go?" Callie asked.

Morell nodded and looked down to Kelly whose intellectual brown eyes, heavily cloaked in kohl, were veiled in a muddled tangle of blatant misunderstanding and self-chastised longing, nearly on the verge of tears.

FiFTEEN

The Lynx, standing some fourteen feet from the elevated platform on which his target would soon be so proudly displayed for the world to see, snapped a few photos with his primary camera as the Convention began with a rousing and supposedly spontaneous singing of the National Anthem and the emcee's subsequent efforts to lay out what would be the evening's order of events. It was the Convention's final day, having run the whole week, and everybody, bearing the dissertations of academics, politics, and policy puppets, was awaiting the town hall-style question and answer session with Mayor Geffington and the interim Police Chief.

The interim leader of Crescent's jumpsuit clad influx of paramilitary cops was a barrel-chested man by the name of Bertolucci, whose smug posture and salty goatee made him appear less overweight than he was. He'd served his time in Crescent and was, if anything, an accomplished Policeman, even though he would be the third interim Police Chief in as many months.

The County Sheriff was also present, but somehow wasn't being given the honor due his rank, as if the Mayor was unaware in his desire to demonstrate procedure of a ceremonious nature that the County Sheriff outranked Crescent's Chief of Police.

And The Lynx bided his time till the perfect

moment would present itself, running the escape plan over and over in his mind.

Madness was about to make a special guest appearance.

It was against a hail of courtesy claps and the introduction of the Mayor that Kelly leaned over to speak with her newly declared *boyfriend.*

"We have to talk." She said.

"Hmm?" He turned and saw nearly the same expression as before.

"We have to talk."

"I know, Kel. Now's not a good time."

Her lovely brown eyes, distending, said: *Really, Hank? Didn't you kind of decide now was the time when you told two strangers something you've never told me? You've got me so confused I don't know what to think. WE NEED TO TALK!*

"Just sit tight." He said, with a slight nod as the Mayor began to speak with the willowy voice no one seemed to be bothered by, save the hard working constituents of South, who didn't really vote for him and were outweighed by those of North four to one.

"Citizens of Crescent, thank you so much for coming tonight and all this week to this…hopefully *transparent* demonstration of our desire as elected officials to keep you, our friends, family, and fellow Americans, safe."

Morell crossed his leg as Kelly sighed and sank in her seat. Callie was sitting to his right and Kelly to his left, Aimee to Callie's right.

"She's so cute." Callie whispered over the Mayor's rambling pontification.

"Kelly or your daughter?"

The Tidebender CEO shot her newest employee a nonverbal reprimand, yet her winding smile refused to leave.

"Didn't I tell you my daughter never listens to me?"

"Something to that effect. She seemed quite pleased with herself…or did you put her up to it?"

"Please. She enjoys debate. Besides, it's not like single women don't notice you. Remember, I know the score and I know you're *not* oblivious."

"She enjoys making me uncomfortable. What have you told her about me?"

"Me?" Callie pointy chin dipped to the left. "I haven't said a word to her about you."

Morell squinted at her but knew she was telling the truth.

Technically.

"I was talking about Kelly." Calabrese corrected.

"I know you were."

"She's really smart, too. I'm sure I could find her a position on my staff when she's done getting those two supplementary *Masters* degrees. The signing bonus alone would wipe out those school debts. She could go just about anywhere in the world, too. Sounds like a good partnership waiting to happen to me."

"She wants to go to D.C."

"Ugh…" Callie shook her head. "So she does have something in common with my daughter."

"It's a *very* small similarity." Morell assured.

"Well, D.C.'s a long way from Crescent."

"I've already told her as much."

Callie smiled to herself.

"By the way, Kelly's ring finger is a size six, her coloring calls for gold, not silver, and her birthstone is amethyst."

Morell rolled his eyes and crossed his arms as Mayor Geffington stumbled over a few notes before finding the desired script.

"It is at this time that I would like to begin our Question and Answer session, and I assure you with the utmost sincerity that when you depart this historic building tonight, you will leave with not only a more honest opinion of myself as a Mayor, but a prouder view of your fellow neighbors and citizens of Crescent," The Mayor's malleable voice rose in pitch as people began to clap. "Who will not be denied our inalienable rights to thrive in a free and prosperous city, not by terrorism or any other threat to our welfare!"

"This should be good." Aimee said to herself, clapping with the crowd, though half-heartedly; nearly mockingly. Her mind was already dissecting Geffington's weakness of intellectual conflict and imagining how he'd handle any directly confrontational queries.

The first question was on how the clean up budget had affected public transportation. Morell couldn't help but laugh about it, considering he was nearly as afflicted by said public transportation as the Crisis itself.

A few questions later there was a stumper about gun laws and gun reform. Knowing the Crisis inside out, Morell realized the climate of the city was more dangerous *now* than it had been *during* the Crisis, and the question was well-worded enough as to cast doubt on all of the time and effort the city had offered to make the streets safer; because more guns, public and private, could in no way equate more safety.

It was then Callie raised her hand and one of the emcee's assistants pointed to her and she excused herself to get to the aisle.

And as it was custom for the inquisitor to state their name and occupation, Callie definitely turned heads, and had a way of speaking to everyone in the room in the gracious and inclusive manner that made them feel as peers.

"My name is Rachael Calabrese and I'm the CEO of a private security firm determined to end the violent culture of the industry by the name of Tidebender International and my question is directly to you, Mr. Mayor, about your appointment of the city's next permanent Chief of Police and the course such an appointment plots for our collective future."

Small murmurs and nods sealed her comments and thousands of eyes were on the Mayor.

"First of all, Callie, I'm glad you could come, second of all, I believe I answered your question last time we met." The Mayor said with the passive-aggressive nature he was known for.

"Well, if by answering you mean *not* answering…"

"Please come up here, Callie." The Mayor smiled and began to clap, thus inciting a riotous round of applause for a woman who was impossible to dislike. Unless one's name was Richard Geffington.

Aimee moved to her mother's seat, still warm.

"Mom's going to let him have it." She said to Morell. "The Callie way."

Morell didn't say anything and caught Kelly wiping her eyes in a sideways glance.

Callie shook hands with the Mayor and interim Police Chief Bertolucci, as well as the emcee and whoever else was on stage, extremely conscious of the fact that she was milking the audience for applause to warm up the Mayor and loosen the smile on his tight face.

"It looks different from up here." Callie said into the microphone at the podium with a smile. "Maybe I should run for office."

An honest laugh rippled in the crowd, followed by two whistles and a cheer.

"No, in all fairness," Callie continued, "I want to commend the Mayor for even thinking of this sort of gathering on behalf of all those who are as tired of seeing talking heads hog up their TV screens as I am and need a human, tactile experience in which to garner the truth. The fact that I'm here and about to pledge a generous donation to the city on behalf of their relief effort clearly constitutes my support for our city's leadership, which it is why it is my most solemn request that the people get a clear and distinct vision of who is protecting them."

No small roar attacked the crowd, as if she'd said in so many words or less what many of the citizens wanted to but either didn't have the guts to say or didn't know how. Her pledge of cash and backing of the authority was in no way revolutionary, contrary, or anarchistic in the tenuous sensitivity of a city of people with a broken psyche, but just the opposite. She was placing herself as one of the pillars of the community and *as* one of the pillars was politely demanding Geffington find his backbone and make a decision, whether it was the right one or not. Public office was not supposed to be a schoolyard merry-go-round. Camera flashes followed, Callie's classy appearance no doubt newsworthy, and if it were the days of the monarchs, Callie's dynamic sense of grace and femininity would've been enough to rule the land in direct contrast to the indecisive and slightly-built, weak-voiced Mayor whose silver hair was in no way a mark of wisdom, but of great stress.

Such things were only a stage for the extreme shockwave of breathless astonishment that stole the heartbeat from the Grand Ballroom with a cruel and cunning split second of silence in the eye of applauses' emotional storm.

Callie stepped back from the podium to let Mayor

Geffington respond to her challenge, which he surged forward to eagerly accept. In practically the same moment, Mayor Geffington's neck received the skin-slicing terminal velocity of the Twenty-Two-caliber marksman's bullet and his body arched with a stiff shudder.

Disbelief forever froze on his face.

Crimson blood trickled down the oversized pinprick and what began as the puffing, reddened mist of a violent entry wound quickly transformed into a permanently staining river of fresh lifeblood pumping with the fervor of a dying man's futility; soaking the fabric of his once clean white shirt.

The fragile cord running from the Mayor's heart to his brain had been expertly cut by the assassin's bullet, as had any and all chances of a brighter future for the dangerously hopeless people of Crescent.

SiXTEEN

Screams and screeches of horror, ripped from the very mouths of those overwhelmed beyond the point of recovery, spread a reckless rage of survivalist fury throughout the Convention's gilded and trompe l'oeil surroundings and some two thousand guests as if a spell of nuclear confusion had been cast over them.

Police Chief Bertolucci was swift to Geffington's side, propping up his neck and shouting orders, which no one heard, because the man had died instantly and there was nothing anyone could do about it. His brain had been unable to tell his heart to stop its pumping, and the Mayor's body had completely exsanguinated itself on the elevated stage.

As The Lynx had planned it.

CPD in tactical jumpsuits were caught in the chaotic crossfire of voices and selfish rushes to what was thought to be saftey, flooding the stage to protect their Chief, funneling the petrified toward one of three exits, and trying to find the shooter, all of which were indelibly impossible.

The result was a stampede.

The Lynx had counted on such dread and panic and fell in step with the other photographers and journalists as two bulky CPD Officers were ushering them toward the exit with the thought that the shot had come from the rafters.

And it wouldn't be irreversibly after the fact, if ever, that they discovered the truth.

Henry Morell was squeezing Kelly as tight as possible, shielding her with his body in a shell of still upright folding chairs, huddled in a half-squat.

"Kelly, are you okay?"

"Yeah, yeah, I'm fine."

Her face in his hands, he saw she most certainly was not, and he stretched to look behind Kelly to see Aimee embrace her mother as CPD escorted Callie off the stage in a crouching run.

"Get out of here!" One of the cops said, rushing past.

"No," Morell shouted, replaying the way Geffington lifelessly fell over and over in his mind and how the shooter had almost killed Callie.

Stage left.

"Stop, the shooter's still here, he's hiding!"

No one was listening.

CPD worked the radio and were establishing a perimeter around the Hotel with a no one out, no one in policy and dozens of CPD cruisers were on their way to the scene, as well as SWAT teams and their command and control armored bus in accordance to CRT protocols.

Both FBI and Homeland Security were sure to be close at their heels with the deadly shooting presenting itself as another horrible event of national awareness.

"Callie!" Morell called and urged Kelly toward her, his mind snapping and crackling at the dwindling prospects of finding the shooter as he or she hid in plain sight. Morell would bet his life on it.

Grief was deep set in Callie's heart-shaped face and though not a drop of the Mayor's blood was on her hands, or any other part of her body, her countenance was as if death itself had stood at her doorstep, knocked, and said, *I'm watching you.* It didn't matter if she felt partly responsible or not, the deed had been done, and anything in retrospect was a foolish way to relive traumatic misery.

Morell leapt to the stage and took a knee next to Chief Bertolucci, who was hollering orders and obscenities into his radio.

"Chief, the shooter's still here."

"Get outta here, now!" The Chief's face was red and taut. "Braden!" He called to a chunky Officer of about fifty years who'd been close by. "Escort Callie to her car and make sure she's okay."

So, even in the midst of other movers and shakers, Callie merited an addendum to the no one out policy the Chief was stressing to his Officers amidst a fusillade of curse words.

Morell ran to her, and was struck by the coldness of her aura.

Her incorrigible charisma and contagious vibrancy had been lobotomized in one single act of violence.

"I'm going after the shooter." Morell said to the girls, making sure all of them understood, and Callie failed to nod, receiving the support of both her daughter *and* Kelly Barnett as if she were an invalid. The younger girls were still in quite a state themselves and Morell spoke directly to Aimee, who seemed to be the most cognizant of the three. "Follow that Officer to your car and get her back home as quickly as possible, okay? Kelly you go with them. Go!"

Morell spun around to face the stage and his eyes bounced between the edges of the room and the three exits.

Geffington's carotid artery had been pierced by a perfect shot, ground level, right? Not from the rafters. It had to be. One shot. One flawless display of marksmanship.

And who or what could conceal such a device but a member of the press?

A cameraman.

Morell took off in a dead sprint toward the service exit behind the stage and vaulted a row of chairs as if they were track and field hurdles as the last stringers of the fourth estate had cleared the Grand Ballroom and its reverberating cacophony of terror.

The Lynx, stuck in the center of a bundle of frenzied media hounds, shed his AP branded vest and white button down-shirt in the blind spot of two security cameras and reached in his camera bag for a wadded CPD windbreaker. The group was tight in the narrow hall of the service exit and, still in the blind spot of a CCTV camera, The Lynx made comments to those around him about having forgotten his camera. Someone told him it wasn't worth it, and others forbade his going back with the fear locked in their eyes, but The Lynx did, and opted for a mundane passageway to the stairs leading to the parking garage instead, affixing his CPD windbreaker so as by the time he was in view of the next camera, in the gray concrete of the garage, his gait and posture had changed nearly as much as his wardrobe.

Jasmine Keelan, rattled as much as any other by the appalling turn of events that had so rapidly degraded the Convention from a chance at returning the optimism the Crisis had stolen to an event of eternal infamy, stimulated even further by the group anointing, had been at the back of the pack and in prime position to see the photographer several feet in front of her shed his AP-tagged vest and wasn't sure anyone else did.

Thoughts tangled inside her as to why and what such action meant and it wasn't until the man in the gray suit came bounding up to the congested funnel of bodies, searching and analyzing them, that it made sense.

She separated herself and caught his eye, Geffington's blood seared in her imagination.

"I saw a man remove his AP vest as we were moving." She said, her heavily made-up features strained. "I didn't see his face, but I think he got something out of his camera bag."

"Where?" Morell grabbed her arms, compelling her to show him. Parting the crowd of tensed elbows and fearful faces was not without difficulty, and mildly forceful jostles and shoves finally brought them to the space in the middle of the pack where the vest and camera bag were lying, strangely abandoned.

"Officer!" Morell called, and the CPD Officer between them and the doorway at the end of the long hall came over, having caught the attention of the reporters and photographers. "Homeland Security, open the bag."

The cop, in the midst of baited breath, did so without hesitation and found a camera, to which Morell told him to pop off the bottom plate.

A small gasp seized the onlookers as the silvery butt of a marksman's pistol was exposed in the hollowness of the camera's shell of a shape and a second expellation of air rifted the crowd as the telephoto lens clattered to the ground to reveal the slender cylinder of the Twenty-Two's silenced barrel.

The cop threw his chin to the radio affixed to his left shoulder, speaking rapidly, and motioned for another Officer trying to work people out of the long and narrow hall to come.

And by the time the first Officer, now surrounded by the overloaded minds of journalists and the nimble

fingers of paparazzi snapping pictures, had opened the
camera and looked up for an explanation from the man
who'd said he was Homeland Security, the man *and* the
tall blonde woman who'd been standing so close to him
were both gone.

Jasmine was only a pace behind the man in the
gray Burberry suit, her height and athleticism somehow
making up for the fact that she was wearing heels and
the man was quite fast and nimble. It wasn't until
they'd reached the small elbow-shaped hall connecting
the parking garage to the old building's foundational
access that she chanced a question, her mind no longer
able to keep her mouth silent.

"Homeland Security? What the hell happened?"

"Geffington was shot." Morell said tersely,
judging between the two doors and what he'd do if he
were an assassin on the run, having planned to hide in
the crowd till the time came to split. "And I'm not
Homeland," He added, with a softer tone, realizing that
if it handt've been for the woman he'd be running
around like a headless chicken, and because of her, he
was certain the killer was close. "I was in the Crisis."

"CPD?" She said, six foot one in her heels and he
stared into the overshadowing of her Hollywood-ready
features as if blinded by them.

"No, Tidebender."

"Tidebender?" She said and her dark blue eyes
began to gleam in the sallow whitish elbow of the
hallway. "I came here to speak with Callie about Maks
Lenkov, thank God she's okay."

Maks Lenkov?

Same killer? Same day…same city…

Coincidence?

Morell's gaze went blank as all three thoughts
made a play for the intersection of his voice and

collided into each other, the result of which left him
staring at the bridge of her nose with his mouth slightly
agape. Her muddled blue eyes darted around his face
for an answer.

"What, what is it?"

"You said he pulled something out of his camera
bag?"

"Yeah."

"Did you see it?"

"Kind of…"

"What was it? Think!"

Jasmine used a brave face to hide an exasperated
demeanor. She'd never been so scared in her life; to be
a rookie Channel Two reporter in a room of such
notable people and then see the Mayor of Crescent, so
alive one minute and then swallowed in his own blood
the next, *and* to be caught in the ensuing pandemonium
while at the same time a trivial, yet ferocious remnant
of her soul had latched onto the story of a lifetime with
a possessive grip of white-knuckles and clenched teeth.

"Come on," Morell badgered, "Was it a phone, a
pen, a weapon, something hand held or concealable?"

"It was wadded up." Jasmine said, grasping at a
hurried memory, as if still considering other
possibilities, and then reestablished eye contact and
nodded to seal the choice.

"Wadded…" Morell turned back to the option of
doors, the unlocked stairs to the parking garage, and the
locked stairs to the building's foundation. Sure the
killer could have a key into the foundation and
would've known another way out if he'd chosen his
way in, but why? What was the point? To wait? He'd
know how many cameras there were, he'd know
everything. The inclusion of the silenced single-shot
pistol in the hollow camera was no way an indicator of
a street punk shooting or even a crazy who'd somehow

made it past security. It was the mark of a professional *paid* hitman who'd executed the plan with as much finesse as he'd executed a fellow human being.

Just like the hit on Maks Leknov and the collateral damage of his wife. So was Geffington a part of it? And if so, how?

Morell couldn't dwell on conspiracy and prodded about the object.

"Was it something dark?"

"Yeah, I guess…I couldn't really see it."

"Dark blue, like a CPD windbreaker?"

Morell didn't need Jasmine's answer, surging for the door to the parking garage. He took the stairs quickly and Jasmine less so, using the rails for stability with her heels and all.

The cold spread of flat concrete gently sloping to lower darkness on the left offered them no direction in which to go, and the garage was silent in contrast to the hellacious display above. A linear string of orange light spilled across the glossed hoods and trunks of blocky automobile shapes and between gray pillars and charcoal-colored guard rails, the puzzle of finding where the man disappeared to had become an instant impossibility, whereas in the narrow off-white funnel of old halls it seemed so close Morell could nearly reach out and grab the back of that alleged dark blue CPD windbreaker.

"He's probably got a badge in that jacket, enough to fool some beat cop who's never seen him, maybe even a gun if he needs it." Morell said, and turned to Jasmine, struck again at how tall she was in her heels, at least four inches above him. "Take my phone," He said, giving it to her. "Stay here, don't move, and call the first five speed dial numbers and tell them what happened and that I'm tracking the shooter down. Got it?"

Morell was about to leave and she grabbed his arm with, to him, what was a surprisingly strong grip, considering her sunny and glamorous Californian features that he assumed would sour if the temperature wasn't above sixty-five degrees Fahrenheit. He didn't know in that moment that she, at one point, was an essential member of a nationally ranked college volleyball team and had transformed her body by an obsessive relationship with beach volleyball, having played it incessantly those four years of absence from Crescent's dark green cage of pines and firs.

"Wait, I don't even know your name."

"Henry Morell."

"Jasmine Keelan," They nodded abruptly to seal fate's companionship, no hand shaking. "I'm with Channel Two."

"Perfect," Morell frowned in the slightest to remember. "And you came to speak to Callie about Lenkov? Well, if this all works out, Christmas is coming early for you."

And with that Morell took off in an easy clip-clopping jog to the lower darkness of the cold parking garage, sealing any further questions in Jasmine's mouth and it wasn't until the shrinking streak of his gray body was gone that her fingers snapped to life and began placing the calls he'd asked her to.

SEVENTEEN

Morell had reached the third level of the parking garage when the rolling ignition of a car engine fired through the dead space of darkened concrete. By the sound of it, it was a six cylinder import, more than likely a rental, and Morell ducked in the narrowness between a Mercedes E Class and a support column as the car, which was either dark blue or black, he couldn't tell, swerved past and the kick of the throttle soaked the emptiness with a nasally explosion of sound.

And with nothing to go on other than gut instinct, Morell stood up and took off after the car, vaulting the guardrail, as the car was no longer visible.

He could reason the lone driver in the vacant garage was cause enough to supply him with a suspect, or the dangerous speed at which the car rose to street level sealed such guilt, but it wasn't until Morell had just barely and somewhat breathlessly reached the ground floor that his suspicions were set in stone.

Huddling against the bubbled yet chunky shape of a brand new SUV, Morell saw the driver park the car with careless haste and slide out of the seat.

He was a short man, with a long stride and militaristic arm swing, and his CPD windbreaker was unzipped and flapped in the breeze he created as he strode toward the dark square of the exit and his dicey chances at freedom.

Morell advanced until he heard voices and held his position near a black Mercedes.

"He's gotta be down there, try floor five..." The man pattered with a New Yorker's flavor, and Morell chanced a view to see the short man in the CPD windbreaker was speaking to a SWAT team of four men as if he was a Detective and had made a superficial sweep of the area.

SWAT already? Morell thought. *Geffington's new policy of tactical action may cost a lot but it's fast. FBI's got to be lurking around, too, and Homeland.*

The girls are never gonna get out. Nobody is.

The FBI is going to have CPD keep everyone inside and process them one by one. They can't see me, they'll never let me out and that bastard'll be gone forever.

Morell clenched his teeth with the rich meal sitting heavily in his stomach and bothering the sharpness of his mind with the slightest whispers of grogginess. The man probably had a badge and a gun and SWAT was on the jagged edge with the shooting of the Mayor only manifesting what had been so intensely anticipated; hell, everyone in the city would be headaches and hangovers for God knew how long, reacting to the shock of the tragedy the only way they could. Regardless of the damage and the chaos already caused, Morell, confident the killer held all the cards and was operating on the premise that he did, resolved to follow the killer *without* CPD, FBI, Homeland or anyone else getting in the way, and get him dead to rights once the killer'd made his escape from the net closing around him. That way, his guilt would be complete, and Tidebender, not Homeland or CPD, would get full marks in a situation where black eyes, bloody knuckles, and forms filed in triplicate were the norm.

And Morell would be damn sure to *interrogate* him properly.

Fists first.

He advanced a few more car spaces as the killer conversed with the four-man SWAT team but their voices were too muddled to hear. He seemed to give them all they needed. Gestures and directional hand signals passed between the heavily armored squad, having chosen to believe the man in the windbreaker and knowing no better, which allowed the killer to head unabated to the exit in a light jog. SWAT then moved toward the lower bowels of the parking garage with the loose shuffle Morell knew so well as an Army Sergeant of six years overseas duty.

Morell cursed and waited till SWAT had passed beyond his sightline to run a decent pace, slowing once he'd reached the mouth of the garage.

The cold air was acutely obvious, chilling his forehead and the sweat that stained it, and Morell squinted to adjust his eyesight from the orangey drear of the garage while still maintaining a low profile. He could only imagine what trigger-happy Officer wanted to be the hero to shoot first the bastard that killed the Mayor, asking questions later with the new policy of anti-terrorism encouraging as much and only having been set in stone with the Excalibur of Geffington's assassination, and with the thought of everyone with a badge and a Glock Thirty in a twenty-mile radius setting up around the perimeter to turkey shoot anyone running where they weren't supposed to was *not* Morell's idea of a good time. The fact that SWAT had come in the garage was of positive note in that CPD must've sealed an area tight enough for SWAT to sweep, which meant there wouldn't be any Officers loitering around to spot him and mistake him for the man who'd killed the Mayor, but it also meant that

since the killer'd fed some effective lines of nonsense
to SWAT, he knew exactly where to go and was doing
just that as Morell cautiously checked his surroundings,
the gap between them stretching with every wasted
second of Morell's vigilance preventing him from
pressing into the cold and glossy wetness of the city
street's awaiting game of roulette.

Morell considered his immediate options, telling
himself how well he knew the area because he'd lived
on Second Avenue since returning home from Iraq;
every nook and cranny, right? Only in theory, flawed as
all theories were. A proverb he'd learned in Iraq, stating
night makes a fool of sunlight only made more sense as
the Continental Plaza's wrap of pavement and the gated
lot that separated it from Second, Third, Dunham, and
Maxwell, might as well've been in Iraq they looked so
foreign, and Morell let the curses fly under his breath as
he pushed out, as straight and fast as possible, across
the double lane of the access road running around the
hotel, to the twelve-foot high ironwork gate to scale it
in three simple movements.

Once over, and avoiding ankle injury and any
harm to the gray Burberry suit despite the iron's
slickness, Morell knew the weakest point in the Police's
perimeter would be the uneven mess of alleyways and
residential blocks in a spread of Second Avenue known
as *hipster hostel* for its glut of starving artists and
message board activists; where the smell of coffee and
nicotine cloaked mortared rectangles of thick tan bricks
like a shroud, and as the black streets gleamed with the
shine of a fresh rain, Henry Morell would take his
chances or die trying.

Kelly and Aimee were guiding Callie by the hand
through the slog of people trying to escape the sight of
Geffington's blood as Officer Braden was carving a

path for them with his combination of uniformed size and supportive remarks about everything being under control and the like, though it was of no use. The people of Crescent had voted; their newly elected Mayor was panic and they were capitulating to its indulgent policies of screaming and hollering as if the very ground on which they stood was on fire.

Braden left the girls near a plaster pillar and a street-side window in the endlessly stretching left wing of the Georgian hotel building with about a thousand others and it was within the throng's manhandling and shoving for an emergency exit door far off in a distant location they'd never get to that an over-muscled man knocked Kelly to the ground, stepping on her left hand and rushing past Callie, elbowing her as well. Callie lost her balance and rammed face-first into one the plaster pillars running along the wall near a window with a sickening thud.

The CEO crumpled in a heap of black silk and Aimee rushed to her side.

"Mom!"

Aimee knelt as blood began to pool and trickle on the corner of Callie's eye and with Aimee's touch of concern and the stinging pain it caused, Callie seemed to gain consciousness from the stupor that Geffington's bleeding out had plunged her into.

Kelly was rubbing her hand with a wince frozen on her face as Aimee helped Callie to sit on the diminutive ledge the window allowed and Kelly's grimace deepened when she saw the clash of red and blue lights and the muffled howl of sirens.

"Every cop in the city must be out there." She said.

"Just about." Callie dabbed her eye and bit her lip at the redness on her fingertips.

"Why won't they let anybody out?" Aimee

ducked into whisper, now ultra-protective of her mother considering the smear staining her feminine visage. The insanity and instability of those around her were bordering on hostility, and Aimee's hands tensed ever so slightly till they were fists.

"I thought you would've been all read up on Geffington's new procedures and strategies following the Crisis." Callie nearly smirked, more at the hideously unfunny side-effects of after-the-fact legislation than her daughter's ignorance on something that was, in many ways, a social phenomenon to Crescent that had yet, until tonight, to be physically enacted.

"In the event of a violent act of terror," Kelly nearly quoted verbatim, eyes darting across the splattered dance of red and blue outside as it extended the full darkness of Second. "The area of immediate threat is placed in static quarantine, subject to the authority of a Critical Response Team with all the constitutional rights of martial law."

"That's an equal blend of FBI, Homeland, SWAT and CPD beat cops armed to the teeth." Callie squinted to recall the stats. "God knows how that perfect plan's going to hell with the man who was supposed to have been in charge of it all being the cause of it…would you believe Crescent took on forty-thousand LEO's and CRT's in two months with a supplementary budget addendum of two billion dollars?" The CEO of Tidebender shook her head and smiled to thank Kelly as the student gave her a tissue. "There goes the rainy day fund."

"It's a real policeman's paradise." Kelly shook her head, staring down the length of the hall as the door everyone thought they'd gain freedom by was thick with an influx of riot-geared CPD cops, their tense faces shielded in glossy masks.

"So, we're not getting out of here?" Aimee asked,

thoughts about her mother's safety at the forefront of her mind, even though she was living in the middle of an event that would gain national recognition for its rarity as the culture of the new age of anti-terrorism.

It was one of those world-changing experiences the ripple of which would *only* continue to spread.

"Not any time soon." Callie sniffed and folded the tissue, continuing her dabbing. "We'll get processed one by one. It could take days."

"Days?" Aimee's exotic features stretched and her voice betrayed her twenty years of age with a harsh whisper. "That's not right! They can't do that!"

"They can and they will." Kelly said, sadness hovering indecisively between leaving her bookish features forever or deepening irrevocably and permanently. Considering the circumstances, she knew bravery would be in short supply, but her was heart set on Henry Morell and his absence was hard to address with exhortation and hope.

It was a bad night and it was only going to get worse.

"I guess there's shoddier places to be held prisoner." Aimee mused.

"It can give us some time to talk about *somebody* behind their back." Callie's subtly winding smile infected the two younger girls, the obvious subtext of which was Henry Morell.

And the smashing of a window just ahead of them by a paranoid citizen crazed to escape the multitude of fellow captives stole their levity as the militaristic hollers and shouts of riot-geared CPD made the girls think, if just for a moment, that they knew what it was like to be a soldier like Henry Morell stuck in the corruptive blast furnace of Iraq.

Nearly half a mile from the Continental Plaza

Hotel and the swirling maelstrom of action it'd been submerged within, The Lynx began to cut through a zigzag of clogged two and three story dwelling blocks with his senses fully alert to any and all signs of life around him. He couldn't shake the feeling that he was being followed, that accursed addiction of adrenaline, of hunter and hunted, predator and prey. In some strange way, the glossy glaze of the day's cold rain showers and the reflective gleam it cast on the greasy pavement and the shoulder-width brick walls he'd chosen to weave through to escape the scene of the crime reminded him of Belfast and the time he'd spent there as a much younger man. He didn't know *why* he was thinking of Belfast in that moment, as bloody images of the late eighties and early nineties danced in the darkness like ghostly holograms, he wasn't supposed to think, he was supposed to *do*. Everything had been planned for success from the confusion of *others*, not accounting for his own, and the odd cocktail of the rat maze's functional similitude to those Northern Irish streets and the perception of a dark and wraithlike presence pursuing him were splitting the shell of sanity that so carefully covered a molten core of the very opposite.

For a moment, The Lynx stopped and looked behind him. His breathing was labored and his eyesight blurred, made clearer by squinting, but still not pristine and crisp as he was used to. Was it the contacts? Must've been. He removed them and saw that he was caught in the direct middle of a long alleyway and with each snap of his head left and right the scene seemed to spin and twist and morph itself into Stockholm, then Berlin, then Paris, Marrakech, Istanbul, Baghdad, and thousands of square feet of unidentifiable geography.

And then, in an explosive flash of magician's powder, he lost his entire sense of direction, so instinctive it was, and slid to the ground as a result.

Over and over his mind replayed splices of the same reels and he was subject to their gruesome images-knives, guns, bomb blasts and blood; the hurried rush past static objects and frozen faces witness to the possessive focus of one man removing another from the planet. Time, itself, dissolved within this prism of violence and the space it controlled within his cerebellum.

And it wasn't until The Lynx heard the soft patter of footsteps and the splishing sound they drew from a nearby puddle that he stood to his five foot six inches of height, eyes dead set on facing the one who'd been following him since his escape and evasion from the Continental Plaza Hotel with intent to kill creeping across his yellowy-green eyes.

EiGHTEEN

Morell had slowed his pace, breathing heavily, to stare down the length of a passing alleyway, darkened by the unnaturally narrow shoulders of its offerings as more of a mistaken gap between buildings and not a viable causeway. Everywhere he looked, the nothingness of darkness glittered and mocked, as did the empty windows and rusty locked doors of the residential maze. He was about to rush past the endless shaft of dead space, knowing he was cresting the northeastern edge the Critical Response Team's perimeter, when the unmistakable swish of synthetic material snagged his ear from behind. He turned and had but half a second to throw his hands up as the dim flicker of a sleeve clubbed him broadside. The recoil of shock and physical force worked in violent tandem to throw him against the wall separating the narrow and lightless death trap in which he already felt claustrophobic just thinking about entering from the broader spaces of conflicting alleyways spreading before him and the man that guarded their freedom from him.

"Come on you nasty litt'l sod," The man said, his features shaded with his back to the naked bulb above a pair of doorways some twenty feet away. "You've been followin' me, have you?"

"You killed Geffington." Morell blinked rapidly

and his arms naturally held a rigid fighter's stance.

"Did I?"

"*And* Lenkov."

"Is that so?" The man said and lurched with a feint that provoked a defensive snap within Morell and the killer laughed, judging in a moment at what level the man he was about to beat the hell out of was at before letting the enjoyment of such commence.

"You've got a bit of the Service in you, mate. I respect that. Hope you've got more t'offer than they taught you in basic."

Morell disregarded him and his accent, seeing that the man was provoking him to fight but had not yet gone about the grisly process of doing so or drawn a gun or done *any* such thing relating to an act of finality.

"I know who you're after but I don't know who you're working for." Morell said as quickly as possible.

"I'm sure you do, but what's in it f'you? Don't you know you could be shot runnin' 'round out here without one of these on?" The killer referenced his fetching CPD windbreaker.

"I just don't want anyone to get hurt."

"People *get* hurt."

"No. We both know you're good enough to leave innocent people alone."

"No one's innocent."

"I can understand Lenkov, he's a member of the Order, but Geffington wasn't."

The killer straightened, yet the threat of his knife-like hands were still at the forefront of Morell's consciousness, and the tiniest smattering of light between them meant Morell could spare the man, who he was now convinced had killed both Lenkov and Geffington, no hesitation.

"So you *do* know. Then you know who's next, right?"

"Can you promise me innocent people won't die?"

"Like your government promises?" He nearly barked, and then quietly added, "Like *any* government promises?"

"Did you kill Geffington just so you could throw this place into chaos? Turn it into a police state?"

"You *are* smart." The Lynx chuckled. "And because you are you'll know there's only one way out of this for you."

"You can walk away."

"We both know I can't." The man shed his jacket and seemed to shrink, his undershirt in no way reflecting tics of light as the CPD windbreaker had. "Pity," He added, rolling up his sleeves. "That *is* a nice suit."

The Lynx feinted with a deep surge toward Morell's left and Morell instinctively unleashed his left foot to kick into the darkness where he thought the man's center mass would be but the killer took the thrust of Morell's leg in a strong grip and yanked with a swift movement.

Morell's consciousness of equilibrium fluttered, becoming parallel with the earth though several feet above the surface of it before the cold unforgiveness of the pavement nearly gave him a concussion.

The killer, still clutching Morell's leg, worked it further back in the crook of his arm and ground Morell's face away from his own with a stiff palm.

"You won't win this one, mate." He growled against Morell's overwhelming flood of primal urges. The man was right, and Morell was at his mercy before the fight had even begun. Even an animal when threatened knew to shut down and play dead. "If you walk away and forget all about it, you'll live, but you'll live in fear of me coming back for you, won't you?

That's because *I'm* the hunter, not you!"

Morell didn't capitulate and whipped free his leg around the man's head and twisted his core with all his might, rolling the killer over and aiming at the darkness of his head to unload his stiffest shot.

He never got the chance. The man's hands nearly whistled in their rushing toward his ears, flat palms that smacked a devastating sonic explosion within his brain as if a riot grenade had been stuffed up his nose.

The killer flicked Morell off of him and Morell rolled toward the light, stumbling upright in a laughably dazed stagger.

His ears rang with the harsh searing of ruined drums. He scrunched his face and shook his head to make it go away but his sense of symmetry was bankrupt and the fight held no prospects of turning his way.

"You've got spirit, mate, and because of it I won't kill you today. But stay out of the way or I won't be able to help m'self."

The Lynx advanced and Morell prepared himself but the light spoke to him in a way he couldn't comprehend in the moment and looking at it blinded him for the briefest second with tiny sunspots but it occurred to him to see the killer's face and he drifted back toward its eerie warmth.

The killer saw what he was doing and took off in a sprint toward him, not wanting to expose his face to Morell, considering the circumstances. He'd never been afraid of showing his face before but he'd lost control when Morell had picked up his trail and if a man were good enough to track him down, then the Lynx would do him the service of keeping his face a secret.

Morell stopped in the only stance he could afford and The Lynx threw an arcing punch which Morell blocked with a high bar and was about to throw a strike to the man's solar plexus in return when The Lynx arched his back and drew in his right leg to stamp a booted heel just above Morell's left kneecap in a chasse bos Savate kick, hyperextending it.

Uneasily lurching backwards in shooting pain with what little balance remained, he couldn't stop the killer's whip-like flick of a kick into his vulnerable fifth and sixth ribs.

The force of impact compressed his chest nearly an inch and Morell felt a squelching fibrillation rush through his heart. The edges of his vision darkened beyond the blackened yet pale haze they already subscribed to and his breathing was shallow, nearly suffocatingly so.

He fell to a knee and the killer pivoted on his right foot to unleash his left into the prime real estate of Morell's face as if it were a soccer ball on the volley.

Energy transfer threw Morell, like a rag doll in which no life remained, to the unyielding brick wall of residential unit Forty-Seven A, where his skull clunked with hollow abeyance against the brick and his eyes shut themselves with the involuntary motion of unconsciousness.

Whether he was in Valhalla or not, Morell knew the killer was no more and after the ten minutes it must've taken him to stand up to the grim reality that he was, once again, as close to death as he'd ever been, he knew why.

German shepherds were barking nearby, though the wet night maze diffused their physical location from knowledge.

Two facts glared in his mind, nearly as loud as the unbearable voice of his own pain.

He was alive and the killer was gone.

Morell stumbled along the lighted alley to where

the wall ended abruptly and another alley from which
Third could be reached extended from it, spacious by
comparison to the others, though it was blocked by
green industrial dumpsters laborious to maneuver
around, and Morell willed his body with everything he
had just to get to Third in order to fall face first onto the
wet pavement nearly ten feet from a pair of CPD
Officers who'd drawn their guns at the sight of his body
spread eagle on the ground.

It wasn't until they searched his pockets and
called in his name to the FBI Special Agents running
command with the CRT force that the black Suburban
carrying Blake Fosnick, Ricky DiMocco, and the head
of Crescent's newly minted CRT force, stood over
Morell's exasperated body with the sardonic
satisfaction of fate intervening on behalf of justice.

"I can't wait to hear the explanation." The CRT
Captain said, a veteran Special Agent by the name
Sheth, whose gravely voice was due to a bullet to the
neck sustained during a joint operation with the DEA
some two years ago.

"I can't either." Fosnick said, nonverbally
forbidding DiMocco to say the joke rising within him
and the tall Junior Agent simply hoisted Morell up to
set him in the Suburban. Morell was barely conscious.

"How do you want to do this?" Sheth asked, his
heavy jacket making him appear larger than he actually
was. His face was creased and worn looking, aged by
stress and a self-fulfilled prescription of after-hours gin
Hi-balls, and what little hair he had left was buzzed to
the nubbins.

"I thought that's what I'm supposed to ask you."
Fosnick said, beginning to catch the drift of Sheth's
subtext.

"You don't think he shot Geffington, do you?"
Sheth was conscious of the CPD Officers' location, and

as they were well out of earshot range, the hard gaze he offered Fosnick demanded an answer, saying, *if you want to, son, you can dirty this man with a suspected murder charge and break him on the crimes we both know he committed so he'll cop to them to get out of the alleged murder of Geffington or you can handle him quietly knowing he'll put up a fight and might wiggle out of your grip for good with someone as slick as Callie in his corner.*

Fosnick sighed to think, stuffing of his tongue against his bottom teeth and puffing up his chin. A four-block radius around the Continental Plaza was officially traffic-free and disconcertingly vacant, spookily offering him no help. Action times for the city's first ever CRT response had been outstanding and at nearly ten o'clock, the city felt more like two or three in the morning.

It was as if no one was watching and the power to do whatever he wanted concerning Henry Morell was *all* his. Sheth was saying as much, and it was to be the new way of life in the psuedolegality of Crescent's new anti-terror policy where decisions of hushed discussions became unquestionable after the fact.

"No, I don't, but we will have a lot to talk about."

Sheth nodded with something of a scowl.

The apprehension of Henry Morell, wanted for white-collar crimes performed under the authority of the US government, was only a strange cherry on the extremely bittersweet sundae, made even more so by the brutal physical damage he'd sustained. He'd been fighting someone, yes, but how'd he get out of the Continental Plaza, and who was he fighting?

Sheth and Fosnick threw a look toward the splayed doors of the glossy black Suburban and the dome light showed Agent DiMocco examining Morell while wearing a pair of blue nitrile gloves.

"Is he okay?" Sheth asked.

"He's okay." DiMocco piped up from the car and sealed him in tight.

Fosnick fastened his black-three button suit and passed DiMocco a hand motion to fire the Suburban.

"We'll let's get him to Precinct Three and process him quietly. He won't put up much of a fight if he wants to use the brains God gave a crowbar but he fancies himself a bit of a tough guy, so we might have to tango."

Sheth smirked, nodded, and stayed behind, considering Fosnick's decision, and, knowing it was ethically correct on behalf of an unethical man, was still silently devastated by what had happened to Geffington and the city of Crescent, knowing damn well he hadn't the slightest idea who was responsible and if Henry Morell did, then chances were the charges against him, despite their resounding clarity, would have to be dropped.

NiNETEEN

Lucy was sitting tall on the edge of her bed, coaxing the tender melody she'd written for a late friend from her oboe when the digitized bleat of the cordless phone put an end to it. In college, she'd tried instruments like other kids tried drugs, in the casual way of a young experience seeker, all the while the distant mountain of the piano and the uncrossable bridge it was between her and her father forbade her from doing so.

First the clarinet, then splitting time between the alto and tenor saxophone and dumping them both for the shiny curves of the French horn and later the bold clarity of the trumpet after a viewing of the movie *Patton*.

Of course, she'd had her fling with tubas and trombones before swearing her senior year to never play anything other than a flute before finally, hearing the sound of the oboe in its simple and lonely purity, knowing that the instrument itself had chosen her as the one it wanted to be spoken through.

When Lucy saw the number her tone adopted the nearly inhuman emotionlessness work demanded of her.

And work was nothing like music, the ultimate liberation of transcendency, releasing one's soul to the moving vibration of sound and the unhindered communication of practiced motor skills with the starry heavens, where the music Lucy played seemed to descend from.

"What's up?"

Lucy's breathing shallowed as she listened to the hideous turn of events that had ensnared the city of Crescent so distant from her in the cloistered knoll of Eavesdale and she was nearly out the door with her badge and gun the moment the Captain had hung up, knowing just how much her city needed her.

After throwing her long, straight blonde hair in a ponytail and changing her clothes to jeans, hiking boots, a thermal knit Henley top and a dark blue CPD waterproof jacket to appropriately tackle the night shift and whatever can of worms it promised to be, Lucy arrived at Precinct Three and showed her credentials to the Desk Sergeant to log her in, telling her exactly what room Henry Morell was being held in.

Cops were like elephants, some said, they never forgot. Many at Precinct Three remembered Henry Morell and his near death experience at PierHouse and were a little leery of Blake Fosnick's enjoyment of sticking him in the Interrogation Room as if he were a criminal. Henry Morell was, in the cops' view, at least the ones who remembered the Crisis and weren't imports because of it, one of the heroes of Crescent and was considered to be one of the good guys, a real cop's friend.

Lucy jogged down the hub of hallways emptying from the broad, yet narrow retrofitted lobby to find an Officer named Horner standing with a Policeman's heavily-geared slouch.

"FBI in with him?"

"No ma'am."

"Get yourself a cup of coffee, Horner. And go see if any of the fleet cars need a coat of wax or something."

Horner, who was fresh out of the academy, only rolled his eyes, knowing a harmless but still demeaning butt-chewing was awaiting him at the hands of the FBI.

Lucy popped in the cloudy-colored Observation Room to see it was empty and stood near the glass to stare at what had become of the man she couldn't deny having strong feelings for. The pain of physical abuse was sore on his features and she fought the desire to rush in and perform some kind of first aid.

What in God's name had happened?

Maybe he sensed as much, because his dark eyes bore holes in the two-way mirror and Lucy left the Observation Room, knowing full well, with no Officers around and no *real* jurisdiction on her behalf, that her conversation with him, whatever it would contain, would be heard by whomever just so happened to slip into the Observation Room while she had her back to the two-way mirror.

She would be going in blind, but she had to. She had to talk to him.

Her face couldn't show the pain it felt for him when she saw his. He looked like he'd gone twelve rounds with a heavyweight boxer.

"Hiya gorgeous." He said as she entered, with a wheezing sort of whisper that was as much as he could offer. The FBI were doing nothing about his cracked ribs, save the one optional painkiller on the table and the half-empty glass of metallic-smelling tap water to wash it down. They had given him a talking to on whatever subject they had detained him, and Lucy, totally in the dark over it and thankful for the Captain's heads-up in light of Geffington's assassination, knew the Captain would want her to get to the crux of it because the FBI was saying nothing in the matter.

It was the way of the new CRT policy, with CPD

on the bottom of it all like menial foot-soldiers to do the suit's bidding under martial law with no mayor.

"This is no time for a bad Bogie impression."

"Bad?" He coughed. "I'm hurt." Then he squinted. "So that's how long your hair is." His small laugh bore a striking resemblance to air leaving a balloon and he attempted to sit up in the uncomfortable chair and held his ribs with his cuffed hands applying pressure to them.

His militaristic curses were murmured and he hunched on the hard metal table.

Why is he cuffed? He's not a criminal and he's not going anywhere, save the ICU...

"You're still here?" He asked, weakly.

"I want to help."

"That's sweet, it is, and I know you mean it, but what can you do? We both know what the *F* in *FBI* stands for. They don't need no stinking..." He laughed again, unable to finish the classic movie quote.

"*I* need you for *my* investigation."

"More than the FBI needs me for scapegoat duty? Baby, I'm UDSA Prime."

"Seriously, Morell, help me help you."

The former Homeland Security Agent and expert Interrogator shut his eyes and let his head fall back to the uncomfortable crown of the chair.

"I'm *doing* that by telling you to leave." He gestured with his chin, wincing at the pain. "There's the door."

Lucy slammed her fist on the table in the same moment her rise kicked the chair back to the wall where the two-way mirror held its obstinate gaze and she rushed to the door and held tensed posture before leaving.

God, Henry, why are you pushing me away? Is it because of the FBI? You don't want me dragged down into your mess?

You've got to let me try to help you! I want to help you, I don't want to see them take you away, don't you understand?

Don't you want my help?

I've got one hell of a poker face, you know.

It was then Lucy got the sense someone was watching them, one of the traits she'd picked up in Vice, eyes in the back of her head. Such senses had saved her life on more than one occasion and she hoped they were strong enough to save his career.

"Is this another Homeland slash Hoover Boy pissing contest?"

Morell shook his head.

"RepMax and Tidebender?"

Morell remained still.

Lucy crossed her arms, taking his lack of a *no* as a *yes*.

"You gonna tell me about it?"

Morell's omission affirmed as much.

"Can't or won't?"

"I…" He trailed off, deciding against it.

"Like Iraq?"

Morell's facial shrug was sheepish, considering the tender bruise on the right side of his boyish features.

"Have you asked for a lawyer?"

"I'm not taking one."

"Why?"

"I'm pleading out."

Special Agent Blake Fosnick entered, bringing a rush of cold air with him. Lucy could tell he'd been outside, as he smelled in the slightest of gasoline. A file was in his hand and he wordlessly split it, slapped it on the table and retrieved a ballpoint pen from the inner pocket of his suit to click it and let it fall to the paper dominating the table.

His voice was as clear as it was quiet.

"Then do it already."

Lucy craned her neck to read the form.

It was a confession to gross miscarriages of justice, usurping the authority and office of Homeland Security to deface one private company on behalf of another, written in first person so Henry Morell had only to sign it to seal his fate in the Federal Pen.

So RepMax vs. Tidebender it is. Callie can't bail you out of this one and I can't either...but I'll be damned if I don't try.

"Is it true?" Lucy asked, uncrossing her arms and clasping them behind her back.

"Lucy...*you'll* need that painkiller if I tell you truth." Morell's joke was empty in its sense of objectivity and he held her gaze, attempting to discern which way her judgment of him was headed; for the nearest exit or straight down the darkness of the night's mysterious highway.

Together.

"We're burning daylight." Fosnick sighed, having his Manhunter quota nearly fulfilled by the corralling of Henry Morell for subsequent processing by the Department of Justice.

"I'm only signing it on one condition." Morell said after carefully browsing the page. "That you hold off your full court press until this investigation is complete."

"You mean Maks Lenkov? His suicide and this supposed assassin of Mayor Geffington you were fighting with? Which *no one* saw, by the way? My partner wrote down everything you were rambling about on the ride over but it doesn't sound like a case to me. Not like the one the DOJ's got against you."

"Listen Captain Planet, you can ignore the facts all you want, but if this guy kills one more billionaire or elected official, the blood's on your hands. I'm going to own up to what I did but I'm probably the only guy in Crescent that can stop what's about to happen. Now you can call it in to your bosses and whoever wants my head so bad they can't stand it anymore can have it after this guy's either dead or behind bars and we figure out what the whole thing's about."

Fosnick chewed on his bottom lip and glanced at Lucy.

"CPD has nothing but the highest regard for Mr. Morell." She added. "Ask around. They'll get prickly if you roll him out of here in cuffs."

"I can handle prickly." Fosnick nodded to sell the point and then probed, his blocky face becoming quizzical. "Stop what?"

"I'm not sure, exactly, could be a terrorist attack or an other assassination, but I can tell you who I think's at risk."

"I want names."

"I want your guarantee."

"Names then guarantee." Fosnick place his left hand on his hip, exposing his sidearm and nonverbally establishing his dominance of the situation. "If it checks out, then it'll buy you some time."

"You're a bastard." Morell growled and shook his head.

"You know the rules." Fosnick chided with condescension. "Don't get all sanctimonious on me. You've been on this side more times than I have, you know how the cards deal out. Debt is debt, Morell, and you may want to gamble, which I commend, but debt *is* debt."

Morell drained the water, leaving the painkiller.

"Yiury Mogilev, hedge fund manager, he owns an apartment near the top of Regency Tower and a yacht moored on the Waterfront named *Adler von*

Pomerelia."

"What's the significance?" Fosnick removed a notebook and took his pen to write.

"He bears certain unavoidable similarities to Maks Lenkov, namely his connection to an ancient religious order of wealthy professional soldiers."

Fosnick only held his pen in dead space and gestured for more, not skeptical of what he was hearing but not yet convinced, either.

"*Alder von Pomerelia* is German for the *Eagle of Pomerelia*. If you find the boat, you'll see there's a small *black* eagle below the calligraphy script of the name and since you won't be hunting and pecking for it in your FBI servers and need me to spell it out for you like the laymen that you are, *Pomerelia* is the original name of *Pomerania*, an area of land that was divided between Germany and Poland after World War Two. Pomerelia was conquered by the Teutonic Order and the Kings of Poland insinuated that the Order was unlawfully holding the land which lead to even greater conflict between the two. If you want to know the significance of the eagle with these people, have Lieutenant Radzewicz show you Maks Lenkov's penthouse on Ninth and Schwartz and if you can't see what I'm talking about from the moment you get off the elevator then have her show you a bottle of *Zakon Krzyżacki* Polish vodka." Morell cast as smirk to Lucy. "Did I say it right?"

Lucy's gray green eyes were wrinkled with the slightest edging of crow's feet.

"Lieutenant?" Fosnick hid his surprise. He could've sworn she was a just Second Grade Detective with how young she looked, or even an off duty patrol cop with whom Morell was in a relationship, considering her wholesome and natural, albeit phlegmatic attractiveness.

"I'd be glad to show you Lenkov's place." Lucy proposed.

Fosnick weighed several options and turned his focus on Morell.

"If you don't sign, I'll tag along everywhere you go and appoint an Agent more annoying than DiMocco to tail you around the clock. However, if you *do* sign, I'll get off your back and you'll be able to freely conduct your investigation, based on the outstanding merits of certain aspects of your service record. But the moment it's over, you belong to the DOJ. Fair?"

Morell looked to Lucy for some form of guidance and the solemn pledge soaring within her gray-green eyes sealed their collective fates.

"Gimmie the pen." He said, and proceeded to scribble, of his own volition, the signature that said his days, as a free man, were limited.

TWENTY

Once Officer Braden had learned there was *no* exception to the CRT's quarantine protocol, he took the girls to the gym near the pool for a bit of peace and quiet, relatively speaking, telling them he would be in direct contact with the Chief of Police but Callie knew a royal debacle when she saw one and took to the bench press to lie down like a wayward mummy. Braden left with the names and locations of Callie's two plainclothes bodyguards in an effort to reunite them. Kelly noticed that Aimee sat close to her mother in a young-person's knock-kneed, hands-between-legs manner, her eyes drifting around the weights and the mirrors to indicate she wasn't the gym type, and Kelly was about to speak with her when her phone forbade her from doing so.

It was Henry Morell's number.

"Hank, where are you?"

"Um…" The voice on the other end of the line was feminine and a bit Californian in that it was tight and hurried. "Excuse me, ma'am, I'm calling on behalf of Henry Morell to let you know that Mayor Geffington has been…"

"Yeah, I know, I was there when it happened, who are you? And where's Hank?"

There was a pause on the other end of the line and Callie sat up from her forced repose, an inquisitive frown highlighting her parallel scars.

"...*Hank* gave me his phone and told me to call the first five speed dial numbers and tell them what happened and that he's pursuing a suspect."

Kelly squinted and checked her watch. He'd been gone for nearly an hour and she was just now hearing about it?

Callie stood and approached Kelly, telling, as was obvious despite her well-trained eye, that Kelly was about to be distraught, even more so than earlier. Kelly noticed the CEO's unobtrusive presence and Callie gently offered her hand for the phone.

Kelly gave her the phone and managed to turn her back before tears fell from her kohl-darkened eyes and stained her cheeks. Her feet were sore in her heels and she walked several feet before taking a seat on an apparatus she had no idea the purpose of and hunched over to stare into the dullness of the carpet.

"I wanted to tell you how much I like your dress." A soothing voice offered behind her, after nearly ninety seconds of relative silence.

Kelly turned to see Aimee standing at a polite distance with a tissue, nearly returning the favor of such that Kelly had provided her mother.

"Thanks." Kelly sniffed and tossed her eyebrows to a space for Aimee to sit down and join her.

"Men." Aimee said.

"Yeah, I know." Kelly removed her heels and curled her short brown hair behind her ears. She felt physically inadequate next to Aimee but Aimee still had shades of her mother's compassion and gentility and that somewhat lessened the severe beauty of Aimee's looks in comparison to hers as they sat in front of a wall of mirrors.

"Listen," Aimee's hand hovered in the space between them before reaching to Kelly's and clasping it. "I'm sorry if I offended you earlier, I didn't know he was your boyfriend."

Kelly's eyebrows leapt in genuine surprise, not only with the stunningly exotic young woman's sincerity, no doubt a genetic copy of her mother's, but the fact that she was *so* wrong about what she was saying.

"Not at all, don't be."

"I'm serious, you looked like you were going to die and I was flirting with him pretty hard. We were even speaking Arabic."

"No, really," Kelly cleared her throat, knowing Hank didn't speak Arabic in America unless he really had to or was choosing to do so on the count of showing off, which, also meant in Hank's military mind that he *had* to. "Hank's *not* my boyfriend."

Aimee's clear blue eyes were caught in a baffled series of blinks and her mouth was slightly agape.

"But even now, I mean, I can see how concerned you are. And back when we met, you guys came from the restaurant…that meal must've cost a small fortune."

"Yeah. We worked together after the Crisis taking down RepMax, but he's *not* my boyfriend. You could say we're…close." Kelly sniffled. "Yeah, you could say that."

Aimee was still a bit confused over Kelly's tears, as if she was having a hard time convincing her own self of what she was saying and then chalked them up to her being in the Crisis and the trauma of such coming back again with the death of the Mayor.

"Then…" Aimee waded.

"He probably thought your mom was trying to set you two up."

Aimee frowned and even her frown was worthy of a magazine cover or the eyes-on-everyone-who-passed-by cosmetic advertisement space and her face seemed to have some sort of light emanating from it, like a pool of pure mountain water catching the morning sun. She shrugged at her mother's tactics, so cerebral they were, and blew a hand her way like she didn't know what she was doing. Kelly was fascinated by the young woman and had never, in her formative schooling days, even *thought* of befriending someone so physically flawless. Kelly's friends had always been people like her, off in a corner types that never caught the eyes of the jock or the class president. And even though those days were *long* over, going back to college was only bringing them back and the soreness of losing her potential fiancée in the Crisis was only aiding and abetting the hollow thump of the refrigerator, the dusty sound of pages turning, and the chilliness of her bed as the night dragged on and on and on.

Her own words seemed to clang and clatter like Medieval weaponry against Henry Morell's.

No, really...He's not my boyfriend...

Hey Kel, have you met anyone at University?

So it was true, he'd just used her to say no to the boss's daughter.

Then he's both a jerk and an idiot. Look at her. She's breathtaking. And I'm the bigger idiot for wanting to be his girlfriend, for being grabby and clingy even though I really do need someone.

But he's my friend, he's a damn good friend. He's nice and smart and we get along so well, he gets my humor and he's never taken advantage of me. But friends can't do that, right? They can't take the leap... it's poison, it's...

"Interesting..." Callie said in nearly a humming tone as she crossed the distance between them, staring blankly at Kelly's phone.

"What?" Aimee fluffed her strawberry golden

curls and Kelly shook her head again at the girl's unconscious beauty and how sore her own heart *still* was because of the Crisis.

"This woman, Jasmine Keelan, works with Channel Two. She helped Morell identify a possible suspect whom Morell believes is responsible for the death of Lenkov *and* Geffington."

Callie judged the facial reactions between the younger women and handed the phone back to Kelly. Aimee was in the dark but had lived her entire life watching her mother speak to others of things she had no idea about.

"So he told you about Lenkov?" She asked, hands moving to her hips.

"Yeah, he wanted me to do some research."

"On the Middle Ages? The Teutonic Order?"

Kelly's chin tipped to the right.

"Yeah, but what does that have to do with this…Jasmine lady having Hank's phone and him going off the grid, so to speak?"

Callie shrugged.

"What can I say? He just…went off, chasing after the guy who he thought killed Geffington." Callie said with a rush of frustration and was about to walk back to her bench and nearly began to wag her finger at Kelly. "You know, if you're going to be in a relationship with a guy like Morell, you should know that he doesn't check in with mommy every five minutes."

"Mom…" Aimee squinted.

"He didn't even hesitate throwing himself into the fire when everyone else just about peed their pants including some of our esteemed public defenders and he could be out there in the dark and the cold, right this very minute, lying dead on the pavement because he can't stop himself from trying to do the right thing when everyone else is trampling each other in an effort to save their own ass."

"Mom, seriously…" Aimee craned her neck and Callie slashed her arms in the air, turning to walk away from them with her left hand on her hip and her right on her mouth.

Aimee shrugged with swollen eyes.

"I'm *so* sorry."

"No, it's okay." Kelly dropped her head into her hands, staring into the floor to contemplate the depth of her own selfishness.

Aimee's frown returned in silent response to Kelly's statement but as she watched her mother pace back and forth near the door of the gym, it occurred to her she'd never seen her mother so distressed about the welfare of another human being while doing such a poor and unpolished job of hiding it.

Jessica Birchall checked the time on her cellphone as the man she'd been speaking with returned from the bathroom of the darkened and intimately lit rendezvous bar near the fourth terminal of Bay County International. The muddled spit of cold rain was beginning to turn to frost on the stretched panels of the windows, making small toys of the line of awaiting airplanes and Birchall's somber face had been twisted more so by the story dominating nearly every available television screen in the airport, from which the reporter couldn't help but feel she was in limbo, literally and figuratively.

"God, what a shame." The man said, his hands smelling in the slightest of soap.

Birchall stabbed her straw past the ice cubes of her third Long Island Iced Tea to get at the last bits of it. Her flight to Boston had been cancelled entirely, and maybe her chance of getting the anchor job along with it.

"Life sucks, doesn't it?" She said and then stared at him.

"What?"

"Can we get this over with?"

"I've told you all I can without actually giving you the redacted files to compare with the original transcripts."

"Where are they?" Birchall's head felt heavy and her penetrating brown eyes were glazed by the steady combination of alcohol and circumstance. The city of Crescent was yet again going to hell when she was trying to find herself a cozy little anchor job and the man in front of her was not only appealing to the very reason she'd become a journalist in the first place, but was taking a chance on her moral fiber as well.

"They're in a safe." He said, with the guarded tone she'd become accustomed to. It seemed the more they'd talked about the CIA-ordered mishap in Baghdad the thirstier she became and after the her third Long Island Iced Tea the man was beginning to appeal to another portion of her soul.

The terrified one, craving comfort in the face of danger, because adrenaline was no drug to rely on in the midst of severity unless one was ready for the frostbite-like crash of coming down to fragility and instability with nothing to rely on but the strength of character one carried deep inside.

And in Birchall's case, that was a flimsy dinghy in the storm.

Birchall's delicate hand massaged her brow, trembling in the slightest.

Perhaps that was the problem. Since the Crisis it'd been one giant adrenaline trip and after her soaring ascension to dominate every newscast with her stories of tragedy and tribulation and then her firing, probably for accusing the man in charge, Hoyt Stanton, of taking the teeth out of the truth, she'd finally come down to the fact that she was petrified to be in Crescent and she was afraid of another series of events paling the first round in comparison.

She was *not* a soldier. She was a reporter; fires and car wrecks, *just* the facts of who, what, when, where, how, and why…and now Geffington had been shot? What was the world coming to? When would it end? Would it ever? Forty-eight people…*slaughtered* in Baghdad at the hand of those sworn to protect and defend threats both foreign and domestic and on and on…

"What's wrong?" The man said as the shaking of her right hand increased.

"Would it be so horrible…" Her eyebrows twisted as she swallowed with difficulty. "If you took me to a hotel for the night?"

The man was surprised to say the least and leaned in closer for clarification.

"Do you need somewhere to stay, or…"

Birchall only nodded, her head heavy on her shoulders with the weight of life making its presence laborious, letting him decipher the fullness of what she was asking for.

"It's just that…I'm *really* scared." Birchall stared deep into the frozen cubes of her Long Island Iced Tea, the alcohol of which ripped the truth straight from her guts without any chance to process it through the formalities she was so bound by. "Especially with what's going on here, coincidence or not…I'm not a combat soldier…with all the death flying around here I'm not going to be able to see this thing through. I know I'm not a very strong person by nature."

Pity deepened across the man's face and he reached within his wallet to leave enough on the table to cover her drinks.

"Are you alright if I buy you a cab?" He asked and she assured him quickly she was and he scrutinized her inebriated features. It was true he'd seen her heavily made-up face on TV many times and had chosen *her* amongst a host of other investigative journalists, maybe with the fact that she was a hundred and ten pound brunette contributing in the slightest, but the man felt far more compassion for her than romantic attraction and would've bet his CIA credentials she was only hours away from crying herself to sleep, to which he would be glad to monitor on behalf of the truth about *Wolf Stone* needing to get out. Honestly, he *was* using her as a means to an end, but he was using her as a voice and a conduit to shine a light on atrocities that could no longer be buried beneath the fog of war, *not* as an instrument of self-gratification. For him, there *was* no gratification, even in the exposition of American war criminals.

The truth was a painful soul mate, and it would be his sole companion till the day he died.

And he knew he had to get the story out before that day came.

He hadn't seen them since he'd left Boston just before the storm front swept in on his tip-toe trip of red herrings and diversions northward from D.C., but he was sure they were looking for him, those men that had begun following him nonstop last week, not that he was an easy man to find in the first place. He did empathize with Birchall but the *last* thing he was going to do, especially on the run, was get into a relationship, despite whatever the looseness of alcohol was pleading on Birchall's lips and the ease in which the procedure had presented itself, and was keen to hear the voice of fear speaking from her lips, hoping that nothing else was wrapped around its plea to be safe from danger.

As a CIA man, he was well accustomed to

immorality offering itself on a silver platter while those
in authority over him looked the other way. After all, it
was the very reason *why* he'd sought Birchall in the
first place.

Someone had to stand in the gap between right
and wrong and not play both sides for the middle.

Birchall grabbed his right hand in both of hers.

"Hey, where are you going?" She nearly slurred,
the evidence of alcohol undeniable. "We're safer
together."

"…Right." He nodded. As much was true. "I'm
gonna leave first and call you a cab, okay? Go get it
about in ten minutes, south concourse. Give yourself
some time. Room Three-Zero-Two, Fifteenth Street
Inn. The cab ride'll be about thirty minutes." The man
spoke slowly and precisely as Birchall's penetrating
gaze gained the tiniest bit of focus and he reached
within his jacket pocket with the hand she wasn't
holding onto for dear life, sliding what looked to be a
an oversized car-key underneath a napkin near her ice-
cube-filled glass. "Here's my room key, okay? I'm
going to go now. Ten minutes."

The man's emblem of stability slipped from the
loose grip of her dainty hands and Birchall watched him
walk away, wishing the small blooming and burning of
warmth the Long Island Iced Tea provoked in her throat
would overwhelm her entire being and she would be
able to wake up the next morning with a handle on the
spiral her life had become.

And what she didn't see, in her self-absorbed
haze, was the two sinister-looking men following the
man she wanted to spend the night with as he left for
the parking garage.

TWENTY-ONE

Lucy got the passenger door for Henry Morell and he hesitated, considering the lowness of the sport coupe, before wincing to slide in the seat.

"Thanks." He said, after she'd walked around, sent a glance to the dark gloss of a Precinct window where Fosnick would be glowering at them with his oddly clever passivity, and buckled herself in to fire the gold Sebring to life in the cold night.

Lucy only nodded, waiting till they were on the road to speak.

"What happened?"

"Didn't you hear?"

"You know what I mean."

Morell gently tapped his sore ribs. His head ached with the dull agony of being used as a soccer ball in addition to the stinging disorientation of still not really having his equilibrium stabilized and the hyperextending of his left leg had thankfully not snapped any cruciate ligaments but would still give him a bit of a limp for a few days.

"I found the guy who killed Lenkov and Geffington. He admitted to it, almost as if he wanted to, he was proud of it…but he was *so* much better than me. I got off easy…"

"You could've died." Lucy's voice was strained with concern though her face was nearly implacable.

"Why didn't you coordinate with CPD, why'd you go lone wolf?"

"Have you ever seen the Critical Response Team protocol first hand? It's absolute *anarchy*. It reminds me a bit of Iraq…guys barking orders, people running and screaming and covering their heads, and enough automatic weapons floating around to turn a steel battleship into Swiss cheese."

Lucy shook her head, as much providing a negative answer as she was stifling a derogatory comment about the entire CRT procedure and the way martial law affected everyone's way of life.

"It was like a pen of sheep in a thunderstorm. Army acronyms come to mind, and they all start with *F*…" Morell stared into the dotting of raindrops on the windshield as Lucy casually flicked the wipers on and off for one broad stroke of refreshing clarity. "And I knew that if I was out of the funnel they were trying to send everyone to in order to control them and lock everything down, some rookie cop might've emptied his gun on me, or at least detained me and stopped me from finding the shooter. No…I saw him fool a SWAT squad in the parking garage and I was on my own from there. He's damn good, this guy…he knew what he was doing, taking out the Mayor. Crescent's ruined now, and he'll use it to his advantage to do something else."

Lucy sighed and rubbed her forehead as they waited for a red light to change and it occurred to her.

"You live on Second."

"Yeah?"

"Then you can't go home. The Continental Plaza's like…two-hundred feet from your place and there's a four block no-traffic zone, forty-eight hour minimum quarantine."

Morell shrugged.

"I didn't want to ask."

"You didn't have to." Lucy's gray-green eyes contained a sly grin as she sat up in her seat to judge the traffic before performing a cop's U-turn. Morell was pushed back in the seat as she accelerated down the nearly empty opposing lane. "You'll like my place." She said. "It's quiet."

Morell's laugh of two wheezing breaths was muted over the acceleration of the Sebring and its fluid route toward Lucy's secret retreat in Eavesdale.

In his state, quiet was all he could handle.

Lucy was sure Morell had fallen asleep with the shutting of his eyes but by the time they'd cut through the idyllically maintained lots dotting the knoll next to Fircrest Hill, he sat up with a slow and strained movement as the Sebring eased to a halt. Lucy got his belt and was quick to get his door.

"Need a hand?"

"Thanks." He said, eager to rely on her strength in his hobbling and tender state of weakness, and the heat of her touch in the falling frost of nearly eleven o'clock. His joke was quite the opposite, and he was sure she saw through it. "I'm pathetic, aren't I?"

"We all have our moments." She said, placing her left hand on the small of his back with her right at his right elbow.

"So this is what it feels like to be old." He said and his sideways glance caught the winking in Lucy's gray-green eyes, considering he was close enough to smell the light vesper of lemon oil that was clinging to her skin and her clothes.

"You're gonna need to dry clean this suit." She said, on their way to the white door, flanked by two well-trimmed perennial azaleas, yellowing in the porch light.

"You wouldn't happen to have any men's smalls I

can change into, would you?"

"Women's smalls. I've got a ruffly leopard-print blouse you could wear."

"No you don't." Morell laughed, pain coughing through his windpipe. "You're not the leopard-y type."

"*Leonine*." She corrected. "And stop that."

She fetched her keys, opened the door and waited, seeing Morell was standing with a slight wobble.

"Won't Fosnick drag you through the mud for this?"

Lucy's simple attractiveness mocked the question and her eyebrows made an attempt at a frown as her voice was nearly a monotone.

"Screw him."

Morell laughed again, despite the pain.

"Stop that." She said, shutting the door behind him, even though her harsh joke was covering the blatant fact that she didn't care about Fosnick, the FBI, procedures and protocols, or anything else in the moment but Henry Morell's welfare and the case they were in, *together*, over their heads.

Morell caressed his facial bruise where the Lynx had taken his free kick as Lucy provided some light in the sitting room. It was small, as was the house itself, but an illusion of extra space was quantified by the lack of clutter so many people used like a drug to make their houses feel like homes. Conversely, Lucy's place was nearly barren, but truly imbued Morell with the relaxing sense of disconnection he so desperately needed and was nearly guilty of embracing. It was as if Crescent was an afterthought and Geffington's blood and his run in with the killer had been smoothed away with the Sebring's swishing wipers.

The very *atmosphere* of Eavesdale was different; liberated from the mind-bending cobweb of Crescent's steel and glass hamster wheels and the apocalyptic frenzy they were about to free-fall into if things got any worse.

"Come on." Lucy tapped the small white couch, indicating Morell park himself there as she unzipped her CPD jacket and disappeared past a low wood-burning fireplace. Her house reminded Morell of a small version of what he'd seen in older television shows and movies and was partial to, though he was never home enough to equate spending money on such a place and had chosen his dwelling in the thick of Crescent's stilted heartbeat for duty's sake. In the stillness of Lucy's place, and on behalf of it, his mind was clear enough to recall Callie's words about CAP Syndrome.

He really was a victim. He would've thought it selfish to take himself away from it all and unplug till the time clock called him back. It was as if he didn't have a time clock, his service was twenty-four seven and he applauded Lucy's self-respect and self-control that she valued such separation.

Lucy was back, shoes and coat gone, and her hair was free of its ponytail; long, flowy and beautiful.

"Hungry?" She said. Morell shook his head. "Coffee?" Again, the same shudder of negation. "Music?"

Morell's eyes wandered to her perfectly organized CD collection and squinted to read the labels and saw Lucy's taste was a few pay grades above his.

"The only music I ever got into was hardcore metal when we were about to take a trip into a hot zone. You could *feel* everyone get pumped up. You wouldn't happen to have a copy of *Shogun*, would you? I'd be ready to take on the world if you did."

Lucy said nothing, leaning in the open doorframe near the fireplace, but her voice quieted.

"Need to call anyone?"

"Oh God…" Morell's forehead wrinkled in grief. "Kel's gonna kill me."

"Girlfriend?"

"No…my partner in crime. We worked together taking out RepMax. We met Callie in the lobby and she got us into the Convention…she's probably worrying her head off right now, how I ran out of there."

Lucy left for the cordless in her bedroom and padded back across the hardwood floors to give him the phone.

"They're probably together, Callie and…*Kel*, you said her name was?"

"Kelly. Kelly Barnett."

"The journalist?"

"Yeah…" Morell dialed. "You know her?"

"I've been reading the CMJ for as long as I remember. She usually covers the Libertarian Party, not that that's a very big crowd around here."

Morell smiled and forbade himself from laughing on the count of the joke about her tainted view on politicians and authority figures wanting to worm its way out of his mouth.

Lucy left for the darkness of her bedroom and the attached bath to get some things and tried not to listen to Morell's call to Kelly, though her CPD Vice habits were too hard for her to break, and if she wasn't his girlfriend, then why was his concern for her and not Callie, whom it sounded like, from the Captain's relation of the events of the shooting to Lucy, had almost died herself.

Jasmine Keelan followed the bear-like Officer named Braden to the gym near the pool to see three women and two men, all of which she'd never seen before, save the woman who'd nearly stolen the show at

the Convention and had been inches from Geffington
when his neck received the bullet. She, Rachel
Calabrese of Tidebender, proponent of anti-violent
defense and security through psychological profiling,
and political lobbying of de-weaponizing the world,
was the woman Jasmine had wormed her way into the
Continental Plaza Hotel to meet and had gotten *so*
much more than she bargained for.

"Callie?" Officer Braden called and Callie pushed
herself from the bench press to greet him warmly as
Jasmine entered the gym with as much confidence as
one of the well-built and semi-military looking men
standing off in the corner near the dumbbell pyramids.
One of the women, a cute academic, was caught in a
serious phone conversation off in the opposite corner
near a leg press machine. Another, perhaps an
international-looking actress or a model to Jasmine's
eye, was nursing a small paper cup of water from the
inverted jug so common to gym and office spaces alike.

Jasmine leaned on the dip machine with which
she was well acquainted, waiting for Callie to finish her
hushed conversation with the Officer before catching
her eye.

"Thank you for coming." Callie said, before
adding quickly with the aid of her finger to point out
who she was speaking of. "That's my daughter Aimee,
those two men are a part of my plainclothes security
detail, the taller one is Imler, the shorter one is Epps,
and the woman on the phone over there is Kelly
Barnett-anything you have to say to me about what Mr.
Morell told you you can say to all of them as well."

"*I can't believe you!*" Kelly's declarative whisper
was nearly as loud as a shout in the relative quiet of the
gym, and she was bent in half, facing the mirrored wall.

"So, if you can, while we're waiting for Ms.
Barnett..." Callie said but Kelly's conversation with

Henry Morell was unavoidably distracting.

"You can be a real dick, you know that! You should be sorry...yes, yes I do, but really...I mean, seriously...why didn't you just tell me? You know how hard it's been...well that's no excuse, okay? Jeez..."

"If you can," Callie motioned Jasmine to sit down with Epps and Imler, "Please tell those two gentlemen *exactly* what happened word for word for our records."

"You know..." Keelan's tone was inquisitive. "I came to the Convention to speak with *you* about Maks Lenkov, do you think..."

Callie's features wizened and her smile was polite, though she wished to have a plan of attack in place before involving the media, especially an outlet as green as Jasmine Keelan appeared to be, for all her attempted polish one of Callie's expertise could nearly see the marks the training wheels still left in her jerky and over-practiced movements.

"We'll talk about it after my associates take your statement for our record."

"Stop saying that! It's no good, you already did it, okay? I'm over it...Yeah, fine...I'm glad you're okay, but...I know, dear Lord, you had me so worried..."

"Got it." Jasmine nodded nervously, unable to avoid the sensation of being in on a secret and the strangeness of trying not to overhear Kelly Barnett's reprimands of Henry Morell. Jasmine had been divided from the miasma of the others and their volcanic tensions by Officer Braden who had been on orders from Interim Chief Bertolucci to separate Callie from further danger. A doctor had come by but Callie had assured him she was okay, and Braden had been able to find Callie's plainclothes Tidebender Shadows. They had the flair of despondent businessmen but they were former US Army Green Berets, both of them, and had nearly scored perfect marks on Callie's extensive battery of psychological tests, proving themselves qualified to identify potential threats via body language and apprehend them, if the need presented itself, in the least violent manner possible.

Callie caught Aimee's eye as Kelly ended her cathartic phone conversation with the swipe of her thumb and at Callie's subtle nod, Aimee brought Kelly a paper cup of water.

Callie waited a scant few seconds before taking a seat opposite the two younger women and hushing her voice.

"Morell gave this reporter his phone and told her to call the first five speed dial numbers," Callie handed the device in question to Kelly. "Do you recognize them?"

"Yeah...Ed McKinney and Joe Hayes. Both served with Hank in Iraq and went in the private sector after honorable discharge, they all worked together in the Crisis, but I'm pretty sure McKinney runs a survival school in Katonah National Park now, and Hayes works for..."

"RepMax?"

"*No...*" Kelly's face was still sour from speaking with Morell. "It's an acronym...SSAR, I think?"

"Scarlett Surveillance and Research, they're an east coast outfit, more private investigators than paramilitary..." Callie said as much to herself in open thought as to the girls. "What about the next two, before yours."

"Uh...one of the numbers looks vaguely familiar but...oh, I know why, the one's a D.C. area code."

"Yes, it is." Callie was puzzled by as much and indicated the fourth number with a thrust of her chin. "What about that one? Crescent area code, right?"

"Yeah, but it doesn't look familiar."

Callie's kind blue eyes gained an ornery twinkle

and Aimee, knowing the look and what it had been responsible for in the past, glanced past her mother's shoulder to where the Channel Two reporter was still going over the particulars with the two tough and dour bodyguards.

"That number left a message…is there any way you can hack Henry's four digit code so we can hear the message?"

"Oh I don't know…" Kelly's fingers were injected by a nearly supernatural pulse, flying to do so. "My conscience might forbid me…and there we go." She smiled and mouthed the word *birthday*, listening to the message and Aimee, who was not in any way, shape, or form, conscious of what her mother was doing on behalf of the death of Geffington and the billionaire Lenkov, or what Morell had purposed in his private spreading of information, saw the color drain from Kelly's cute and humble face.

The message was nearly a minute in length and Callie's scars were as strong as the question possessing her face.

"Dear Lord…" Kelly said in the clutches of disbelief, staring at the phone as if it what she'd heard was scientifically impossible, like the sun reversing its course in midday.

"Who was it?" Callie leaned forward in her seat.

"A voice I haven't heard since November." Kelly stared at the phone, heavy in her hand.

The voice belonged to Sierra Marland.

TWENTY-TWO

Henry Morell was staring into the ceiling when Lucy returned with a small hamper basket and clicked on a selection of barely audible piano instrumentals. The nearly watery sound of the pianist's touch spilled through the speakers and alerted Morell of her return in the softest of ways.

"Unbutton." She said, taking a seat next to him, though he was in the small couch's direct middle.

"Aren't we skipping a couple of steps?" He smiled, about to chuckle and her gray-green eyes forbade him. "…Right." After his phone call's abrupt end, he'd been relaxing with his head propped on a pillow, arms outstretched on the back of the couch to ease his breathing motion and the slightest movement of his left arm from that position jabbed a knife of pain in his ribs.

"Okay." She said. "If I must."

Lucy took great care in unbuttoning his white collared shirt and wrapping his ribs tight with gauze while taking his mind off of such.

"Talk to me about the assassin. Did you get a good look at him?"

"No."

"Can you describe him?"

"About my height…British."

"English, Irish, Scottish? Welsh?"

"Oh gosh…" Morell frowned to think, which then twisted to a wince. "Oww…"

"Sorry." Lucy said, having to push with her thumb to attach the metal fastener that would keep the gauze in place. "No sudden movements, alright?"

Morell's eyebrows juggled as if to say, *yeah, sure, I'm gonna do cartwheels across the floor* and his vision waned to repose and darkness with the comfort of the pillow, the light smell of lemon oil and Lucy's body heat in close proximity doing their restorative work as the chord progression of A minor, F, C and G Major inversions thrummed in the background.

"How'd he fight you?" She asked. "Did you grapple? Did he know any Asian disciplines?"

"Gosh, that's a blur." Morell grimaced. "I'll take a pass."

"Let's go back. How'd he get past SWAT in the parking garage?"

"CPD windbreaker. I'm sure he had a badge, too; that and a little brazen confidence was all he needed but I didn't see a badge or hear what he said to them. I was too far away. You know the gun he used for Geffington was a Twenty-Two single shot hidden in a camera? He was standing right there with the press, stage left the whole time, and nobody saw him…bold to have only one shot…"

"Yeah, the Captain told me as much but he also told me the FBI's running the investigation. You know they'll slow down and go to cameras and lose him for good, so…I'd love for you to contribute the missing piece of the puzzle."

Morell tipped his head down to look at her with weary eyes, unaware that she had also removed his shoes, placed his left leg across her lap and rolled up his pant leg during the course of their conversation.

"What?" She said, reaching for a knee brace from

the basket.

"You're really something, you know that?" He said.

Lucy would've blushed but her paralysis wouldn't allow it and she averted her eyes in the near violent stretching and placement of the neoprene knee brace.

"Now for your head." She said, removing a bottle of cold medicine.

"No. It's got alcohol in it."

"You sure? It'll help you sleep."

"No."

"It's mint flavored."

"Positive." Morell assured. "But you could sing me a lullaby."

Lucy rolled her eyes and inverted the hamper basket to place his left leg on it to elevate it and keep it straight, setting the cold medicine beside it if he changed his mind. She took the fleece blanket she'd also placed in the hamper basket and draped it across him and though it pained him to do so, Henry Morell caught her right hand with his left and held it before she was about to leave.

"Thank you, Lucy." He said, the painful throb in his facial bruise nearly echoing the pulse of blood rushing up and down her radial artery.

"It's the least I could do." She said.

"We both know that's not true. *You* came to get me. Nobody else."

"I don't think anybody else could."

"You want to try that same logic with the car crash? Or the fact that if Callie *was* going to dump me because I was late on the first day you were going to move mountains to get me into CPD? Not to mention how you just about flipped over the table when I was trying to protect you from getting on Fosnick's bad side." Morell chuckled, knowing he had her in his sights, and as mysterious and emotionless as her pleasant complexion was, he was addressing her feelings eye to eye, man to woman. "God knows you would've done anything to get me out of there, even *after* reading that affidavit. You stuck your neck out for me and I want to thank you for it, as much as I want to thank you for taking me into your beautiful home and patching me up. And trust me, Lucy, a soldier doesn't forget either. *Ever*."

Lucy stared at him, cognizant that with his hand around her wrist, thumb at her pulse, he was well aware of her acting out of attraction toward him and that she didn't make a Good Samaritan habit of taking every injured co-worker home to nurse them back to health. In fact, her home was off limits, just like her heart was, and the coldness people read from her was as much a front as it was a natural reaction to keep all that was tender in her heart locked inside of the bank vault she relied on staying sane by. *Someday*, she always told herself, someday, there'd be a reason for not being loose like everyone else, for not barflying and bedhopping and it was as if the solemn pledge in her eyes back in the Interrogation Room of the Precinct was just as much about truth and justice and the vindication thereof as it was about the deepening bond of partnership she was saying *to hell with the rest of them* by seeking and her words at Victory Park echoed in their truth within Henry Morell.

I trust you. You're the kind of guy I wish there were a lot more of...

I'm on your side...

I trust you...

Lucy's blinking eyes were blank and she simply left him where he sat, his left hand limply falling from her right arm to sit lifelessly at his side as she switched off the lights, one by one, and finally, the elegant and delicate piano music to leave him in the blackness of silence and the unshakeable knot choking up his guts with its stony sense of sickness.

In the relatively unaffected freedom of the Waterfront, its clean up and reconstruction efforts stillborn for the evening, The Lynx walked with little or no consciousness of the numbing cold, considering his lack of outerwear.

He'd survived the Fan Dance in the Breacon Beacons during Escape and Evasion, though one wouldnt've guessed it just by looking at him, and his militaristically purposeful stride was an indicator, as was his indifference to the wet and frosty chill, that he was once, British Special Air Service.

But he was Lithuanian, in his heart, in his soul, always had been, always would be, though again, no one would guess as much when throwing him a passing glance.

He was the kind of person that garnered no second appraisals and could've been the scion of any number of European genealogies and the cocktail thereof, when in truth, he was immovable in the beliefs of his ancestry, made even more so by his vehement hate of governments and worldly systems.

The Lynx surveyed the winter-swollen greenish vein of industry that was the Targus River, running parallel to the city skyline, and the darkened hulks of logging barges eager to trudge freshly-shorn firs and pines up and out along the Bay north to the Mill in Ram's Head.

The Ferry Terminal, close by the looming orange cranes and boxed mazes of shipping containers, for the islands up north, hid a clustered crop of moored ships, most of them of the sailing variety, and it was near the Ferry Terminal at a derelict oyster bar that The Lynx found another of the rare payphones he loved to use.

Convinced he'd done the right thing by fleeing when he had, rather than killing the man that'd so expertly tracked him down, with a small stroke of luck as was always the case in combat, The Lynx attached his illegal device to the phone and placed a few quarters in the machine.

Though he could've killed the man in the blink of an eye, the clock inside forbade him from doing so, as time was the only voice the assassin listened to in the limitless recesses of his psychotic brain.

"…Yes?" The American voice employing him, speaking all the way from Estonia, garbled after coughing.

So it is flu…pity, all that mucous, such a nuisance, really…but, it'll make it easier on me when the time comes, The Lynx pondered.

"Watchin' the news, mate?"

"Yes." The American said, nine hours ahead. "It's breaking now. Did you really think that was necessary? I didn't pay you for that."

"And I didn't charge you for it, but it's only gettin' worse from here. The chaos makes me feel at home. Number two's about to hit the bottom of the Targus, so, enjoy your breakfast. The next ones'll just be flies in a jar, no worries."

With that, The Lynx hung up and breathed in cupped hands as he left the booth and walked along the peeling paint of the old oyster bar for the rental SUV in which was hidden his diving gear, removing the device from his baggy cargo pants that triggered the explosives in the rental he'd strategically placed near the entrance of the Continental Plaza's parking garage.

The result, horrific to those involved in both gross extremes of physical, psychiatric, and logistical damage, would be the architecturally catastrophic

collapse of a building Crescent regarded as a symbol of
the way things *used* to be.

The deafening concussion of The Lynx' remote-
controlled explosion, amplified by the echoing canyon
of the subterranean five-story parking garage and the
greedy ignition of trapped oxygen, nitrogen, and
methane car exhaust it housed, rocked the Continental
Plaza like a small earthquake. Those caught in the
service passageway behind the Grand Ballroom were
struck anew with nauseating floods of dismay and the
paramilitary Critical Response Team outside the Hotel
were as startled as any by the shockwave of the blast
and fireball that followed, until the rubble buildup of
the Hotel's structural cave-in hid the flames from view
in a grisly mess of half-ton chunks of concrete and
stone.

Clouds of dust whooshed from the opening of the
parking garage in a giant sneeze, and the first floor
followed suit with an exhalation of masonry and
crushed glass, pinching underneath the weightlessness
it had been forced to accept till the portion sitting
directly above the garage sagged in a broken v-shape.

The SWAT Commander, a former Marine, rushed
to CRT Captain Shane Sheth, cursing about how his
team was down there and his voice only added to the
dissonance assaulting Sheth's ears, making already
impossible administrative decisions worthy of a
pulmonary embolism.

Sheth swore to himself in disbelief as the
crumbled grave of stones choked the black smoke of
the explosive conflagration.

There was no good way to handle it.

Crescent was once more clamped in the cruel
vampire's bite of terrorism.

And as the clock ever so slowly approached the

midnight of a bitter January evening the citizens of
Crescent would never forget, Sheth couldn't shake the
sixth sense haunting his vastly experienced mind that
whispered, ever so softly against the maelstrom of vain
emotion possessing Second Avenue, that the
destruction was far from over.

TWENTY-THREE

The cab ride from the airport was slow and laborious with detours to thousands of cars disrupting the flow of traffic as far as Bay County airport, twenty miles south of the riverside city of Crescent, upon which midnight was approaching like a thief in the visceral form of a cold, dark wind.

Jessica Birchall, cozy in the cab's relative stuffiness, had taken the time to sleep off a small portion of her alcoholic stupor. She was still buzzed, not that she'd ever really been over the limit before, with all the rules she had to abide by to stay in the television's judgmental eye, and when the cab finally did reach Fifteenth Street Inn, she was ready to call it a night.

The cab ride'd also cleaned up her sense of perspective, the solitude of it, and even though exactly *what* she'd said at the table evaded her in the moment, she remembered the kind and nearly pitiful look on the CIA man's face and in the back of her mind was cognizant of the fact that he'd sought *her* out to shine a light on a very dark secret, knowing she'd been fired and was in a state of limbo.

You handled that very well, Birchall told herself as she paid the Pakistani driver a few dollars more than she should've and left the cab at the corner of Fifteenth, so congested it was she knew it'd take the cab awhile to go any further if she needed to hail it again for any reason. *Very professional, Jessie…I'm sure he still wants to work with you, seeing as you're flakier than puff pastry.*

He's CIA.

He's not a fake?

No, he's not a fake, couldn't you feel his sincerity?

I could feel something alright, it's called gin. Don't they train that, anyway?

What?

Sincerity.

Who?

The CIA. He's trained to dupe people to get what he wants.

That doesn't make sense. You're saying he is CIA if his sincerity was false? A fake would've pushed the fact and tried too hard. He showed you his card because he wanted to get your attention and what he wants exposed could change the way America views the war in Iraq. Besides, he wasn't desperate for some company, there Miss Iced Tea…

Birchall blushed with no uncertain shame at what'd brought her to the Fifteenth Street Inn in the first place and the chill of near freezing midnight only added to the redness of her face, stealing the lingering heat of the cab from her. As if it were a cold shower, she stood in the wind with her satchel and carry-on bag, letting the stiff breeze flip-flap her heavy brown hair to and fro, until she was clear-headed enough to go in and talk to the man about the war crimes he was so brave in wanting to expose.

But was the timing right?

Crescent was under attack again, and whether she called in a favor at Channel Two or passed the story on to the independent press, Crescent was in the thick of it,

déjà vu of the Crisis and she'd have one hell of a
headache the next day; not because of the shooting she
could be reporting, but because of her disassociation
from it all as if the frenzied muddle of thoughts and
voices swirled around the atmosphere. The whole thing
was just so…*odd* to her now, knowing that blocks
away, HD cameras were up and running to film the
stilted conversations ping-ponging between field and
studio, and in whatever downtime could be found, the
camera crews that weren't recharging their equipment
were rushing to get loads of B-roll footage for the
weeks ahead. It was as if retiring from the adrenaline
rush and the *stop go stop go* aspects of it had switched
off an entire portion of her soul and the rest of her
functions were running at half capacity, including, most
importantly, her sense of reasoning. During the Crisis,
Birchall had fallen into knowledge by way of wrongful
assumption and having learned her lesson, had grown to
be so severely factual that it caused a falling out with
her boss, the arithmetic of which was untethering the
reporter's balloon from the stable to float freely into the
cloudy skies of joblessness.

So, purposelessly, she continued in the strange
limbo period of waiting for her contract with Channel
Two to be terminated with interviews for softer
postings, knowing fulfillment would be found in none
of them. If she couldn't be in the thick of the fire with
the dance of red and blue lights splashing off her
overcoat, what was the point? Her old boss had infected
the ears of those in the business with the stigma of her
being hard to work with and impossible to manage,
demanding far too much personal input and never being
satisfied with the result and rejection after rejection
only proved as much.

But it was true. Especially where the truth was
concerned. The truth was the truth and couldn't be

changed, and reporting something less than, an edited version, cut and pasted for itching ears just wasn't within her heart.

Fifteenth Street Inn was a three-star hotel masquerading as an old building replete with the tropes of a depression-era flophouse, including an intentionally flickering sign of neon pink. The tall and narrow block, set back from the street amidst an overstretched row of international eateries and reasonably-priced apartments, was the dream of a local real-estate developer obsessed with film noir and was popular with travellers because of the Inn's vintage tour package as it exemplified the ghosts of a city by the water whose past was rife with immigrant success stories, hole-in-the-wall big band and gypsy jazz clubs, and zoot-suit gang wars. Only, the tour had a way of leaving first timers sucked in to its marketing brochures with an empty feeling upon completion, because nearly all of the sites in the tour were covered with fifty-story buildings, leaving the guide to state the fabled happenings more out of conjecture than fact.

Birchall leaned into the revolving door and, finding it nearly too heavy to push, tossed a fatigued smile over to the sharply dressed concierge in his dimly-lit bracket of dark wood, plum paint, and hanging key rings. The Inn's peak season was closer to summer, and, as hundreds of other small businesses were, rolling their dice in corporately-controlled North Crescent instead of meting out equal portions with those in South, the Inn was tightening their belt.

Taking the stairs, the Inn nearly reverberated with the soundless echo of its own vacancy, and the sentiment registered an honest pitch within Birchall.

Reporting was a lonely job, but somebody had to do it.

Jessica Birchall had to do it.

Room Three-Zero-Two was on the third floor at the very end of a hall in which black and white photography sat in tarnished gold frames as would a gallery of progressive history. Birchall wandered down the hall, taking in the Ford Model T's and the dirty faces of construction workers sipping coffee from a thermos on the naked edge of a thirty-story building, with the seemingly tiny specks of the younger generation below them looking up in awe. It was a time when children believed in Superman and Santa Claus in equal parts, with the innocence of their youth, and their parents, wherever they were from, believed the only future was the one they built for themselves.

The coppery-colored key was cold in Birchall's hand and the door was thick and heavy, opening to a dark room that smelled in the slightest of bleach and cologne. Jessica stood between the threshold of the open door and the black and white-lined hallway and flicked on the light, taking the bareness of the narrow room in one glance as the overhead draped warm orange light over a floral-patterned queen.

"Hello?" She called, and waited, her eyes blinking away what numbing sleep was trying to creep through the edges of her vision. "Hello?"

No answer.

She tried a final time, not wanting to step foot in the room if she didn't have to.

"Hello?"

So the man was not there.

Birchall shrugged and gravity sucked her to the doorframe, her head feeling heavier than ever. Perhaps the man was giving her the hotel room to spend the night in, *alone*, knowing she'd made plans to take the flight to Boston and sleep on the plane. He hadn't given her a phone number and the name on his card was more

than likely not his real name. God knew where he was
or what he was doing, and seeing as he'd found her for
his purpose he was more than likely going to provide
somewhere for her to be in the interim, not wanting to
have to track her down again the old fashioned way
because…

Birchall began to think as she entered the room,
letting the weighted door shut itself behind her and her
eyes tracked down to the coppery room key in her hand.

It was a key. Not a card but a real, machine-made
key. And speaking of cards, he'd showed her a business
card. Nothing from his phone, if he even had a phone.
He'd even checked a hand-written piece of paper inside
of his jacket for some reason.

No technology.

Why was that?

Birchall sat gently on the edge of the bed, having
left her luggage next to it.

Technology made communication easier;
networking, tracking, coordinating. Why hadn't he
shown her any footage on a hand-held device or
photographs of any documents?

His words and their guarded tone came back to
her.

They're in a safe.

A safe? Old school. But why?

With the frown of critical thought crossing her
face, Jessica stood to remove her jacket and heard the
subtle *plink* of water dance through the sonically bright
tiles of the bathroom. The sharp, rippling sound cut
through her mental haze and directed her attention to
something she hadn't noticed upon entering the room.

The bathroom. It sat directly before her. The door
was shut and the light was on.

Birchall stared at it until another *plink* of water
forced a blink from her eyes.

Technology...communication, networking, tracking, coordinating...

Tracking?

Water dripped again and Birchall rushed to the door only to hesitate before twisting the knob.

Could it be?

Her heart fibrillated a pair of beats and the deep frown of critical thought sunk to a grimace too numb with the straightjacket of inebriation to be horrified.

That would all come later, as she thought about the sight over and over and over, replaying the episode in her mind.

The CIA man who'd been so intent about shining a light on his own indirect involvement with the tragedies of Baghdad was himself, a member of the departed, submerged in the bathtub with an expression of indifference frozen on his cold, dead face. His eyes were open, and his painless gaze was locked on the bland and pallid colors of the ceiling with no further questions or answers to the woman standing before him.

Birchall's hand came to her mouth and the *plink* of water from the faucet of the full tub forced her to wake from the stupor of her life's spiral.

A CIA man was dead. Crescent was under terrorist attack. To hell with feeling tired and wanting to curl up in bed and make it all go away.

It couldn't. It wouldn't.

Evil had a way of becoming the default, and the static and bloodless extinguishing of the man's brave existence gave her the courage to, herself, be as brave as he had.

Birchall swallowed hard and rushed back into the bedroom to get her phone from the satchel bag to take pictures, and as she did, one small fact weighed itself against a litany of others in the crowded train station of her thoughts.

What good would it be to call CPD? What would they do? What *could* they do? They were already overburdened with the great distress of tragedy and if there were more attacks to come, the chronic overwork of crisis management mode would return again and the individual would lose out over the greater good. A home invasion robbery or a domestic disturbance had no way of comparing with a detonated bomb or a public shooting. And whatever ID the man had, if any, wouldn't help a local Homicide Detective placing calls to Langley where the only answer he'd receive was a big fat runaround. No, it was a federal matter, if even *they* could do something about what foul play was afoot with the man's inferred suicide, and the only federal connection Birchall had, a happily retired one at that, had put in a good word for her transfer to Boston.

Birchall checked the time on her phone but knew, no matter what, Sierra Marland would have her back.

Before retiring for the night and letting her last interaction with Henry Morell bloom within her heart, Lucy shut her bedroom door and called the Precinct to ask them to send a squad car to the Marina at the Ferry Terminal. She figured Henry Morell'd researched whatever thread connected Maks Lenkov to the man he'd mentioned to Fosnick in the Interrogation Room, Yiury Mogilev he'd said his name was, a hedge fund manager, before he'd attended his ill-fated dinner date at the Continental Plaza. Whether he was yet another Russian billionaire or a member of a secret society remained to be seen, and Lucy wanted to at least have an Officer or two stay down at the Marina, just in case the ghostly assassin who Morell was convinced had killed Lenkov *and* Geffington used the chaos of the CRT induced and dominated police-state to his advantage.

The desk sergeant relayed the deteriorating severity of the situation at the Continental Plaza to her in great detail, now that the parking garage was blocked and the thousands of guests were being detained at an offsite facility and in no certain words, spelled out how there was no one to spare, especially not without higher authority stating why. Concerning the Marina, he was sure, after clicking and scrolling through computer files, that the Ferry Terminal and the Waterfront in general would be deemed as high priority areas and would, in the days and weeks following as the Feds did their thing, receive armed guards and twenty-four hour patrols.

Even so, two Officers could not be spared for the night. Lucy had no place to authorize such. She could only put in a request through the overloaded CRT command center and hope for the best.

Again, Lucy felt nullified in her lame duck position as a Lieutenant, with her clock-out during the CRT's takeover placing her on the very bottom of the Precinct's duty rotation. In so many ways, her outward lack of responsibility was in complete opposition to the immense weight of gravity pressing down on her shoulders as she grabbed her CPD jacket, badge, and gun. As if by default, she was reverting to her practices as a Detective, maybe even proving that she was not qualified to be a Lieutenant, giving the fullness of her intense focus to a narrow bandwidth of dutiful obligation as a true soloist, instead of sitting behind it all telling who to go where and do what as would a conductor.

And if her facts on the case were simply the brazenly confident words of a man threatened with a prison sentence by the Feds, a man she had feelings for and was sleeping off his injuries on her own couch, well, then that was all she had to go on.

At the end of the day, what more was there than trust?

She thought about waking him as she passed by him and stopped, for a silent moment, to watch him sleep and listen to him breathe, and, deciding against it, she clicked the oil heat up a few notches and zipped up her waterproof CPD jacket against the frosty chill of midnight, firing her gold Chrysler Sebring for the Marina.

TWENTY-FOUR

In a somehow cozy private room in Corazon's naturally secluded Rehabilitation, Therapy, and Recovery Ward, the irritably blinking green light of a smart phone forced the woman with jewel-blue eyes and wavy jet black hair to rise, check that her husband, who had his back to her, was still sound asleep, and skulk into an empty hallway to address whatever issue couldn't wait until morning. The phone was the woman's only link to remnants of the past, having removed herself from the life of clandestine service to tend to her husband's wounds, now strictly the psychological kind since his body had fully recovered from its STRIC-R-induced coma.

His mind had not.

And she would be by his side until his mind had received the careful fabrication of truth she was working hand in hand with the CIA man who'd adopted her from the bridge-burning Homeland Special Assignment Branch campaign she'd waged in order to save the sovereign information of the United States' millions of inhabitants in the terrorist attacks of November with an *ends justifies the means* sort of fighting fire with fire approach.

But the phone calls, first Morell, who'd been one of her most trusted subordinates in the Homeland operation, and now Jessica Birchall, the reporter who'd walked straight into her hand like a wild card back in November, all of it was pulling at Sierra's feet like the centrifugal swirl of a drainpipe.

She was *retired*.

Whatever fight was to be fought was not hers and though it was tragic that Crescent's Mayor had been shot and the city cast into a state of panic that would spread like a cancer, the former Homeland Security Special Assignment Branch Agent by the name of Sierra Marland was no more.

She was Sierra *Erland*, now; a wife whose sole desire was to start a family, with the insanity of her duties in the Crisis being meted with absolution by the secret adoption of the CIA and swept under the proverbial rug to be forgotten forever, leaving her content to carefully monitor her husband's mental health so that they could live out their days as a normal couple, even though she hadn't yet been able to consummate her marriage to Michael Erland, on the count of his mind still being built one puzzle piece at a time, she knew the time would come when they could leave Crescent forever and start a family.

Regardless, *she'd* passed on Jessica Birchall's name to the CIA whistleblower named Berenguer, and somehow it'd all gone terribly wrong. Sierra shook her head as she listened to Birchall tersely relay the events of the hotel room to her, not that Birchall knew Sierra had set the meeting up, only that Sierra was the only person Birchall knew she could go to for help in such a grave matter. The picture of Berenguer cold and lifeless in the bathtub only drove the point home with the thunderous whack of a deadblow hammer-the corruption she'd fought so hard to remove, at the risk of her own life and everything she loved, was far from it; still, just lurking in the darkest corners of the government, waiting to snuff any torch that passed by.

Don't kill the messenger, Sierra thought and gave Birchall specific instructions and ended the call, tip-toeing to the doorframe to peer up to the stairs where the silence of her husband's sleep bore the only confirmation she needed.

He didn't have to know.

Ever.

Despite her attempts to sever herself from November of the past year and all it represented, she had to do *something*, retired or not.

The distant hum of a buffer being cranked to life to keep the floors waxed and shiny gnawed in her ear as she placed a call to the CIA Extemp man who'd adopted her from the debacle of Crisis-era Homeland into his own liability as an offer of gratitude for services rendered to the United States of America.

For in whatever threat sat outside of Crescent like a storm front, waiting for the prevailing winds to push it over the edges of the skyscrapers, Sierra truly was powerless.

But the man she was about to call, was not.

Shane Sheth, rubbing his creased forehead in a strange combination of shame and sleep depravity, strode up to Fosnick's black suburban. DiMocco was in the driver's seat, with his eyes closed, waiting as would any other Junior Special Agent and Fosnick was seated comfortably behind him.

"What's up?" He said, his blocky features naturally pensive and inquisitive, which added to his subtly stony demeanor of confrontation when he clamped down on those in his sights.

"I have something I want you to see." Sheth shut the door behind him and took a tablet out of his heavy overcoat, tapping and swiping several times before cursing and continuing to do so till he appropriated the app that he wanted.

"Does it have to do with the bomb blast?" DiMocco asked, still resting in the driver's seat like a statue.

"I'm not talking to you, am I?" Sheth growled in the gravely voice Junior Special Agents didn't want to get on the wrong side of.

Sheth held the tablet out to Fosnick who took it and already began dissecting the images on the screen as they flashed forward, jump cuts of security cameras at several places throughout the hotel, all of them time-stamped. Immediately, as if a mathematical savant had been awakened in his cerebral cortex, Blake Fosnick began analyzing the man in the footage with the primal instinct of meeting his prey for the first time glazing his eyes like eerie mist of a late winter night.

Even though it was *not* the first time they'd met.

Fosnick was a lead field operative in the FBI's Manhunter Squad for a reason, a damn good one; despite his thirty-one years of age there was none better.

"Is this the guy?" Fosnick's speaking tone was a near whisper.

Sheth held an appraisal of Fosnick before answering. His focus was already razor sharp and even as the new day began at midnight, his slow-burning fuse showed no signs of slowing down. Giving the skilled Manhunter the raw footage and letting him head the investigation before all of the details were ironed out was not traditional, but Sheth knew by doing so he was perfectly delegating his resources, allotting himself more time to spend on cleanup, recovery, and crisis management.

"McNeil went through the footage with that new algorithm he's been testing out and the parameters for the man Morell described fit this man."

"So he was right."

Sheth's hoarse voice took on a nearly fatherly cadence.

"Now listen Blake, despite what you might think about Henry Morell, he does have legitimate skills and if this really is the man that shot Geffington, fooled SWAT and blew up the garage, then not only was Morell on the ball for finding him but damn good not to get killed by him."

"Would've made it easier..." DiMocco mumbled.

"Or," Fosnick handed the tablet back. "He's lucky. I read the after action report of when his Stryker vehicle was hit in two-thousand four and I happen to know that earlier this morning he got T-boned by a bus. It's what makes me dislike him, if you catch my drift."

Sheth did. By using Homeland's resources and authority to dismantle RepMax and set up a cozy job for himself at Tidebender, Morell was abusing karma, or any other *goes around comes around* sense of fatalistic inertia men who had guns strapped to their bodies knew was as strong of a physical force as gravity itself. When one had a habit of laying their life on the line with some consistency, it was foolish to take advantage of whatever providence was responsible for life when an inch or two or a split-second separated such from death for one's own selfish gain.

After all, Sheth believed that the gunshot wound to his neck two years ago had not killed him because earlier that same year he'd refused to shoot a teen who'd pulled a gun on *him*, and instead, talked him out of it to end the day with a series of handshakes and no loss of life.

Funny it was that way, now that Sheth was known for a tone of voice that others said, behind his back, sounded as if he had throat cancer, when it had been his talking that had saved *two* lives, his own and the teen's.

"Well, at any rate," He continued, "We've got this *because* of Morell and you know as well as I do it's enough for you to go on, so a bit of gratitude is in order."

"When can I go inside?" Fosnick asked, disregarding any form of agreement.

"When everybody's out. 'Bout half an hour."

"Where are you moving them to?"

"Municipal Arena."

Fosnick nodded.

"Thanks." He said. "I won't let you down."

"Sure." Sheth nodded and again, his cadence showed genuine care for the highly driven yet imperceptibly callous and merciless man next to him. "Blake, I just want to warn you now, Henry Morell was level three US Army combat school qualified, which is all volunteer training and qualifies him to be a combat instructor, not to mention whatever black magic they taught him at Homeland and he got his ass totally kicked by this guy, so if you *do* find yourself face to face with him, you've got the green light under the constitutional CRT policy to pull your service weapon and drop him, no paperwork required."

Fosnick's blocky face bore signs of misunderstanding but then the episode of Henry Morell's apprehension came back to him, and how Sheth had given him the option, due to the cyclone of chaos, to take Morell in legally or illegally, and how the choice truly was in Fosnick's grip. The FBI didn't just run up to people, criminal or not, and put a bullet in them. It was against the laws *they* had to abide by to separate themselves *from* the criminals they fought to keep the country safe. But the constitutional anti-terrorist protocols of the CRT merited extreme prejudice on the grounds of extraordinary circumstances exhausting themselves so that no other option would be viable for the safety of the American people.

As clear as the policy was, the responsibility was no less grave, and in all the men and women Fosnick had hunted in his short and illustrious career, he'd never encountered the need to pull his gun on one and squeeze the trigger.

"Yes Sir." He said and shook hands with Sheth before falling back into critical thought about whether he would or would not, given the circumstances.

Killing a man and capturing him for the world to see as he stood on trial for his crimes against an indignant nation were two *very* different things. One lead to mountains of paperwork and psychological evaluations.

The other lead to immortality.

Casey Sullivan covered her mouth as she yawned uncontrollably and blinked away the gluey stupor of her self-imposed graveyard shift in the lower bowels of FBI Headquarters in Washington D.C. Her lone friend in the coffin of forms, records, documents, and other items of extreme banality she was swamped in was a janitor by the name of Peter Daniels. He was a portly man with a southern accent, from Louisville as she was, and the age gap between them was so great he found the need to talk to her about everything and anything for some purpose of education. Checking her Tag Heuer Aquaracer, the Junior Special Agent knew it was time to go home, since Rome hadn't been built *or* conquered in a single day and she told the janitor she'd hear more about the history of rock and roll the following evening. The janitor drawled his goodbye and Casey responded in kind.

But Casey's southern accent, the husky kind that burned like a smoky glass of bourbon and didn't give a damn, had been unconsciously hidden, or at least watered down, by the nasally semi-Californian lilt of a girl who'd once been a spoiled rich teenager and wanted way the hell out of the south, on to bigger and better things, only to find life was just a slow and dripping thaw like an icicle on a barn gutter no matter what package one stuffed it in to sell it to those who knew no better. Life itself, she had come to learn, was the only thing of value in life, and the human beings that it belonged to, no matter what their situation or condition. Her moment of lucidity in the matter had slugged her over the head when she was seventeen years old, staying with her grandparents in the one-street town of Bent Spoon in rural Iowa, as she watched one man shoot another dead. She knew, in that moment' when it'd happened, and her extraordinarily beautiful almond-shaped blue-green eyes captured the image of the man's flesh exploding from his chest as if he were a cast-off winter squash, that she would never *ever* be the same.

She didn't know, however, that seven years later she'd be a Junior Special Agent in the FBI's Manhunter Squad.

Casey stopped by the ladies room to wash her hands and examine a pair of paper cuts on her left index finger. She was a statuesque woman, five foot nine, and always wore ballet flats to keep her height as such. Her casual black business suit and simple white blouse were of the highest quality and in no way presented her athletically trim body in a titillating way, and her physicality of class and refinement were, always, shockingly opposed by the caustic and often foul-mouthed sharpness of her politically incorrect tongue. Her naturally sunny blonde hair was cut short and swooped across a broad forehead and her shapely cheekbones looked soft and springy to the touch. A straight and well-balanced nose, ending in a naturally sulking mouth of impossibly kissable lips exemplified the hidden knowledge of a soul that'd looked so much older than her age most of her life and had finally made the transition to the adulthood of a nine to five, or rather, twelve to three-thirty professional woman. One with any skill of perception, however, would know, passing Casey one glance, and she received plenty as she ran up and down Headquarters on clerical errands and legwork sidejobs from the time-in-grade elders in her expansive squad, that she was a woman with secrets, and her secrets were always hovering behind a pair of guileless pupils in the symmetrical fullness of a blue-green sea. As Casey stared at herself in the mirror, she told herself she'd get through the probationary period of toil and wheel-spin and sooner, rather than later, she'd be able to track down the people that'd killed the man who'd saved her life that balmy summer night back in Iowa and sparked in her the tinder to become something other than the rich and aimless debutante her parents would've had her to be.

As tired as she was, *she'd* chosen to be so.

For there was nothing in life Casey hated more than the endless army of thieves and murderers hiding like recluse spiders in the industrially fabricated webs of corporate capitalism, smiling through bleached teeth as they pressed a button or flipped a switch and turned a blind eye to the world beyond them as it burned like a dark and endless fire of hell. She'd been raised by two of them; the man who'd saved her life had eventually had his taken from him by them, and they were back, seeing as they never left, these legions of corrupt and faceless marauders and manipulators, these evening wolves of biblical proportions, to ruin the career of a man she knew bled red, white, and blue.

And as Casey finished washing her hands and

signed out with the night watch crew to locate her
BMW in the parking garage, she knew she'd do
whatever it took to save Henry Morell of the incredibly
lopsided and morally ambiguous case against him.

For he had become the target of character
assassins and corporate duplicity, its tainted tracks
leaving footprints all the way up to the Director of the
Bureau himself.

TWENTY-FIVE

Yiury Mogilev squinted at his timepiece, a custom-made Rolex, and in consideration of his busy day on the morrow, closed the novel he'd been reading in the stateroom of his one hundred and eighty foot yacht, named *Adler Von Pomerelia*. It was his family's land, Pomerelia, conquered by blood at the request of the Pope hundreds of years ago, and one day he'd have it back and was content to wait until that day made itself manifest. Before Mogilev retired for bed, he checked his email one last time to see if any new developments had altered his upcoming meeting with the other members of the Order. It seemed, though tragic, that the suicide of Maks Lenkov had been taken in stride and his other brothers were on schedule for world domination, though Lenkov's obvious contributions would be missed.

It was war. Death was as natural of a byproduct as carbon emission from an automobile.

Yiury pondered what effect Lenkov's suicide would have on the Order and poured himself an unreasonably large glass of vodka from the bottle featuring a muscular and utilitarian brown castle on the label and as he sipped at it, he stared at the black eagle governing the skies above the castle with one lone thought stealing away his mind.

The Lynx, once in sight of the unpopulated west shore of Christmas Island, some four and a half miles from the Marina, removed his aqualung and mask to let them sink to the bottom of the Bay. Upon doing so, The Lynx reverted to a comfortable backstroke, nearly reveling in the gentle lapping of the Bay's frosty waters. The oblong voids and ominous shapes of the sleeping timber barges dotted around the greenish waters and the twinkling orange lights of the expanse of wealth and labor stretching behind the Waterfront released a smile across his face, and in the still of the frigid night, The Lynx knew he was truly all alone, his favorite feeling in the whole world.

It all looked so trivial, at a distance, the towers of those scraping their nickels together to stay in the middle class, spending money they didn't have as they lived a cashless life of plastic and credit, and against the barren desert of cold water, Crescent seemed such a futile endeavor. The CRT paramilitary squads of suits and SWAT were wasting themselves on the life of their leader and so distraught over a small car bomb, how could they leave the Waterfront so vulnerable? Especially when the man preparing himself for bed in the belly of the gleaming white yacht with a small black eagle near the script of the vessel's name owned nearly a quarter of North Crescent's commercial real-estate, not to mention substantial positions in São Paolo, Beijing, Guangzhou, Moscow, and Tallinn, the very same yacht that had nearly ten pounds of Semtex plastered to its hull and wired to a remote detonator in The Lynx's drybag?

Soon, the world would wonder what became of him, and, as any two-edged sword in the hands of a skilled martialist, the city of Crescent would receive the blowback of yet another seemingly random act of terror performed with the impunity of the shadowed hand that slowly siphoned away their lust for life in its terminal grip.

    Rubbing praying hands together with a brisk movement as she left the gold Sebring for the Marina, Lucy was surprised to find that the Ferry Terminal, though boasting a host of security cameras, only held two night watchmen. They were polite and accommodating in their small space within the Ferry Terminal's post-modern building, aesthetically incongruent with the nearby cranes and crates of the Docks, but Lucy's badge-heavy presence worked hand in hand with the disturbing images of the small television in their security alcove to stir within them a fawning sense of dread, though they tried to cover it with smiles and waves as she left for Yiury Mogilev's yacht, and while Lucy walked, she thought of Henry Morell.

    Why had he signed, in so many words or less, his own death warrant? The document had clearly plotted out his indefensibility in an extremely invasive fault-finding tribunal and the mere mention of such would slap a sticky black streak of mud on anyone even remotely involved with him. There had to be a reason beyond the obvious, since it didn't seem like money was an issue for him. But what was it? The further Lucy strayed from the Ferry Terminal and the parking lot where her Sebring was still relatively warm and cozy, the more her mind locked on to the fact that if she wanted to know one why, she had to first figure out another.

    Why had Henry Morell dismantled RepMax?

    If it was for selfish gain, for Tidebender's success, then, Lucy had been wrong about him in so many ways, and he was the kind of man she was a fool for letting in her home. She'd never actually stopped to think about the possibilities but the more she did, blocking out the chill as her brain leapt from one scenario to another, she began to consider the chance that he was *still* a Homeland Security Agent and that Tidebender was as equally corrupt as the private gun-toting army-for-hire RepMax had been.

But Fosnick stole such ruminations from her. His swooping in for shackles and chains had coincided with Morell's first day at Tidebender for a reason, had it not? So was the FBI then *protecting* Tidebender from a clandestine Homeland investigation, or were they, themselves, one of the corrupt parties, knowing RepMax was a Pawn in the game and if a Pawn was taken from the board, every piece behind it, the more important and dominant they were, still, that much more vulnerable.

Lucy stopped on the squeaky causeway, cold salt air curling toward her nose over the sour odors of rotten seaweed and diesel fuel.

The chess board in Lenkov's office, Morell had said it himself, how the message had been sent there.

The Black King has been defeated at the hand of the White Pawn.

But who was black? Who was white? And who or *what* was the King? Was it not a matter of perspective? And was Lenkov's killing the fulcrum of a giant lever balancing between two powers in a struggle for supremacy? So much more was at stake than met the eye, and Lucy was convinced, as she spotted the one hundred and eighty foot yacht belonging to Yiury Mogilev, that if Morell wasn't going to tell her the guts of the truth, she would have to trust that his choosing not to do so was for a damn good reason, because it made no sense for a man who was born to fight for the freedom of others to cave in the moment a pair of red tape and procedure cowboys lassoed him in order to brand him a traitor to the office he'd had the honor of holding with such distinction.

Yiury Mogilev was about to retire to his bedchambers for the night when he returned to the stateroom to douse the lights and spotted, through the window, the strikingly odd and incredibly unexpected image of a pleasantly attractive blonde in a dark blue jacket studying the stern of his one hundred and eighty foot craft. What little light there was on the dock provided him with all he needed to see and since his crew was in town for the night, and he was alone on the ship, Mogilev quickly made his way to the deck.

"Hello there." He called down, cloaked in a heavy claret-colored velvet robe, moving toward the gangplank that connected his floating palace to the dockwork of the Marina. His English was thick from his early years as an affluent young Muscovite even though most of his life had been spent splitting time in the largest cities of America, China, and Brazil as a true international, and forgoing the tendencies of one, he had a weakness for women reminding him of the Mother country.

"Hello." The woman said flatly and turned to stare down the causeway into darkness. "Are you Yiury Mogilev?"

"*Da.*" He said, standing tall in his red velvet robe with hands easily as large as the woman's head bracing his weight between the guardrails. "And how can I help you?"

"I just wanted to see if you were okay."

"How can you see from down there?" The billionaire chuckled.

"I can see just fine. Have a good night, Sir." Lucy said, and turned to leave before Mogilev continued.

"Won't you tell me what this is about?" He said.

"Please, come inside where it is warm. I can make you coffee, if you like."

Lucy stood her ground and examined him in a pensive and guarded sideways glance, noticing, as he began to slowly descend the stairs with leaden steps, that he was a *very* large man, so much like Lenkov, and the observation began to unnerve her. She'd lived through a harrowing spell of close calls during several undercover Vice operations and the man's lascivious nuances were conjuring nostalgic images of the time she'd spent with the Departmental psychologist, trying to forget. Their solitude in the Marina only seasoned the moment with the bitter flavors of the memory, and the shells of sailboats and smaller fishing craft bobbing in the gentle river current like oversized decorations, in their own way, were no different than the lamps, picture frames, and wallpaper patterns of an hourly motel room.

Lucy was about to show her badge when her eyes caught the man's shiny platinum Rolex, a custom-made model for sure, black diamonds studding a white diamond backing to form an asymmetrical cross, much like the shields and surcoats of the ancient Teutonic Order.

"It's too late for coffee." Lucy said, stuffing her hands in her jacket pockets, wondering how she should proceed, and if she did probe a bit, if Mogilev would get wise to the fact or not. In Vice, she had learned, men needed to be strung along to incriminate themselves, and as risky as it *always* promised to be, it was still a woman's natural ability to do so.

But now she wasn't staring back at the nervous eyes and twitchy hands of a ladder-climbing stockbroker cheating on his wife before sneaking back home after a day of trading the Hang Seng, but a man who gave off the aura that he *owned* the world, if not certain parts of it and had the power to do whatever he wanted with it.

"What then?" Mogilev stopped on the very edge of the gangplank, towering over her by at least a foot. His head was an inverted eggplant with a tuft of gray hair to cover his scalp, and the bulge of his brow shaded deep-set eyes the color of dirty snow. His neck was pockmarked and curly brown and gray chest hairs were attempting to poke out from the collar of his robe.

"Do you have any vodka?" Lucy asked.

At first, Mogilev smiled and let salacious thoughts drift across his mind before the small print of her jacket became legible to his sixty-two year old eyes.

"Crescent Police, eh?"

"And?"

The billionaire crossed his arms, as if a candle had been snuffed in his vicinity and he was waiting for the sulfuric smell of the smoke to dissipate. His tone had been sucked dry of whatever had influenced it and his brow sagged with the perfunctory route his conversation with the woman had fell victim to.

"What do you want?"

"I told you," Lucy said, "And I see you're fine, but…do you have security of any kind?"

"Yes, they are in town right now. Is this about Maks Lenkov?"

Lucy didn't say anything, the impartial mask of her face ever cool in the confidence of knowing *no* man could read her, no matter how much money he made.

"He committed suicide." Mogilev continued. "I will do no such thing."

"Are you staying in Crescent for long?" Lucy asked.

"I will be leaving tomorrow."

"Where to?"

"You're welcome to inquire with the

Harbormaster's Office, Ms…"

"Lieutenant." Lucy said, as if it were her name and added, "Have a safe voyage," turning to leave. As she walked and walked she could feel the gears of the billionaire's intellectual brain wizening to the subplot of her visit. Mogilev's voice stopped her, its bassy notes clear in the relative quiet of squeaking hulls, well-tied knots and ship's rigging.

"Why did you ask me about vodka?"

Lucy never got the chance to answer. The detonation of the Semtex stuck to the hull of the one hundred and eighty foot yacht lifted her two inches off the ground and in the same split-second, pushed her back some twenty feet head over heels into the concrete of the nearby parking lot. The last thing Lucy saw before the blinded sunspots of a nearly concussed tumble on the pavement possessed her faculties for good was an arcing fireball of deadly afterblasts spitting liquid streams of diesel fuel and freshly-kindled flames across the welcoming tinder of lacquered wooden sail boats and smaller motor vessels as if they were kindling awaiting accelerant. Lucy pushed herself up with tremendous difficulty, feeling the cool trickling of blood chilling her face in the fallen frost, and watched, in the stoic and eerily still silence of one who'd lost her hearing, as the billionaire's yacht flickered with the blazing torches of hell and had transformed the Marina, in one simple second, into the lake of fire.

TWENTY-SiX

Rachael Calabrese, perhaps paying her way out of the disastrous and life-altering situation befalling those who'd signed up, not many hours ago, for a suit and tie Convention, with her generous monetary support to the city's relief fund, had been able to save her daughter and herself from the trouble of being transferred to the Arena for further detainment and processing by the Critical Response Team that had taken over Crescent, leaving Jasmine Keelan and Kelly Barnett in the protection of her Tidebender shadows to see them both safely to their homes, whenever that moment came. National Guardsmen had been deployed from a nearby base, thundering out the backs of heavy camouflaged trucks and hastily-built retainers and checkposts had been put in place to isolate three blocks of Second Avenue from the rest of the world. Aimee Jaziri comforted her mother as a CPD motor pool car took them to Callie's home in Fircrest.

"You haven't held my hand since you were twelve years old." Callie said, pain in her eyes though she hadn't yet shed a tear. Aimee was very sensitive to the fact that, *on top* of her mother nearly taking a bullet to the neck, she was in the thick of the plot surrounding the terror that had befallen the city. And she would've been, even if she wasn't so close to the shooting, though not to the degree that she was now, as

Tidebender's entire business revolved around the admirable yet dismal attempt to keep people safe in a world as destructive as it'd ever been. Aimee studied her mother's kind face in the back of the motor pool car and wondered why she didn't look a hundred and five with the constant bombardment of stress she had no choice but to deal with every single moment of her life, and how, in her father's world, points of conflict came from the distant print of the headlines or the back-handed remarks of a dissident student when Callie, day in and day out, ran an extremely profitable and classy *business* that attempted to take the dogs of war and physically and emotionally repurpose them to become unarmed silent protectors in the civilized world. Not only was Callie trying to salvage the souls of men who'd thought their lives were over when they left the military, but she was trying to change the culture of an ethos so fused with the rapacious imperial economies of world history, saying that guns and other weapons of mass violence, murder, and destruction *didn't* have a right to be in the world, and in doing so she was a martyr fighting a fight she would never *ever* win.

"I'm so sorry, mom." Aimee said, and pulled Callie's hand to her so that Callie, still shock-stricken in the depths of her being, curled her legs to her chest and laid her head across Aimee's lap in the bench seat of the Ford Crown Victoria.

"Now you know." She said.

"I think I always did." Aimee ran her fingernails through her mother's hair, her therapeutic touch making the lightest scraping noise as Callie's fingers had combed through Aimee's then black hair when she was just five years old and, in a way, neither had yet made a decision about their life's work, but were still, simply, mother and daughter. "That's why I was mad at you for so long. You weren't my mom as much as you were that woman on TV trying to change the world."

"Some people love me. Some people hate me."
Callie said, her voice a detached tone, floating from a
flat face as her eyes had slowly closed shut. "But
everyone respects me..."

"I'm sorry it took *me* so long."

"You know, your father and I have always fought
over you. He wanted to be the one to change the world
so that I could raise you but you and I both know he
married me because *I* wanted to change the world. In
psychology it's called *The Law of Tragic Attraction*.
Some people have it written into their DNA to fall in
love with a hopeless case; pity becomes so extreme it
transforms itself into a possessive desire to become a
caretaker, hoping that affection and support will make it
all better. But it's like gravity...like *The Call of the
Wild*. Man's relationship with animals have been
fraught with LTA for centuries. There's nothing you
can do in the end but just let go."

Callie twisted in Aimee's lap to gaze up into her
eyes, so much the same they were, blue and pure, yet
unlike her mother's they were free from the intense
burden of responsibility; the eyes of a virgin who'd not
yet been sullied by the savage whirlwind of life where
the woodwork of personal connection had dared to
stand in the way of destiny's vicious buzzsaw.

Callie's hand reached up to cup her daughter's
face and traced the beautiful line of her chin.

"There isn't a day that goes by that I don't regret
choosing a social agenda over choosing to spend time
with you. But, then I think about how many lives have
been saved by the humanitarian work I've done
worldwide, the millions and millions of dollars spent on
medical care and food distribution to war-torn areas,
not to mention the fact that I give soldiers a purpose by
hiring and training them when they're vulnerable to

suicide after leaving the service, and I always believed that you'd turn out the right way *because* of it."

Aimee smiled with teary eyes.

"You were right."

Callie's eyes faded shut once again and Aimee peered out, through the misty blur of the backseat window, letting the truth bruise her heart, to the city of Crescent and the stilted parapet of tall buildings that had been made small and insignificant by the gradual ascension to the crown of Fircrest hill.

Pupils shrinking in the concentrated focus of the EMT's penlight, Lucy sat on the edge of the ambulance huddled beneath the thin comfort of a shimmery silver space blanket, reliving the moment of the explosion again and again, though now it was only a flash in the dimness of her mind, as if the more she thought about it the fuzzier it became, shrinking and degrading in length and clarity. Thus was the way of trauma. It would all wash out. Eventually. Even though three ladder trucks had formed a containment zone to stop the fire from seizing the industrial space of the docks and the masses of pitch-covered timbers awaiting shipment up north, the Marina was a total loss, and the painfully cracking roar of the conflagration could be heard from blocks away, not to mention what illumination it spread across the blackness of night as some sort of malevolent beacon of death and destruction. A news helicopter hovered high overhead, its blades gargling in the darkness to keep it from the volcanic cloud of smoke, and Lucy couldn't help but feel like the Crisis had returned to Crescent with the vengeance of one that would not be denied total annihilation.

It was a sobering thought.

The EMT nodded his head and told her she didn't have a concussion but she could only read his lips in slits and slices of red and blue CPD lights as they formed a bracket along the edge of the parking lot to keep the bystanders at bay, their breath visible in congested coughs of pale fog. The cold was undeniable, cutting like a knife against the right side of Lucy's neck where the skin had been scraped raw by the unyielding pavement and the brutality of momentum. A second EMT applied a bandage to the cut over her eye, thankful that it didn't need stitches and left at Lucy's request for a bottle of water.

"I'm fine." Lucy told the man checking her ears, though the ringing tone gnawing through her brain was disconcerting to say the least and she waved him off to stand and stretch away the soreness in her left shoulder, staring with a vacant pair of grey-green eyes into the devastating dance of light and heat for some time.

"So I was right." A light smoker's voice said behind her.

Lucy turned to see Henry Morell standing next to Blake Fosnick, the light of the fire casting their faces in an arbitrarily similar manner, as if they were related in some strange way.

The immediate thought on her tongue was to ask Morell *why aren't you back home?* But she didn't. She couldn't say as much in front of Fosnick even though a man like Fosnick would know, regardless, and there was no reason to try and hide such things from him. He reminded Lucy of a fox in every way, a slick black fox who hunted his prey when the light of the day had reached its nadir. Perhaps it was the strange marriage of past and future that had her in its grip, since her father's favorite piano piece was a little known Chopin sonata about the nocturnal Fox King of the Black Forest.

"His taxi drove up about the same time DiMocco dropped me off," Fosnick said, hand in the pockets of his pants, his suit carelessly unbuttoned in the cold so that the orange illumination of the crackling fire glinted off his FBI shield, "and considering the circumstances," his eyebrows tipped toward the inconsolable damage of the blaze, "I not only owe Morell an apology but I'm in *his* debt, because without his attempt to apprehend Geffington's assassin, I wouldn't have anything to go on, and if I'd been quicker I might've got the bastard."

"I told him that's total crap, but..." Morell shrugged, hiding a grin at the fortuitous turn his standing with the government had taken. Lucy squinted to see he was wearing a waterproof CPD jacket, much like hers, no doubt appropriated by Fosnick with his CRT status of being able to do anything he wanted.

It was then Fosnick removed the signed affidavit, ripped it in half and gave it to Lucy, who received it gingerly, as if it were dripping with poison.

"What are you doing?" She said, in the shock of misunderstood thankfulness, the ringing in her ears making her feel as if her voice was coming from somewhere outside of her body and the whole thing from her meeting with Mogilev all the way through was crawling through her psyche like some strange dream.

"I was supposed to sign my contract with Tidebender today and I didn't." Morell explained. "That means I don't work for them and never have. They've never paid me a dime."

"I don't follow..." Lucy stared at the papers in her hand, aching in the frost-bitten chill. Like the city itself, in half a second's precious time, they were torn asunder, irrevocably ripped from top to bottom.

"With the way Callie had been covering for him for about two weeks now I thought Tidebender had already pushed their chips to the middle of the table for him, but that wasn't the case. I have no legal right to prosecute him as such and he knew it, especially if he signs a contract with me saying he never will work for

Tidebender, thus nullifying the whole damn reason that brought me out here in such a timely manner." Fosnick hid a smile, eyes darting between the Lieutenant and Morell. "And now he's got my full attention with this new threat. So," Fosnick continued, and again sent a searching gaze past them through the curled spray of fireman's hoses as if he was justifying his reasoning for doing what he was about to. "This is how it's going to be. You're going to give him a provisional status with CPD as a part of the CRT protocol. He'll have all the proper credentials, a sidearm, everything, but it means that *you'll* have to stick with him because *you'll* be under CRT protocol too, as his superior." Fosnick smiled, a shallow thing considering his block-shaped face. "I'm going after the madman but I'd be a fool not to requisition some help to do it. You two are the closest thing we have to experts in whatever links Lenkov and Mogilev, and this tragedy only proves it. Thank God you weren't any closer, Lieutenant."

Lucy nodded graciously.

"You'll have your way in the case but no matter what, you *can't* widen the loop. That's imperative. It *has* to stay between us." Then Fosnick leaned toward Lucy, still speaking in the soft and controlled manner in which all of his words were carefully weighed and judged before leaving his mouth. "And since Mr. Sheth is in command of Crescent, you'll have to take it up with him if you don't want to do it. Chief Bertolucci has no say so in the matter, but *you* do. I don't want you on board if you don't want to be but if we want to save the day, it's got to be done this way."

Lucy's face was impassable, shaking her head, but Morell saw the hint of crow's feet wrinkling her eyes. Her desire for duties meritorious of her rank had been met and exceeded in the call to investigative arms in a time of extreme emergency and made her role as an

administrative and clerical traffic cop pale in
comparison.

So eager she was to take on the case with Hank
Morell, that she completely missed Fosnick's undertone
of suspicion about widening the loop for safety's sake,
especially with such a diabolical threat striking the city
and God knew what else at will.

But Morell caught it. He was keen to the fact,
pulled back from the machinations of the moment in the
recesses of his mind, that the rotten apples had been so
well-waxed and shined up they looked no different than
the good ones, and that most of good apples were so
beaten and bruised by trying to do the right thing they'd
left the barrel altogether.

"No objections." She said. "I'm in."

"Good, then both of you need to get some sleep.
I'll be working out of Precinct Three and I'll see you
both at eight sharp."

Fosnick chose not to shake hands and only
nodded, slipping off towards the rounded gate of CPD
squad cars separating first responders from bystanders
and camera crews, the dark shape of his body failing to
push out wisps of white fog breath as did all those
around him.

Lucy let her legs kick for a moment as if they
were on the edge of a pool and stared at them, still
attached to her body and functioning perfectly when she
very well could've been an amputee or a paraplegic.

The thought scared the hell out of her.

Perhaps Morell felt this because the distance
between them sealed itself and he sat next to her in
silent support. Disembodied shock slept in the jagged
obscurity of the looming skyline and its chatoyant
menagerie of windows and glass panels, each building
catching the ghostly glow of flames like the eyeballs of
a hellhound.

"Why aren't you back home?" She finally asked, as he ran his gaze across the bandage above her left eye.

"You expected to find me reading the paper, waiting for breakfast when you came back?"

"Sounds nice." She said, as he was close enough to give off body heat, and such warmth reminded her of her beloved escape from the world in Eavesdale.

"I didn't think he'd strike so soon."

"I didn't either, but, the more chaos the better." Lucy swallowed with a dry mouth, and wondered about the EMT with the bottle of water, assuming he'd been tasked to do something more important. "Who's next on your list?"

"God, I don't know. I don't think there's anyone else in Crescent. I didn't have enough time to check after I left you at Victory Park…he wouldn't take out Lenkov's kids, would he?"

"It's not about their businesses, it's about members of the Order."

Morell wheezed as he twisted to shield himself from the meandering dance of red and blue lights and distraught civilians captured in their vision-altering colors.

"So you believe me?

"Of course I do.

"I didn't mean it like that.

"I know." Lucy chuckled. "It sounds farfetched to the traditional ear but I'm the kind that *assumes* conspiracy until proven otherwise."

"How do you know then?"

Lucy turned her gaze to Morell for the moment and wondered, of the pain would not leave his face, if it was physical or if it was, instead, directed toward her, and the consideration that she not only would've been dead, given the slimmest margin of circumstances, but would've been completely vaporized and gone forever.

"I saw his watch." Lucy said, swallowing at the cloying dryness of dehydration in her throat. "It was a custom-made Rolex, white and black diamonds forming a cross, like the Knights' surcoat."

"No kidding." Morell said, his eyes falling to the pavement. "You got that close? What happened?"

Lucy sighed.

"Let's just say he wanted to show me the state room and I'd bet every dollar I have that if I found that same bottle of *Zakon Krzyżacki* Polish vodka I probably would've smashed it over his head and pulled my service weapon on him."

Morell gathered what she meant in as many words and knew that she'd cut her teeth in Vice with the youth of her face and her pleasantly timeless bone structure. She'd caught the eye of many a lusty man with a slathering of makeup and the right clothes, not to say that her duties in Vice came easy to her, just that she was very good at them and had been victorious in lurid situations that had every right to have left her scarred for life.

"I can't protect you from this guy." He said, with the brokenness of now knowing *why* he wanted to protect people and would give his own life to save theirs.

Morell's face fought a grimace and his dark eyes studied her face and its leveled objectivity.

"What?" She said, her grey green eyes shutting out the world around them.

Morell only shook his head, keeping his silence, with his eyes inspecting the cut on her forehead before standing up and ushering her, with the knock of his chin toward the confused sea of onlookers past the police barrier, to find the gold Sebring and carve out a path for Eavesdale.

TWENTY-SEVEN

Homicide Detective First Grade Steve Romero was walking to his office next to Homicide's Conference room with a pair of file folders when he spotted Lieutenant Radzewicz sitting inside the impoverished space of HomCon amidst the perfunctorily stiff blue carpet, not quite clean dry-erase boards and uncomfortable chairs, swiping at a tablet.

"Lucy." He said, standing at the door, "Can I have a word?"

Though the undersides of her eyes were puffy from a long night and a few hours of forced sleep, Lucy reminded Romero of when she was a Vice Detective and a damn good one. Her lips were cherry red with a slathering of lipstick, her generous lengths of blonde hair were curled, and her gray-green eyes were callously objective beneath a delicate ceiling of sky blue eye shadow. Makeup had covered the scratch above her eye and her black turtleneck, form-fitting brown pants and mid-calf black leather boots sealed the fact that she would've been a tremendous black and white movie star, especially in the way she could shut down a man's come-on without moving a muscle.

Romero always wondered how she could do that. Most women were so transparent in the games they played, which was why he'd married a woman that reminded him of his mother. But Lucy, well, either she really *was* an impenetrable cold fish kind of soul or that Award-winning black and white actress come to life.

Romero wished she was still in Vice, though, and in a fatherly way he knew it was better for her, but in a time-in-grade Detective sort of way he resented her leapfrogging and her leadership style was so far from micromanaging it appeared at times to be apathetic.

But then again, her face, in its comeliness, was also framed with an air of misanthropy, as if the shell was so tight one could only guess if there was a pearl inside or not and if one dared try and open the shell they'd lose their fingers in the process.

"What's up?" She said, after checking her watch, the Roman numerals on the squarish eighteen-karat gold Cartier Panthere proving she was of unmodern tastes. It was seven-fifty five in the morning.

"Dead body, Fifteenth Street Inn, bathtub."

Lucy's eyes narrowed.

"I thought you'd taken the day off?"

"Couldn't." Romero said, still in the doorframe as her prettiness made him feel a bit awkward in the building nearly vacated by the stresses of the previous night's anarchies.

"Doesn't Lowery want it?" Lucy asked, returning her attention to the tablet, miffing Romero in the slightest by doing so.

"He's busy." Romero nearly grimaced, speaking of another young gun that'd been unduly promoted, even though his role in the Crisis had been crucial. And Lucy would know all that if she were at her desk like normal Precinct Lieutenants, making it easier for the hierarchy above to do their job by going above and beyond in hers, especially in times such as these.

"Keep me posted." Was all she said, and Romero swore quietly as he left, nearly running into a cheeky-looking military man who only exemplified the fact by making a well-fitting blue suit look as if it were a dress uniform. He entertained a quick thought why Lucy was dolled up with the stoic and somber attitudes possessing the new morning and convinced himself it was on behalf of the man in the blue suit who was more than likely one of the Bureau boys and his curses turned to smiles at the thought of her wanting to leave CPD for a spot in the FBI where she would be, not only a better fit, but out of his hair forever.

"Hey." Lucy said, setting the tablet aside. "Fit's alright?"

"Yeah." Morell sat next to her, smoothing out the pants. "It was the best they had."

Since Morell would be unable to return home for an undisclosed period of time as CRT had locked down a good portion of Second Avenue, Lucy had brought him to the Precinct early to hunt through Vice's collection of undercover apparel, and he'd opted for the daytrader special, not tailored to perfection as his gray Burberry had been, but still tight enough to make him feel the functional comfort of sharpness a true military man craved.

Fosnick entered the room at eight sharp before they'd time to say anything of meaning, as they'd both slept like pieces of dried-out driftwood on the beach once entering the hushed cocoon of Lucy's home and had barely made it to the Precinct with the harsh chill of a new winter morning making the thought of deep sleep that much more inviting.

"Black." He said, handing Morell a sixteen ouncer of coffee. "And black tea." He said, with a twelve ounce for Lucy, the string and the tab of her favorite brand dangling out the side beneath the plastic lid.

A wary glance passed between Lucy and Morell because Fosnick was a Manhunter and knew men were animals, creatures of habit to be captured by their own lusts, tastes, habits, and seeking of certain comforts; thus, Fosnick's mind was apt to pick up on the little details of one's existence and his knowledge of their favorite morning drinks was a small, nonverbal declaration that he knew a great deal more about both of them and was leaving it at that, asserting his psychological lordship over them by such.

Fosnick went to the dry erase board and began scribbling with an italicized hybrid of cursive and print, slanting to the left as he was a lefty.

A few minutes later, the board had established the simple facts of the case in a series of bubbles with lines connecting to more bubbles and the blankness of their questions.

"What am I missing?" Fosnick asked, capping the marker.

"Nothing." Morell said, massaging his left knee.

"So who's behind it?" Fosnick returned his attention to the board. "Two billionaires...who stands to gain the most? An ally or a competitor?"

"We're going to interview Maks Lenkov's children today." Lucy said. "They have an estate just a couple of miles outside of the airport."

"What about this whole...Order thing?" Fosnick mumbled with a lack of eloquence incongruent with what Morell was used to and he nearly winced in saying so, but whether it was on behalf of the buckwheat pancakes he found in the cafeteria or the possibilities of a secret society, Morell was unsure.

"I spoke with Mogilev before the..." Lucy motioned with her hand, and nodded, as one did when not wanting to speak of something traumatic they were still forced to reference. "And I saw his watch. It was a custom made Rolex with diamonds in the shape of a Teutonic cross, black and white. Lenkov had a custom made Rolex as well, with a Deepsea with a Russian flag motif. Different model and different theme but same idea. I know a good deal about watches and I've never seen either. I'm sure the other targets will have similar Rolexes."

Fosnick nodded pensively, knowing better than anyone how deep the canyon of personal artifacts could run and what space they managed to carve out in a case, especially in lieu of an investigation into one's buried secrets.

"I believe what Lucy is getting at is that whomever is being targeted is a member of an underground branch of the Teutonic Order, which to public knowledge in today's society is a bankrupted charity of Catholic subjugation, nothing equating Russian billionaires and *certainly* nothing worth killing for. We'll only know if they're a part of the *underground* portion of the Order if we get close enough or find a connection with those who have already been taken out."

Fosnick nodded, looking not in one iota different than he had last night, as if he was the ageless kind that hung upside down from the rafters of a cathedral and Lucy avoided the thought of what he'd look like with the collar of his black suit flipped up.

"So is the killer one of the Order or an enemy of the Order?" He thought aloud with the soft tone he'd gained in FBI meeting rooms. "And was Geffington a member of the Order or an accelerant of chaos? Because the pride of Crescent claiming to come back stronger with the right to live in liberty doubled their fall last night and killing the man responsible for preaching the message of retaliation against terrorism by the aggressive pursuit of freedom was just as much a message to our freedom as a nation as it was the planned collapse of an economic superpower."

"It has to be the money." Lucy said, after Fosnick's words hung heavily in the air. The thought of Crescent falling any further scared her. It would affect the stock exchanges, the real estate markets, the GDP of the nation and ultimately the world economy, as the ripples of psychological deterioration pinged through Wi-Fi hotspots and wireless routers where tensed fingers twitched their emotional reactions to the scrolling tickers of half-truths and initial reports.

For if more attacks were to come, then the only people who would be roaming free in Crescent would be terrorists, striking the city at will.

"Well I've got a bit to go on at the Continental." Fosnick said, meaning an initial forensic team had found DNA on a half-eaten meal left by the man who'd killed Geffington, solidified by the fact that the man had been playing games with the security cameras but still couldn't escape a proprietary new visual search algorithm.

"There is also the vodka." Lucy said, bringing up a picture of the castle featured on the bottle on her tablet. "The Teutonic Order is of Germanic heritage and assimilated much of the Baltic, but one of the items connecting Lenkov to the Order was a bottle of Polish vodka. Being half Polish myself I noticed it right away. I'm positive Mogilev had it in his yacht but…maybe we can check his apartment in Regency Tower, and see if he has one there, too. If we can trace the origin of those bottles we can find out who else has one and where they came from."

"I like it." Fosnick nodded. "Because alcoholic imports are heavily monitored. If you write the name down for me I'll have something for you before the end of the day."

"What about those black eagles?" Morell interjected.

"The granite ones? Those might be harder to trace." Lucy stood to show Fosnick the picture of the castle on her tablet, which he studied with great consideration.

"Still, if the artist responsible has made others like them, they were probably commissioned by the same people."

Lucy nodded in agreement but didn't want to divert any manpower from the investigation into the vodka.

"Where is this?" Fosnick asked.

"Poland."

"Do you read or speak Polish?"

"Just enough. I am fluent in Italian, though."

Fosnick hid a smile in a yawn. He already knew that. Furthermore, he'd assumed that her father had taught her the language through music instruction, hoping she would one day rule Vienna as the pianist of the century. But she had spoken the fact for Morell's ears, not his.

"Have you been there?" Fosnick handed it back.

"No." Lucy shook her head. "I've always wanted to go."

"If it comes to it you just might." Fosnick assured, reaching for his vibrating phone. "Okay then." He said, after noticing the number. "Hopefully you don't strike out with the kids. Keep me posted."

Morell stood and nodded as Fosnick left HomCon with little to no noise underfoot and Morell turned to see if Lucy was ready to hit the road for the twenty-something mile drive through dense traffic and did a bit of a double take at what he saw, still getting used to the fact that Lucy's expressionless face, in a way, was a blank canvas and she had doctored it as such to be an alluring and cultured counterpoint to the rich scion of an assassinated Russian billionaire in a battle for the truth about a secret that had all the potential to be nothing more than a strange and fruitless coincidence.

And as Morell winced in politely helping Lucy with her belted tan trench, his left knee still tender but his ribs even more so, he couldn't avoid the thought sneaking across his mind that she'd taken advantage of the situation to change her appearance for *him*, too, to tell him that as perceptive as he was as an expert interrogator, there was far more to her than met the eye.

TWENTY-EiGHT

Casey Sullivan was brooding over a bowl of arid-looking All Bran when her cellphone nearly buzzed itself right off the kitchen bar top. Her apartment was on the third floor of a hotelish sort of place in the middle of Eleventh Street Northwest, half a mile from the White House, with a horde of smartly dressed doormen as portly as they were curt. A post-Georgian façade protected a stanchly formal sense of decorum, and even though Casey's young and still *slightly* rebellious side wouldnt've been caught dead in such a place, she'd wizened in her parent's graduation-from-the-Academy gift of it, seizing its ridiculously strategic proximity to FBI headquarters and the National Mall in a city so plagued by the daily slide puzzle of traffic it bordered the absurd. And, in keeping to herself as she had learned to do so well in the past, it reminded her of her affluent upbringing as much as a zoo reminded a regal African lion of the Serengeti. She nearly always walked to work, which was a healthy practice, though she usually caught a cab home, given early hours of her departure and she often cleared her head, the Louisville girl that she still was deep down, with daily walks around the monuments and their surreal presence.

Casey frowned at the number on the old flip phone's screen and a one-time leftward twitch bit at the side of her mouth. It was an unconscious tell she would never be able to quell.

"Fosnick?" Her smoky voice crackled and squeaked with inquisition, still dry from the late night's sleep, not that the bowl before her would help.

"Good morning Ms. Sullivan."

Casey stared down into the bowl of squiggly brown shavings and their unappealing promise of healthy fiber instead of the craveable sweetness of the dozens and dozens of other boxes in the grocery store and pushed the bowl from her, as if it were a metaphor for the course of her destiny since she'd graduated the Academy.

Casey then strung together a fowl litany of colorful adjectives about the state of the squad without him there to run the ship and how she couldn't stand the sight of his favorite morning cereal anymore.

A small chuckle cut through the receiver over the low-pitched acceleration of a car engine, perhaps that of an SUV.

"The day they put soap in your mouth is the day I quit." Fosnick said, and barely audibly at that, as if he were with someone else and loathed them listening in. "Are you still working on Morell?"

"Yeah, and seriously..."

"No, it's okay Casey, my assessment of him wasn't *entirely* correct."

Her naturally sullen and nearly pouty lips twisted in a proud smile and she sat tall on the barstool.

"Woah, Nicky, I think I hear angels singing in the heavens. You actually agree with me for once. Where's my calendar? I'm gonna go mark it down..."

After all, it was Fosnick whose eye she'd caught rushing through the Academy as if she'd trained for it all of her life, since the expert Manhunter was always scouring new classes for the best, and Fosnick had been, to date, some sort of brother to her, though she frequently disagreed with his assessments, the Morell case proving it. He'd always encouraged his *entire* team to speak their mind but knew she was the only one he could count on to do so and he was constantly amazed at the potential she showed, though, privately knowing her resolve was a result of her seventeenth summer and not some desire to be a Capitol Hill career go-getter.

"But I've got something else…"

"Something else? What am I, a computer? Open a new tab for whatever pops into your head? Yeah, like I'm just over here sitting on my ass, watching tour busses of Chinese people take each other's pictures in front of the IRS building. Do you want me to lean out the window and say, *hey guys, enjoy those ten-year visas, swim lessons are on us!*"

Fosnick laughed again, airlessly, so refreshed to hear Casey's sanguinity in such a dour situation. She was predictably *unpredictable*, a smack of fresh air in a world stagnated by reams of printed rules and the grim-faced enforcers thereof.

"It's just a bottle of Polish vodka, okay? Once you're done you can practice up for that surprise firearms evaluation I'm not supposed to know about…"

Casey rubbed the last remnants of sleep from her extraordinary almond-shaped blue-green eyes. They didn't need liner or mascara to be as beautiful as they were and they had a way of brazenly defying those who tried to decipher their mystery with a glossy loveliness one could see their own reflection in, as if Casey was so adept at hiding her true self there were mirrors glued to her soul.

Only Fosnick knew who she was, where she'd come from, what she'd been through; he'd been in the operation himself, the one that Casey'd found herself in as a normal citizen that balmy summer seven years ago, the very same operation that'd sadly facilitated the loss of one of the Department's best undercover agents at the hands of Chicago mafia.

But from that fallow ground a seed had found new life, and the death of one Agent had made way for the burgeoning career of another.

"I'm just playing with you, Nicky, you know I'm here to work. And shutup about guns, you know how much I hate them. Whatchu got?"

Fosnick smiled in the backseat of the Suburban as DiMocco eased it through the National Guard-flanked checkpoint along Second Avenue, cutting a clear route through the morning-after CRT cleanup of the Continental Plaza to find a parking space.

"Do you have a pen handy?" He asked.

Fosnick heard rustling and the rolling of ball bearings and the banging of kitchen utensils as DiMocco switched the SUV off and left to find a somewhat sleepless Shane Sheth.

"Okay, shoot."

"Pchow…" Fosnick made a fake gunfire sound.

Casey shook her head.

"Leave the jokes to me, Nicky, they fit you like a pair of *Frozen* leggings…okay, what's the name of this Polski firewater?"

Fosnick squinted to read what he'd scribbled in his own notepad, shaking his head at the sight of himself in such attire.

"*Zakon Krzyżacki.*" Fosnick said, and waited for it.

"Schieße…would you mind spelling that?"

Fosnick did, with an airless chuckle, never having asked her exactly *what* the German word meant, though he was sure it was perfectly consistent with Casey's unabashed *Casey-ness,* and its context had already been well deciphered by his sharp and swift mind.

As much as Maks Lenkov's apartment attempted to make one believe they'd stepped foot in the Russian embassy, his estate three miles south of the airport was some sort of time capsule to the days of colonialism, where Europeans lived as giants, kings, and gods in lands they had taken by force though such lands would never belong to them.

The pale white mansion itself was an oversized three-story construction replete with columns and louvered windows spreading from a central rotunda that gave it a flair of being the capitol of a long lost woodland empire, steeped in the heritage and tradition of proud forefathers. Bordered with a few pines and firs as if to prove the area had once belonged to the Katonah tribesmen and the deer they bowhunted, the house stood as an arrogant monolith, incongruent with an otherwise beautifully sweeping vista of green hills and small creeks, and the fences of stables and training grounds for the horses raised there.

"I couldn't live in a place like this." Morell said.

"Neither could I." Lucy slowed the Sebring on the crest of a small knoll and peeled off of a left hand corner sharp enough to be dangerous at the right speed, and no guardrail was present to encumber the view just over the treetops.

Lucy unbuckled herself and Morell clued in on the fact that she had something on her mind and waited for her to say as much as they shared a bottle of water on the hood of the car, as it was still warm from the drive in the crisp clarity of a new morning.

"I'm in the lead of this investigation on paper because Fosnick said so and I'm a CPD Lieutenant but you know as well as I do," she said, eyes on the distant scene of horses grazing, most of them still in their jackets, puffs of mist clouding their muzzles. "You're the expert. I trust you to take the lead."

Morell swallowed a swig of water and crushed the bottle, sealing its emptied skinniness with the cap.

"I respect that." Morell said. "But you have to have more faith in yourself. Your instincts are sharp and you have to trust them."

Lucy nodded.

"And..." Her voice was hushed. Morell knew she was weighing the scales to say something part of her didn't want to, something that shouldn't be said.

In the end she stared at the concrete of the road and let it out.

"I just thought I should tell you. I've never worked with anyone I've had feelings for."

"I have." Morell let his eyes drift off to the forest because the gnarled drill tip of CAP Syndrome had already ground itself in his stomach on the couch of her living room and he wanted to steer the conversation away from its burned out canyon of historical failure.

For *both* of their sakes.

Because that ache wasn't going away.

"Feelings of deep admiration and respect. Green Berets and Rangers come to mind."

"But not..."

"No. The only women that ever gave me the time of day were, um...loose types, you know. Not the kind to sign up for my line of work. Most of the women I served with were actually wives and mothers, believe it or not. Brave as hell...*incredible*..."

"Homeland?"

"No." Morell said, his imagination considering a few unforgettable faces.

"That's interesting." Lucy said. "I would think that serving together in such extreme circumstances would...*anyway*," She shrugged. "I've always been a loner. A soloist. I've never had a partner long enough for them to realize I'm not cold-blooded. I've even had a few life threatening moments in this business, but I've had to deal with them alone." She turned to face him. "I usually don't allow myself the option, but, you're not an everyday kind of guy, so…" Then a muddled chuckle came from her lungs, deep down, and she said. "I've been on the force a long damn time and I'm still just a rookie in this department. I promise you it won't get in the way of our job, but with Geffington and the Waterfront fire and all you've been through in the Crisis, I just think it's important for you to know that when the heat dies down, if it ever does, I'd love to go out to dinner with you, and get to know you."

Morell beheld her glamorous appearance and heard the pain edging her voice, though her face would've fooled the world's finest of poker players.

"Yeah." He said. "We'll do that."

"There's something else I have to tell you." She said. "Because I've misjudged my whole life and I want you to know upfront, since we're working together. It's not something I've ever told anybody else."

Morell bit his bottom lip, the knot returning to his stomach.

It was a specter of relationships past, indelibly unshakeable for a man who relied on natural reflexes and the repetition of training, and that sickening knot was, *always*, an indication the abrupt, misguided, psychological pretzel that CAP Syndrome was, whether the attraction was one sided or not.

He'd dealt with its sleeplessness when been there to nurse wounds the FBI coldly refused to be attended to, and was unable to ignore its haunting pang as it returned in the razor's edge of fresh cold air like a shapeless ghost cutting through the surrounding brackets of evergreens.

The knot had never been wrong.

"You have to know that…when I was a child, I

had an accident."

Morell's face twisted, his thoughts racing to wonder if she was going to confide in him the horrors of parental abuse, or of something relating to the inability to conceive children and the poison it'd pumped into her self-esteem and her soul.

A single, salty tear slid down her cheek as she was finally able to release the burden of rejection at the behest of others; their comments, their sniggers, their thoughts.

All of her life, she'd suffered their judgments about her, shouting at her in the silence of their glares when she wouldn't laugh at their jokes and never smiled in their pictures.

"I have near total facial paralysis." She said. "It's why I look so young. It's why I was good at Vice." Her eyes became wet as her memory sifted through fate's blessings.

And curses.

Lucy sighed with her gray green eyes to the sky, forcing all the air out of her lungs and turned to Morell for his response.

Morell's dark eyes were warm in the chill of the morning and Lucy gathered from their gaze that she didn't have to prove anything to him.

She didn't even have to try.

His eyes said she wasn't the Dalit she felt like inside and she gathered, from his slight smile, that he liked her honesty, so much it worked hand in hand with the affirmative promise of that far off dinner she'd already vociferated a desire for to help focus her on the now and the task at hand for them both.

It all made sense in that moment, the moment that belonged to them in the breadth of the crystalline vista.

"We should probably get going." He said, the aridity in his smoker's voice stronger than usual.

Sergei Petrovich Lenkov was shaving the hard edge of his jaw in the broad space of the master bath when Alexis Maksimillia stirred awake with a moaning yawn.

"What time is it, brother?" She asked, and he snorted to himself. She always called him that, as if to make fun of the fact that they were, beneath the world's infinite microscope, brother and sister, when in fact they were not and bore no relation to each other.

They were lovers.

It'd been the late Maks Lenkov's idea against the wishes of the Order to find his son a suitable mate and had done so through the careful process of ancestral investigation, thus finding a woman of royal descent, the purity of her heritage linking the boundaries of space and time to a period when the Order was thriving in the gauntlet of conflict and war. But because the Order had not wished Lenkov's son to be married, he had to adopt Alexis as his own daughter, knowing that they could never truly be happy together.

Perhaps, subliminally, it was why Alexis Maksimillia wore the oversized and multi-faceted green oval chrysoberyl ring on the middle finger of her right hand, as if to immediately antagonize her enemies, defiant in the fact that she was the royal princess of an ancient kingdom about to seize power from those who'd so unjustly taken such from her ancestry centuries ago.

And sadly, the rich man who'd raised her as his own had not foreseen what she was capable of and had suffered the consequences as would all others who dared stand in her way.

"Between eight and nine." Sergei said, "Why?"

"I'm so terribly cold." She said, her voice purring with suggestive undertones as she was far from it in the capacious clutches of their King-sized bed and its wealth of comfortable coverings.

"We have a long day ahead of us, so get dressed." Sergei countered, always having to negotiate with Alexis about such things, as he was a prisoner to her appetites.

Especially those concerning world domination.

When Sergei had completed shaving and primping, making sure not a single jet-black hair of his watch and cuff-link model coif was out of place, he found Alexis rolling her neck around in circles in the seclusion of the walk in closet. Her silk robe was the color of pink pearls, and, feeling his presence at the open doorframe, the robe fell from her with the slightest shirk of her broad shoulders, allowing a curtain of auburn hair to cascade down the pale nude skin of her back. She then walked from the smooth fingers of the robe as if she'd shed her skin.

"What should I wear?" She said, sensing the lingering eyes of her *brother* trace the corners of her hourglass figure.

"Something warm." Was all he said, his words injected with the callous abruptness of his father.

She'd always hated that about him. Business was business, pleasure was pleasure, and the twain should never meet. How dull men could be.

But like everyone else, Alexis thought, indulging a serpentine smile as her lips transmuted some hedonistic gratification, *his day too will come.*

Alexis' eyes were closed as she stood like a stoic tree in the still space of the room, meditating. Her breathing slowed so that her heart barely beat and her arms outstretched unevenly like willowy limbs. Her body became cold and her face vacant and void of the emotion she could so easily flood its deadly beauty with.

Soon I will be alone in my reign as the Queen. At

*the sound of my voice, they will bow or they will feel my
wrath. They will give in to my every whim and fancy
and it will still not spare them from the vengeance my
blood seethes within my bones to take. Soon they will
know who is their master. Soon they will all curse the
day of their birth.*

And as the doorbell rang from a distance, echoing
through the cavernous spaces of the mansion, Alexis
Maksimillia selected an outfit of formal function,
betting every dollar in the family trust as the gambler
that she was that the doorbell represented some form of
law enforcement eager to witness firsthand the tears
spilling from her provocative emerald green eyes over
the tragic *suicide* of her adoptive father, Maks Lenkov,
for whom she was named.

TWENTY-NiNE

The six-foot two patrician businessman of thirty four years greeted the man and woman dwarfed under the high arch of the doorway with the tight bow of his head and turned to allow them to step in from the cold.

"My head of security informed me you are both carriers of the new Critical Response Team variance of your Police Department's badges and I am to answer all of your questions since my lawyer is enroute." Sergei Lenkov said with the resonance his father's genetics allowed, though he would forbid himself to grow fat in his old age as did his father. "And I shudder to think what would bring you here if not for the untimely suicide of my late father. Forgive me, but it is still a sore subject."

Once seated, an imperceptible wince flashed across Lucy's gray-green eyes.

Sergei held a defensive posture behind a Parisian-style chair in the limitless sitting room of the rotunda where he'd forced them to gather by one of his broad hands and the scrutinous gaze of the younger Lenkov's eyes were reminiscent of the Teutonic black granite eagles flanking the doorway to his father's penthouse on Ninth and Schwartz.

Predators, unmatched in the food chain, sleek and effortlessly carrying out their deadly duties, designed to the endth degree for the fluid processes of one masterful function.

Survey. Select. Kill.

Seated at her immediate left, Morell sensed the nervous agitation rising within Lucy, as an athlete would of a fellow teammate. But turning to view at her and her appliqué of makeup and her lovely platinum blonde curls, he knew she'd steal the show if she gave herself a chance. Yes, Lenkov was intimidating, intelligent, and internationally-minded, but Lucy had hidden any and all signs of the previous evening's physical damage, unlike Morell, his tender injuries still apparent, and having run a hundred good-cop-bad-cop routines in the military, Morell would bet the farm Lucy's first impression on Lenkov would pay dividends as long as she stayed natural with him and trusted her instincts.

That was, until his sister entered the room.

It was clear, from the moment her emerald green eyes, layered and telescopic in their chatoyant depth, caught Sergei Lenkov, that he was under her spell, and she was in control of his *functions* as if he were a marionette. Lenkov brightened, straightened from his defensively hunched posture on the back of the chair and took her hand, offered and accepted in an antiquated display of manners akin to some Elizabethan pavane.

"Sister, how good of you to join." He said. "We have visitors."

Morell swallowed with difficulty as the woman silently judged him, the heat of her nonverbal study bordering feelings of personal violation.

And so the table was set in the oddest and most uncomfortable of ways, with Lucy turning to quietly survey her partner's unease at the electric green eyes indulgently caressing his handsome toughness as if he were a Michelin star meal for her to savor between her teeth, across her palate, and down her throat.

Morell crossed his leg and Lucy caught the flash glance of grit teeth.

Physical pain?

Extreme disdain.

"Yes, we are CPD CRT," Lucy said in the affable and unconcerned manner she could afford, knowing her face would give nothing away as her body language was proper in the presence of such elitists. "But we're not here to question you about your father or your business. Our presence is more for your well-being than anything else."

"Oh." Sergei's granite-lined face softened, if only for a fraction of a second. He sat down next to his sister on an unreasonably comfortable couch the color of polished steel. "I'm touched."

"He's taking it well." Alexis said, nearly doting, her gaze washing over him and returning to Morell. "And though we have our own security team, we could always use another man around the house."

Morell squinted and attempted a different avenue, knowing her knee-high brown leather boots and tight mossy green cotton twill pants were not for gardening.

"I couldn't help but notice how many beautiful horses you have." He said. "I'm sorry if we interrupted you."

"Oh no." Alexis leaned back in her seat, expanding her chest and fluffing her curtain of auburn hair with a consciously demure technique that hardened Lucy's eyes like brass knuckles. It was as if she could feel an energy emanating from Alexis, a channel of it, attempting to burn through Morell's chest like reflected rays of the sun through a mirror.

And as a student of history, Lucy noted, Morell would remember Archimedes had burned the sails of Roman ships that way, sinking them and their attempted amphibious assault dead in Syracuse harbor.

But what could she say? *Hands off, he's mine!* No, and Lucy had no experience in the matter, such possessive feelings for another man were completely foreign to her and she was doing her best to stay focused on gleaning information without evoking the Lenkov sibling's right to lawyers and processes that would surely, if not indefinitely, invalidate them from the time-crunched hunt for a terrorist.

After all, the city was on her shoulders, and any feelings toward Morell would have to wait. It was as if expressing them and setting some far off dinner date had helped her focus on the case all the more, that was until Alexis showed up and started oozing that sensual slime from her skin.

Even though Lucy knew how to play that game, too.

Lucy nearly leapt out of her skin as strong fingers brushed her right elbow.

"I like your watch." Sergei said, motioning with his chin.

"Oh." Lucy held her left arm at a rigid angle, the squarish eighteen-karat gold Cartier Panthere catching light from one of the louvered windows.

"My father and I are...*were* both timepiece enthusiasts." Lenkov stood tall next to her, his waist eye level as he sipped at a glass of water. She was unaware he'd left, being so drawn to Alexis on her partner's behalf, even though Alexis was strangely magnetic in her own way, the kind of person one found themselves staring at, blankly.

"I am as well." She found herself saying. Lenkov was keen to the make and model.

"Is it a family heirloom?"

In a way it was, but why would she give personal information to such strange...*feeling* people?

"It was a graduation gift from my late father."

"And he was Polish, I take?" Lenkov smiled. "The gateman phoned in your names."

"Half." She said.

"What's the other half?" He asked.

"Swedish."

"Ah, then we're practically neighbors." Lenkov returned to the steely blue couch and had all but made himself comfortable when his sister's icy words provoked him to rise again.

"Brother, why don't you show Miss…"

"Radzewicz." Lucy said.

"Why don't you show Miss Radzewicz your watch collection?"

"Great idea." He said, and nudged his head toward a broad doorway just off the rotunda, flanked by the limestone sculpture of a gnarled, leafless tree, beautiful in its large scale and capturing of movement and energy as it stretched to fill empty space in the hollowed courtyard of the rotunda, nearly to the roof three stories above.

Lucy stood and met Morell's eyes, briefly, seeing in them the conflict of a daredevil readying himself for a world-record base jump.

Alexis smiled, the joke of her words somehow salacious on her lips as Lucy turned her back on Morell to follow the tall Russian.

"Take your time, Miss Radzewicz."

Morell nodded in thanks, accepting a glass of water from the royal princess and Alexis had taken the opportunity to shift from the steely blue couch to the black one Morell was seated on. She did so with one leg under the other with a cushion between them and stretched her left arm across the back of the couch.

Morell steadied himself with a sip of water.

"Are you sleeping with her?" Alexis asked, puffing a mist of water from Morell's choking attempt at swallowing.

"Excuse me?" He said, wiping his mouth with his sleeve.

Alexis' eyes were curious on him.

"Um…" Morell cleared his throat. "We have a protocol in place that would prosecute us both for gross negligence, especially in light of last night's terrible events." He said, leaning forward to set the water on a low glass coffee table.

"The same protocol that gave you this?" Alexis touched the right side of her face with her right hand. The chrysoberyl-ring caught Morell's dark-eyed gaze like a hypnotist's charm.

He touched his own face, like a mirror of her movement, having forgotten, since soldier mode had taken him over, that a purplish-yellow complexion stretched from his temple to the stubbled line of his chin where The Lynx had attempted to kick his head well into the next county.

"It was my fault." He said.

"It *is* tragic about my father," Alexis let her green eyes fall to the floor and trace around the lines of the immense rug covering most of the rotunda, the purity of its true image obscured by furniture and other unimportant decorative items. "But my heart breaks for the city of Crescent. I can't imagine what it's like for those who can't afford their own private retreat like myself, those who rely on welfare and government-sponsored programs…"

Morell was instantly taken aback by the breath of humanity that'd made an appearance in her nearly bony face, severe in its supermodel-like thinness and its framing of her enormous eyes. Quickly, as she was still dwelling on her thoughts, he flashed a head-on picture of her in his mind, and attempted to ascertain a few facts about her heritage, as she looked *nothing* like Maks *or* Sergei Lenkov.

"But, it does get lonely here, in this castle." She said, nearly beginning to ramble as Morell processed what information his brain was swift in assuming. "Everyone has their version of riches and wealth but they fail to realize the immense burden of responsibility that comes with such an office, such a price, it is…ironically." She turned to him as his eyes were on the floor. "Am I boring you, Mr. Morell?"

"No, but…" A grin crossed Morell's face, though the tenderness of his bruise cursed him with a dull gnaw. "I wouldn't mind a tour of the…castle, as you called it." He said, and was rewarded with a glimmer of delight in the telescopic green prism of Alexis Maksimillia's regard.

Wondering several thoughts about Lucy during the course of the tour, and carefully noting everything he saw with the belief that it bore a thematic connection to the thread surrounding the Teutonic Order and their medieval conflict, Morell knew he had one shot at ascertaining the answer to a question of incongruity, and the answer to the question lie around Alexis' neck, no doubt nestled between her breasts behind a velveteen brown blouse with ruffled silk sleeves.

Nearly everything Alexis showed him, with a growing sense of pride as the tour passed from a mini art gallery of paintings, sculptures and antiquities, to the pristine grounds of the horse farm, hinted at something cryptically *anti*-Teutonic, as if her antagonistic pride was eager to demonstrate the fact with articles that could be interpreted to be, on their own, innocuous, but really were not.

It was on the third floor of the rotunda and

Morell's winding eye line of the chandelier down to the
rug on the floor that he finally understood what had
been evading him.

But he had to be sure.

"I guess our tour is complete." Alexis said,
joining him on the balustrade. "Unless you would like
to see the walk-in freezer."

Morell had been holding his breath and squinted,
pretended to lose focus and shook his head, swaying
dangerously over the balustrade and back. He blinked
his eyes rapidly, seeing Alexis' own swell as his
swooning reached its zenith, and he twisted from the
railing of the third floor of the rotunda as if heroically
saving himself from a great fall and smacked into the
hardwood floor, face first, making sure the left side of
his looks took the fall with a double-edged ploy, not
only to save his already bruised right side from more
damage, but to make sure Alexis saw his eyes seal shut
above the nasty-looking contusion.

She swore in her native language which he was
pretty sure was not Russian and took quickly to a knee,
rolling him to his back. Bending over him with helpless
worry, the velveteen fabric of her blouse sagged and
Morell counted out a realistic string of seconds in his
mind before fluttering his eyes to clarity and swiping a
hand at her blouse as if he'd recovered from the
shocking throes of the panic-stricken blackness one
helplessly enters when passing out.

The success of the ruse, as he sat up and
pretended to catch his bearings under her warm half-
embrace, was galvanized in the fact that Alexis stuffed
the necklace back in her shirt so that its exposure
wasn't more than a blip across his vision.

But he'd seen enough.

"Are you okay?" She asked, and he felt the heat
of her breath and the beat of her heart as it skipped

against his shoulder.

Nearly face to face, the emeralds lodged in her skull appeared in a way to be inhuman, as hard and cold as the ring on her middle finger, mined from an antediluvian vein of gemstones as old as the earth itself.

Morell shot to full height, noticing strangely as he did Alexis was a bit taller than him, and the facts of his findings burned within Morell as they would within a young child eager to tell a newly acquired secret to his best friend.

"I'm fine." He said.

"No, no…" Alexis cooed and her hand grazed his bruised cheek as her grip pinched his chin and she turned his head left and right. Though he was sure she was no medical professional, he had no choice but to reciprocate as though she was, and in her touch was a numbing warmth that reminded him of the perilous grasp of alcohol. He fought the urge to shiver, but couldn't, causing Alexis to coo again as he blinked away thoughts he didn't want to think, thoughts that Alexis subliminally cast upon all men like some sort of advanced psychological warfare.

Morell cringed to think of the way his former self would've handled her, and sighed, nodding that he was okay.

"My personal physician lives five minutes away." She offered, holding his right arm in hers and guiding his left hand down the stair rail as if he were ninety-years old. Strangely, he did need the help, as his ribs were sending solar flares of pain in all directions, making his breath shallow in his chest, and Morell was reminded of the great care in which Lucy performed a similar procedure to get him from the car to the restorative confines of her Eavesdale home, sharply contrasting the rigidity of Alexis' posture.

"So this is what it feels like to be old." He said,

wheezing out a laugh.

On the crest of the second floor, the soothing and nearly spongy tones of an old piano spread through the wooden expanses of the mansion, minor chord tones blooming with a dramatic sense of beauty and struggle.

Alexis' concern for Morell halted abruptly, if only for a split second, and she continued to help him till they reached the ground floor.

"Wait here." She said, passing him a hasty smile and leaving the rotunda for the direction of the music.

But Morell did not wait, and hobbled after her with the lengthy tour of the three-story building and nearby horse stables having severely aggravated the hyperextended left knee Lucy had so cautiously applied a brace to the night before.

THiRTY

With the erect back of a concert pianist, Lucy lolled her neck to and fro as the music drifted directly from her soul into her fingers to begin the seamless transmutation of performance she'd been so aptly trained to achieve by her father. Except, the tattered and aged museum-quality piece of music before her, one of Rachmaninov's originals, was not the music that flowed from her fingertips as her father would've relished, but rather, a song that *she* enjoyed playing *herself*, knowing full well the psychological power of its melody.

Thus, somehow, she'd exorcized the memories of the musically religious brutality that'd severed her tactile love of the piano from her life, and the voice telling her that *if she could never be the best then she didn't deserve the right to play* were drowned out with the piece's final chords.

When she'd concluded the piece, six eyes were on her and the clapping of hands that followed deserved only the lowest of bows.

Despite her reservations over splitting up and having a crack at Sergei Lenkov alone, she was overwhelmed to find the ease of being herself had not only garnered her a wealth of information but lead to the payoff, deeply rewarding in its meaning, of playing such a priceless antique Bosendorfer the color of the smooth scotch.

"That was brilliant." Sergei said, and quickly motioned to his sister. "You should invite her."

Alexis' mouth opened and closed with brief hesitation before smiling.

"Yes, our guests would love to hear such beautiful music."

"She was playing the Rachmaninoff." He said, proudly beaming over the glass that had contained water as he'd left his sister's presence and now was tipped to the brim with Pinot Gris, not his first by any means.

"Oh?" Alexis smiled at the manuscript. "Yes, did you know it was handwritten by the composer himself?" She turned to Sergei and lowered her voice. "I think Miss..." Then she turned to Lucy with her eyebrows raised.

"Radzewicz."

"I think Miss Radzewicz will be quite busy tonight, brother. The city needs her, now more than ever."

"Not at all." She said, quickly crossing her arms, letting Alexis' green eyes bore into the skin of her face as the woman attempted to decipher if she was lying or not. "It's not everyday you get a chance to play such an instrument of this age in perfect condition. Besides, our monitoring of your well-being is more of an off-duty consideration than anything. But I'd be glad to play a dual-role at your party tonight, coordinating safety monitoring from inside the house at the helm of this beautiful old thing."

"I was thinking of having the tuner come play for our party tonight." Alexis lied, slipping her arm through the keyhole of Sergei's, resting on his waist, as if to assert her power over him.

"A *tuner*? For the fundraiser? Can *he* play the *Rachmaninoff*?" Sergei said, whatever indeterminate amount of wine he'd snuck away from the prying green eyes of Alexis freeing his tongue. "Besides, look at her…let her borrow one of your evening gowns and put out the hat, they'll think we've snuck in one of Moscow's finest right under their snooty little noses! And just how much would it cost to fly a concert pianist in here from back home?" Sergei turned to Lucy. "Can you play Tchaiko?"

Lucy chuckled at the pet name of Peter Ilich Tchaikovsky, one of the greatest composers in the history of music.

"With one hand." She joked, and knew *Dance of the Sugar Plum Fairy* was in her near future, though folks were probably sick of it after the passing of Christmas.

"It's a fundraiser…the money we'd save on hiring a Moscow-based musician means Alexis would be able to buy more Ossetia caviar…"

"Howabout Liszt, Brahms…Chopin?" Alexis reached, not wanting Lucy to attend the fundraiser for reasons belonging to her and her alone.

Lucy shrugged.

"I'll bring some sheet music from home," She said, "you can select what you'd like."

"Wonderful!" Sergei exclaimed, and Lucy caught Morell's glance as they moved to leave. Morell made a few comments about returning later in the week for a formal deposition with the family lawyer and spotted a hint of surprise on Sergei's face at the mention of legal representation, meaning that he'd been bluffing about the lawyer at their initial arrival.

Lucy sighed deeply on their way to the car, checking the gold Cartier Panthere. It told her the time was nearing eleven.

"You're floating on a cloud." Morell said. Lucy turned back for a lingering survey of the mansion.

"Yeah...so how'd it go for you?" She asked, insinuations of a smile shading her face.

"Wait till we get in the car." Morell said, shaking his head at the gravity of his findings.

The country roads swirled before them at Lucy's lead-footed appraisal of their wooded crooks and apexes as the terrain steadily rose to leave the Lenkov's palace in the distance.

"Where do I begin?" Morell searched the tree line, still shaking his head.

"Howabout the fact they can't tell the difference from classical and post-grunge neo-prog?"

"What?" The former soldier frowned. His view on music was strictly beat-based, and had, as most soldiers of the desert and dust, utilized the smashings of drum symbols and guttural crunches of down-tuned electric guitars as adrenaline-amping drugs to enter combat like Viking berserkers.

"I wasn't playing Rachmaninoff." Lucy said. "I was playing a song I'd transposed from *Origin of Symmetry* called *Space Dementia* by the British band *Muse*. Certain chords bear a similarity to Rach's Second, but...any Russian who knew their classical music would know I wasn't playing *that* exact handwritten sheet music in front of me. It's one of his most recognizable pieces and sounds nothing like his Second. The damn thing must be worth a fortune." It was Lucy's turn to shake her head. "My dad would've flipped if he'd seen that set up, Rach's own penmanship atop an eighteenth century Bosendorfer..."

"They're not Russian." Morell corrected. "That's just like...clothing and makeup. It's an act."

"Right." Lucy nodded. "Teutonic. Anyway, what about the party? She didn't seem too keen on me coming."

"No, but you *have* to go. Especially after what I tell you about what I found in that place. Fosnick might even compel you to do some…reconnaissance."

Lucy took her eyes off the road for a second and swallowed. It was one thing to conduct a friendly yet clandestine interrogation while talking to the six-foot two billionaire inheritor about watches, old books and pianos, entirely another to play spy in a house that uncannily reminded her of *Clue* on uncut crack cocaine and Medieval iconography and art. Besides, Morell was the expert, *not* her. He needed more time in the place, *not* her. The piano had been some strange warp zone back to reality and she'd literally ended the difficult process on a high note.

"I've got a lot to chase down." Morell said, his brow heavy with thought. "Like that giant *Tree of the World* sculpture in the rotunda and Alexis' creepy owl necklace."

"Pardon?" Lucy leaned forward in her seat, slightly preoccupied with the limping slowness of a random dump truck hogging up their side of the two-lane country road.

"And that rug…that damn rug, bigger than my entire apartment…not to mention her choice of paintings. And the horses, don't even get me started on the horses…"

"Hold on." Lucy said, sticking her foot nearly to the floor as the Sebring gnawed through the powerband to pass the dump truck on a lengthy straight.

"What were you saying?"

"First of all, they're not related. It's impossible. And Alexis isn't Russian *or* Teutonic. She's…"

Lucy swore and pumped her foot on the brakes several times but the car refused to respond, almost as if the car's sudden and furious acceleration had caused the life-threatening turn of events.

"What's wrong?" Morell asked, his eyes darting between Lucy's foot and the road, and the quickly approaching corner at which they'd shared a quiet moment before entering the Lenkov's private world of horses and thematic artifacts, the clarity of which would be forever hidden in Morell's mind if they didn't make it safely back to the Precinct.

"The brakes are shot!"

Morell swore and faced the inevitable, the traumatic episode of his own car crash suddenly fresh in his mind, despite all that he'd gone through since then. Even with Lucy's more than competent skills at the wheel, the corner ahead of them was far too sharp, and its increasing proximity at Lucy's chosen passing speed wasn't about to give them time to weigh their options.

Lucy shifted to neutral and swerved lightly left and right to cut some of the speed but it was of no use. The nearly ninety-degree corner forced Morell's hand and he reached over to Lucy and manhandled her out of her seat to the small space in the back of the coupe.

Morell then kicked at the wheel before Lucy could speak and the Sebring twisted to take the edge off of its missile-like projection from the precipice and instead, spun to slide down its face with an ungracefully bone-jarring series of rattling shatters and metallic crumpling noises, as if they were inside of a rotating piñata.

The extreme pain seizing Morell's chest with searing discomfort made it hard for him to breathe in the disorienting somersault but he held onto the seatbelt in the crook of his left elbow and armpit with all of the strength his body had to offer as its tough fabric was woven around his arm like a thin gray python. Over and over the Sebring arced and fell, cessation of movement a far-off fantasy, and Morell tried to shift his body weight with the sway of the violent momentum, pressing his left shoulder into the back of the passenger seat with what little control remained, his right leg as rigid against the opposite side of the car as his less-than healthy physiology would allow.

Finally, as the car came to a halt near the base of a stout old pine tree, hesitating for a moment before resting on its roof, blonde curls smelling of floral notes and spices encompassed his vision like a lemon-white canopy.

Lucy groaned, struggling to prop herself up on her elbow, and pulled her hair back from her face to catch her bearings as Morell steadied his breath. Her brain was spinning within her skull and felt like a liquefied smoothie, ready to spill from her ears at any second.

"That's two in two days." Morell said, chancing a thin smile at Lucy. "Thank God you're alive." He brushed her hair back and saw the shock in her eyes. The cut above her eyebrow had been split open in the brawl of man and machine and she collapsed against him with a feeble embrace of lost strength and living shock.

"Not too hard, Lucy…" Morell wheezed.

She propped herself on her elbow again and searched the windshield tattered and split with spider-webbed fissures.

"You're alive." She said, feeling the tangible rush of living when death had made other plans as she lowered the driver's seat. "If you weren't, I'd have to fill out paperwork."

"No you wouldn't." Morell reached for the lever to flip the passenger seat down. "I don't really work for the Department anyway."

Once they were free of the wrinkled and steamy heap of the gold Sebring and had taken a few steps

from its sour smells of spilled brake fluid and gasoline,
Lucy spotted the parade of thoughts rushing past
Morell's eyes like the plastic horses of a carousel,
alternating in height over the same sickening melody.

"What now?"

"The fact that the car was sabotaged means we're
closer than I realized."

Lucy dabbed at the cut with the black cuff of her
turtleneck.

"You think?"

"Yeah…" Morell bobbed his head and squinted
back up the ridge and its vacancy, failing to address her
sarcasm. "That was no accident. I didn't have eyes on
the car at all, did you?"

"You kidding? I nearly went cross-eyed over
Sergei's watch collection. Do you know how many
potential Order-specific custom Rolexes that guy has?
Not to mention Omegas, Breitlings, and pair of Patek
Philippe's underlit in shadowboxes he worships as if
they were Church relics…"

Morell brushed his hands together and motioned
for her to follow him through the trees to a field
clearing not half a mile away.

"Fosnick'll take it in stride, I'm sure."

Lucy noticed that Morell was hyperaware of their
surroundings as she pulled her phone from her pocket.

"Damn…no service." She said.

Morell's vision waxed cold in the eerie silence,
cut only by the random pops and crinkles of the
deceased Sebring, wondering if the lack of service was
on the count of their tree-ridden location or some sort of
signal-jammer.

"I underestimated these guys." He nearly
whispered to Lucy as they took to the cover of a
gnarled maple tree and drew their weapons, Lucy
following Morell's lead. "And if we get out of here

without getting shot to bits by some sniper we're going to barricade ourselves in my apartment till we can figure this mess out and nail them with everything we've got."

"Your place is on lockdown." A smile was hidden in Lucy's eyes.

"I've got CRT clearance." Morell smirked back.

"I thought you didn't work for the Department?"

Morell nodded after his eyes scanned Lucy up and down and the brave and fearless figure she was becoming in the wake of Crescent's newest Crisis.

He pointed her toward a groove in the maple tree, eyes jabbing left and right into the woods, nearly cornering her with his body, protecting her, turning serious despite her desperate attempt to be light in the face of peril when he knew full well all she wanted to do was hang on to him and teleport somewhere warm and sunny.

"Keep your head on a swivel, okay?"

"Absolutely." She nodded, muscles tensed.

"Come on." Morell said, wetting his lips as vigilance entered his eyes and he fell back from the cover of the giant maple. "Let's go see if we can get cell phone reception in that clearing."

"If not?" Lucy said, nearly breathless.

"Well then, how do you feel about acquisitioning a horse?"

THiRTY-ONE

Kelly Barnett's eyes were puffy by the time she stepped out of Municipal Arena in stride with a dreary trickle of pedestrian traffic finally cleared by the CRT mosaic of CPD, FBI, and Homeland Security operatives and employees.

Throughout the mandatory questionnaire slash interrogation at the hands of a terse-faced female FBI woman of nearly fifty years of age, probably most of them in service, Barnett's thoughts wouldn't stop drifting toward Henry Morell, not that it helped her focus when confronted with the woman's more invasive inquiries.

Waiting for Jasmine Keelan near the ill-equipped bus terminal, Kelly was struck by the amount of citizens stuck without rides or transport of any kind back home. The Convention had drawn constituents from out of town and even out of state, eager to hear what would be done about the shock of domestic terrorism, and Kelly struggled to remember how many cars had been buried underground in the Continental Plaza's parking garage, and was confronted with a bodily clogging of the bus terminal. She quickly remembered to call a number she'd been given about which cars, parked off-site and out of the doomed clutches of the Continental Plaza's subterranean garage, had been fully checked and transferred to the lot spreading around the Arena.

The monotone floating over the speaker of her smartphone could not help dismiss the tears forming in her eyes as recollections of the past Crisis of months ago suddenly became a ghostly reality in the new light of the day.

It wasn't until she reached the Verdoro Green Nineteen Seventy Pontiac GTO that she broke down and let her tears stain the blanched concrete of the spreading stadium lot, a cold and salty wind from the Bay nearly freezing the teardrops to her cheeks.

"Are you okay?" A feminine voice asked, startling Kelly.

Barnett was shocked to see Jessica Birchall, her own cheeks reddened with patience under a high ponytail of dark brown hair. Her delicate hands were stuffed deep in the pockets of one of her colored overcoats and her smile to Kelly was considerate, if not conciliatory.

"Oh my God." Kelly reached out to hug Birchall. The Crisis had united them in clandestine service under Sierra Marland's guidance, and they had both been instrumental, though secretly so, in her efforts to stop the terrorist attacks of the man named Jupiter. "What are you doing here?"

"It's a long story." Jessica said, her voice tight with bound-up pressures, the drowned CIA man at the forefront of the storm inside. Kelly wiped her astute brown eyes to free them of their stinging emotions, only to see Birchall's own eyes were rimmed with the dark circles of sleepless stress and strain.

Kelly sniffed and dug in her purse for a tissue, searching the grounds for Jasmine Keelan who was not supposed to be *that* far behind her in the cue, and in doing so, spotted Birchall's Subaru parked near the GTO.

"I'm here to speak to Jasmine," Birchall said, as Kelly blew her nose. "But, once I learned you two were together, I knew it'd be a case of the Musketeers. I saw your car immediately and thought I'd wait for you both."

"Yeah…" Kelly sighed away the ghosts of November and shivered in her eveningwear. She wanted a shower and a cup of coffee, and a good two and a half hours kicked out on her couch to make sense of it all. "Just like last time. Except for Tabitha Grey. And Darren…"

The savor of pain spelled out her late boyfriend's name. Her only peace was in knowing that he'd expired without pain in his own home, and would forever be a hero to her, having played an integral part in saving the United States from the most brutal information drain it'd ever seen. Before today, the last time she'd driven the GTO was, in fact, to pick the car up from the Arena to deliver it to him at his house, as he had completely forgotten who he was and, in the throes of amnesia, was unaware that such a beautifully babied muscle car belonged to him.

Jasmine arrived with a well-conditioned lope, developed by her height in accordance to running up and down sandy Californian beaches for volleyball training. Her features, aided by her youth, looked unabashedly fresh and sunny, and her broad-mouthed smile was genuine at the sight of her mentor.

"Jessie!" She said, and gave Birchall a hug. "My God, I got your message, what's wrong?"

"I'm glad both of you are okay, but we need a safe place to talk," Birchall said. "Sierra's orders."

At the mention of the Homeland Security Special Assignment Branch Agent who'd been victorious in a deadly chess-match against the terrorist responsible for the Crisis of November, Kelly straightened her cutely

petite posture and her scholarly brown eyes gained a bit
of clarity, knowing that if she wanted to again, be a part
of serving *and* saving the freedoms of the United States
of America, she would have to shelve the seasick sway
of emotions that wanted to swallow her whole.

"I volunteer my place." Kelly said, reaching in
her purse for the GTO's keys. "I'll make a fresh pot of
coffee."

Shane Sheth was as sleepless as any of the first
responders from the redeye flight that'd brought him to
Crescent to begin with and was running on fumes when
Fosnick urgently requested his presence inside the
hotel. Sheth had been briefed on the historic building's
structural damage, and was miffed, as he made the
journey to the killer's room alone, with the collection of
his thoughts, that the building would have to be
demolished. Attempts were being made to clean the
rubble blocking the entrance to the garage, but coupled
with the death of four SWAT members *on top* of the
Mayor himself, Sheth was beginning to see there would
never be a brighter day for Crescent, no matter *what*
happened. The smoky demise of the Marina was only
fuel on the fire and he felt as grimy as he did ashamed,
for himself, and for Crescent, working his weary ass off
to gain ground in managing the limited resources of a
losing conflict whilst dodging cameras and
microphones that demanded answers at the risk of
hysteretic unrest.

Upon his arrival at the hotel room the killer had
used to prepare himself and his diabolical plan, both of
the dour-faced forensic scientists left abruptly and
Shane Sheth carefully scanned the room, in its
simplicity, with his eyes ending their perusal to land
heavily upon Special Agent Fosnick.

The Manhunter was leaning against the computer

table next to a broad window, arms crossed, chin jutted in an extreme underbite.

"Blake?"

Fosnick only stared into infinity, as if he'd been given the news that the terminal disease of a loved one had taken a turn for the worst. At times, Sheth was jealous of the kid's motor as it only *enhanced* his natural skills, but at thirty-one, Fosnick's age, Sheth had still been working himself to the bone for peanuts, running around greater Maryland at the whims of Capitol Hill time-in-grade good old boys calling in favors with each other.

What he'd give to do it all over again.

"Blake?" Sheth croaked for a second time, and Fosnick remained a hardened statue of chiseled stone but his eyes rotated in their sockets to bore with laser-like heat into the dead space of the open door behind the CRT Captain, forcing him to close it shut.

"It's my DNA." He finally said, as if the earth itself was headed for a black hole in the universe.

"What?"

His blocky faced remained passive and his voice was a near whisper.

"On that damn burger...*my* DNA."

Sheth looked at the dried out mushroom-Swiss black angus cheeseburger and the collection of still-edible steak-fries next to it, served above a bed of Bibb lettuce.

"The swab processed that fast?"

"Look at the pattern." Fosnick urged with his chin and Sheth swallowed with difficulty when he realized that the bite-mark pattern was a startling replica of the image in the open file folder beside it, and the DNA had processed in the mobile lab so quickly because CRT policy forced all CRT members to have both their DNA and biometric data used in a sample database as

baseline points for rapid field testing, thus enabling a
multi-million dollar new computer algorithm to isolate
unique strand variants from more common parts of the
complex code shared by thousands, if not millions of
others.

"It's yours." He said, just like that.

"That son of a bitch is setting me up, antagonizing
me." Fosnick nearly growled, standing next to the ill
omen on the white ceramic plate with his left hand
resting on his belt just above his Glock Eighteen. He
wanted to empty his magazine into the burger, the
haughty emblem of impunity that it was.

"How…"

"Look at it!" Fosnick roared, though Sheth had
never heard him shout before, and had never even seen
him get riled or lose his cool. "Mushroom swiss and
French fries, he's calling out my French-Swiss heritage!
My mouth, my DNA, he's sending me a death threat!"

"Blake, calm down."

"Don't tell me to calm down! What the hell else
does this guy know, huh? My medical history? Check!
Howabout the retirement community my grandmother
lives in back in Great Neck, or the girlfriend I had last
year in Baltimore?" Fosnick nearly bowed on Sheth,
trying to get him to see the seriousness of the fact that
the man could not only kill an elected official of one of
the country's largest cities and richest economies but
stalk and hunt a man who made his living stalking and
hunting, and was *very* good at it.

"Don't you get it, Shane? This guy's got me dead
to rights! It's not an *if*, it's a *when*; and let me tell you,
I'm not gonna sleep a wink from now till that day
comes, by God, it's gonna eat at me every waking
moment till that bullet or bomb or whatever the hell this
guy's MO is catches up with me, because someone *way*
the hell up the damn food chain gave this guy the secret

to Samson's strength."

And with that, Fosnick left, his breath as tight and fast as it was shallow, his skin paler than usual in the stubbled confines of his blocky face.

For in the business of hunting, there was no worse feeling than to have the very same philosophies of such used against you. It not only made the job *impossible*, but it made *life* impossible. Fosnick's ultimate end would come in a severe lapse of judgment at the hands of schizophrenic tendencies as his mind raced to ascertain questions that had no answer unless the man was caught and caught *yesterday*.

To know the limits of the human psyche and to explore them day in and day out, delving into the detritus of the human brain to discover the motives for illogical patterns of action and ultimately, turn the tables on the target by using the repetition of their own predictive psychology to cheese their own rat trap was what Fosnick knew better than any other.

And the man who'd killed Geffington was saying, without a doubt, that he was better at this horrible game than Fosnick, and was waiting patiently, as the clock spoke to him with each thunderous shifting of its gears and spinning hands, to strike.

THiRTY-TWO

    Threading the thick and twisted trunks and limbs of the Lenkov estate's private forest, Morell kept his eyes peeled for signs of life in the surrounding hills with furtive glances, static slivers of cold sunlight his only illumination in the clinging dimness. He was unable to avoid the nostalgia of Baghdad returning; even the drastic differences of the landscape's colors and smells were powerless against the prickling sensation of devilish eyes squinting through hi-powered sniper scopes, greedy for the kill. His mind had been racing throughout their cautious trek amidst the trees, trying to ascertain *how* the Sebring had been sabotaged and by whom, and Morell swore to himself as the clearing appeared suddenly, even though it was the place they'd been trying to get to all along. It was a spacious green of nearly three football fields in length, and its mid-section was cut by a marshy splat of reeds and lily pads.

    The temptation of the unfiltered blue sky above and what cell-phone coverage it suggested bit Morell in the back of the neck like a wayward mosquito. Half a mile away, it'd been the only logical choice, and now, it seemed so foolish with the prospect of either the man who'd killed Geffington or his cohorts, if he even *had* or *needed* any, ready to rain down molten lead upon his unprotected body, and the supremely obvious fact that the Lenkov's private security guards had been so present and pleasant upon their arrival and all but vanished upon their departure loomed ominously in Morell's sharp mind.

"Give me your phone." He said to Lucy, who complied quickly. "I'm going to call Fosnick and he'll send a squad car. If someone *is* after us and starts shooting, just pull back into the woods, keep your head down, and keep your eyes open. If I get hit, don't worry about me. Whatever you do, stay back. Got it?"

Her complexion was grave at the thought of paramilitary action and more realistically, of Morell getting shot in the nearly soundless remoteness of the Lenkov's property, and it occurred to Lucy that she hadn't heard a single airplane since leaving her home in Eavesdale even though the estate was three miles from the airport. Sheth must've upped the Threat Level considering the Marina fire and was probably flooding the airport with National Guardsmen to lock it down in anticipation of another attack-no incoming, no outgoing flights.

In retrospect, no one had it easy, not Sheth, not all the tireless men and women under him, not the mothers and fathers that had to wonder if their children were going to be safe at school or not; nobody. Lucy inhaled sharply through flared nostrils to prepare herself for violence and was grateful Morell didn't give her the time to let her emotions for him take over.

By the time Morell reached the center of the field, completely exposed, he realized he'd been paranoid, and rightly so, given the traumatic sabotage that equated his second near-death car accident in as many days, and the density of the woods and the old property that it was had been to blame for the loss in coverage, no jamming equipment necessary.

Unless, of course, there *was* someone jamming

them and *wanted* him to make the call, only needing the few seconds Morell would have to be still enough to do so to take a shot.

Regardless, Morell laid down on his belly in the stringy arms of the reeds and the chilly dew-glazed bog grass, dialing up Fosnick.

The reception was scratchy and muted, but perfectly legible, even with Fosnick's naturally controlled and soft-spoken diction.

"Go." He said.

"We need an emergency pickup off of SR Six-Seventy-Nine, mile marker twenty-two, ASAP."

Fosnick was caught off-guard for the briefest of moments before snapping into action as Morell knew he would, and their conversation immediately clipped itself with a military flair for brevity's sake.

"Roger…is your GPS on?"

"Yeah."

"Okay. Give me a sec…"

Morell held on and soaked in the eerie stillness of the clearing. With his chin on the grass he could pick up the faintest movement of puddly bog water and the nearly indiscernible frequency of the earth itself, the low hum of mass and energy beyond human comprehension, spreading beneath him as it rolled its way up to the shouldering hills on either side.

"Black and white en-route. ETA seven to ten." Fosnick said. Then, "What happened?"

"Sabotage. Brakes. Car's toast. Possible tangos at my nine and three o'clock."

"Confirmed?"

"No."

"You guys okay?"

"Not a scratch." Then the bloody re-opening above Lucy's left eye came to Morell's mind. "Well…"

"Sit tight." Fosnick said, ending the call and all

but throwing his phone across the grand lobby of the Continental Plaza for anger's sake.

Whoever was responsible, they were making a fool of him and the Manhunter stood as a statue in the unlit vacancy of the richly decorated lobby, wondering how much he would have to lie, cheat, steal, and gamble *just to break even.*

No...Fosnick negated, thoughts colliding with each other in his head, as if the white-hot heat searing his brain on their behalf would split open his skull.

I can't. It's too dangerous. Too risky.

Too risky? So just how many more have to die? You signed an oath, now uphold it! If you sacrifice yourself and the threat dies with you then you've won the battle, but the war on terror will never end. You know that. It gets worse and worse every day, all you ever do is bat clean up. Why don't you go on the offense for a change? Take out the terrorists before they can leave their mark in history. You'll just be another statistic in the great database but damn it Blake, you'll be listed under the wins, not the losses.

Face it, you're going to die sometime anyway, do you want it to be as a crippled old man, losing your eagle-eyes or do you want to look death in the eyes one last time and set the chess board for another duel.

Fosnick slid his thumb across the screen of his phone, the ripples of clenched teeth bulging his cheeks with a reptilian rhythm.

Fortune favored the brave, the bold, and the well-connected, and while Fosnick didn't consider himself any of those, he certainly wasn't going to stand by and watch Crescent burn in effigy because he didn't give all there was for a man in his position to give.

The temperature downtown had risen but a few negligible degrees by the time Special Agent Blake

Fosnick met Morell and Radzewicz at the National
Guard checkpoint on the North end of Second Avenue.

"I thought you'd want to talk about it at your
place." He said, as Morell stepped from the police car,
and Fosnick noticed the suit the former US Army
Sergeant had made look relatively dapper at the
beginning of the day was now soiled with green
smudges and dark stains.

Fosnick also spotted the fresh bandage above
Lucy's left eye.

"You hanging in there?"

She nodded, her face unfeeling in the harsh light
of winter.

She's tough, that one... Fosnick thought,
remembering how life-threatening and life-ending
circumstances tended to separate cops into two
categories *fazed* and *unfazed*, with Lucy looking like a
member of the latter, even though as the trio silently
eyed the cleanup and entered Morell's hip five-story
cottage building, Lucy was still getting over the
sabotage and Fosnick would have to discern as much
from other indicators since he was completely unaware
of her facial paralysis.

"You guys hungry?" He asked, once in the
elevator and on the steady rise to Morell's third floor
apartment. Morell and Lucy both nodded, and Fosnick
reached for his phone, dialing a number that he'd seen a
few blocks back from memory. "Curry In A Hurry okay
with you guys?" After another round of nods, Fosnick
turned to the door and dipped his head, waiting for the
dial tone, his blocky face blank in the reflection of the
brushed bronze elevator.

Morell's apartment consisted of a large white-
walled room overlooking Second Avenue with a blonde
pine floor and a jagged bookshelf staircase to the

immediate right of the entrance, leading up to a very low twin bed, isolated in the frosted glass-hidden space on a plush white rug and covered with a smoky gray duvet. A circular white table connected conversation between a blue paisley loveseat and a brown leather beanbag and four orange bar stools lined a curved bar in the kitchen area to the left. Lucy's eye immediately went to the modern art triptych above a slim gas fireplace, not much different from the giant piece that hung in Callie's private office retreat.

"I knew it." Fosnick said, choosing the loveseat so that he could read the spines of Morell's books in between bits of conversation.

"Knew what?" He said, grabbing mugs of water for each of them and bringing a filtered pitcher to the circular coffee table.

"You don't believe in TV."

"Don't have the time to."

Lucy hadn't taken a seat yet and Morell noticed her reticence.

"Bathroom's upstairs there." He motioned, wincing as he massaged his ribs.

Fosnick slowly drained the mug of water, sipping at it as if it stung his throat throughout the course of Morell's report on the accident.

"It could've been a remote detonation, a small charge on the brake line." He surmised, setting the empty mug in front of him and crossing his leg European style. "But it's the style that pisses me off. We can't charge anyone without thousands of man hours and thousands more taxpayer dollars of forensic investigation. If I could I'd move mountains to get a tap on the estate's communications but there's no way in hell that's within my reach, even with CRT status."

"It could've even been last night at the Marina." Morell offered. "It could've also been set with some kind of tachometer to break at a certain speed…and if that's the case, then that dump truck we had to pass was no natural occurrence."

Fosnick stared at one of the paintings and was about to say something when Lucy returned and sat next to him. The cut above her eye had been cleaned and was well on its way to leaving a faint, nearly unnoticeable scar.

"Tell me what you found." He asked her, instead.

"Four custom Rolexes of note, three men's, one ladies'."

Fosnick retrieved his notepad and pen and scratched his chin quickly before flipping to a new page.

"Go."

"The first one was gold with a dark blue face and had a red lion on the left of the face and a gray gryphon on the right, and three gold stars above them both."

"Right…"

"Second was kind of a stainless steel with Polish flag face, you know, red and white, only the bottom half of the face was black like a ship, and the Polish flag looked like a sail and was more on the right side."

Morell left to answer a knock on the door and Lucy continued.

"Third was black and had a coat of arms kind of thing with three blue lions in a shield and a lady with silver hair and a gold crown wearing a red dress above them."

"And those were all men's watches?" Fosnick asked, the smell of curry preceding the swishing of plastic bags as Morell busied himself in the kitchen with the quick distribution of food onto civilized plates.

"Yes. All were in cases, set aside from the others, but I'm sure the rest of them had significance too, because they all contained varying degrees of medieval icons, you know, like dragons and castles and stuff."

"What about the ladies' watch?"

"It was white, the whole thing and everything on it. I think it was a ceramic band, anyway, everything on it was white, and it had an owl perched in a tree."

"And why'd you pick this one out over the other medieval ones?"

"Because it was the only one like it."

"The only ladies'?"

"Yes, and the only white watch."

"I see." Fosnick carefully set his notepad on the arm of the loveseat as Morell brought their food. Fosnick had chosen a creamy Chicken Korma for Morell and spinach-laden Lamb Saag for Lucy.

He was sure his predictions were accurate as they tucked in like veterans and he followed suite with his own Lamb Vindaloo.

"Okay expert, let's hear it." He said, blowing on a steaming forkful to cool it.

"First, that watch belongs to Alexis. It has to."

"Why?"

"As I was about to tell Lucy before we crashed, Alexis isn't Teutonic or Russian or Polish or German or anything even *remotely* related to the Order. I bet *Alexis* isn't even her real name or her family name, because *Maksmillia* is a patronymic possessive, insinuating that she belongs to her father when in fact I'd bet my Commendation Medal she's the one that had him killed. She's Lithuanian, and everything she's proud of and uses to represent herself is *anti*-Order, so distinctly so that it'd be like a pastor's kid drawing pentagrams in Sunday school."

Morell took a bite and continued.

"The Lithuanians were the area's last pagans and adhered to a sort of hybrid nature worship and pantheistic mythology that bears resemblance to ancient

Norse traditions, the latter being the reason why I know any of this to begin with." Morell stood and walked a few paces for a book and returned.

"Their estate is in the middle of the forest, much like a temple or sanctuary to one of the Lithuanian gods. The giant *Tree of the World* sculpture, dominating the not so insignificantly round shape of the three-storied rotunda only seals it. The *Tree* is itself is a three-tiered symbol, and each one of these points were reflected on the corresponding floors. The leaves and branches stretch up to heaven and connect the celestial realm of the gods with the realm of men, the earth, or the trunk, and the roots stretch down to the underworld and the place of the dead. Case in point, living quarters are on the second floor and all of Alexis' Lithuanian-themed art is on the third. Also, the ground floor is covered with the ancient *Tree* weave pattern indicative of the earliest period of craftsmanship via verbal heritage. I don't think it's original but only someone with knowledge of the ancient art could've replicated it, it's all hand knotted. I checked."

Morell splayed an old encyclopedia for them both and placed it between their mugs, refilling Fosnick's with filtered water.

The picture on the page was an artistic rendering of exactly what Morell had explained, both a technical drawing of the tree's spiritual conceptualization and the gold and red weave of the rug, which looked more like fuzzy snowflakes.

"Alexis was also keen to show off her beautiful horses, and they were gorgeous, and if you know the Lithuanian creation mythos, sparks from the thundering hooves of Perkunas' horse, Perkunas being their version of Thor, sent lightning to earth and so on."

Morell took the book back and flipped a few more pages.

"The worst is yet to come, and is about to shift a serious spotlight on the one more than likely responsible for the Order killings and future Order killings, not to mention God knows what else."

Morell waited to speak till a disturbing image had run its course through Lucy and Fosnick's minds and Lucy pushed her food away and curled up in the corner of the couch with the mug in her hands as a result.

"I noticed Alexis was wearing a necklace and it was hidden for a reason, so I faked passing out and managed to get just a glimpse of it as she bent over me, trying to help me up, and she stuffed it back down her shirt as if her life depended on it. It was an amulet of an owl, and it looked like an old coin, *extremely* aged, probably original to the medieval period of this spirit's zealous followers."

"Giltine?" Fosnick frowned, finishing his rice.

"Gil-tee-*nay*." Morell corrected and Lucy was tired of looking at the picture and turned her attention to the window and the cold diorama of Second Avenue, which instead, bore witness to the aftereffects of what the grotesque image of a witchly woman with a snake-like tongue drooping from her mouth was supposed to control.

"Goddess of death, huh?" Lucy said.

"Yeah, the owl is her animism…but not so much a deity but rather a spirit, kind of like their grim reaper." Morell nodded.

"That's twisted." Fosnick admitted, knowing full well what qualified for such.

Morell continued.

"She always wears white and supposedly has a poisoned tongue that she can use to choke her victims or even stab them…she subverts that whole underfed scarecrow motif with the thought that she's not so much a skeletal apparition *sent* from the underworld to bring souls back, but rather, a physical embodiment of death, appearing to be beautiful and desirable to the naked eye, and selecting victims for the grave of nothing but her own sadistic volition and pleasure..."

Lucy shivered.

THiRTY-THREE

Fosnick received a call from DiMocco and slid his thumb across the screen to hang up on the Junior Special Agent before even hearing what he had to say.

"Was she wearing white when you saw her?" He asked.

"No, but that's what I was getting at. The watches have to represent time, and whatever obsession the Order has with it, as if they're waiting for something, and there'll be a time when she puts that watch on but I'll be damned if I know anything more than that…although, I will venture as far as to guarantee that all of the other men's watches, the ones with the dragons and what have you, represent smaller subsections of the Order's hierarchy and the levels of authority they represent, districts and what have you."

"Expert opinion?"

"Yeah. The Third Reich used the Order's structure as a template. It's one of those simple but still complicated things, so I won't explain it, but I'm pretty sure I can give you the other three men's watches. In fact, I'm positive."

"I thought you…"

"No, it just came to me." Morell left the beanbag for another book. "I was just…ruminating."

"You should've seen him at Lenkov's apartment." Lucy said, with pride. "It's great to watch someone who's good at what they do, regardless of what it is."

Fosnick gave a morbid thought to her statement, seeing as his job involved inhuman amounts of thinking, the byproduct of which being a complete lack of girlfriends yet not for a lack of trying.

If only he could find one like Lucy who shared the sentiment.

In fact, the only girl that really respected what he did and hung on his every word was Casey Sullivan, but then, she felt confident enough to disagree with him as well, and Fosnick believed if two people didn't learn how to properly disagree about something then they had no hope of a relationship.

"Okay, here you go." Morell offered the images of another old book.

Fosnick peered over his food to see the crests.

"Estonia, Latvia, and the Hanseatic League?"

"Yeah. The Hanseatic League was like the day's Amazon dotcom. They were their own sovereign sort of economic superpower, kind of like an economic version of the Order, except their range was ten times as broad; from Arhus to Minsk, Oslo to Gdansk. They ruled the seas, they funded the largest ship ever built at the time and their warehouses of choice goods were guarded by private soldiers, so…"

Fosnick dabbed his mouth with a napkin, wondering how Crescent fit into the grand scheme of things and how many *followers* Alexis had working for her.

What further destruction was planned for the city of Crescent? And why?

Crescent was an economic superpower, a haven for Fortune Five-hundreds and private enterprise Kings and Queens.

"If that doesn't fit with a pack of billionaires, I don't know what does." Lucy said. "But the edges of the puzzle are only exemplifying the missing pieces in the middle."

"We need more information." Morell said, sitting back down on his beanbag.

Lucy saw Morell's food was nearly cold from the historic dissertations and sat up in her corner of the paisley blue couch.

"Alexis…or whatever her name is is having a fundraiser tonight and I managed to get myself invited somehow. Whatever information we need I'm sure I can get it."

Morell's revelation of the historical ties rippled in Fosnick's face, considering more information could be divined from within the pale walls of the self-perceived death goddess' palace, though he knew the danger, especially after the sabotage of her Sebring.

They were closing in on the truth and those responsible for an endgame yet to be realized were closing in on *them* for doing so.

"Really?"

"Yeah. Just another pianist succumbing to the pull of an empty bench and a handwritten piece of Rachmaninoff. They want me to play piano for some shindig but I'm sure I can slip away for a bit of recon when the canapés and champers come out."

"Wow, well…you'll have to go."

"It's not safe." Morell said.

"You're damn right it's not." Fosnick agreed, standing. "But the guy who killed Geffington called *me* out with my *own* DNA on a burger he was supposed to have eaten over at the Continental Plaza, replicating my dental pattern and everything, just before he teleported between security cameras like the bastard son of Harry Houdini…" Fosnick's blocky face was fatalistic and his tone was barely audible. "So, I'm going to have to go back to D.C. and run things from there. *None* of us are safe now. So we have to do everything we can, chips to the middle. It's just us, anyway."

Morell frowned and filled his mouth with food.

"I'll run it." He said after swallowing, a simple plan of attack beginning to take shape in his brain.

"I was hoping you'd say that. What do you have in mind?"

"Nothing fancy, just more information gathering; see who's at this *fundraiser* and what it's for. I'll get the goods from Callie."

Fosnick nodded, taking twenty-two dollars from his wallet and laying it on the table to pay for the lunch.

"Typical BSP?"

"I don't know if the one they taught me in Homeland is typical…"

"Right…just, whatever you do, *don't* widen the loop."

"Are you kidding?" Morell smiled. "She's trying to set me up with her daughter. All I have to do is ask nicely."

Fosnick shook his head at Morell's cavalier streak, seeing that the man's reputation didn't *exactly* match up with his service record and the fact that he even *had* a reputation as a skirt-chasing hot dog meant that he'd ticked off a few very important people along the way but those very same people hadn't been important enough to do anything about it, save the spreading of rumors about his personal life and his appetites.

Lucy, however had the benefit of only his military service records and the Police reports of his actions during the Crisis to formulate her opinion, not to mention his conduct thus far. If Fosnick was to let her in on the interdepartmental water cooler talk about him, as FBI and Homeland weren't exactly friends, buddies, or pals, Lucy would rightly disagree.

But Fosnick assumed she was biased toward Morell, even though he didn't have much to go on to believe as much. After all, she *had* been the only one to show up in his time of need back in the Precinct, and whether that was on a personal or professional front remained to be quantified in Fosnick's abacus of a mind. Did she know how he'd bent and broken the rules to destroy RepMax?

Morell moved to lock the door once Fosnick had left for the elevator and darted up towards his bathroom. Lucy threw away the trash and returned to the books as he showered.

When he returned to his loft, perfectly shaven, he spotted Lucy staring at the paintings above the fireplace, the open books splayed before her.

"Find anything else?" He called out and she began folding up the books, trying to stick them back in order and caught a peek of him up in his loft. He was wearing only his black suit trousers and the fresh scent of shampoo still hung in the air, wafting through the half-open bathroom door.

He walked to his thin and humorlessly professional closet for the appropriate attire and could feel Lucy's eyes on his lower back through one of the cracks in the bookshelves.

"I thought only girls got tattoos there."

Morell allowed a chuckle. The phrase *Non nobis solum nati sumus* was written on a banner stretching the span of a cross about the size of a middle finger at the base of his spine.

"Can you read it?"

"Only lawyers and Popes read Latin."

Morell chuckled again and threw on a military-issue white t-shirt before reaching down to a rip stop duffel bag on the floor for a thin bullet proof vest. It would only stop Nine millimeter-caliber rounds and smaller, but it was comfortable, ergonomic, and didn't change his physical silhouette in the slightest.

"It means *we are not born for ourselves alone*...I got it with a buddy of mine when we both got deployment orders for our second combat tour." Morell dropped his focus to a pair of leather slip-ons with a rugged tread. "He didn't make it out of that one. RPG from a rooftop took out our Stryker vehicle and last thing I remember he was pulling me out. The Doc told me I was scrubbing his blood off of myself with a sponge for a week afterward but I don't remember that. I just remember him pulling me out. I had to read about the second RPG in the after-action report, but the whole thing's like fiction to me after that last image of his face, you know..."

Lucy was touched that he'd finally, in the comfort of his own home and his own secluded bedroom space, spoken to her about his experience in Iraq and she walked up the stairs, still keeping her distance. She could only hope, for his own health, there would be so many more stories like it in evenings to come and she watched him dress himself in the way an athlete would for a game, or a knight would prepare for battle, and she knew he was a knight that needed no squire, but rather, a princess, to hold him and comfort him and facilitate the release of battles past and the many traumas they'd caused.

It had occurred to her before that she wasn't the nurturing kind, and she crossed her arms and stared at the two neckties he'd selected and set on the duvet, falling back to business.

"What am I going to have to do?" She asked.

"Just play the part." Morell smiled, buttoning up his shirt as reached forward to pick his tie. "I'll be in your ear the whole time and I'll find you some sort of costume jewelry piece that we'll use to hide a real-time camera, unless, of course, you'd rather wear glasses."

"I don't like glasses." Lucy admitted, holding up two and deciding that Morell's crisp black suit and dark blue shirt needed a silver and sky blue patterned tie to give it a businessman's flair, just in case he had to rush in to the fundraiser to help her.

A thought crossed Morell's mind.

"What?"

"Glasses." He said. "I've got to talk to Kelly."

"Phone?" Lucy motioned her head to the cordless on the nightstand.

"No. I've got to go see her before we go…I was going to buy her car. She never uses it."

"Oh…" Lucy's eyes hid a smile, full confirmation received that this Kelly Barnett, a sharp young political writer whom he'd wined and dined at the Grand Ballroom and who was no doubt foxy in her own innocent and nerdy way was really his girlfriend and he was just being polite to her about her confession of attraction and desire for dinner. "Good thinking. PC Three must be a zoo. No motor pool cars for us."

Morell frowned as Lucy wrought a perfect four-in-hand knot.

"Funny you should say that, Kelly lives in The Zoo, just above the old theater…hey, why do *you* drive a POV? Gold isn't Department issue, is it?"

"No more than Victoria's Secret." Lucy's gray green eyes twinkled and then she shrugged. "I like to have *just a bit* of flair." She held up her thumb and forefinger inches apart in her right hand while her left brushed off Morell's shoulders and lingered on his chest.

"That's good." He smiled. "Our new wheels certainly won't be lacking for that."

Lucy then crossed her arms as was her habit.

"You don't have any size fours from Vera Wang

in that closet, do you?"

"No." Morell smiled, "But I'm sure the boutique downstairs could use some business in this trying time. National Guard posts and bombed out parking garages are generally strong deterrents for roving packs of spoiled North Crescent tweens on the rampage for Prom dresses that make them look like professional weekenders at the Nexus Club."

The previous twinkle in her eyes magnified, and she turned to avoid his scrutiny, finding her glass of water at the table. Just spending time together, away from it all, made their near death experience with the Sebring's loss of brake fluid not much more than a bad *Giltine*-inspired dream. Lucy tapped manicured nails against the water glass as if it were a piano. She'd window-shopped the boutique before, knowing that the day she'd be able to get fancy for her man was the day every acrid trace of playing the role of a prostitute for the likes of another Vice arrest would leave her palate for good. And that day would come, sure enough, but she wasn't going to greedily shoehorn it into the now, as if stuffing herself in a garment that would never fit.

"I'll be quick." She said, rapt in thought.

"You'll have plenty of time to try stuff on while I go get the car. That way neither one of us has to sit around. What's the most comfortable thing to play all that fancy music in, anyway?"

"Batman onesies."

Morell laughed, heading for the front door, holding it open for her to follow.

"Sounds distracting."

Lucy's eyes twinkled again.

"Hey, I'm not the one with a lower back tattoo."

THiRTY-FOUR

Kelly Barnett refilled Jessica Birchall's coffee as she'd all but finished her account of what'd happened to her, sparing no detail as Sierra had instructed. She was weary, but determined not to show it, and made a joke about being able to nap later.

"She said she's sending someone who'll handle it with CPD but she wants to meet us and give us a plan of attack. She said these kinds of things take a great deal of effort and careful planning, or else they get nipped in the bud with legalities and blowback and just get swept under the rug."

The surrealism of the present moment coinciding with dreams of sleepless nights past forced Kelly to take a seat at the kitchenette, and as her eyes drifted over the textbooks she'd buried herself in to *prepare* herself to one day enter Capitol Hill politics. The suspicious circumstances surrounding her opportunity to follow Birchall and Keelan to Washington D.C. only etched in stone the gravity of the work she desired to do but reservations of leaving the cozy treadmill she'd built for herself after the Crisis were weighing her down.

And the moment of decision was knocking on her door.

"Are you going to get that?" Jasmine Keelan asked, her eyes on the big-screen TV, set to Channel

Two News and muted. Hogging up the screen with the
raw footage of a live feed, camera far too close for
comfort, the craggy face of Shane Sheth answered the
questions of a determined pack of reporters to the best
of his ability. Each of their arms were stretched to their
limit to stick their microphones in his face and he, as
hindsight would commend, was wise in conducting as
organic of an interview session as possible instead of
rigidly reading off some podium-armored figurehead
address, written for him by the first available underling
he set eyes on.

"Hmm?" Kelly snapped from her transitionary
haze.

"Are you going to get that?"

"Get what?"

The thumping noise rapped three more times on
the door.

Standing up, she pulled at the black leggings
she'd changed back into and adjusted the oversized
graphic t-shirt that showed an image of a Godzilla-like
ginger cat with laser beams gushing from its eyes and
the silhouettes of tiny people running away from its
wrath.

Standing on her tiptoes to see though the
peephole, Kelly opened the door wide for Henry
Morell.

"Hank!"

Morell received her tight embrace as she nearly
knocked him over and she stepped back into her place
quickly, pushing her glasses up her nose, as the floor
outside was cold on her bare feet.

"Gosh, Hank, come inside."

He did so with muted humility, kindly thanking
Keelan for the return of his phone after obligatory
hellos. He also took it that Kelly'd only chewed him out
and hung up on him on their last conversation because

she cared so much for him and was worried about his health and safety with death and destruction flying around and his penchant for getting sucked right in the middle of it.

Birchall gave him a quick rundown of events, assuming he'd be able to do something about it after seeing the badge on his hip. What she didn't catch was the ripple of shock that ran through Morell's face at the mention of the military operation that was supposed to have contained war crimes, designated *Wolf Stone*.

"Why are you wearing that?" Kelly asked, knowing that Morell had a history with *Wolf Stone* as checkered as the tie around his neck.

"I'm on provisional CRT status with CPD," He told her "And it's a long story that I don't have time to tell right now, because I just came to see if you're doing okay and wanted to let you know that I need your car ASAP."

"Hold on." Kelly's patted his chest and eyed him up and down, knowing that he'd been assigned by someone in authority, whether FBI or Homeland, and bore no signs of a private citizen acting on behalf of a private security company. The air he'd carried during their work on the RepMax case, relentless inhumanity on behalf of the truth, had returned, and the man she'd had dinner with last night was all but stuffed away in the bottom of that thin little closet in his sleeping quarters where that mysterious black rip stop bag slept, zipped open, waiting for him to exchange identities.

Kelly left for her own bedroom and returned with keys clinking in her hand and a pair of slippers on her feet, motioning to continue the conversation outside.

Morell waved silently and waited till Kelly shut the door.

"I'm finally gonna do it." She said. "I'm going to Washington."

"Good for you." Morell smiled but the gesture was laced with concern. "Did you get a job? Or…?"

"Yes and no." Kelly toyed with the keys, thinking of how her late boyfriend would flip them around his thumb and get distracted by whatever rant he was riding the rails of and the keys would fly away from his grip and end his rant.

"Is this about that CIA informant?"

"Yes. Birchall's been in contact with Sierra."

"Thank God." Morell sighed. She was the best of the best and was someone whom Morell held in the highest regard. "Whatever she says, you make sure you follow to the letter."

"Yes Sir." The side of Kelly's mouth twisted in a smile and she held out the keys with a coy satisfaction.

"And I can wire you the money tomorrow."

"No." Kelly shook her head. "It's like your papers back home when you were in Iraq. You waited and waited for them and when they actually came, you realized what you'd dreamed about was finally upon you, but you were so stuck in what you were doing and had gotten so used to it that you were afraid to leave it."

Morell only nodded. He'd confided in her as much. Without his transition into Homeland Security, Morell believed he would've drifted into obscurity, as so many returning veterans re-entered the land of their birth like untethered balloons.

"I'm cutting all ties with this place and never coming back." She said. "That means you can have it."

Morell's eyebrows leapt in surprise but he understood the sentiment. There was a time when the value of worldly possessions were completely negated by the greatest spiritual force a human soul could receive and found itself longing for in the hollow solace of sleeplessness.

Change.

"I don't know what to say."

Kelly rubbed her arms to warm them.

"I'm gonna jump out of the plane, Hank." She said. "No matter what the ground beneath me looks like. I'm tired of being afraid of everything and sitting in my room, thinking I've got to formulate some ten year strategy to everything in my life."

Kelly's intelligent brown eyes noted the clean shave of his chin and the perfect four-in-hand knot. He wasn't wearing the gray Burberry suit she liked so much, but rather, one of his black over blue blend-into-the-background standards, and she knew he was preparing for war.

"I'm happiest when I'm in the moment. Like last night...*before* it hit the fan. Thank you for showing me that."

"You're welcome, Kelly."

The journalist's eyebrows pinched in the middle, as if entertaining a ridiculous idea.

"You don't mind if I? What the hell..."

Kelly stood on her tiptoes and kissed Morell on the lips with equal amounts exuberant gratitude and romantic curiosity, whetting her lips with a cheeky grin as she returned to her shorter height.

"I always wondered what that would be like." She said.

"I can't say I didn't wonder myself." Morell admitted.

"It doesn't have to be goodbye." Kelly removed her vanity glasses and slipped them in the kerchief pocket of his black suit, patting them. "You're a good man and a good friend. I'm gonna miss our Chinese food dinners together but I have a feeling I'll be busier than I've ever been in my life. If you're ever in town, though..."

"I'll take you up on that." Morell said. "And one

more thing," He added before he left, with a bit of reticence. "*Wolf Stone…*"

"When we're ready to blow the lid on *Wolf Stone* you'll be the first to know, but the informant supposedly had possession of communication transcripts and photocopies of satellite photos of the operation and they *clearly* cut a stark contrast to redacted after-action reports and create some pretty heavy discrepancies with the version of events the President received. The guy was apparently just some low-level normal joe like you, brought into the fold at the last second and he's been compiling information about it ever since. If we do it right, the State Department will be able to take over, some power tigers over there will get to take full credit, and no one'll ever know who was responsible for blowing the whistle because we'll have shined the light before anyone can snuff it out and say what happened officially never happened."

"I really wish I could help you more. I'd be right with you if it weren't for the new wave of terrorism here in Crescent. I guess I'll just wait to be interviewed. I don't know how this whole thing works, but I do know that it's rare to get a story out without it being smothered to death or watered down so badly it doesn't mean anything anymore." Morell held her shoulders at arm's length. "You promise me you're gonna be careful. That informant was CIA and God knows they're a rough crowd."

"I'd be shocked if you said anything less…but, I surprised myself during the Crisis, and afterward, helping you with RepMax like your own personal secretary…I guess I just have to *do* things and not think about them. If I give myself too much time I'll talk myself out of anything. I guess writing about stuff was always safe, to me, but it's a lot of work to track people down and get them to talk and to make sure your editor isn't playing politics when you finally get to print the story that you feel's taken half the year, twenty-four-seven, to write. I'm so glad to be going about it a new way. It'll be a challenge."

"And you'll knock it out of the park." Morell smiled but his face quickly soured as his eyes drifted toward the glass door with the colorful playbill adverts stuck to it. "Kelly, there'll be a day when I get called to the carpet about having taken my anger surrounding the injustices of *Wolf Stone* out on RepMax, who were bad men nonetheless but technically still did nothing wrong. I might go to prison, I might not, but in the end, *everything* comes out, and I'm just trying to clean the world up as much as possible before the checks and balances track me down and figure out that I falsified evidence against RepMax."

"They were bloodthirsty soldiers for hire walking the streets of America's biggest cities with concealed weapons like gangsters, guarding investment bankers like they were military commanders." Kelly nearly argued, as if that made it okay. Especially with being muscled to keep his mouth shut about *Wolf Stone*.

"It was still wrong. I hope it doesn't sully the revelation of *Wolf Stone* at all…" Then Morell shrugged as not to think too much about the unwritten future. "Just follow your heart and keep your head down but be ready for the fallout of serving the truth. It has a way of making some people mad as hell."

Morell nodded with finality and Kelly reciprocated, hugging Morell quickly before he skipped down the stairs.

"Take care, Hank."

He waved and she understood that he was a snowball heading for the precipice, and his only consolation in the incarceration awaiting him would be

the fact that he did good work in protecting the liberties
of the American people, using whatever tool was at his
disposal, often at the risk of his own life, even if he had
bent or broken the rules.

Because the young corporal who'd been hastily
assigned as a translator to the time-sensitive CIA
operation named *Wolf Stone* had learned that if he kept
his mouth shut when bad men did bad things of their
own perverted justifications, his reward was a speedy
promotion, and if he, in turn, wanted to be a good man
in a bad world, he had to be ready for the consequences,
whether they be a bullet in the back of the head while
he slept or a grand jury indictment with the ravenous
lips and prying eyes of the many news cameras that
accompanied such a liberally-seasoned spectacle.

At any rate, he couldn't let the thought of what
was to come stop him from living in the moment, and
for that, Kelly was grateful.

She may've given him a classic muscle car but
he'd given her a new lease on life.

THiRTY-FiVE

Homicide Detective First Grade Steve Romero stifled a yawn with the clicking of a ballpoint pen as he received three sets of stapled papers for signature and began to scribble his name against the flatness of the wall just outside the door of room Three-Zero-Two of the Fifteenth Street Inn.

"We got room downtown?" He asked the forensic scientist that had zipped up the body of the man identified as David Browning; cause of death, asphyxia by inhalation of fluid.

"No." The forensic scientist said as a bent over man approached them from the stairs down the hall, a County coroner by the looks of him, and an aged one at that. "This old dude from County's taking him. Geffington's autopsy is all CRT-FBI territory and whoever's in charge of it kicked us out."

"Meh." Romero said as the bent-over man came in focus with waddling steps, the County credentials around his neck seeming to weigh him down even more so than the struggle of age and the depravity of his line of work.

"Spare me the trouble." He drawled, his voice dripping with a Texan's slower pace of life. "Wet or dry drowning?"

"Wet." Romero said, ushering the scientist to leave and settle the paperwork because of the CRT policy's backed-up sense of due process and waved the old Texan into the room, where they'd moved the stiff body of the man identified as David Browning to the floor next to the bed.

"Poor bastard." The Texan shook his head, already rapt in the fullness of his act, knowing full well Detective Steve Romero had no idea the *poor bastard* had been a member of the CIA, and if everything worked out, never would. "Who was he?"

"David Browning, forty-one years old from Cambridge, Mass. Advertising salesman. We're working on next of kin and all that."

Romero knelt and busied himself with the pulling back of the zipper and revealing the corpse with intent and practiced focus, while the Texan, whose name was Mark Loomis, though his laminated credentials stated otherwise, straightened, if just a bit, and searched the room with a pair of wise blue eyes. The disguise, one of his favorites, consisted of a gray-blond but neatly-trimmed Amish beard and nose and eyebrow adjustments of his favorite temporary cosmetic enhancements, flesh-like silicon nobs and flaps called *skinplants*, upon which makeup was applied to blend the augmented facial topography with the rest of the face for a natural and human disguise.

Mark Loomis was a skilled tradesman, adept at changing himself to fit the moment, and often inhabited his characters so deeply that it was hard for him to come out of them.

The old Texan was an easy sort of everyman he found himself going back to like a favorite movie.

"Positive it wasn't secondary?" His drawl, relatively unchanged from his natural voice, probed the Detective to remove a pair of latex gloves from his pocket and offer them for Loomis' further inspection.

"Positive."

"How so?"

"No other explanation for the moment."

"What's your take then?" Loomis rambled on, his eyes quickly scanning across the room.

The CIA whistleblower named Berenguer had been assassinated by those wanting to keep *Wolf Stone* a secret, but Loomis, a master operator of CIA Extemp, which meant *without planning*, knew the killers had been unable to locate a simple piece of paper containing the location of the safe in which was stored the damnable evidence of the truth. They hadn't the time to torture him or take him to a black site, due to his contact with Jessica Birchall, and the fact that if they killed Birchall or involved her in any way they would be overstepping their secretive bounds. Loomis had a man tailing the killers and, for the moment, they appeared to be as in the dark as he was about the location of the simple slip of paper Berenguer had been safeguarding, and thusly, the location of the safe containing all of his damnable evidence.

"No sign of a struggle. We'll have to wait for the autopsy to see what was in his system, but…I wouldn't be surprised if it was an alcoholic suicide with the events of the day, not being able to get back home and all. He could've gone to vomit and took on water instead. I've seen it happen before. Eighty percent of drowning victims are male."

Loomis considered the possibilities.

Knowing the killers, they'd used a ninety-percent lethal injection known as STRIC-R, and unless one was looking for it, they'd never find it in Berenguer's blood.

Detective Romero stood up, showing his own age by bracing his knees. His wooly suit looked itchy to Loomis, and Romero had the kind of stiff, black hair that never changed as if it were a baseball cap.

"I'll be right back."

Loomis nodded and waited till the Detective was out of the room before turning Berenguer's head to the left and shining a penlight where mother always said to wash.

Sure enough, the tiniest pinprick hole sat in the soft skin behind the ear just above the jaw where the sensitive lymphatic system could be skewered for a surgical strike.

Five to ten minutes of unconscious submersion would render no marks, leaving the initial image of a peaceful suicidal passing hard to avoid.

Mark Loomis studied the bathroom.

Splashes of water on the floor appeared consistent with the twitches of a final life spasm but Loomis would bet the wad of cash in the back pocket of his ill-fitting costume-appropriate black slacks that one of the killers held Berenguer down with his foot while counting the time on his watch as the other carefully searched the room, making sure to return everything the way it was.

Loomis left abruptly, long before Romero had returned from whatever need had pulled him from his misinformed explanation of events, and was quick to place a call once striding the building's back alley, reaching his rental Lincoln sedan as the dial tone was still humming in his ear.

The killers were waiting.

But if they were waiting for Birchall to realize the piece of paper had been passed on to her and tail her for the purpose of stealing the information, Loomis couldn't be sure.

However, the gnawing sense in his gut, throwing lead into the accelerator and fluidity into the hand holding the steering wheel, was telling him the killers, who had dozens of CIA-sanction black ops under their belt, were only biding their time to initiate forceful contact, having been cleared by someone *far* up the food chain to do so in the first place.

The Lynx cast a sideways glance down the highway, where, cut in and amongst the jagged green and nearly black shapes of pine trees stacked like medieval soldiers marching to battle, the dirt road to the staging area awaited his arrival. Timing, as always, was both his enemy and his friend, and he was positive that his choice of walking to his destination rather than stealing a car and having to sit around and wait was a good one.

Christmas Island was appropriately named for the *other* side of the tree-covered lump of rock and the yearly tourist attraction that gave children and their childishly-minded parents a gaudy taste of the North Pole, leaving the rest of the island a no-man's land of long-retired hermits and their forest-secluded catchall properties.

One such pine-caged splat of land, owned by a man that had been dead for nearly a year though no one had noticed, consisted of an old turn of the century granary building and several empty barn-like structures. The hulks of rusted-out diesel busses, tractors, and other restoration projects caught in the permanent futility of good intentions dotted the landscape like the remnants of an old battlefield, and The Lynx easily hopped a chain-link fence boasting a sign that read *First Amendment Rights WILL be exercised on trespassers with extreme prejudice.*

The Lynx laughed silently to himself, perhaps because the blunt message of such a sign had been neutered by the legal speech it'd been written in. The original must've been something along the lines of *Intruders will be shot.*

Jaroslaw, a compact blonde man of twenty-seven

years, his head buzzed to the nubbins, greeted him with
a quick salute and a handshake. A heavy brown three-
quarter length oilcloth jacket covered his tactical black
BDU's so that if there *were* any prying eyes about,
though such was unlikely, they wouldn't immediately
spot the garb of a counterterrorist operator, complete
with level two body armor, an equipment harness, knee
and elbow pads, and black combat boots laced up tight.

"Ready when you are." He said in Lithuanian, to
which The Lynx was glad to finally drop his adopted
Britishness and respond in his native tongue.

"Excellent. We haven't long to wait now. Soon
we'll all be back home where we belong."

After all, the man that British Army and SAS files
knew as Ridley Sorber, an adoptee of displacement by a
liberal British family at the behest of Soviet oppression
in Vilnius, was *not* Ridley Sorber, and certainly was not
British, though it seemed he'd trained his entire life,
waiting for the moment to return home as a conquering
hero, having bided his time with inhuman patience to
one day restore the land of his ancient ancestors to its
rightful sovereignty.

After all, once freed of Soviet oppression,
Lithuania had entered the stilted state of EU servitude,
hoping to carve out a hard-earned niche in a space
where capitalist Russian oligarchs and corporate raiders
still called the shots in former principalities of Soviet
rule with long-stretching tentacles from their armored
palaces in Moscow. Perhaps foresight of such was
behind the collapse of the USSR, as most of Lithuania's
economy had been privatized overnight and the social
reformers that had appeared to have instigated calls for
independence suddenly lost control of the government
with proto-Russian shell companies and the hierarchy
of Russian moneymen stepping in to snatch up the reins
of the pyramid with their newly acquired billions. The

Lynx's hate of Russians was in his blood, dating before the oppressive rule of the Czar's, to a time when horses ran free in the forests and men were allowed to sow grains and raise cattle in peace. It was a shame that the ancient Lithuanian King, Mindaugas, had been assassinated by greedy nobles, and The Lynx drew a dark parallel to the vicious capitalist societies of the modern way, where business, companies, and brand names were more powerful than governments and their castrated leaders; a world where Kings and Queens were all but two-dimensional faces on decks of playing cards.

Jaroslaw caught the door to the granary for his Captain and the squad of men inside smiled at his coming as they prepared and re-checked their equipment around the sleeping frame of a matte-black Sikorsky S-Ninety Two, fueled and ready to be wheeled to the flatness of a nearby slice of turf for takeoff. The helicopter had been EMP hardened and fitted with radar deflection modules to give it the electronic signature of a large bird.

"Your rifle, Sir." Jaroslaw smiled, proudly presenting his Captain with the Heckler and Koch MRA Seven Six Two One, scoped and laser-sighted. "I can't wait to see you in action."

"And I you." He said, staring down the infrared scope and judging the heft of the ten-pound weapon, as he'd be operating the sniper rifle from the open bay door of a moving helicopter.

The Lynx handed the rifle back, received his tactical gear, and stripped to don the stealthy garb, finishing with the neoprene balaclava to complete the fearsome appearance of a modern knight, armed to the teeth and ready to ride into battle on a wraithlike black steed as it surged from the split silhouettes of the treetops with a thunderous *thwop thwop thwop*.

Jaroslaw was staring at the perfect to-scale model of the compound they'd be assaulting under the cover of darkness.

"Is your knife sharp, young man?" The Lynx asked him.

"Yes, Sir." Jaroslaw nodded grimly, knowing full well to what he was referring, and how much blood would stain the floors on the count of their grisly objective.

"What about BZ?" The Lynx asked, thinking about the army of nondescript semi-trucks strategically interspersed throughout parking lots and roadsides surrounding the city of Crescent.

BZ stood for *Balta Žaibus*, meaning *White Lightning* in their language.

"Ready to deploy."

The Lynx took stock of the men and could nearly taste their anticipation as it watered their mouths and coated the nerve endings in their fingertips.

"Good. Then let us take our revenge."

One of the men brought Ridley Sorber a satellite phone and he frowned to take it.

"Yes?"

Sorber listened carefully and laughed as his new orders were given. It was strange, to change the plan so late in its operational development, but he was a man who followed orders and did as he was told. Thus was the mark of a leader of men-the ability to obey those in authority over him.

"Gather round." He said as the call concluded on the other end from the haste in which it was made, and The Lynx turned his attention to the to-scale compound mock up.

"New plans?" Jaroslaw asked, seeing his Captain's face was rapt in a fit of humor and making no attempt at hiding it.

"Most assuredly, young man." The Lynx said, eyeing his team with finality and posing a question to the group. "How's your German?"

"Nicht schlect." Jaroslaw shrugged, more than likely speaking for the group as they were all residents of Europe's largest cities, having lived in the shadows of normalcy most of their lives, training for the day of their revenge with lonely self-motivation.

"Howabout your Russian?"

Jaroslaw frowned as the men gathered around to hear the changes in the plan.

"Just what are we doing, Captain?"

THiRTY-SiX

Blake Fosnick had been given special clearance by CRT Captain Shane Sheth to take a private jet back to Washington D.C. and waited till he was in the air to give Casey Sullivan a call.

"Hold on, Nicky…" She said with a beleaguered moan, as if having to clean up a puppy's untrained mess and Fosnick's keen ear detected the squeaky wheeling of her office chair, a hand me down from higher time-in-grade Junior Agents that hadn't yet shaken their probationary tags as her conversation with a young-sounding male co-worker peppered the receiver.

"Can I help you?"

"Yeah, I was wondering if you wanted to grab dinner together?"

"Well, keep wondering."

"I've got tickets to the Symphony."

"I'm sure you and your grandmother will have a lot of fun."

"Well howabout just a drink after work, then? You can bring a couple of your friends if you want. It doesn't have to be anything serious. You know, just a drink…"

"I don't drink."

Fosnick could picture her leaning on her desk in her classy black and white business suit, holding the sarcastic deadeye of swollen pupils beneath an endless

bank of insultingly dim overhead fluorescents in the
confines of her cubicle.

Fosnick bit his lip as footsteps clip-clopped into
the distance and yet another insecure hopeful fell victim
to the stymying honesty of an unattainable woman not
giving a damn.

"I've got something for you, Casey."

"Oh really?" Her voice perked up. "Like
something from the duty-free or a one-of-a-kind
tchotchke like a…hand-pounded copper salmon wind-
chime or something…Crescent-y."

"Research, Casey, more research."

"Bastard…"

Fosnick smiled as a cascade of unmusical
squeakings preceded the clunky hammering of keys.

"You wanna hear about the vodka first?"

"Sure."

"Zaykon Kerrzacky or however you say it is
Polish for *The Teutonic Order*, or more specifically *The
Order of the Cross* and the castle on the label is
Malbork Castle in Malbork, Poland, about forty miles
from Gdansk. It used to be called Marienburg, back in
the day when the land belonged to the Order, and I
don't want to get off on a history lesson so I'll just take
a left turn after saying it was the seat of the Teutonic
Order during their crusades and wars. Their leader was
called the *Hochmeister* and the castle is just a museum
now. The vodka is *not* produced there. However it *is*
produced in Gdansk by some guys that look like heavy
metal monks and have a really strange website, kind of
like beard and tattoo Portland beer crafters after too
many readings of *Beowulf*, anyway, it's distributed
worldwide by a shell company of HansaVolk GmbH,
based in Estonia, which, strangely is a company of
German origin, but its headquarters are in Tallin, and
it's owned operated by a Russian named…" Casey

paused to squint. "Stanislav Veremecek."

Fosnick's mind was racing at the ramifications. Veremecek was one of the richest men in the world and a very public figure at that. He owned a top-flight English soccer team, multiple modeling agencies, and God knew what else since he'd made his money in all of the former Soviet-satellite states after the fall of the curtain in the not so glamorous privatization of utilities, garbage collection, and the necessities that separated third world countries from first.

And, it would be a failure to omit the fact that HansaVolk owned roughly ten percent of the world's bulk container ships and approximately twelve percent of the world's deep sea drilling platforms.

So Veremecek was a part of the Order. Had he united the Order *with* the Hanseatic League for some sort of economic control? Was he the Hochmeister? Maybe, and such would explain why he was still alive *if* the killings were contracted by an enemy of the Order, as Morell suspected Alexis was. Fosnick made a few quick calculations, knowing that the best way to find out what was going on and who was behind all of it and why remained the most dangerous of options.

Find the killer.

If Stanislav Veremecek *was* on the killer's hit list, then his death would be a tragic and extremely public one, unable to sweep under the rug like Lenkov's suicide and Mogilev's misfortune of the Marina fire, which Sheth had informed Fosnick before his departure was the work of Semtex, though Sheth was going to keep such details to himself. Both Lenkov and Mogilev had made their money in more linear pursuits and their assets were not as spread out as Veremecek's, thus, they didn't assert as much power in the scope of world policy.

"Nicky, you still with me, bud?"

"Yeah," Fosnick rubbed his eyes, knowing he'd sleep like a stone in his seat. "And the black bird on the vodka label is HansaVolk's logo?"

"Yes. It reminds me of the cover of that one *Queen* album." Then Casey muttered a few curse words. "Hold on…Adams, I'm working."

"Just a drink, Sullivan," The young systems analyst nearly whined, "It can be a Diet Coke if you want, I mean, we went through the Academy together and I swore to myself if I didn't have the guts to ask you out I didn't have the guts to work for the Bureau."

An irritated squeak indicated a rise in posture and many caustic remarks flooded Casey's mind. But in the end she only shook her head *no.*

She didn't mention how short Adams was, maybe five foot four with his small feet stuffed in an oversized zip boot.

Adams swore in frustration and left and Casey took to her seat again to hear the sound of Fosnick chuckling to himself.

"You really cut him off at the knees, didn't you?" Fosnick attempted.

"Nicky, please. I can't believe they gave him a gun…anyway, what were you saying?"

Fosnick opened a bottled water as he explained a few of Morell's theories.

"What angle do I take?" Casey asked when Fosnick had concluded. "I mean, it reeks of being pretty time sensitive to me…and Morell sounds like a sharp cookie, but I guess I already knew that, now didn't I?"

Fosnick ignored her because they had disagreed on Morell's handling of RepMax and Casey had begged Fosnick to go to New Mexico to chase down meth cookers instead of wasting his time with one of the good guys.

Though Fosnick knew she was right, he also

knew she was wrong, because she didn't know the whole story, and would soon find out why rules were rules and what happened to those in their line of work that broke the rules.

Deep down, Fosnick was sure Morell knew, too, like a man with a terminal disease, and that he'd made some nonverbal plea that Fosnick couldn't ignore, and Fosnick was glad that Morell, despite his obvious abuses of procedures and the reputation that followed him, was the only man who'd deciphered the ghostly threads connecting the threats responsible for raising hell in Crescent, schemes promising a far greater catastrophe in the near future.

He had said in so many words or less, *just let me serve my country this one last time…*

Whether that threat was again surrounding Crescent or targeting parts unknown in a world so inextricably connected remained to be seen.

"First priority is who's at that fundraiser so we can give Morell and the Lieutenant a heads up and they can filter their recon. Then we'll try to track down all the members of the Order. Has the paperwork come through on the vodka purchases?"

"Not yet."

"Well, that'll give us a good bearing when it comes. I'll catch some sleep on the flight over and we'll go over what you have at dinner."

"Finally." Casey said. "It's about time."

"Well, you've been beating me over the head with it."

"Nicky, they're the best wings in town. They'd cure a health nut like you quicker than…" Casey shrunk in her shoulders as Director Mellinger walked by with two bulky Special Agents.

"I'm a tough nut to crack, Sullivan."

Casey laughed, to which Fosnick smiled because

he loved to hear her initial raspy cough and the
pneumatic *rat tat tat* of unhindered sanguinity that
followed in a building where the courteously plastic
appliqué of sycophantic suits and ties bubbled and
gurgled like a festering swamp.

She was a breath of fresh air.

A *beautiful* breath of fresh air.

And the fact that Fosnick was her quasi-big
brother only helped to intimidate those who, unlike
Adams, though nothing came of his brave attempt,
couldn't work up the moxie to ask her out. People were
afraid of Fosnick and his slow burn, his track record of
capturing every man woman and child he set his mind
to, and Casey had informed him, over such a snapping
rat tat tat laugh, that they called him a vampire behind
his back.

"What about this…assassin guy?" Casey asked,
and Fosnick heard the subtlest hint of a fearful quaver
in her smoky voice, since the laughter had run its
course and her hollow timbre was hushed and personal.

"That's why I'm coming back to D.C." He said.
"To take care of him once and for all."

Casey Sullivan nodded on her end, trusting the
skilled Manhunter to do exactly what he said as he
always had.

But Casey had no idea what ramifications
Fosnick's statement contained and how deeply
possessed FBI Special Agent Blake Fosnick was to
eliminate the man that was so efficient, himself, at
ending the lives of others.

Morell couldn't ignore the strange feelings rising
within him as he ascended the brown glass cylinder of
the Tidebender building in the solitude of the elevator.

Lucy's admission of personal attraction and
sharing with him the secret of a disability that'd colored

her life with the prism of deep rejection while at the same time making her a damn good undercover Vice cop was a big deal for her, but he wasn't about to pass on his own half-formed confession that his brain was warped by some character-altering Syndrome he didn't fully understand and that his stomach was housing the aggrandizing ache of its psychological inadequacies.

Morell swallowed hard as the elevator emptied to Callie's private office, and back in the throes of Callie's subliminally hand-crafted cradle of false peace in a world literally burning and dying around her, he wondered, if he told Callie about Lucy, if she'd have any sound advice.

Not that he wanted to talk about. The lump of nervous energy didn't go away by talking.

Just swallowing harder and moving on.

"Hello." He heard from his right, up in Callie's raised seating area where she could watch businessmen and local residents flit around Victory Park below like ants.

"Hey." Morell said and came to stand at the edge of the seating area but not take a seat. Callie was stretched out on the chaise wearing a funeral-appropriate black skirt and double-breasted suit and her face was compressed in the loss of a whimsical innocence, traded in for a grim sense of reality and he guessed she may've recently shed tears.

"What do *you* want?" She said.

"How do you know I want something?" Morell took a seat across from her.

"Everybody wants something. I just wish they were more honest about it." She turned to him and he felt the scrutiny of a schoolmaster, and perhaps the sensation was such because of the negligence of his mother. "Like you, for instance. You never wanted to work for me."

"No." He said. "I did. I wanted to plan my revenge while earning enough money to carry it out."

Morell's sincerity caught Callie off-guard and she sat up with a spike of concern. Violence was her enemy, the bane of her existence.

"For what?"

"CAP Syndrome may or may not've taken that giant irreversible hit you talked about during a classified operation in Baghdad where a lot of innocent people got killed and the course of a lot of destinies were forever altered as a result. That's a lot of weight to carry around and if you think you know what makes me tick, you might as well hear it straight from me. I dismantled RepMax illegally because I hate the idea of soldiers of fortune and soldiers for hire who have no flag to prosecute them when they exceed their authority and no flag to cover their coffin when they die in conflict running around our largest cities at the behest of multi-billion dollar corporations, and I plan to kill, in the cold blood that he deserves, in a country from which I cannot be extradited, the man who killed all of those innocent people in Baghdad and swept it under the rug and lied to the President about it in order to intensify our foreign policy."

Callie blinked and her eyes drifted down his body to the floor. She looked like she aged overnight, and the stress of the city was to blame.

"What are you saying?"

"I'm saying that before I go to white-collar prison for knowing how to work the system and falsify evidence against a multi-million dollar private security corporation, that I'm going to de-classify a CIA operation that altered the course of the war in Iraq. Sure, more RepMax's will spring up to fill the void as is the case with all supply and demand, but I'll have done my part to rid the world of a cancer while I had the chance."

Rachael Calabrese could only shake her head, the granite of *no return* already cut and placed in Morell's dark eyes with the expert masonry of careful strategic planning, and the hardness of his cleanly-shaven jaw and sharp suit gave startling clarity to the sentiment.

The soldier had snatched the body of a private citizen, and the spirit of purpose burning within him didn't give a damn at the consequences, be it the court of public opinion or physical imprisonment.

"You'll be worse than Snowden," Callie said. "With enemies public *and* private. They'll hunt you down like a white buffalo."

"I don't care." Morell shook his head. "And if it weren't for Special Agent Fosnick being so understanding with the threat we have now I'd already be on my way, hog-tied and helpless."

Callie stood and smoothed her black skirt, shifting positions with her feet as if they were too tired to hold her up anymore. Her voice was distant and her eyes drifted over the small shapes of Victory Park stuck in the transit of the lunch rush.

"I guess this is goodbye, then."

"Why, where are you going?"

"Aimee and I had a long talk last night and she wants to suspend her Ivy League studies and be a part of my humanitarian work, and she wants to go to Egypt."

Morell smiled.

"So she is Egyptian."

Callie walked to the window and disregarded Morell's comments, sucked back inside to the capacious palace of anguish she'd lived in most of her life, trying to do the right thing and feeling forever stuck in the mud for even remotely wanting to do so.

"Aimee's a twenty-year old pro-life virgin who

wants to change the world worse than her mom and dad. If she's not the minority in this day and age, I don't know who is, especially with the fact that she could go to Hollywood with those looks of hers. She told me with tears in her eyes that ninety-one percent of Egyptian women have had genital altering surgery, and she shared with me several horror stories of the barbaric practice of removing the clitoris…like the use of kitchen scissors, pocket knives…pruning shears. I couldn't make a fist hearing the first-hand accounts but reading them empowered her, stoking the bellows, so to speak. She had this light in her face when she told me she wanted to help those women. She also told me that only eighty-one percent of women who are aged fifteen to nineteen have been mutilated, so there's hope for normalcy in the coming generations, but in a culture as old as theirs, I told her it could end up being a life's work that had little to no effect. It still didn't shake her. Her mind was made up. Her dad'll understand, I hope."

"How do you mean?"

"She's basically turning down the cushy two-point-o life of an academic, you know, marrying a Wall Street broker and living in a dollhouse, for the pain of face to face humanitarian work. She doesn't want to be a businesswoman. She doesn't want to be a politician. She doesn't want to be a doctor or a nurse. Just a voice for those that have none, a voice that'll never shut up."

Morell stood next to Callie and spoke in a muted tone.

"You should be very proud."

"Mom, are you…" Aimee said as she entered through the side, past the series of empty desks where Callie performed many of her dizzying formalities with an army of helpers. "Oh, hello Mr. Morell."

"Henry." Morell said and stepped down from the elevated seating area to see she was ready for travel, with a layered outfit of blacks and greys and denim and her uniquely-colored strawberry blonde kinked curls were in a ponytail beneath a perfunctory *Tidebender Intl.* baseball cap. "You look like an employee."

"I am." She smiled. "Volunteer nonprofit."

"She told me." Morell smiled and held out his hand and she shook it. "I'm honored to have met you and I'm sorry if I gave you the wrong impression. I hope everything works out for you and I'm sure if we'd spent more time together you'd come to realize that you're the kind of person I wish there were more of and I'm the kind of person people like you shouldn't hang out with." Morell nodded as their handshake ended. "I think what you're doing is tremendous and if our paths ever cross again I hope you'd be gracious enough to let me buy you dinner. Salam alekum, Aimee."

Aimee's smile was genuine, a heart-warming display of pristine teeth and the light of her pure blue eyes radiated with the gratitude of a deeply received compliment.

"Mom doesn't know but I read your file and I know about your service to this country…"

"You what?" Callie stepped down and rushed to her daughter. "That's classified information."

"Who am I going to tell?" Aimee shrugged, and then tapped her watch and her mother nodded, grabbing an overcoat from a nearby chair. "Maybe Henry can *debrief* me."

Morell laughed and reached for his phone.

"You ladies are trouble, you know that?"

"Speaking of trouble." Callie crossed her arms. "I seem to have spied a blonde woman in a tan trench coat leaning on the hood of a green muscle car across the Park staring up this way, you wouldn't be testing her patience, would you?"

"No need. The government beat me to it." Morell

said and showed Callie his phone, the CEO's eyes quickly ascertaining the reason for the list of items on the screen.

"There'll be some paperwork." Callie said.

"I was hoping for a charitable donation. You know, seeing as I'm kind of a nonprofit volunteer myself."

And though Morell smiled for Aimee's benefit on the count of the levity she brought, Callie saw the steel in his eyes and knew he was doing a job he'd get no credit for, and giving him a couple of thousand dollars worth of personal surveillance equipment would be like a hospital handing out free band aids.

"ASAP, I assume?"

Morell nodded.

"I'll pass you on to Meg, my secretary. We've got a bit of a drive ahead of us since the airport's on lock down but just remember, Mr. Morell…" Callie shook the former Army Sergeant's hand, an ornery twinkle taking residence in her blue eyes above a winding smile. "You have my number."

Morell bowed his head politely knowing full well she held no grudge against him for using her corporation as a pillar to hide behind. Quite the opposite.

He'd come to her to form an alliance of hopeless cases and burning candlewicks, the resonance of which being that no matter what the consequences, evil could not be allowed to triumph, and the *good men* of the timeless maxim sometimes had to break the law in order to see the precious light of a new dawn.

THiRTY-SEVEN

Morell drove overcautiously on the winding trek back to the Lenkov's private estate, the GTO's pristine waxy green sheen catching the pale orb of a nearly full moon when the low cloud cover of another passing rain shower permitted.

Morell let his eyes drift, once or twice, to the passenger seat. The moonlight, cutting through the clouds and the stretching fingers of scratchy pine tree silhouettes smeared by wind-fanned raindrops on the window cast a cool glow on the pale skin of Lucy's chest. Her low-cut purple velvet V-neck three-quarter sleeve maxi dress fit like a glove, even further cementing the thought in Morell's mind that she was a swimmer, and the third time his eyes deviated from the road, she caught him.

"Checking out the hardware?" She asked.

"Excuse me?"

She tapped the web of glittering pear-cut cubic zirconia around her collarbone, the airiness in which her flittering touch brushed the jewelry prophesying the success of her coming duties with the Bosendorfer grand piano.

"Um…y-yeah." Morell nodded.

Lucy's necklace held five sequentially-spaced MicroHD cameras, the Wi-Fi feed of which Morell's computer could splice together to receive an extended

panorama of uninterrupted real-time surveillance.
Lucy's earrings, old-fashioned clasp and pendant style
colored gold and forest green like Faberge eggs, hid
condenser microphones so that Morell could eavesdrop
on the conversations around her so that Lucy didn't
have to and Morell would be with her at all times via a
two-way flesh-colored earwig.

Upon leaving Tidebender with the surveillance
hardware, Morell had driven Lucy back to her home in
Eavesdale to give her time to run through a few scales,
stretch her fingers on difficult arpeggios, and gather the
sheet music she wanted to play. He'd instructed her
briefly on what he thought she should look for at the
fundraiser, but again, was quick to remind her of how
skilled a Vice Detective she was and that her instincts
were solid and to be trusted. The same disability that
had made her an outsider had made her a speculative
observer, and her time in grade with Vice had only
made those hinting thoughts and assumptions more and
more accurate. The time had passed quickly over a
dinner of frozen pizzas and equipment preparation,
most of Lucy's time taken up by the necessities of
evening wear.

Lucy checked her Cartier Panthere to see it was
nearly seven o'clock. Her curled blonde tresses spilled
over the back of the seat.

"I have to tell you while I have the chance." Lucy
said, squinting through the trees and the rain-smeared
window to eye the rotunda and pillars of the three-story
structure hovering ghostly across the grounds of the
property in the darkness. "Going back home made me
want to say to hell with it, because whenever I step
through that door part of me wants to shut down until I
can prepare myself to do it all over again."

"I know." Morell nearly whispered.

"It's been hard to get it out of my head, you

know, to stop thinking about it…at your place it was easier…but the moment we stepped inside mine I couldn't help let it clamp down on me. Maybe it's because I've lived there for thirty-eight years. I'm damn nervous about tonight, you know. Call it performance anxiety. I don't know if I'm ready but we don't have a choice. There's a lot of people relying on me, even if they don't know it."

Morell sighed.

"I don't have any magic words for you."

Lucy's head lolled across the seat and her hand reached out to curl over his as his was firm on the gearshift. Compassion was in her touch, echoing the care in Callie's voice.

It was as if his six years of overseas service to his country had carved a special place in their conscience, and they, in their own way, respectively, whether personally or professionally, were going to make sure he knew how valuable he was to them and the community, even though the dangerously selfless mind of CAP Syndrome wanted to blaze on and help the helpless and remediate the spilled cup of injustice before its cause and effect soaked into the parched soul of the city; they were going to stop him long enough to tell him how much he mattered, and tell him they cared about his well being.

"How did you do it as a soldier? How do you do it now?"

Lucy pulled her hand off of his to set it in her lap, with one cradling the other as if they were made of porcelain, and had to be babied before her spell at the piano.

"Dammed if I know." Morell chuckled, pulling off to the long country road cresting its highest point to roll down to the low, gated entrance of the horse-pasture valley. "You just do. You don't think about it.

You have the rest of your life to get over it, I guess."

Morell paused as the gate security, consisting of four muscly men in tuxedos with squiggly earpieces running down their necks to the starched collars of their white shirts, verified Lucy's name on the checklist and nodded when Morell showed his badge and told them he was only driving and wouldn't ruin the party by stealing the free champagne and canapés.

The space designated for parking, a horse-racing track not two hundred yards from the grand pillared entrance, underlit, for effect, with swirling floodlights, would effectively corral the automobiles responsible for transporting those wishing to attend the swanky fundraiser in such trying times.

Perhaps it was an elitist escape, much like video games would be for the many children of those parents stressed beyond the capacity of normal function as terrorism had again mindlessly returned to Crescent, or even as alcoholic beverages were for those parents as they sought to gain space from the world around them with the numbing cloak of inebriation.

Morell shut off the car and turned to Lucy, arm around the back of the seat so that not much more than an inch or two hovered between their noses.

"I believe in you, okay? You're gonna be great."

Lucy's chin jutted in the slightest as she nodded, as the thought of him in her ear would be an aspirin to help her stand the unbearable headache of expensive perfume, cosmetic surgery-enhancements, exclusive designer label clothing, opinionated duels of conversation, and the lurking threat of whomever had sabotaged her car.

She tapped his hand on the shift knob and grabbed her wrap from the small space in the back, handing Morell an umbrella with crow's feet nipping at her eyes.

"Aren't you going to get cold out here?"

"Trust me Lucy," Morell chuckled. "When you spend a night in Baghdad, America takes on a very different appearance. I'll be plenty busy in this comfy leather foxhole, don't you worry. And remember if you feel the least bit uneasy, let me know and I'll come get you. We're just doing recon, after all."

"...Right." Lucy nodded.

Morell exited the GTO first, extending the golf-sized black umbrella to run around the hood and save Lucy's purple velvet dress from the drizzling rain falling aimlessly from a muddled blanket of gray clouds and black winter skies, behind which the nearly full moon watched, objectively, anticipating the jagged dissonance of lightning's searing white streaks and veins splitting the sky like the hooves of a Lithuanian deity's fearsome horse.

Sergei Lenkov spotted Lucy nearly the moment she entered the rotunda.

"Isn't this weather just awful," His father's resonance rumbled like thunder. "Please come inside and have a splash of vodka to warm you up."

Lucy was going to make a comment about being unable to drink alcohol before playing and Morell was quick in her ear, not yet to the car.

"See if he's got the *Zakon Krzyżacki*."

"I'd love to see what you have." Lucy lowered her wrap and held the oversized clutch in which she had placed her sheet music with two hands to survey the large seating area to the left of the rotunda, which, in the daylight, was an entirely different space.

Where were the couches and tables?

Where was the rug?

Except for the lone piano, the floor was bare, stripped to the originality of its beautiful wooden purity, and though Lucy couldn't ignore the multi-tiered butterflies taking sanctuary in her stomach, she knew her piano playing would never sound better. The richness of one *single* note of the perfectly preserved and expertly tuned work of art would saturate the stilted conversations and static statues near the open bar as it flooded the room, and Lucy told herself to take it slow and act like she was sitting at her dusty upright at home, tucked off in the corner of the office by the laundry room, facing the window.

"I should hope for a bigger audience." Lucy remarked as they reached the open bar, which had repurposed the kitchen space with a staff of tuxedoed security guards, indivisible with those taking trying to take cover and sneak in a smoke break as they patrolled the grounds and guarded the main gate and other areas of egress.

"Trust me, you'll have it." Sergei promised ostentatiously, motioning for one of the menus.

Lucy noted his watch selection for the evening and twisted her body to catch the shiny face of it in the mood lighting.

"I see it." Morell said, back in the car, at his computer. The volume of his voice was well dispersed in her inner ear, not too loud over the ambient noise. "He's chosen to wear the Estonia watch. Pretty bold of him. Ask him if there's a schedule."

"Would you happen to have an order of events so that I know when I play and for how long?" Lucy asked, as she received the menu, for which Sergei looked flustered and stifled an excusatory statement with a cough.

Lucy followed his exit with her body.

"Someone's been hitting the sauce already."

"Do you see Alexis?"

"No. Just a lot of security guards and some early

birds, pretty cliquish by the look of them. Should I go see who they are?"

"No. Wait till he comes back. Fosnick told us Veremecek will be there, and Fosnick thinks he might be the *Hochmeister*. After all, he was recently at Malbork Castle. Fosnick said his visit was in the back pages of *The Guardian* last week."

Lucy quickly scanned the menu and found the *Zakon Krzyżacki* Polish vodka, continuing her observations from the open bar till Sergei returned. He was wearing a sharkskin tuxedo with a black bowtie and not a jet-black hair was out of place. The thin cut of his jacket made him appear cartoonish and top heavy as did most of the other Russian bodyguards, damn near all of them his size and bigger.

"Have you decided?" Sergei said, shielding Lucy from the rotunda and the staircase and halls beyond where, somewhere, Alexis was doing God knew what. Strangely, it was *her* Lucy was the most concerned about, the most concerned *and* the most interested, as if everyone else in the space were cutouts of cardboard and she was the master of the marionettes. "Quickly Ms. Radzewicz, so we can toast your wonderful performance before my sister chides me for drinking too much."

Lucy pointed.

"How do you say this one?"

"*Zakon Krzyżacki*? Oh, you don't want that one, Polish though it may be. It'll rip your throat out. Something with strawberry and anise, perhaps? And though it's not on the menu, I'm sure I can find you some Aquavit. I was in Stockholm last year and I remember purchasing a few special bottles."

Lucy nodded and eyed the schedule he'd placed on the bar top.

"You're auctioning your watches?" She said with

the best attempt at genuine surprise she could muster, hearing a snickering smoker's cough waft through her ears because of it.

"Yes." Sergei Lenkov said, straightening as one of his minions provided him with a bottle and a bucket of ice in which were set hand-blown glass vials, awaiting tastings. He took two of them in his massive hands, splitting them between his upturned palm like a Vulcan salute as he poured with great expertise. "It is a welcome addition to the addendum." He smirked and performed a flamboyant flinging motion after returning the bottle to the bar top, and his voice became derogatory. "*Artists*...the lot of them give me the creeps. Anyway, Alexis is selling most of her horse and forest nymph paintings and I will be tossing back whatever I can get my hands on until it is my turn to take over the auction. It is a pity Father is not here...he would've had all of his soldier buddies belting out the National Anthem by now."

Lucy took the vodka and clinked vials with the Russian billionaire inheritor and Order member and nearly shivered at the odd confluence of sensations, the initial stab of arctic chill on her lips and the numbing warmness that followed, sliding down her belly like a soothing ointment on sunburned skin.

Sergei checked his watch with a brusque movement and stood.

"I must go. Please begin at your earliest convenience...you know," A giant finger whirled around his head. "For the atmosphere."

He offered his hand and Lucy took it and instead of shaking it, he kissed it with the lingering lips of one who was bordering drunkenness and was comfortable with its lascivious undertones.

"Did he just do what I think he did?" Morell asked as the tall Russian walked away to greet new guests, the squeak of leather audible in Lucy's ear as Morell adjusted positions and reached in a satchel on the passenger floor for a pair of binoculars to examine the routes of the Russian security guards from his primo spot in the horse track parking lot.

"He did." Lucy said, moving to the piano with her clutch and the precious music it contained, as if it were the musical embodiment of Prince Charming awaiting her awakening.

"Bastard…"

"Easy…" Lucy said as she arranged her music. "He's European. They can get away with stuff Americans can't."

"Heh…" Morell chuckled, peeling the glasses from his eyes to flick the wiper blades. "And Americans can get away with stuff Europeans can't, like *real* football. Could you imagine me trying to pull that stunt on Callie?"

"I don't think she'd have a problem with that."

A mutual smile held silence between them.

"I see it wasn't too hard for you to get the surveillance equipment." Lucy said, having neatly arranged her music before her and adjusting her posture so that Morell could watch the rapid influx of faces corresponding with the new cars piling into the lot.

"Yeah." Morell traded looks between the computer screen on the passenger seat and the rain-smeared car windows. "She donated it freely. She seemed…different."

"Different how?"

"She's going with her daughter to Egypt for some humanitarian work. I think…outside of her generous monetary donation, she feels she can't do anything else for Crescent, and Crescent is only a microcosm of the modern way. Look at RepMax." Morell squinted into his binoculars, set on the forest, not adding that the

psychologically restorative work Callie wanted to
perform within Morell and his CAP Syndrome was
also, in her mind, a half-formed attempt stillborn in its
conception. "Until I came along they were taking her
lunch money just because they carried Glocks.
Businesses are so afraid of the next jihad that they fail
to realize how many criminals private enterprise
attracts...how many parasites, and they'll hire whatever
gives them a sense of protection even though it's a false
parameter. To quote a passage from one of Callie's
books, *life with a gun is endemically, systemically, and
fundamentally more dangerous than life without a gun.*"

Morell dropped the binoculars and waited for a
response, wondering if he'd stepped on a soapbox that
sat in a sore place with Lucy, considering the paper
he'd signed with Fosnick and the ghostly thought that
Fosnick's ripping up of the damning contract was,
itself, a temporary reprieve that would, in the end,
justify much stiffer action.

"Lucy, you with me?"

Morell heard nothing in response, save the
opening measures of Polish composer Frederic
Chopin's *Nocturne in E flat Major*, though he didn't
know that was the name of the piece, he was convinced,
as the wind whipped up the rain and slapped it across
the roof and the green turf of the horse track, that it
was, without a doubt, the most beautiful piece of music
he'd ever heard in his life, and could only imagine how
beautiful Lucy looked, in turn, as she played it.

THiRTY-EiGHT

Tipping the bottle of honey wheat ale to her naturally sulking lips, Casey Sullivan attempted to quench the fiery tang of the hot wing sauce she was trying to get Blake Fosnick addicted to as another basket of natural cut French fries, smelling more like donuts than potatoes, came to the table at the hands of a broadly smiling waitress, confident that the indulgence before her would yield a substantial tip.

"Thanks, Tiff." Casey winked and stifled her own smile as Fosnick's eyes rolled around in their sockets.

"You expect me to eat all of this? I'm gonna die."

"Nicky, you and I both know you've been working yourself to the bone, so…isn't it about time you come down from the rafters and act human?"

Fosnick rolled his eyes again, and drained his soda, to which Casey deftly caught the dark haired waitress on the way back and asked for another bottle of beer and a refill on Fosnick's soda.

"You know, it's really nice of you to do this for me." Fosnick ate three fries at once, house-made ketchup dripping between them like a shared knife-wound, and Casey was keen to notice that with each otherwise off-limits calorie he ingested, he seemed to loosen and inhibit the long-sleeve t-shirt and jeans that he wore with a foreign discomfort. "One gets so sick of salads and…and quinoa and stuff like that…and those little gritty round balls of gluten-free products…" His eyes drifted around the hole-the-wall bar and its intensely reddened wood panels, as if the entire place had been stained in the sauce they were famous for. The stage next to the bar was empty, save the house PA system and the place would be standing room only in a matter of hours. The white Christmas lights behind them glittered and twisted through the rows of pint glasses above the bar and cast a soft glow on their secluded booth. Casey knew the influx of eager new drinkers and partiers would psychologically seal, along with the fats and sweets of the food, Fosnick's feeling of *leaving* something and escaping it, back to the apartment he rented nearly two miles from hers.

"And I haven't been on a date in a long time."

"Oh God…" Casey shook her head with her chin tucked down in her neck as if he'd missed the mark on a trivia question, waiting till the honey wheat ale had cleared a bit more of the special chili d'arbol and habanero sauce from the back of her tongue, as the apple cider vinegar and honey rounding out the sauce spread across the rest of her palate. "This is *so* not a date."

"I know," Fosnick quickly corrected with apologetic hands. The purplish-tinted circles of tireless work resting beneath his eyes and making him appear to be in the clutches of the flu, what the team had termed *dark shadows*, exaggerated the three days of growth that had made his face appear less blocky and robotic. "What I meant to say is I haven't been on a date in so long I forgot how much fun it is to just kind of…you know." He shrugged his way out of anything definite as his soda arrived, as if Casey knew the dating scene so well with all of the eyes drifting her way, when in fact Casey'd never been on a date, save that once when she was seventeen and it all fell apart.

Even then, it wasn't *really* a date.

Casey jutted her chin forward and flashed her lower incisors with it. Her husky southern voice and the presence of alcohol only hyperbolized the lilting Transylvanian accent so many adopted the moment Fosnick had given the team's orders and left the room, though no one did as good as Casey, a natural actress.

"Igor, I*vant* to have some fun…" Casey's eyebrows then climbed up her forehead, one hiding behind the swoop of blonde hair as an idea caught fire in her mind, sharp beyond her years, but not technically so, so that thinking was not, as it was for Fosnick, such a heavy process. For Casey, thinking was more like running track hurdles. It just sort of…worked, and when it didn't she fell down hard and skinned her knees or her elbows. Things made sense. No further processing, contemplation, pontification, or in Casey's hybridized Ger-Merican vernacular *Quatsch* required.

"Oh, Blake's just wanna have fun," She sang with a tinny scratchiness, snapping her fingers. "Yeah Blake's just wanna have fun."

"Stop!" Fosnick shook his head, as if his ears had been subjected to the proverbial chalkboard and nails. "Please…that song brings back bad memories."

Casey lowered her voice, with her lips nearly puckered like pouting trumpets.

"Now son, I know you've been back in D.C. for roughly fourteen and a half seconds," Casey slid into mocking the FBI's Adjutant Chief of Operations John T. Gold with a passably goofy impression, nailing his overbearing demeanor with perfect comedic timing.

"Stop, you'll get me in trouble…" Fosnick managed to say through small spasms of choked laughter, stimulated by his sleeplessness and the mass of food he'd taken in.

"Shutup and listen, okay, good, we've got another

case for you. Nope. Don't change your underwear.
Don't even draw breath as I speak to you here in this
ostensibly formal office in which nothing's moved a
fraction of an inch since the Reagan administration.
Inside this envelope I hold in my hand are your plane
tickets, via as many connecting flights as possible, to
Armpit Junction, USA. I hope you don't mind I've
upgraded you to business class. Nope, don't thank me.
It's the least I could do considering the bang up job you
did." Fosnick curled in his side of the booth with his
eyes squeezed shut in laughter till his head hit the table
as Casey frowned and picked up a French fry and let it,
overwhelmed with a coating of grease, droop as her
hands became demonstrative. "Why the hell does he
always say that, *bang up*? What in God's name does
that even mean? Bang up…does he, like, sit around and
watch World War Two movies while he's waiting to
meet with the President, I mean, seriously…*bang* up…"

Casey smiled as she nibbled at her fry and
watched Fosnick try to recover. Buying the meal and
giving him the gift of laughter was empowering her,
fueling her to continue but for some reason he looked as
if *he'd* been the one drinking and she knew to pull back.
Still, she felt responsible to bring levity to his extremely
stressed way of life, and she liked the duty in the most
protective sort of way, knowing that their relationship
had been built on two *very* non-negotiable terms;
looking out for each other, and disagreeing with each
other, and it was as if Fosnick telepathically knew what
she was about to say when her third beer came to the
table.

Casey asked for the check and stared at him as the
waitress uncapped it.

"What? You've got that look."

"What look?"

"That *I'm about to analytically vociferate a*

highly processed pattern of reasoning look," She tried to mock his dry and nearly whispery voice. "That *check your pulse and pinch yourself* look. That…"

"Okay okay." Fosnick nodded with heavy lids and picked at the basket of fries and gave his statement a final once over before releasing it, seeing as the waitress had ducked off to the register. "It's about Morell."

"Yeah?" Casey wanted a sip of tasty beer but refrained and let the resounding heat bloom in her mouth with the slightest throb the moment his name hit her ears. The tiniest hints of a buzz were gnawing at her temples and she wanted to make damn sure she understood everything he was going to say on the subject of Henry Morell.

He was a hero. A real live hero.

And when it came to heroes, Casey had a sort of a complex.

A serious one.

"He's kind of a problem."

"How so?"

Fosnick slowly pulled his hands across his eyes in a smoothing gesture and then rubbed small circles on the edge of his brow.

"…I feel…" Fosnick began, distant gaze proving that he was having a hard time condensing what he wanted to convey and Casey's own brows were slowly creeping together, hanging on his words.

"I feel that I'm giving him a chance to make a better case for himself in the days to come."

"What do you mean?"

"If he can take this terrorism tied with the Order and loop it up in a package with a nice little bow, I'm sure the DOJ will view his case in a different light."

"But he's innocent. You know that."

"No, Casey." Fosnick shook his head. "He's not."

"Müll." Casey hit the table with her hand, causing the silverware to clink and leaned forward. "Do you know what that guy's been through?"

"In the war? Yeah."

"With *Wolf Stone*?"

"Yes, I read your notes. I know how you busted your butt to get the information, too, asking around and phoning people off the clock. It showed a lot of moxie, for such a young Agent, but…"

"And so you know…" Casey's whisper was hoarse as she was not much of a whisperer. "That the JSOC General in charge of that operation, Wendell Mellinger, is the current Director of the FBI, and the CIA operative running the operation, Frederick Percival, went missing two years ago?"

Fosnick sighed.

"Casey, we've gone over this. It's easy to call conspiracy where there is none."

"Did you know," Casey tilted her head, conscious that Fosnick was staring directly into her swollen pupils and the blue-green seas they floated in, working their indelibly convincing magic as only they could. "That Director Mellinger owns a ten-percent share in RepMax."

Fosnick frowned.

"No. How'd you find that out?"

"It's called the freaking Internet, Nicky, and don't you dare tell me it's out of your hands and the moment he comes here to D.C. they're gonna slap him in zip ties like he's some cartel gun runner and stuff him in the broom closet till they figure out how to blame *him* somehow for RepMax and *Wolf Stone*."

"Okay then." Fosnick shrugged. "I won't."

"But it's true."

"Yeah."

"How? How's that even freaking…*remotely*

possible?"

Fosnick rolled his eyes as the check came and waited with an idle tapping of his fingers till she'd counted out a hundred dollars in twenty's and told the waitress to keep it.

"So who owns the other ninety?"

"Percent?"

"Yeah?"

"Do you need to see the hard drive in Mellinger's bedroom computer or something? Is that what it'll take?"

"No, Casey, I want you to realize that *hundreds* of millions of dollars went down the drain because of what Morell did and counterclaims of him falsifying evidence in a court of law strike a serious sentence, even if the whole thing still is under the radar, and nobody's really taken up sides yet. Once it hits the airwaves though, his life'll never be the same. That's a fact. No matter *what* conspiracy you may want to read into, such as a...*severely* redacted CIA report you had some washed out former Agent hand you in some diner or circumstantial evidence surrounding a money trail that can more than likely be explained six ways from Sunday, you have to realize that even if Morell, whom I believe is a good man at heart, had a *justifiable* motivation for falsifying evidence, that's for the courts to decide, *not* us. I agree, certain things can look fishy from certain angles, but I'm giving Morell one hell of a break in seeing what he can do with this terrorist threat running rampant in Crescent, and I swallowed my pride on that one, because at the beginning of the week I didn't like the guy...but if he doesn't deliver something fast, the Director's going to have me get his ass over here pronto, and it's going to be in cuffs, NQA, and I'm not going to get full marks for bringing him in because I'll have fudged the rules enough myself and Gold will send me up to Mellinger who'll rip me a new one and I'll limp back down to my office to see you leaning on my desk, pouting about it all because you didn't get what you wanted and in your mind you're always right." Fosnick took a sip of soda, sad to have sobered Casey's mood with his cutting sarcasm and aridly by-the-book personality. But her beautiful face was like the coast the way it could be cloudy and overcast one minute, and then split by pure, unfiltered sunshine the next, and back again, so much so that her mysterious sense of unpredictability was more maddening than attractive to many members of the opposite sex and he knew she'd see the facts of the quicksand Morell was sinking in and get over it.

She had to. It was their job to get over it.

"So that's it then?" She nearly mumbled. "Dead man walking? American hero goes to Supermax for trying to sucker-punch corruption while it slept on the job? Nicky, he could get *killed* in prison by someone he helped *put in there* and no one would blink an eye, but the system would tick another notch in their belt because the case goes in the record books as another sterling example of truth, justice, and the America way."

Fosnick hid a shrug in grabbing his coat. He did not defend *the system*.

He only enforced it.

"In the end, Casey, we're all just soldiers, doing our jobs." Fosnick began with heavy lids but his speech was as harmlessly-toned and passively confrontational as ever. "The minute we start questioning where the orders come from is the minute the *system*, as you call it, breaks down. My job is to get those people that are a product of a fallen system diametrically opposed to the inherent morality of the one we serve, whether it be drug-dealers or serial killers, arsonists and bankrobbers-you know we see the worst the land has to offer, and let me tell you, for a fact, that I uphold the law and by no means seek to interpret it. If you want to make this job your life then you have to break, deep down inside, to the fact that you're a glorified cop and if you want to argue the semantics of social policy and world issues, I'll be reluctant to take your badge but I'll have no choice, because you belong, with all of your talents and forthright passions, in *another* field. If you ask Henry Morell, he'll tell you that's the way it is, and he knew damn well what he was doing before he did it. I applaud his balls because I wouldnt've been able to in his situation. I know this country's a mess but I keep it to myself and do the job I'm asked to."

Fosnick departed with a hasty march after prying himself from the cozy booth, leaving Casey to dwell on his words with clasped hands.

Her soul motivation for becoming an FBI Agent was so intensely linked with the desire for vindicating a fallen hero and it was as if, sitting in that wood-paneled booth, soaked in a ruddy stain that looked like dried blood in the peppering of the Christmas lights, that she was forever going to wage the war of a dead-man, a legend, on behalf of everyone that fit the profile.

Was Henry Morell a bad man, having abused the powers of oath and office, badge and gun, to wage his own private war against a security company known to hire ex-mercenaries and soldiers that he may've served with in Iraq and seen the worst sides of?

Or was he on the wrong side of a tempestuous sea with no life raft and no more strength to tread water?

The one-time twitch bit Casey's kissable lips, betraying her uncertainty.

Of herself.

Of life.

"Schieße…" She muttered and grabbed her own

jacket, a fitted leather motorcycle-style, colored maroon.

Casey Sullivan, woman of magic and mystery and the poetic profanity that punctuated it, was not about to be told her feelings were *wrong*, even though she was still, despite being wise beyond her years, a young woman who may or may not've been blinded by the thoughts blossoming in her heart; thoughts that those in more romantic lines of work had the luxury of calling *love*, and the possibly false hope of character such thoughts of love had assigned to the decorated Iraq war veteran and Crescent Crisis-scarred hero by the name of Henry Morell who reminded her far too much of a late friend she couldn't bring back from the dead but still hadn't allowed to fade away from her mind.

THIRTY-NINE

Hanging out the door of the Sikorsky S Ninety-Two with the savage fingers of the night wind tearing at his obsidian-colored body armor and loving every visceral second of it, Ridley Sorber turned to Jaroslaw to give him the go ahead with nothing more than a sangfroid dip of the chin. The blonde Lithuanian quickly gave the radio order to initiate the *Balta Zaibus* protocol and then the universal hand signal of comprehension back to The Lynx, who pondered the appropriate nature of his pseudonym as the black Sikorsky cut across the fuzzy treetops of the northern island chains splitting across the Bay. In medieval times, the *lynx* was seen as a metaphysical creature, with the ears of an owl, the fangs of a snake, and the eyes of a cat, and the tongue of a man. It was a go-between of the spiritual and physical realms, a foreteller of the future and was believed to have the power to see through stone walls. The morbid humor of the situation would only be amplified by the team's equipment, stored, as it was, within the shell of the EMP-hardened helicopter, and their tactical advantage in the aftermath of BZ would manifest itself as otherworldly, as if they were operating on an inhuman plane and controlling life and death with the impunity of dark spirits that didn't give a damn about the laws of physics.

Sorber slid the door shut and took his seat,

waiting for the show to begin.

Long had he dreamt of this day, and even with the small changes to the plan, it had finally come, in all of its gratuitously sky-shattering glory.

Strategically placed in and amongst the parking lots and roadsides of Crescent, an army of nondescript semi-trucks, each with a hole the size of a dinner plate drilled into the top corners of their trailers, the location of the hole dependent on their own location within the quadrants surrounding the city, began the process of *Balta Zaibus*.

Requiring strictly a crew of two, an operator and a driver, with the driver keeping lookout, though not necessary with the frenetic dissolution Geffington's assassination had spurned within CPD proper and the densely populated city, the operator would activate the terawatt lasers manufactured exclusively by the Veremecek Technology Group's off the books Research and Development Program.

The lasers, firing insanely fast pulses of invisible plasma into the low and heavy clouds surrounding Crescent, would create tunnels of ionized molecules, scientifically known as filaments. These filament tubes of ionized gas would hollow out spaces in the naturally occurring rainstorm clouds, and act as channels to ground, *lightning rods*, so to speak. By the sheer force of number and repetition, it would only be a matter of time before the first flashes of artificially manufactured lightning would begin a chain reaction the city of Crescent would be unable to stop as it forever altered the city with the cataclysmic effects of an electromagnetic pulse-triggered blackout, frying transformer grids, skyscraper generator units, and service industry utilities, thus reducing Crescent, until such parts could be replaced, to the dark ages in which the myth of Perkunas and his lightning-sparking horses came from.

The devastating effects of the lightning-triggered blackout would turn Crescent into a cesspool of chaos, and would brilliantly, in more than one meaning of the word, cover the tracks of a devious plot as if the complicated procedure was simply slight of hand in a giant magic trick.

Morell yawned and covered his mouth from the toasty comfort of the GTO.

"Tell me about it." Lucy whispered near the grand entrance of the front door, free of her musical duties. "This guy responsible for selling the paintings is putting me to sleep."

She'd received several compliments in the time following her final notes, and stayed in the main body of guests so that Morell could work on identifying the various faces she encountered with information emailed to him from Fosnick. Since locating Stanislav Veremecek, indicated by his six-foot five frame and handful of dapperly-dressed former Spetznaz security guards, and small entourage of cosmetics models, Morell instructed Lucy to stay close and find out what she could, if anything, and keep her eyes out for his possible assassination.

Alexis' art auction began shortly after Lucy'd ceased her playing Rachmaninoff's extremely melancholy *Prelude in B minor Opus Thirty Two* to a host of applause, and not to be outdone in some strange psychological way, Alexis patiently waited till the applause had run its course to make her grand introduction to the swanky party beneath the glimmering thousand-pound chandelier and the eerie light it cast across the stretching and stoically writhing arms of the three-story *Tree of the World* sculpture.

Her sleeveless white dress, complete with a wooly mammoth-tusk bone corset and studded with hundreds of chatoyant Swarovski crystals, dramatically drug a train of fabric that would make the richest of brides envious. Lucy'd made a comment to Morell about the descent of a goddess into the world of mere mortals, and Morell fired back a sardonic observation about mourning daughters traditionally wearing black.

Alexis seemed to steal the oxygen from everyone in the room as she nearly levitated down the stairs, her dress covering her feet, and a knot seized Morell's throat as he watched her do so via Lucy's necklace cameras with the perspective of such a diabolical identity tainting the technical merits of her severe, runway model-like beauty.

Throughout the course of the art auction, which Morell knew was innocuous in its boast of raising money for the late Maks Lenkov's favorite charities, as each sibling was putting up their most valuable possessions to honor the legacy of their father, the former soldier couldn't help but think the fundraiser was a front to a private meeting of some kind when a flash of light panned across the sky.

"Oh, hello." He said, dipping his head to see another follow it within seconds, illuminating the forest like a tactical flare.

"What's up?" Lucy whispered back.

"Lightning. Did you see it?"

"No." Lucy's gray-green eyes rolled to the louvered windows to see they were closed shut. "I didn't hear any thunder either."

"I'm no science geek but I know you don't always have one when you have the other...try to hold out for the watch auction, the whole thing may be a ploy to officially distribute new seats in the Order, so to speak, with Sergei taking over Estonia. Is Alexis wearing her watch?"

"What else can one wear with such a dress?" Lucy muttered, feeling like a peasant in the luxurious velvet Morell had purchased for her with a gift card, and she meant to ask him why he even *had* a gift card to the women's boutique ready to go in his wallet and was sure there was a great explanation for it, surely conversational fodder for that far off dinner they'd have when the case, if ever, allowed it.

Morell took his eyes off the computer as a series of brilliant flashes snapped across the sky, coloring the thick blanket of clouds with the nuclear white heat of the sun for a nanosecond, only to be seemingly outdone by subsequent explosions of the same, magnificent intensity. The sheets of camera-like explosions seemed to be contained within the heavy clouds, unable to break free of them, and the pace of the flashes increased in frequency and succession as if driven by an inaudible drumbeat, mounting in its silent fervor.

The display carried on for a good ten minutes, capturing Morell's attention with its awesome power, and at the sight of the first shorn curtain of lightning descending to earth, Morell let out a whistle.

When Lucy didn't respond, he said,

"You should see it Lucy…it makes the fourth of July look like child's play."

Fizzling white-hot teeth ripped from the gray-black sea of fog with an otherworldly sense of catastrophe.

Morell pondered the staggering frequency of the lightning strikes and immediately considered the possibility of a blackout, remembering blackouts in Baghdad and how sensitive certain electronics were to greater frequency charges, whether they came from launched missiles, as had the Baghdad power loss, or the electromagnetic pulse charges of the sun, and on a lesser scale, ground-reaching lightning strikes.

His mind then shifted to Lucy.

Perhaps, he thought, *she can't talk. Or, she isn't happy since I'm rubbing in how nice it is out here. She's doing the heavy lifting while I get to sit out here in the on and off rain and listen to music. A peaceful reprieve from the stress of the job, that's for sure. God, lightning this heavy's got to be rare, like, once in a lifetime. And she's stuck in there with a bunch of rich creeps keeping their balance with champagne glasses.*

What custom Rolex was Veremecek wearing again? He'll probably be buying the Hanseatic one. Lemme check my notes...

Morell turned his attention to the computer screen and didn't see anything, so he twisted the device thinking that the illumination splitting the sky like the first kickoff of the Superbowl on steroids was casting a glare across the screen.

"That's strange." He said, more to himself than anything, even though it occurred to him Lucy would hear his words as well and hadn't responded, because the computer had shut itself off. A scowl stretched across his face when he realized he'd lost audio with Lucy.

Morell leaned forward in his seat to survey the brilliant splashes and jagged streaks of lightning crashing from the sky and wondered if it were possible that the sheer voracity of the electrical currents zipping toward the surface of the earth had caused some kind of frequency overload. He fired the GTO, thankfully free of electronic ignition, to quickly check the area but received his answer to the situation as the stretching darkness of the Lenkov's estate was stripped of its power.

Lucy felt the gasp for breath ripple across the

room as it was plunged in a thick, obscure gloom.

"Everybody please remain calm, we'll have the power back on in no time." Sergei quickly promised with a booming bellow, and the remaining eyes of the party's wealthy constituents were drawn to the windows Veremecek's bodyguards quickly began to flip the louvers of, to watch the unnatural display of lightning as it ripped across the length of the cloud-covered vista with random precision.

"Henry." Lucy tried her comm at conversation volume, since the party was consumed with *ooh's* and *ah's* and the smatterings of slightly inebriated conversation.

Nothing. Not even static. It was as if she didn't even *have* a comm in her ear.

Lucy gathered her dress like a prom queen and clicked toward the door in her low heels, following a pair of tuxedoed security guards out the giant door to search for the GTO with some stealth, as a pair of guards inside the party had ordered everyone to stay inside for safety's sake.

Henry Morell was bounding up the steps to greet her, having stuffed the GTO near the gate, away from the other cars to run back to the mansion.

"The lightning must've knocked everything out." He said.

"Yeah, but comm's?" Lucy trailed off as Morell pulled her toward one of the entrance columns to keep away from any prying eyes scouring the windows. "Aren't those battery powered?"

Morell scanned the parking area behind him, intermittent flashes of light and dark stabbing his eyes and making it impossible to see clearly. He could only attempt to ascertain the suspicious thread sprinting through his mind by analyzing brief snapshots of the staid vista as it slept under the dizzying spell of the storm.

"Do you think someone's jamming the signal?" He whispered, wondering if the killer and any associates, if he even needed them, were awaiting their moment to strike in the back of one of the many limousines dotting the racetrack parking lot.

To think he had possibly sat among them as they waited...

"I think *something's* going on," Lucy shook her head, the gist of it evading her. "But I don't know what."

Morell watched as two tuxedoed security guards met up with a pair of anorak-cloaked guards near one of the horse stables, nearly a half a mile away.

"Their comms must be down too...strange, we're on *way* different bandwidths..."

Morell grabbed Lucy by the arms, bending close as the lightning strikes lessened in frequency.

"The killer's got to be here, at the party."

Lucy's breath shortened.

"Who's the target?"

"It has to be Veremecek, especially if he's the Order's *Hochmeister*. I'm shocked that he's here with what happened to Lenkov and Mogilev, but, he's not the humble type."

"Maybe he doesn't know about them. It all happened so quick...and we've been stuck so deep in the case to have any perspective, especially with all the coverage around here centering on Geffington and the CRT takeover."

"Are you kidding? A guy like Veremecek knows everything, or else he wouldn't be one of the richest men in the world."

Lucy shivered in the cold and Morell studied the scene as the security guards broke up their meeting and rushed back to the house with the haste of people losing control. Lucy could imagine him in fatigues, M-Four strapped to his chest and tight in his fingertips.

"That's not right." Lucy nearly whispered, processing the veritable kaleidoscope of possibilities as Morell's proximal warmth and the light scent of the GTO's blue tree air freshener comforted her beneath the waning stabs of deadly light far up in the sickened sky. "If Alexis is behind the Order killings, then she's got to have something planned, something big. She's got all her ducks in a row here, right?"

The tuxedoed guards approached the entrance steps.

"Please," A burly man with a crew cut strangely contrasting his dapper black split-lapel tux tapped Morell's shoulder, his English muffled with a heavy Russian accent. "Inside."

Morell looked up with bewilderment, blips and fizzling slashes coloring the sky.

"I just wanna see the lightning." He said incredulously, as if the guard were a caveman.

"Da. Inside." The burly man ushered with a hand that looked as if it could break boards with one chop. The two anorak-cloaked security men brushed past him, leaving the door open. Morell spotted the beads of water on their jackets and knew they'd been patrolling the furthest reaches of the property and wondered how many of them were out there, stuck in all of the little nooks and corners of the sheds and stables and the dense thickets of pine forest trees.

A thought crossed his mind about the killer sneaking in with the security detail. It'd be a replication of the Geffington job, even though in Morell's mind, he'd stick out like a sore thumb being so small in contrast to the collection of bodybuilders Sergei Lenkov employed.

Chaos, a new jacket, and the blind bluff of

confidence to sell it all, that's all the killer needed, and Morell's service weapon began to burn inside of his suit in the discreet hip holster right next to a shiny gold badge that wasn't really his.

But Morell could ID him, he was sure of it, and prevent another brutal assassination.

That was, of course, unless Lucy was right and Alexis really was the master of puppets, ready to slice her knife into everything that moved as they were all boxed in the mansion like a neat little horror movie.

"Lemme get to my car first." Morell nodded.

"Nyet." The guard urged, and wouldn't move till they complied. "Inside."

"But..."

"*Inside.*" The guard's voice was laced with a sense of finality Morell didn't want to argue with, and Morell split his gaze, with swift eyes, between the ever-placid face of Lucy Radzewicz who tipped her vision to the darkened sky, now strangely void of the lightning that had once so frenetically consumed it.

FORTY

The impervious skin of the nightmare-black Sikorsky crackled and buzzed with the fizzling ice-blue worms of directionless electrical pulses as the highly-modified civilian helicopter's angled rotors sliced through the static sky.

Eagerly awaiting the go ahead from the man coordinating the *Balta Zaibus* Protocol, Jaroslaw opened the slide door to a grim and sedate gunmetal vista, having tallied the laser pulses devastating success rate, thus beginning the operation's second phase.

"Greatness awaits you, Captain." He shouted over the wind, as the Sikorsky began its final approach to the Lenkov estate, sliding through the gray fog till the scent of fresh pine began to rush into the cabin.

The eight men eager to touch their boots to the ground and spill Teutonic blood echoed their agreement with a shout of thunder, reveling in the freedom of speaking their native language with the frigid wind tearing at their eyes, and the black fringe of trees below beckoning their ghostly presence as warriors of the forest, kindred spirits of ancient brothers who had fought and died in bitter battles against their Teutonic oppressors.

The Lynx, Ridley Sorber, stood.

All five foot six inches of him.

In their eyes he was a giant, a *killer* of giants; a

hero for a people that had none, and a symbol of the patience necessary for the fruitful harvest of revenge.

Sorber wordlessly moved to the door to sit on the edge of the chopper bay, his legs wide on the rails of the fixed landing gear for balance.

Jaroslaw strapped him to the floor and doorframe of the helicopter with a nylon rope and a karabiner, tightening the rope with a click pulley till Sorber was secure.

"Eyes." Jaroslaw called out, and the soldiers flipped down the night vision goggle units fitted to their matte black helmets.

With the dispelling of the retina-burning lightning, their advantage had been set in stone, and Sorber loaded a twenty-round magazine into his H&K rifle as his squad members attached silencers to their nine-millimeter MP-Fives.

His accuracy would be one hundred percent, and not a single shell would be wasted.

For Sorber was no longer the pawn of the chessboard, but the *Žirgas*, the Knight, and instead of a blunt and simple single-square procedure, like a pawn was forced to engage, his attack would be a fluid, multi-tiered display of cunning and tactical aptitude the ripple of which would never subside.

And as the Sikorsky rounded the breadth of a hill, it twisted sideways to hover above the treetops with serpentine grace, allowing Ridley Sorber to exact his first deadly murder of the night with a deafening echo.

But the gatekeeper's head, caving in with the bludgeoned mess of overripe pumpkin as his body arched and began to fall to the ground, didn't hold the bright green tint of The Lynx's scope for long as the gatekeeper's partner, jarred from his static position by startling splatter of the shooting, jerked and stumbled to the ground as Sorber centered the man's neck in the rifle's bull's-eye and pinched the trigger with the simple facility in which a classically-trained pianist struck middle C.

Inside the building and huddled near the bar shielding the kitchen from the ballroom with the light of a smartphone that had no service, Lucy's eyes met Morell's on the second gunshot. Though Lucy'd never discharged her service weapon in the line of duty, she knew the sound of gunfire all too well and the unattractive snarl working across Morell's mouth let her know just how accurate her ears had been.

"It's an H&K." Morell said as the deafening *thwop thwop* of the Sikorsky ripped across the property, punctuated by two more crackling shots. "And the caliber's a hell of a lot bigger than my vest can handle."

Lucy's gray-green eyes flit to the windows and the blackness that consumed them and back to Morell, whose nostrils were flared with an indefinite sense of adrenaline, as if it had snapped awake and been shaken up like a chemical tube light, tossed down into a pit of snakes.

"Talk to me." Lucy begged, as pandemonium began to seize the room. Morell's vision snapped between Lucy and the small throng of directionless riches standing in the rotunda.

He wanted to give her an answer, but the chaotic tones of Geffington's assassination were returning, and the self-serving cries of madness engulfing the partygoers only slowed his soldier-sharpened functions like rubber cement.

Who's the target? I can't help them all!

The powerlessness gripping his ankles and wrists was the blindness of pure darkness and isolation as ignorance forced him to imagine the parameters to a host of factors, finding clarity of direction in no certain thought.

Each question echoing through his mind like the rotating chamber of a fired revolver left him with the blank gaze of a dead man.

I can hear them but I can't see them. I don't know how many there are. I don't know who they're here for, or where they'll hit. I don't know if there's an inside man or if a forward observer on the property is calling the shots. Do they have satellite? Infrared? There's no power. Phones have no signal. I've got a pistol and a badge, but this isn't Baghdad.

It's worse.

And just what am I supposed to do? My own government wants me in jail.

There was nothing for him to do, no action for which he could equally and oppositely *react*, save continue studying the flight plan of the distantly ominous *thwop thwop* of a helicopter impervious to the lightning and the blackout it had caused.

Panic instantly asserted itself as the master of ceremonies; clacking heels and slick-soled dress shoes attacked the hardwood floors in an effort to rush to some deceptive safety, sounding like fusillades of returning pistol fire. Sergei Lenkov's resonant voice demanded attention as his men and Veremecek's pulled their weapons and tried to maintain order, with half of them corralling the weak-minded for the basement and the other half taking futile peeks at the window to see the disturbingly incoherent diorama of death and darkness.

"Is it civilian or military?" Lucy asked, her Detective mind cautiously alert and focused, though Morell could feel her heart race as she stood close. She knew without anyway to contact help they were on their own, and the overwhelming caveat to their loneliness was the fact that the city itself was sinking under the helpless hell of powerless blackness.

The chosen swordbrothers of Giltine had arisen.

"Civilian." Morell said without thinking, his mind locked on more of the *what* than anything else, even though the *who* was at the forefront of his thoughts.

"Tell me what to do, Henry." A quaver riddled Lucy's voice, and he knew if her face could make an expression it would be a twisted display of fear, despite her fortitude developed through experience.

They were all in over their heads, for ghost-like life-stealers had come for blood, and nothing but, ready to slice the spines from their victims with the sharp sickle of Giltine's tongue.

The helpless shroud of execution slowly fell on the mansion as the security guards, at Lenkov and Veremecek's bidding, grappled for some kind of order.

Morell stood close. Lucy didn't fight the feeling of drowning in something far greater than herself.

"I don't *know* what to do." Morell said, with clenched teeth, as she steadied herself and attempted to tap into the mental fortitude of a combat soldier, needing it now more than ever, even though she'd never seen combat and didn't know what it was like.

Running out to the car would guarantee certain death, with the man operating the H&K from the belly of a helicopter obviously being equipped with NVG's.

Whomever was coordinating the special-forces flavored assault was operating on concepts Morell had yet to grasp, but was sure he would see the brutal fullness of if he stayed smart despite the fibrillating thrum of his heart telling him to run like hell.

Lucy seemed to shrink tightly within herself as another shot echoed through the forest while the mechanically flawless concussion of the chopping helicopter blades eerily drummed out their cyclical cadence, as if a band of native cannibals were trudging through the forest to skewer the rich colonials of the capacious fortress of a house on the tips of their spears and knives and would not be content to do so till the psychological mind game of the circling drum-like noise had fully wrought its paralytic effect.

Sorber squeezed off a dozen more shots in the once-over sweep of the perimeter, knowing that the remaining two bullets in his cartridge represented the hardest two targets to hit.

The damn CPD CRT cops.

The one, of course, he'd fought and let live, once, not long ago, and wouldn't do so again.

The other, well, he was sure she was the silly kind of girl who believed in heaven and would be able to play her beloved Chopin up there.

With every deadman's flailing silhouette, stretching to clutch at the futile gray-black blanket of the blank sky with a final flash of life, and every thunderous crack preceding the dismal crumpling of death, the squad of soldiers cheered with wholehearted approval, as if The Lynx was the king of a type of sport hunting they found endlessly entertaining.

Long had their enemies lived in opulent arrogance. Forever would they receive the punishment due the careful planning of vengeance.

And as the Sikorsky banked for a tight return to the racetrack parking lot, with the squad sucking up frosty breaths of night air as if it were a drug to get high from, Ridley Sorber steadied himself for his final two shots before the *Mjslingumas Karalienė* would finally rise to the dreadful sense of omniscience only a terrorist who could call down lightning truly deserved.

For when *Mjslingumas Karalienė* came to power, all the world's chess pieces, both great and small, would bow to the eternally damning check-mate of a

Queen who sat on her throne with no sorrow, but rather, waxed intoxicatingly fiercer with the quenching of her vampiric appetite for blood.

The deep rift of thought capturing Morell's focus finally broke with a hasty summation of probable calculations and he swore as he twisted Lucy around, pushing her toward the kitchen.

"What? What?" Her whisper was harsh, and Morell refrained till they were out of earshot of the confused huddle of partygoers still wondering about the loss in power, the gunshots and the helicopter.

"Giltine…" Morell rasped, his dark eyes flashing left and right to show the sclera in what Lucy might've suspected was fear, had she not've had as much faith in him with the encroaching claws of combat closing around them as humanly possible.

"What?"

"Come on." He pressed her down and grabbed her wrist, ushering her through the kitchen of marble and stainless to the butler's pantry, nearly four feet by four, as Veremecek's former Spetznaz men fanned out along the window in the ballroom with their nine-millimeter pistols at the ready.

"Giltine what?" Lucy asked once Morell had slid the walnut panel door shut behind him and tugged at the pull chain to wash the shelved-out room in pale orange light.

"Lenkov's Order, right?"

"Yeah?"

"And Veremecek, right?"

"Yeah?" Lucy's gray-green eyes danced around his face.

"They're *all* Order, right?"

"Yeah?" Lucy said, frustrated with Morell's lack of explanation.

And then it hit her.

They're ALL Order. Everyone at the damn party.
Every last one of them, rounded up with a cute little
bow like grain-fed beef cows for the bone saw of the
butcher. It's an execution. Not one, not two.

All.

"Where is she?" Lucy asked.

"I don't know but nobody's getting out of this
place alive. They've knocked out the power, cut the
comms, phone-service, everything! You can't see your
own hand in front of your face outside, and I'll be
damned if they haven't got two four man squads with
silenced machine guns and night vision ready to turn
this place into a shooting gallery."

"Giltine…" Lucy whispered as if it was a
summons, and Morell took her hand as it began to
tremble.

The hideous two-dimensional image of the history
book was dancing around Lucy's mind, cast in the
unnerving light of a thousand pound chandelier and a
glittering white dress.

"Listen," He said, his skin sticky with the sweat
of adrenaline's intensity. "I've got a way out of it but
you have to do exactly as I say, understand?"

"Of course, of course, anything." His request
snapped her back to the pulse of the moment.

"No, Lucy, it's not like that." He gripped her
velveteen shoulders. "You've got to trust me."

"*Henry*…" Her voice nearly broke with
exasperation, and her hand leapt to cup the shadowed
bruising of his face. "You *know* I trust you. You *know* I
do."

"Good." Morell pulled back from her, removing
his service issue Beretta from the holster with steel in
his dark eyes. "Because I'm going to go kill that crazy
bitch."

FORTY-ONE

Ridley Sorber scanned the windows running east from the columns of the grand entrance and counted four buzz-cuts holding defensive positions, smiling that they would not die at his hand.

One could never understand the empowering *feeling* of sparing life till one stared down the barrel of a rifle.

Unlike in closer-quarters combat or the fervor of pursuit and a hand-to-hand fight to the death, the satisfaction of snuffing someone's candle in the blink of an eye, thus *stealing* their soul from the very bones and skin in which it lived, always gave Sorber a rush.

"Owl One, deploy." Sorber commanded as the Sikorsky leveled off four feet above the deck, twenty yards south of the fenced-in car lot.

Two soldiers simultaneously leapt into the cold on each side of the chopper bay, followed by two more. Sorber's goggles colored the soldiers grainy and green, amplifying the lightlessness, but to the buzz-cut security guards in the window, the slick black shapes were mere specters made indistinguishable by the murky blanket muting the light of a nearly full moon. The distinctive gargle of the chopper would only add to the defensive disorientation consuming the mansion, as they could hear and not see, and the isolated fear of the unknown was a proven battlefield superweapon, eroding the mind like a malignant cancer.

The chopper rose steadily and stealthily, shrinking the four men of Owl One in Sorber's vision as they charged along the parking lot fence line in a hasty shuffle, silenced machine guns leveled and ready to fire.

Their time would come.

Morell leapt up the stairs in twos after showing his badge to the towering duo of men trying to maintain order in the rotunda.

Veremecek and a former Colonel in the Spetznaz by the name of Popovic had finally convinced the partygoers to head to the basement where they would be safe, letting the armed security detail do their job, though no one, save Morell, knew what the hell was going on, other than bullets and helicopters and the severing of all power and communication were horribly *abnormal* and life-threatening things.

Morell was thankful for the darkness to hide his facial expression about the chances of the security guards doing spit as far as some gesture of armed defense in the lack of illumination and had learned from Popovic that Sergei Lenkov had gone upstairs to convince his sister to join them, as she'd bolted off with the initial pandemonium of the sniper rifle's ominous finality, leaving her drunken brother to further frazzle himself and fight for control.

*Her first victim…*Morell thought, bounding up the heights, with the oddly feminine static undulation of the *Tree of the World* sculpture soaring to the roofline next to him and reflecting the colored light of nearly a hundred dazzling smartphone screens huddled at the base of the tree.

Morell stopped on the second floor, leaning on the balustrade.

A sharp pain flared in his not yet healed ribs, and his heart fell as the masterstroke of Alexis' metaphorical tactics hit him with the weight of an ash baseball bat.

The door to the basement was hidden from the grand entrance by the roots of the sculpture as it clambered up and up the giant hollow tube of the rotunda.

According to the *Tree*, Alexis had rushed up to the third floor, the celestials, where she would be surrounded by the subversive art of the deities she worshipped.

Where she believed she belonged as one herself.

That meant the door to the basement was the door to certain death.

The door to the underworld.

One grenade and they'd all be blown to bits, or worse, the Order members could be locked in as the assault team set fire to the house, whereupon they'd suffocate to death, stepping on top of one another to claw at the door like a scene from a horror movie.

Morell's equilibrium suffered with the tactical possibilities flooding his head and he pulled himself up the stairs with the pain of his separated ribs slowing him down.

He had to stop her.

After stealing a large overcoat from the cloakroom, Lucy ducked out the service door used to quickly access the horse stables from the kitchen, as per Morell's choleric instructions. With the overcoat creating an unbroken gray silhouette between her head and the ground, the arms of it tied together behind the back, Lucy gave the eye the flashing shape of a unicolor gray blob, and could fall to the ground and cover herself if she had to, with nothing resembling a human body poking out.

Slipping out into the frosty night air, its unnatural stillness cut by the rumbling chop of the Sikorsky blades to the south, Lucy shut the door and crouched to survey her surroundings in a squint.

Don't think. She remembered Morell's instructions. *Just get to the car.*

If it weren't for the helicopter, Lucy could've sworn she was alone in the forest, with the distant hum of Crescent's metropolitan-area power grid having been utterly silenced.

It was as if Lucy'd been transported to the Lithuania of Alexis' dreams, and her homestead truly was a shrine, hidden from all unbelievers in the dense and fertile arms of nature.

Lucy calmed herself with a steadying breath and pulled the overcoat above her head.

One step at a time Lucja...her late father's advice resonated in her mind as she began making her way slowly toward the nearest stable. The severity of his instruction style had perverted Lucy's mind into thinking that *everything* she put her hand to was a matter of life and death and Lucy couldn't wait to be free of the heavy, musty-smelling cloak as it reminded her so much of him.

Her heels shortened her stride and with each step the thick opaqueness of the stable seemed to swell and stretch and the darkness between them expand to mock her attempt to reach it. How she wanted to cast them off and sprint but Morell had assured her she needed perfectly dry feet to operate the stick-equipped muscle car and couldn't chance the numbness her journey through the cold wet grass would facilitate.

Tactically, Morell explained, *they won't bother with the stable because they've already cleared the area. Their focus is the mansion. Wait till they've*

committed inside and then run to the car. I know it's a long way all the way around the side of the house but no one will see you once you get to the trees. It'll be just like earlier, except there'll be no dump trucks and no sabotage.

Don't worry about me. I'll find you.

Just drive it like you stole it.

She barely remembered what she'd said in response, voicing her obvious concern for his own well-being.

It took everything within her to stuff her own selfish desires to be with him back down inside. She didn't want him to go alone to confront Alexis and her planned execution of the Order's highest echelons.

She wanted him in front of her, leading the way to safety.

His hand holding her own.

Whatever he said she *had* to adhere to. *He* was a battle-hardened solider, a *decorated* one, and in throwing herself out, *alone*, into the cold muddle of the lightless night she was trusting in his ability more than her own.

It was as if he *couldn't* fail, as if he didn't know how.

It may've been blind faith on Lucy's part but it was faith, nonetheless, and would not be shaken.

The voice of Krančjar, Owl One's point man, crackled across Sorber's comm.

"Owl One, in position."

"Copy, Owl One, hold position awaiting deploy of Owl Two."

Sorber shot a tight fist to the co-pilot, who nodded and the chopper began to break from its guardian hover toward the north side of the house, near the horse stables where the secluded service entrance would catch the partygoers in a pincer, if they hadn't already stuffed themselves in the basement, and if they had, then the former soldiers and cops flanked out along the windows would be caught in a nine millimeter buzzsaw, the only escape was the blank gaze of death.

"Copy Lynx. Eyes on four tangos, first floor." Krančjar muttered from his cover near the bumper of a hot pink Hummer Limo. Behind them, windshields were shattered with Sorber's killshots of the hired drivers who hadn't been able to leave their cozy cars.

Bodies intermittently dotted the east corner of the house where Sorber had cleaned up the forest and outbuilding guards as they'd come to conference with those assigned to the mansion.

Fools, they were, *all* of them, and Sorber was licking his chops for the CRT cops, especially the one he'd tangled with in the alley, the man who might've actually known what was befalling the doomed fundraiser.

Not that he could do a damn thing about it.

"Confirm four." Sorber said with the last shapes of the men at the windows disappearing from the crosshairs of his scope, and more importantly, his remarkably keen yellow-green eyes.

He could *feel* the gnawing ache of Owl Two's four soldiers in the bay behind him, eager to spark the static hush of the waiting killzone to fire as a cruel wind sliced through the open Sikorsky.

Understandable, it was.

He had his own appetites to appease.

"Owl Two, prepare deploy." His voice crackled across the comm, and he lowered his rifle as the Sikorsky cut a fluid path around the east side of the mansion to the stables cluttering the north side.

The remaining four soldiers took to the edges of the chopper bay, consumed with the moment when their boots would hit the ground, the safety catches would nick their thumbs, and the service door would finally be the only thing standing between them and ancestral revenge.

FORTY-TWO

Lucy had cautiously made it halfway to the stables when the Sikorsky swept around the east corner of the mansion in a graceful arc, the looping crescendo of its cyclical *thwop thwop* gradually increasing as she instantaneously threw herself to the cold, wet ground and remained motionless till the immense vibrations shooting through her ears and her bones became an overwhelming irreversibility.

She was in no man's land, equidistant between the past and the future, stuck forever in what felt like a shallow grave.

Lucy held her spot in the flat, damp turf, its numbing coldness raging against the burning heat obscenely accusing her of failure. The thought that every breath would be her last and that she'd been spotted and it would all be for naught refused to leave her mind, no matter how hard she tried to cast it down or how still she told herself to be.

But the chopper's earsplitting thunder, carrying a whining musicality denoting a powering down of the engine, told Lucy the helicopter had touched ground long enough to load or unload, and whoever doing so would be focused on such.

She had to make her move.

Twisting on her belly in a back-breaking semi-circle, Lucy peered under the heavy wool top coat she

was hidden under on the broad plain of grass separating
the mansion and the stables to see the blinking landing
lights of the chopper not a hundred feet away from her,
and in the scant illumination such offered, the
deployment of four CT-style Operators, two on each
side, as if they were a SWAT team come to save the
day.

The chopper was facing the mansion.

The men were running *to* the mansion.

She was on their six, their only blind spot in a
pitch-black world in which they held the arbitrary
advantage of night-vision goggles versus the naked eye.

And in the odd combination of knowing her only
chance at doing *any* good would be to risk her own life
with the sound reasoning that she was *still* undetected,
Lucy pressed herself up from the wooly gray shroud
and grabbed the fabric of her dress to take off,
fearlessly, to the stables, as fast as her low heels would
allow, leaving the gray overcoat behind.

The pain was constant, rhythmic and knife-like by
the time Morell reached Alexis' room, and he knew it
was hers because she had told him as much on the tour
and had not allowed him to enter, but rather, reveled in
a glorious explanation that, from the deck of her room,
she could watch the sunrise each morning and set each
night, and that she did so religiously.

Morell tried to control his lungs and shook his
head, gently twisting the knob to find it locked and
readied his Beretta with a final huff of breath, the pits
of his underarms scratchy with the lathered exertion
required to stop the unstoppable.

The wood near the lock splintered as the door
thwacked open under the force of Morell's well-placed
kick to it and Morell quickly processed the scene before
him with the horror of one who had no choice but to

react.

"Drop the knife!" He hollered, and it hurt him to do so, the severity of his own words jabbing him with flinch-worthy discomfort.

On a hand-carved four poster bed of dark wood, Sergei Lenkov was prostrate, on his back, and the expression frozen on his face was one of disgusted shock, as what appeared to be nearly all of the blood in his body stained the white sheets and dripped to the carpeted floor with the plink of a leaky faucet.

With Teutonic blood squirted across her once immaculate white dress of sparkles and mammoth ivory from the savage undoing of Sergei's neck, Alexis' face reflected the flickering glow of the dozens of candles illuminating the room from the mirrored boudoir next to the bed.

"Dammit, I said *drop* it!" Morell shouted again, his body rigid as the porcelain-doll face of the Lithuanian Princess turned to register his words, and her enormous emerald-toned eyes, telescopic in their slivered facets, locked on to his own with the paralytic gaze of Medusa herself.

"Shoot me." She said, and Morell frowned as the woody smell of incense became unreasonably intoxicating. "Or listen to what I have to say, it is your choice."

Morell's eyes tried to break from hers to check on Lenkov but he was far beyond saving, and from his peripheral vision and his initial assessment of the murder scene, Morell knew the dagger glued to Alexis' hand was straight out of one of his history books, and by the jewels encrusting it he was sure it belonged to her royal line and would be responsible for the night's *every* single ritual execution.

Unless he stopped her by becoming the executor himself.

Morell swallowed hard.

"What the hell are you talking about?" He growled, more for the pain of separated ribs refusing to allow him a clean breath, and the soft, orangey light, like the color of Baltic amber, only adding to the heavy, lethargic atmosphere.

"You don't know what's going on, do you? But you want to. You can't just shoot me. You have to know why." She said, her accent tight and articulate, as if she'd studied English all of her life in the way that a hunter studied the habits of their prey.

"They're all Order, every last one of them," His smoker's voice rasped, "And you're going to kill them all."

"True." Alexis said, still poised on the bed on her knees with the metallic odor of blood undergirding the spices of incense. "But it is only the beginning."

"Beginning of what?"

Alexis seemed to rotate on her knees like the Sikorsky, void of physics.

"Of the end. I'm going to change the world. Forever. For the better."

"You're gonna drop the damn knife, Alexis, or *Giltine* or whatever the hell your name is."

At the name of the pagan deity, the woman in white arched her back and swelled her chest.

"So you *do* know."

"That you're a psychopath? Yes. Now drop that knife or you're getting a hollowpoint to the knee cap, the femur, the ankle, or whatever part of your leg you want me to hit, understand? Or do you need that translated into Lithuanian?"

Alexis laughed, a small bubble in her throat, as if she was amused by his manner because he was a shivering Chihuahua squaring off with a polar bear.

"Do you know," Her chin dipped toward her

swollen chest, and her free hand curled before her as if she'd plucked and imaginary piece of fruit. "That *I* command the lightning?"

Morell frowned as if it was a tactical euphemism or some code name for the man that had killed Maks Lenkov, Yiury Mogilev, *and* Mayor Geffington with the ease of picking produce at the supermarket, and was no doubt operating the sniper rifle from the belly of the Sikorsky and coordinating the corralling of Order members for sacrifice.

But as Alexis rose from the bed and stood, easily taller than Morell, the flickers of candlelight zipped through her corset as if jagged shards of light had ripped across the sky.

Alexis smiled broadly, the pale coldness of her white teeth relishing in the astonishment dispersing across Morell's face.

The sudden starting and stopping of the circuitry-frying lightning strikes, free of thunder and rain, echoed through Morell's mind with the blankness of one facing an impossibility, such as anti-gravity or teleportation.

"Yesss..." The woman's voice drawled with serpentine sibilance. "You comprehend but you do not *understand*. Where do I begin?"

"How?"

"How does not matter. It is why." She said, flipping the knife over in her hand so that she held it by the blood-smeared blade, the handle extended toward Morell ten feet away as if she were looking down a bejeweled scepter.

The gun tensed in his hand with a plasticized rattle.

His body language said he'd pull the trigger before she could work up the motion to throw it but his eyes and the eye-lock neither could break the connection of, said otherwise.

She knew he couldn't shoot *until* he understood.
He was a soldier, a do-gooder, a hero.

Unlike her, he abode by the rules. Rules were made for those like him, and she would've applauded the balls it would've taken him to unload his cartridge into her, dealing with the punitive consequences of justifiable murder later, in front of a self-righteous panel of talking heads and she would've respected him for it. It was *her* way of conduct, fighting war with war, steel with steel, and where steel didn't work, the honeyed tongue and the plan of patience would never fail.

But she saw the weakness in his eyes, the weakness of the Constitution and the Judicial branch of watered-down Greek philosophy, Anglo-Saxon romanticism and Biblical principals.

"As *Mįslingumas Karalienė* I control *Balta Zaibus.*" Alexis took a step forward, her voice carrying a hypnotic lilt with the introduction of her native tongue. "And with *Balta Zaibus* I can cripple the world economy one domino at a time. By creating an electromagnetic pulse blackout in the world's major cities as if the hammer of Perkunas has struck the anvil of his father's forge, death and destruction will grip this world as an invisible specter; and one city at a time, every tower will fall, every street will be emptied, every stomach will starve, and those who I have chosen to sleep through this rebirth with me in our forest kingdom will reclaim this earth and rebuild it in the way of our ancestors, having the unopposed power to do so."

Morell swallowed, so gravely shocked that the woman not only believed in her mythology but was facilitating its eschatology for the purpose of a new age, with, of all things, a synthetically-produced natural phenomenon.

"You're talking about…*Ragnarok?*"

The *Mislingumas Karalienė* shrugged and tipped her head to the left, peering down at the former soldier nine feet from her.

"I have a different name for it."

Morell shook his head and disregarded her, still baffled. His own voice sounding foreign to him.

"You want to bring about the end of the world, where…where the gods and giants will kill each other off? So that man and woman sleep in the forest and the earth, cleansed by fire and made fertile again, will begin a new age, void of evil and treachery, to go on forever?"

The *Mislingumas Karalienė,* the *Mystery Queen*, smiled.

"And you wish to stop *this*?"

Her mind-altering green eyes said it was a good thing, no, a *great* thing that corporations and governments, the *gods* and *giants*, who had so rapaciously ruined planet earth would shrivel and starve to death as she stood in the gap and pressed the reset button.

And everything that had made life *so easy* and information *so* self-gratifyingly quick, and every process of life *so* overregulated and overstimulated, would fry like mosquitoes in an outdoor zapper, and those hooked to such ways of life as if they were maternal breasts would finally awaken in a world in which they knew not how to live and, finally unplugged, suffer and die as co-dependent babes.

Morell grit his teeth and readied himself to fire straight through the black hole of her heart.

"You're damn right I wanna stop it you crazy bitch."

The Mystery Queen shook her head, her porcelain doll's face looking eerily ageless and sensual in the candlelight, as if she'd stepped straight from an oil

painting hanging on the wall of the Louvre.
    But her voice was harsh and mechanical.
    "Too late."

FORTY-THREE

Hearing Sorber's order rifle through their comm, Owl One charged forward at a steady pace from the gated enclosure of automobiles, single file, only to fan out on the cold ground twenty yards from the louvered windows and await the snapping concussion of Owl Two's breaching charge.

"Confirm targets." Krančjar said, lining up a buzz-cut in the iron sights of his MP-Five. The blocky and grim Russian face in Krančjar's sights kept furtively jabbing around the corners of the window, trying to see what could not and *would* not be seen and was the human embodiment of insanity, performing the same action over and over and expecting a different result.

"Confirm." The soldier next to him crackled.

"Confirm." The fourth soldier called out.

"Owl Two ready for breach in thirty." Jaroslaw's voice rippled across their ears.

"Three of four confirmed. Holding." Krančjar shifted his body a fraction of an inch to the left, and knew he'd get a clean head shot with his target where the others could only manage a shoulder or an elbow. He tapped the second man on the shoulder who tapped the third man, thus shifting him to get a better angle. They were still waiting for the third man in line to acquire his target but if the target had moved somewhere else in the broad space of the mansion with the frenetic confusion that possessed it, Owl Two would be more than capable of cleaning up the trash with their reverse-entry assault.

"Breach ready?" Sorber crackled over the comm from the Sikorsky.

"Breach ready in three, two, one…"

"Fire at will." Sorber ordered from above as the helicopter set itself on the flat roof of the capitol-like structure, disregarding the fact that only three targets had been acquired. An assault was an interplay of timing and momentum, balancing disorientation with tactical aptitude, both of which were heavily on Sorber's side.

On his order, Owl One snapped off their silenced shots with a pelting volley of *kthk kthk kthk* noises, nailing their targets through the open slats of the louvered windows as shattered glass and slivers of wood misted with spits of crimson. Why they hadn't shut the windows, Krančjar would never know, and refused to think about the arrogant stupidity of his foes as he threw himself to full height in the same moment Jaroslaw detonated the breaching charge on the opposite side of the house.

"Go, go, go!" Sorber shouted, watching the men of Owl One sprint up to the grand entrance, knowing the adrenaline rush of the choreographed assault bore no resemblance to their careful practice of it, and was a sensory envelopment the men would never forget.

Jaroslaw was first through the blackened splat of the service door and thrust a fist to the left to split his team in half. He knew by the time he rounded the kitchen with the frontal cover of the bar from which he could shoot behind, he'd hit the flank of the ballroom security guards who'd taken defensive positions along the window, and those that hadn't been eliminated by Owl One would get a fusillade of nine millimeters in the back as Owl One entered the exposed space of the rotunda and the other half of Owl Two slid around the back of the rotunda to rush up the staircase and clear the higher floors.

Once the second floor was secure with a cursory sweep, Jaroslaw would rush to the third floor to locate and escort the *Mįslingumas Karalienė*, the very one on whose orders they were operating as if the soldiers themselves were militaristic marionettes in the ambidextrous fingers of a musical maestro and master manipulator, to the ground floor to proceed with the planned executions of *Operation Giltine.*

Krančjar, point man of Owl One smiled as he spoke.

"Tangos down, count two. Rotunda clear. Hostiles in basement. Split for ground floor sweep, holding the door."

"Roger." Jaroslaw said as he rushed through the kitchen and popped a round into a tuxedo-clad man, writhing on the ground near the piano with a nine-millimeter already lodged in the socket-joint of his shoulder.

He made it to the mouth of the rotunda to see Krančjar kneeling near the open door, with another squad mate flanking it.

"Rotunda secure." Jaroslaw called to Sorber, up above.

"Roger." Sorber nodded with a tightness in his voice, scanning the dark terrain below him with his scope. "Secure MK and commence Operation Giltine."

Jaroslaw stopped and his MP-Five sagged in his grip. He could detect something amiss.

"What's wrong?" He asked.

"Possible runaway." Sorber's voice was terse as

he was trying to focus on the grainy green circle of land in the crosshairs of his scope, constantly lifting his head to survey the breadth of land before him from the bird's-eye view of the roof and going back again to the increased magnification of his rifle.

He'd spotted the coat on the ground and was furious that he couldn't ascertain *who* it belonged to, or where they had gone *to*. It hadn't been there before, he would've noticed it.

No, it had to've come sometime *after* he'd shot all of the exterior guards and secured the lot.

He was sure of it.

The lot *was* secure because *he'd* secured it.

If it wasn't secure, then *he* had failed, and Sorber, SAS-trained, did *not* make mistakes.

"Shall we wait?" Jaroslaw asked.

"Negative." Sorber put the scope to his eye again, letting his rifle drift across the nearest horse stable one last time, having a feeling whomever fled the house would hide there and try to contact make with the outside world beyond the forested killzone for help, which, for all intents and purposes, was just as helpless. "Proceed as planned. Owl Zero will hold the roof."

"Roger." Jaroslaw shrugged and walked to the door of the basement, hidden by the beautiful and awe-inspiring *Tree of the World* sculpture.

Someone's out there, Sorber thought, staring into the limbs and leaves as he panned across the fringe of foliage surrounding the mansion and the almost treeless plane of grass that it sat on. *I can feel it.*

You can't hide from me, Sorber promised whoever it was and lowered his rifle to move to the other side of the roof.

No one hides from me.

At the sound of the breaching charge, the sonic

signature he knew so well, rocking the hollowed-out
caverns of the ground floor, Morell twisted his head
behind him to the irreversibly splintered door and the
three-story staircase that stood between him and certain
death.

Time had run out.

A solid object thwacked his chest and bounced off
with a dull clatter on the count of his body armor vest,
as if a hearty piece of marble had been thrown his way,
and the object pulled his attention back to his own
safety because the safety of others was forever out of
reach.

Like Lucy, where was she?

Is she still alive?

And by the time he'd processed the fact that some
form of assault team was on the ground floor, ready to
shoot anything that moved, and the helicopter had taken
to the roof awaiting the Mystery Queen's planned
escape, Alexis was on *him*, and he threw up his left arm
to block the arcing blow coming his way.

It did nothing to stop it.

Maddened that the knife she'd zipped toward him,
center mass, had bounced off as if he were the man that
changed his outfit in a phone booth, Alexis' fist crashed
a disorienting blow near his temple and her knee was
not far behind it, doubling him over with a clean shot to
his manhood.

The scant candlelight dimmed in the edges of
Morell's vision as he lost nearly all control of his body
with the airless and sickening heat of nausea as it
collided with the overwhelming stress of circumstance.

He couldn't stop Alexis' second kick, and it tore
the Beretta from his hand to send it skidding to the far
corner of the room.

Morell fell forward on his knees, desperately
grasping at the snowy expanse of white fabric before

him. Alexis screamed as she toppled back into the foot of the solid bed with a *thunk* that echoed inside of her own head.

Dizziness spurned her into further rage.

Morell rolled to the right, off of her legs and on to his back as she stretched for him, the shiny nails of her fingers extending in his blurred vision like retractable cat claws.

The thought of his skin peeling under the swiping razors of her cruel talons flared his primal survival instincts and he tried to gage her position in between the stabs of ceiling, floor, and the orange light of the credenza as he forced himself to roll and roll and roll away from her.

The solidity of the credenza finally halted his efforts.

Alexis leapt at him, knowing all she had to do was hold him down till the assault team reached her room, and the furor coursing through her veins as if she were a creature transformed by a full moon attached itself to the smaller Morell with a ferocious grip, the years of obsessive planning finally coming to a fanatical reality.

She would not be denied the vengeance written into the very code of her DNA.

With a swift movement, Alexis straddled the former soldier and viced his arms in a narrow Y-shape above his head with the surprising strength of a smothering broad-shouldered hug, interlocking her fingers behind his head in a white-knuckled fist.

He couldn't see the candles anymore, or the softly refracting stars of light in the credenza mirror.

He couldn't see *anything* past the murky curtain of auburn hair whipping against his face as he reached to break free and he realized he was powerless against her, physically compromised by her advantageous position.

He remembered his many times grappling combat instructors on the mat, and heard their voices rattle around his mind about how some holds were *impossible* to break.

Morell refused to accept it.

But his muscles foundered in resistance with the lack of a good, clean breath and the sensation of his life leaking like helium from a balloon began to consume him.

Alexis' legs, made strong from riding horses, crushed his lungs and with his last breath he forced his rib cage to swell and hold.

Alexis used the muffled momentum of his resistance to lock her legs together just above the small of his back.

It was then she clamped down on him as if she was trying to kill him with all of her might and her anger and rage, instead of just trying to hold him still.

Morell's body responded to her python-squeeze with the foily-potato chip bag crackling of his fifth and sixth ribs.

Flaming shards of pain ripped through his core as he squirmed and twitched to free himself of her leeching deathlock.

Morell shifted, straining to free himself but she remained rigid and stiff, not allowing him an inch.

He felt as if he were drowning in a gluey sea of Baltic amber colors, coagulating to irreversible hardness in heavy wafting of incense and his hands wriggled above his head, reaching for something, *anything*, to smack her across the face with but the only thing that filled them was the densely spiced air and the mocking futility of its emptiness.

Suddenly, the airlessness in his brain began to mix with the *thwop* of the chopper above them both and all senses faded in Morell's focus.

He was lost in a claustrophobic tangle of pale skin, blood-stained white fabric and auburn hair.

Lost in the arms of secrets and lies, greed and revenge.

And a captive of such, the icicle-sharp sting of horribly painful separated ribs seemed to extend through the soft tissue of Morell's quivering lungs, and, without repentance, pierce his heart with the leprously frozen touch of death.

FORTY-FOUR

Instead of meticulously working her way around the forest and climbing up the small incline that lead to the windy country road in her low heels to work her way back to the car lot, Lucy had taken her chances with a sense of rebellion and drummed up a brazen burst of speed to follow the assault team into the darkness like the lone last place participant in a track meet sprint.

It all hit her as she was running for the stable, thinking about the time it'd take her to do such and to finally reach the car, time neither her nor Morell nor any of the not-yet murdered Teutonic Order members had to bargain with, because their time had run out.

Stolen from them all by the perfect execution of a plan years in the making.

And she could no longer follow Morell's orders because time had presented her with an opportunity, that, instead of hesitating to follow, she'd sprinted toward, with the full capacities of the ad-lib skills and instincts she'd survived on in Vice. Thus, doubling back from the stables, she followed the small squad of Lithuanian Operators into the black furnace of the mansion.

And with their intent focus *on* the mansion and their technical procedure of clearing it, as Morell had explained, the assault team never *once* looked behind them, and had charged straight through the charred doorway into the mudroom's preamble to the kitchen and on to the ballroom.

She had to keep telling herself, they could see, but still in a *limited manner*, like racehorses, blinded but to the singularity of their objective.

The helicopter, as well, had kept its tail rotor to her position, lethargically ascending to take up residence on the flat rooftop and after the assault team had entered the house, Lucy took full advantage of their glaring blind spot and rushed to the door.

There, she had removed her shoes, thus stepping to the hardwood floor in the silence and slickness of nylon stockings.

Lucy frowned, holding her hidden position near the open doorframe of the large mudroom, more than likely an area of egress for the movement of furniture in anticipation of the fundraiser.

Fundraiser...Lucy thought sardonically with fingers of cold air pricking her skin as if the blades of the chopper were the spokes of a box fan.

More like honey pot. There has to be a way out of this...think Lucy, think!

Henry said to get to the car but if you could create some kind of diversion, you'd buy him some time and whatever plan these guys've got going would go south, just far enough to ruin...

That's all you need to do, break it apart; throw a wrench in it and watch the sparks fly.

Sparks???

Besides, Henry just doesn't want you to get hurt. He's afraid you'll die. Keep the cop out of trouble and take all the punches for her like a human speed bag.

What, like he's are made of stone and I'm made of silk?

Lucy ducked her head out of the doorframe of the

mudroom, knowing nowhere was truly safe to stay.

She had to keep moving.

I'm coming for you Henry, and not all the hounds in hell can stop me.

Hold on, Henry.

Hold on.

If we're dying here, tonight, then we're dying together, fighting to the last breath.

Lucy strained to hear the voices of the assault team over the heavy blows of the chopper above and knew they were advancing through the house, having split themselves in half.

It doubled the risk of discovery, but she was well beyond risk aversion and was rapidly venturing into reckless gambling, with her own life as the all-in chips-to-the-middle caveat.

If Morell was right, their entire focus would be on the party guests, and Lucy moved stealthily to the kitchen as two shapes entered the ballroom in favor of the rotunda beyond.

She was operating on the assumption the hundred and some guests had finally locked themselves in the basement, with Veremecek as their de facto leader, barking out orders and mentally preparing a speech to offer a payoff or negotiate some kind of limited release, so there'd be no point in the soldiers hastily doubling back to patrol the rest of the house.

The assault team was there to get something. To *do* something.

To kill.

Quick in, quick out.

Like lightning.

And just like the jagged spits of nuclear energy that had cracked the sky, an idea asserted itself in Lucy's brain and she followed it, thus, overriding Morell's orders to get to the GTO.

Clicking on all four of eighty thousand BTU burners of the gas range to their full power, she stripped as quickly as possible, though the zipper provided some difficulty, and threw her purple velvet dress on top of the burners, bunching up its soft fabric.

Stripping for her government was nothing new to her and though she was grateful to be doing it in the dark for once, her mind was vacant of all other thoughts but the one that mattered.

The loss of power had cut the range's sparking functions and she'd have to somehow procure a catalyst to the awaiting inferno *before* the assault team became keen to the smell of gas.

It would only be a matter of minutes.

And Lucy knew exactly *where* she could find a light, even if she didn't quite think getting there and back would be physically possible, considering the damning guarantee of exposure.

Adrenaline began to crackle across her skin to combat the stinging cold surging through the gaping hole of the service door just beyond the kitchen.

Darkness.

It was all darkness, though the harder she tried, the better she could begin to distinguish between the opaque shapes of inanimate objects in which no light could pass and the faintest guess of the frigid air that separated such indeterminate masses.

Her strapless thirty-two C bra and nylons encouraged inane shivers and she knew they'd only worsen till they risked sabotaging her efforts.

To hell with it... Lucy thought. *To hell with them all.*

I should've known better then to let Morell go off alone. I should've trusted my training and experience, despite this insanity.

He paid his debts before he committed his sins.

He's a decorated soldier and a hero of the Crisis. He's the only reason anybody's here to stop this mass murder.

And whoever's not dead by the time the smoke clears I'm slapping in handcuffs for the duration, Lithuanian or Order, black chess pieces or white, I don't give a damn. They're all getting locked up till we figure this mess out.

And if the FBI wants to come and take Henry from me for some spat over past sins, then they've got another thing coming.

No one knows how to bend the rules like a Vice Detective.

Because our motto in Vice was, 'nothing ever goes right'.

Lucy grabbed two bottles of vodka from the thick bar guarding and hiding the kitchen from the broad space of the ballroom and snaked off for the butler's pantry, planning out her escape.

For once the science of her simple endeavor had manifested itself in the form of fire, chaos would be the feverish cadence of the song circumstance had forced her to play, and though she believed herself to be poor at improvising in the face of chaos, and even poorer at operating in haste, her highly successful career in Vice had been nothing short of a sterling textbook of such.

Maddened by the lack of physical evidence filling his scope in response to the sensation of escaped prey flooding his subconscious, Sorber rushed back to the Sikorsky and ordered them to lift off for a sweep of the car lot, and as the pilots nodded in the hasty response of his off-comm fury, Sorber rushed back to the rear of the chopper for a set of thermo-imaging goggles in order to spot the heat signature of whatever straggler had escaped his masterful net.

Once, he thought of holding Owl Two at the base of the *Tree of the World* and sending Owl One around the house again but decided against it.

If someone was out there, it was his mistake.

It was on him.

And the *Mįslingumas Karalienė* didn't take kindly to mistakes.

Quite the opposite.

FORTY-FIVE

Though his brain function was, at best, limited, it became readily apparent to Henry Morell, in the final moments of his ironic death in the arms of an austerely beautiful and exotic, though cerebrally psychotic woman, that his only method of escape would be an excruciating one.

But he had no choice.

Morell brusquely released all the air he'd forced his lungs to hold as long as humanly possible with pursed lips and though the bone of her knee and all the strong ligaments attached to it seemed to squish shattered bones further into the soft goo of his lungs, he twisted with all of his might in the newly slimmed space between her legs.

Alexis' fingers, interlocked behind his head, slacked as Morell's altered physiology stretched the distance of her arms and shoulders and with his midsection not in the same place that it had been her legs quickly attempted to compensate, but her body had slid too far forward to retain the death grip and her feet broke their stifling vice as his roll painfully bent her left knee and ankle beneath him.

On his right side, Morell pressed his right knee into the floor with a jarring jolt to nearly complete the roll to his stomach, managing to further assist momentum with the return of a right arm that had once been so helplessly extended above his head by sliding it across the floor till the bony fulcrum of his elbow could press him up from the hardwood.

Alexis screamed as her neck and head bent in with the strain of his reversal, and like a rollercoaster on the last clicks of its ascent before its eventual plummet, Alexis hovered with her legs flying through the air before Morell could push himself up and away to his full height of only five foot seven and a half.

As he did, drunkenly staggering backward from the suspended animation of her demise, he saw her long legs and four-inch heels clumsily swipe the bevy of candles and the tiered sticks that held them from the flat desktop of the boudoir.

The jarring explosion of light and flame blooming like a small nuclear flash in the refracting eye of the mirror juxtaposed the dark asphyxia of musty incense, metallic Teutonic blood, and curry-spiced American sweat.

Miles of expensive fabric damned her as some sort of deep-sea fishnet and her deadly catch landed around her with the random precision of gravity's impartial choosing, setting her hair and her dress alight on behalf of its chemical encasement in expensive perfume and cosmetic enhancements.

Her screams pierced the empty hollows of the house as hot wax splashed across her skin and her furious fight to free herself of the flames, only spread further by spasms and convulsions and the slick futility of swishing fabric scratching across the hardwood floor, pushed Morell to the darkest corner of the room, where he could barely manage to bend to the floor and retrieve the salvation of the CPD service-issue Beretta.

The prickling shiver running up Lucy's spine had nothing to do with the cold as she held her position against the cloistered cover of the giant Bosendorfer near the corner of the ballroom, but with the words rippling through the Lithuanian voices guarding the rotunda.

Giltine! Giltine! Giltine!

Lucy knew they were speaking of Alexis. Morell must've done what he said he was going to.

Or something else'd transpired.

And though it had nearly given her a heart attack, Lucy'd managed to grab the lighter that had been left on the Bosendorfer without signing her own death warrant by the wayward plunk of a piano key, the single sonic detonation of which would resonate through the semi-silence like a tolling bell.

She even remembered Morell's funny joke when one of the party guests had schmoozed her after her playing and offered her a cigarette to try to get her outside for some extracurricular activity and had been so befuddled by his own charms that he had left his custom mother-of-pearl Zippo on the piano at the announcement of Alexis' art auction.

Giltine! Giltine! They shouted, bringing her back to the moment. Lucy could hear the creaking of stairs, the rushed swishing of fabric, and the plastic muffle of gloved hands on machine guns. Whatever had befallen Alexis had diverted the assault teams and their well organized full-court press, and though she couldn't *see* them, soon it wouldn't matter because they wouldn't be able to see *her* either.

Now or never, she thought, just barely able to detect the scent of gas under the gagging of her velvet dress.

Clicking the lighter on, she gave it a practice heave and let it fly.

Her hopes of getting the lighter *over* the hefty bar had only been exceeded by her hopes that the Zippo wouldn't roll and click shut or flop to the floor and such negativity was completely and irreversibly obliterated by a surprisingly loud sucking of wind and the subsequently curling spires of blue-orange flames that promised unhindered destruction.

Lucy felt the heat nearly immediately and grabbed the two bottles of vodka she'd procured from the bar as the plinking and crackling of glass began to rock the kitchen with dangerous diamond-like bits of shrapnel.

God forgive me, she thought, as she doused the front of the priceless antique piano with whom she'd instantly fell in love and wished to play everyday for the rest of her life with a bottle of *Zakon Krzyżacki* vodka and hunched near the cluster of the stool and the legs, where rollers had been attached to both, to shift the piano in position to catch flame.

With the conflagration of the kitchen, and the cold funnel of the open service door through the linear space of the mudroom, Lucy squinted against the sweat-provoking heat and the welcome light it provided.

As the tip of the Bosendorfer caught flame, Lucy's feet slipped to halt the rolling momentum she'd created and shoved, from the core of her guts, to redirect the awe-inspiring piano to the spreading picture frame of a target, and once acquiring her target, sent the flaming piano off toward the rotunda with a stiff push that caused her to lose balanced and skid across the ground.

Lucy watched, from her belly, for a scant second as the rush of oxygen stoked the rippling flames of the seemingly motorized grand piano and swept them back into the uncovered cavity of the strings where she'd left another bottle of vodka to leak like a time fuse.

Then she pressed herself up and rushed to the

nearest slain former Spetznaz security guard to commandeer what looked to be a Forty-Five caliber Sig-Sauer P-TwoTwenty.

Since she'd already qualified for Sig-Sauers, Berettas, and Glocks on the range, she hadn't been the least bit worried when the newest interim police chief wanted to replace all of the Department's Forty-Fives for Nine millimeters to the dismay of many beat cops.

And all that didn't matter a damn as she wrapped her fingers around the durable all-weather coating of the grip and felt the tacky sandpaper-like polymer mix with her sweat and adrenaline and grip her back.

Lucy dropped the cartridge to see an unadulterated row of solid brass and copper, and knew she had eight well-placed man-stopping shots if she needed to before any sort of plan B had to be addressed, and rushed after the piano to anticipate its gratuitously explosive impact against the *Tree of the World.*

Swinging wide of the north side of the house for a panning view of the car lot, which he was ready to unleash his intense focus upon to find the stray he felt had evaded the wide net of his rifle scope, Ridley Sorber cursed when he heard the frantic calls to save Alexis.

Through the rush of voices clogging up the comms he heard something disconcerting about *fire,* and his hollers back to establish some semblance of order and figure out what was going on to administrate a strategic outcome were obliterated by the panic that had taken hold of his men.

Sorber ordered the chopper to return to the roof and immediately saw the nearly white splash of heat split the otherwise reddened angles of the mansion, made so by the thermal-imaging goggles, which divided heat into a light spectrum image.

"Hold it!" Sorber ordered and required the pilots to lower the Sikorsky and land nearly two hundred yards from the grand entrance.

Sorber kicked his compact frame from the chopper bay in a dead run after grabbing a go-bag of grenades and slinging them around his shoulder, having two rounds in his rifle and the comfort of a Nine-millimeter pistol at his hip.

Sorber felt the immense thrust of gravity slap at his back and buffet his shoulders, trying to knock him over as the chopper powered up and desperately shot toward the roof.

His unnatural sense of focus was on the louvered windows and the foamy-white crackling of the fire that seemed to be engulfing the kitchen past the ballroom, but the Lynx stopped and raised his rifle studying the hot and pale streak of something else consumed with fire flashing across the louvered window slats toward the hollowed space of the rotunda.

It was being pushed by the heat signature of a human shape.

FORTY-SIX

Both Krančjar and Jaroslaw had rushed up the stairs to catch their squadmates with a pair behind them each, leaving only two soldiers of the eight deployed inside the mansion on the ground floor, and had nearly reached the door to Alexis' room when Lomonosov, one of the two men sweeping the backside of the ground floor, reported the gas fire in the kitchen.

Halted by indecision and paralyzed by the possibilities of *who* was capable of performing such destruction under the perfection of their sweep and the complete absence of any life in the ground and first floors, not to mention the incredibly broad and coverless terrain *outside* the mansion, Krančjar stopped near the balustrade as the others surged past him for the door.

Krančjar called out to Sorber, garnered no response over the swirl of voices stacking the comms, and cut his own comm.

He strained to listen for the chopper and the cracking of the flames at the same time, but the disconcerting voices of his squad mates echoed through the door as Jaroslaw heroically doused the flames burning the Mystery Queen to a crisp, leaving a thick bunch of men in and around the door, stunned and static.

The crackling staccato of gunfire whipped

Krančjar's head around.

But by then he could only see the blur of a green humanoid shape charging his way and the simultaneous star of washed-out green light emanating from the tip of a concussing pistol, shells rapidly ejecting from its shakes and squeezes with snaps and pops.

Krančjar raised his MP-Five to get a shot off, flicking his thumb on the side of the gun from single-shot to three-round burst but the man, who'd launched his attack from an open door behind the cluster of men half-in and half-out of the Mystery Queen's room, had already sent six or seven bullets downrange to devastating effect.

The man leapt headlong at Krančjar.

The muscle and bone of shoulder and skull crashed against the MP-Five and the hands that so tightly held it, sending Krančjar to his heels with an uneasy and incorrigible wobble as he still attempted a shot to kill.

Three rounds spat from the machine gun and bit into the floor, and the recoil of another three misaimed bullets pushed Krančjar over the edge.

The sensation of falling was nothing new to Krančjar as he was a trained paratrooper, but the sickening separation of losing all control of his equilibrium and knowing that his untimely end would be a harsh and unforgiving permanency, filled him with incredible fear as every shape flashing across his green night vision goggles became one in the blender of a gravity-bound death.

Morell didn't know how many of them he'd killed or even hit with his wild volley of shots into the plugged up funnel of Alexis' door, and couldn't stop to think about it, grabbing the *Tree of the World* with his right hand as he vaulted over the edge of the balustrade, muttering every form of curse he knew at the pain taking dinosaur-sized chomps at his ribs. He holstered his gun with a firm leg hold on one of the *Tree's* many climbable angles, and took one last look at the door to Alexis' room and the empty hallway, and then back down at the body of the assault team soldier that would never rise again.

Morell heard shouts from inside the room, masculine *and* feminine, and was sure he was about to be distracted by the horrid screech and wail emanating from Alexis' throat but his vision was diverted by the swell of light zipping across the hollowed diameter of the rotunda like a medieval siege weapon.

Shifting his position with great difficulty in the darkness and the pain to remove himself from the line of sight of whatever soldier still drew breath on the third floor, Morell watched in awe as the Bosendorfer Lucy played so well hurtled across the slick floor, and, like a shopping cart, knocked the side of the *Tree* sculpture and twisted to the right to skid into the hallway leading to Sergei's wood-paneled watch museum.

Shocked and dismayed, the blonde Lithuanian named Jaroslaw held what remained of Alexis in his arms.

He'd been the first to rush into the room, cast his MP-Five aside, and douse the flames at the risk of his own safety.

At the sound of gunfire he'd turned to see four of his men hit the ground, and his soldiering senses were torn asunder by his duties.

It would all be for naught if their ancestral ruler by right of blood was dead.

Jaroslaw hoisted her traumatically burned body in his strong arms, throwing darting eyes to the splintered doorway, and rushed to the French doors of the balcony to spread them wide with a swift kick.

Alexis coiled and twisted in his shelf-like grasp against the stinging cold of the night air and whatever spillover came from the chopper. A wounded moan resonated in her belly and drifted through clenched teeth.

Jaroslaw knew it was an involuntary sound, something that she had no control over.

The tight frown of one trying not to cry stretched beneath the black mask of Jaroslaw's balaclava, as her charred and tattered dress, once so stunningly perfect, had become smudged and stained with ugly maws of black burn marks, as if a tar-like cancer had eaten through the pure white fabric of a bride awaiting her beloved.

And her face, it was hard to look upon without contending against stomach turning bile.

Her dramatically silky curtain of auburn had been reduced to an ashen fray of singed clumps, and the puffy and fire-wrinkled redness of her heat-sore skin bore more in resemblance to the rippled husk of a baked tomato than the beautiful complexion of Baltic royalty he so eagerly waited to gaze upon with pride.

He told her he was sorry as he climbed up the lattice-work to access the roof, but knew she could not hear.

The Mystery Queen was hopelessly caught between the land of the living and the dead, and if she did, by some chance, pull through, then the otherworldly pain of her existence would fall upon the world like a meteor storm from which there was no escape.

And as Jaroslaw held her close and rushed toward the chopper, she wriggled with the whimpers of an injured child, cast into delirium by clawing throb of third degree burns.

Though he was not in charge, Jaroslaw made the executive decision, holding the reticent pilots at gunpoint, to abandon his squadmates, his Captain, and rush south along the freeway to find a city the EMP blackout had not reached in order to save his royal leader.

If there were consequences for such course of action, Jaroslaw decided as he slid the doors of the Sikorsky shut and wiped the sweat from his forehead with a backhand, then so be it.

Lucy counted seven shots and knew they were from Morell's Beretta from her time on the range.

She wanted to shout to him so badly, to reach out to him and clasp his hand, and would gladly carry him out of the fiery grave one dragging step at a time as the building collapsed behind them if she had to.

He was so close, she could nearly *feel* him, and her heart leapt inside that he was alive, but yet, he was still so far away, and the distance between them was a hollowed-out division of darkness, of shadow soldiers shuffling and sweeping around blind corners for the kill, and the time-fuse of carbon monoxide poisoning promising to impartially extinguish any and all parties involved after prolonged exposure.

Throwing squinting vision to the door of the grand entrance, and its blank openness of frosty night air, then to the hall in which the flaming Bosendorfer was lethargically rolling, and back, Lucy popped up from her enclave on the left side of the ballroom opening and sprinted across its exposed face to baseball slide to the right corner, twisting to her belly as she did.

In a flash, she allowed her eyes to track up the staircase with the passing light of the fire and she thought she saw the monkeyed shape of a man clinging for dear life to the *Tree* but couldn't be certain.

Of the man on the floor, however, she was certain, and his night vision goggles and MP-Five tempted her with departing the safety of her cover but the reward of patience outweighed the rash risks, despite the fact that she'd gain an irreversible sense of clarity with the grainy-green goggles.

Lucy'd never been so enticed to flirt with danger in her whole life.

But, reason prevailed. Whoever was left in the house would be caught in the frenzy of the fire she'd started for such a purpose and the sabotage that had so devastatingly skewed the assault teams plans, capped by Morell's silencing of the attempted *Giltine* saviors with his Beretta.

She was sure he was the one holding on to the *Tree*. He *had* to be.

But she waited, and didn't call to him, telling herself there was a creature on the prowl darker than the night from which said creature came, and it would take everything she had to gain a tactical advantage over a man who, with his thermal goggles equipped, truly could, *see through walls*.

Lucy stood and decided that if she was going to die, she was going to die fighting alongside a man she just might've loved beyond explanation, for it was such love that caused people to do such strangely irrational and heroic things.

Lucy bolted for the stairs and the fury of adrenaline surging through her veins overrode that sixth sense of survival she'd built up during her time in Vice, thus, negating the consciousness of certain death aiming at the base of her spine through the open frame of the grand entrance by way of a sniper's scope.

FORTY-SEVEN

The moment The Lynx held his breath to fire the first of his last two armor piercing bullets into his female-shaped target, having followed the faint heat of the shape that'd pushed the flaming mass across the ballroom, through the rotunda and beyond, was the self-same moment in which the slick black of the Sikorsky helicopter uncharacteristically rose from the roof to fly towards him at dangerous speed, and like that, over his head and off into the slate gray smoke of the night sky.

Sorber tried his comm but it had been severed, cut off or *turned* off, without *his* go ahead or authorization, and in the gutting isolation of a child being left by their parents, Sorber's yellow green eyes swelled with distraught apprehension and irreparable abandonment.

For an orphan, who'd finally returned to the family of his dreams, the definitive blood ties and sole identity of a man who carried so many false ones, there was no worse feeling in the entire world.

It was as if everything had been a lie, everything he believed in, and Sorber tried his comm one last time, more of a hopeful prayer than a cursing whisper, as the last blinks of the Sikorsky's landing lights were swallowed up in its ascension to the misty clouds.

Sorber turned back to the scope and saw nothing but the aggressive pink of the kitchen fire to his far left and knew he was too far out for the registering of any

human shapes with his one chance gone and slid the
rifle crossways around his back, on top of the grenade-
laden bag, letting the demonic wrath of being left
behind by the royalty he'd given his life to protect and
kill for consume him.

And once he'd killed *everyone* in the mansion and
watched it burn to the ground, he'd track down Alexis
Maksmillia and whomever she'd convinced to abandon
the team with, severing the comms and departing as if
she had no part in the operation named after her alter
ego, and kill her too.

No one crossed Ridley Sorber and lived to tell
about it.

No one crossed The Lynx.

Sorber removed the Nine millimeter pistol from
his hip and bounded forward in a loping jog, placidly
surveying the thermal-reddened façade of the grand
entrance as the heat signatures began to divide
themselves behind it as if he had some sort of alien x-
ray vision.

Lucy had reached the crown of the second
staircase when she called for Morell.

"Lucy!" She heard him shout back and knew he
was hanging on to the slick limestone *Tree* as if riding
out a hurricane.

Her slippery steps ended on the third floor and
she squinted down the iron sights of her Sig-Sauer in a
looping arc that took in the hall to Alexis' room and
beyond.

She flicked the safety and oddly jammed the thick
pistol in the waistband of her underwear.

"Come on." She reached over the balustrade,
fumbling in the darkness.

The smoothness of the ivory-toned *Tree* sculpture
slipped against her clammy, sweat-smeared skin, and

she knew if she could only *reach* Morell, and hold on tight, she'd be able to help him, as any cursory grip would fail.

Lucy pulled back and wiped her hands against the thighs of her nylons and stretched out again, as Morell had clambered up.

"Henry…" She reached.

"Lucy, duck!" He shouted and she crumpled in a ball as Morell's gun whipped from its holster and shattered her ears with a snapping concussion.

Lucy twisted her head in her huddle against the flimsy safety of the balustrade to see the stunned-stiff body of an injured soldier who'd tried to rise from his leaking of life for one last battle fall helplessly to the ground.

Morell's bullet had speared the space between his eyes.

Lucy was quick, wordlessly regaining her composure to help Morell over the tangled slickness of the *Tree* sculpture not meant for climbing.

"Thank y…"

The gratitude was stillborn in Morell's throat as a volley of light speed Nine-mils spattered around them, howling past the fractured cover of the pale *Tree* to bite into the wood of the third floor's edges and right angles.

Lucy grunted to heave Morell's arms toward her, slipping on the wood in her nylons, skidding to anchor her weight against the balustrade and finally strained to drag his legs over the sharpened slickness of the sculpture for a flopping launch over the waist-high handrail.

Splinters and shards of detritus flicked and zipped through the air as another stifling shower of shots tattered maddeningly around them.

Morell heard shouts of Lithuanian knifing through

the ground floor and it took everything within him to catch his breath.

Lucy's left hand was hot on the right side of his face as he lay on his back, fighting for control of his lungs.

"Come on," She said, and it occurred to him in his slushy mire of physical pain as she helped him up and saw her belly button and her breaststroke-slimmed physiology, that she was lacking the purple velvet dress he'd purchased for her.

God knew how...

Her skidding steps were quick and she pushed him into the first room she saw, kitty-corner to the mouth of the stairs, shutting the door.

"We've got about two seconds." She said, drawing the Forty-Five from the small of her back. She assumed he had something left in his Beretta but couldn't calculate how many rounds in the buzz of the moment.

The intensity of her focus was on *Morell*, himself, who he was, his safety.

She couldn't see him in the heavy murk but she knew he was gone, spent, exasperated.

But something *beyond* that was broken within him.

As if he'd been violated.

"We can't hide." He wheezed. "We should..."

"We're *not* splitting up." She nearly growled, cutting off his weak and pathetic attempt at speaking.

Lucy chanced a thought at his condition, far beyond the physical. It was as if he'd been transformed into a mumbling, despondent teenager, slump shouldered and heavy.

He was spent.

"Then...what?" He asked, no longer in charge. "We're out...gunned."

"Then we make our stand *together*. There's only two or three more of them. If we can get one of them, we can get their NVG's and get out of here before the carbon monoxide gets too bad."

"What about the…Order?" Morell's smoker's voice was merely a faint breeze in the dark and static landscape of the blackened and windowless room. Shapes were with them in the room, shapes of softly rounded objects and musty-smelling angles.

It was as if his voice had no tone, no definable musical *note* and Lucy shoved the pain that it caused her to hear him so destroyed further down into the gaping arms of her heart.

"They're on their own." Lucy nearly barked with a hushed whisper, moving Morell away from the door. Certainly the Order was not without their sins and it took two to make a fight. She was not about to risk her life for them and hoped for their own sake as human beings they'd give their own safety a shot.

But her hope was hollow.

Her faith, however, was fully activated on Morell's behalf, and she truly believed they could make it out.

Alive.

She tried to sense where the bullet-spitting soldiers were and how many of them were left but between concerns for Morell and wonders if they would change their tactics, her brain was just about spent.

"Blood and guts and a little bit of danger…" Morell muttered.

The Lynx, detecting the stifling sourness of butane gas and carbon monoxide already drifting through the air, stopped as the remaining two soldiers, Lomonosov and Bauskaite, rushed up to him in the broad space of the rotunda.

"What the hell?" Lomonosov hollered. "Comm's gone and the chopper too!"

"And there's a burning piano blocking the other way." Bauskaite added, wondering how such came to be with the befuddlement of one so committed to the drill that any alteration to it would shake his confidence.

"It's okay, we've had a change of plan, but we're *still* on track. Don't worry about the chopper and we don't need comms. We're all that's left anyway." The Lynx lied, knowing he'd be the only one escaping the mess alive, and that, to close the situation off so that he would be in control of his *own* revenge, seeing how the Mystery Queen never meant to exact revenge but had always designed to throw the noose around his neck and pull the floor out from under him, he'd work out a plan with the remaining two soldiers and then pull the same reversal on them.

Perhaps it was just fury, though, blind rage at what'd befallen him and it was somehow reasonably *half*-right, and it was really the CPD cops that'd caused all the mess.

But that was laughable, especially with former Spetznaz guarding Veremecek.

The Lynx shook his scrambled head. Too many thoughts, not enough tactility, not enough stimuli.

The men before him waited for a response.

Veremecek. Kill the Order. Kill everyone.

Kill.

The Lynx looked behind him at the open door of the grand entrance and knew that if the fire went unchecked, the entirety of the house would catch and burn.

So the plan formed itself on the spot, standing in the stretched and rounded tube of the rotunda, the pale *Tree* making its symbolic presence known near the staircase.

After all, it didn't really matter if *Alexis* had screwed him or the *CPD cops* had foiled the plan, they'd all die in the end.

All of them.

It was the natural course of life, and The Lynx promised himself that somehow, some way, he'd make it the purpose of his remaining days to end theirs before his own time clock ran out.

"You two go up to the third floor and scan room by room. They're up there somewhere, there's no way out."

"Who?" Lomonosov asked.

"The CPD CRT cops undercover here. They don't think like soldiers and they weren't under Veremecek's guidance. They're smart. Be careful."

"Right." They nodded between themselves.

"Here." Sorber gave them a few grenades, just for grins, not that he cared.

His plan was already rock solid. Air-tight. Amusingly so.

"Use these if you need to."

The soldiers were eager to accept them. Their spiking adrenaline had gone through the ringer with the unexpected twists in the controlled dispensation of their planned assault and this was their reset, with a new battle beginning, a new chapter of warfare.

"What will *you* do?" Lomonosov asked, the de-facto leader of his shrunken unit of two, including himself. In a way he subliminally felt The Lynx's detachment from them and their mission, but was so consumed with the gravity and prestige of his orders as a follower shoved to the place of leadership that he couldn't quite put two and two together, and even if he did, he might end up with twenty-two instead of four.

But if he could, he would've shot The Lynx

himself.

"I'm going to stay here by the basement door and make sure no one comes out." The Lynx said, grabbing Krančjar's MP-Five from his twisted body, ignoring blood and brain matter sticky on the floor. "If they do, I'll get them. Be quick and we'll get out before the air becomes too bad. Hurry up, go!"

Lomonosov nodded and tapped his squad mate on the shoulder to begin their controlled ascent of the stairs, with The Lynx watching their heat signatures glide up the heights, all the while sneaking into his pouch for grenades.

And when the two remaining Owls had reached floor three and steadied themselves for their tactical sweep, the huddle of their fallen comrade's bodies reminding them of the danger they were dealing with, The Lynx expertly lobbed the first of two grenades their way, and did not turn to jog from the house till he'd spent nearly all the palm-filling explosives in his bag by tossing them in each balustrade-guarded level in the house and watching the splattering flares of white they caused spike his blood-red thermal vision.

The sound was unreal, reminding him of the canon fire concussions of Tchaikovsky's Eighteen-Twelve overture, and smirked at poetic justice of such a song capping the Order's demise, rolling a frag to the door of the basement as he ran from the cacophony of searing hot explosives and dust.

If anyone *could* escape the obstacle course of hell he'd hand crafted as a result of being sold out and left by the one he trusted, then, by The Lynx' fatalistic view of life, they more than aptly deserved to live.

The Lynx then took a few seconds to scan the parking lot with the dismantled mansion falling apart as gravity saw fit behind him and chose an appropriately black BMW Seven series in which the driver had been

outside of the car when shot. He casually removed the
keys from the driver's pants pocket, and formulated
new plans in his mind as he tossed the rest of the
grenades in the car lot from the space between the lot
and the mansion before he sped off into the cold black
recesses of the night with the explosive roll of thunder
ripping apart the car lot with successive blasts of
bloated red-orange at his back.

FORTY-EiGHT

Lucy could've told herself it was an earthquake, a simple shifting of plates with the determinate outcome of reparable structural damage, but that would've been wishful thinking.

The first detonation nearly knocked her sideways in the chilly void of the room with an enormous jolt of energy, bruising her patella in the process, and once she'd caught her balance, heading toward Morell's darkened mass as he ushered her to the corner of the room, the second detonation sent them both sprawling to the ground in an ungraceful heap of body parts.

Couches leapt from their weighted positions and slid across the floor. A heavy oak table flip-flopped toward them with a whooshing whistle, end over end as if dropped out of an airplane.

Wood and drywall compressed and puffed across the room in a blinding flash of white-orange, searing the air with dusty splinters and zinging metallic fragments, and Morell moaned as he stretched for the corner of the room, dragging Lucy with him.

He tried to shield her scantily-clad body with his own, though his own felt inconceivably spent and deflated, and the pain in his side cursed him with every breath.

It was as if a volcano of construction materials was erupting inside of the rotunda instead of molten lava, and the explosions continued on and on, mindlessly and innumerably in their sense-consuming magnitude, rattling the massive frame of the house like a gale-force wind to split glass, crunch and shred definable right angles as if made of paper and cardboard and spew metal fragments into the gaping black maws that had been created in their absence.

Deafness plugged Lucy's ears with a flubby *boom* directly below them, as if she'd been dunked underwater, leaving her with the lingering drone of returning pitch and the whiny drawl it carried.

Then the floor gave way.

Lucy felt her mouth open in a wordless scream meaningless to her own ears as the floor tossed her up like a rag doll, where she lost all semblance of equilibrium in the lightless confusion of their exploding prison.

The floor that'd thrown her up had split under the strain of deadly force and a rush of dirt and dust sliced at her wrists and elbows like the violent crash of seawater on a rocky shore.

Her weightless hovering seemed to end as soon as it began and a strong grip secured her fall away into the endless darkness in which the definable shapes of shorn drywall and furniture had been made foolish and frivolous, as if hand-carved credenzas and bureaus had been merely boxes of scattered toothpicks and randomized sawmill castoffs.

Lucy coughed at the black smoke beginning to twist through the artillery-sized holes gnawed and clawed through the mansion with the gross inefficiency and mindless hatred of ambivalent destruction.

"I got ya…" Morell strained, huffing and puffing and Lucy's legs dangled in the air for a foothold, searching below her through the jagged maze of tears and spreading spits of fire.

"I'm okay, Henry…let me go."

"Hell n…no!" Morell strained, feeling as if he held on for one second more his arms would fail him with tattered and unlaced sinews slipping out of their sockets, and Lucy would helplessly plummet to the ground floor, hitting God knew what on the way down like a pinball smacking whatever wanted to smack back.

"No, I'm good." Lucy took hold of the charcoaled teeth of the floor. Morell's grip was slickened with the slime of having fought for his life and she told herself to think fast.

Window. Find a damn window and jump the hell out of it.

You can live with a sprained ankle but you can't live without oxygen.

"Do you see a window?" Lucy asked, looking up to him as she hung limply on the edge of the floor of what had once been the room they'd ducked in to hide from the soldiers that'd been blown to bits.

Lucy chanced a glance down. The spreading jungle of detritus and sure death flickered and fizzled below her with small fires and choking smoke.

*We've got about two seconds…*Lucy reminded herself, and it seemed more of a prophecy than an evaluation.

"Yeah," Morell gasped. "Next room over."

Lucy strained for it and saw the telltale shape of a louvered window, colored bruise purple in the black, holding what appeared to be a static pose in a nearly undamaged room, the *nearly* being that half of it was completely blown out and had fallen through the second floor where bitter septic fumes were mixing with burnt insulation and lacquered wood.

By the time Lucy shimmied across the dangerously jagged teeth of the ledge, making sure not to take any undue risks, the smoke was boring into her gray-green eyes with an unstoppable vehemence. It was as if the unhealthy air had sought her out and wanted to take refuge in her lungs in the way an invading army wanted to capture a city fortress, and she could only imagine how hard it was for Morell.

Almost there...

Lucy pulled herself up, so thankful that she'd forced herself to go to the pool three days a week, first thing in the morning, no matter how much she felt like sleeping in, and her new role as Lieutenant had tested said schedule changes with an unbending temptation, and she'd sadly continued her regime for vanity's sake, not wanting to get fat, unaware that the strength of her twelve mile a week swims had saved her life.

And Morell's.

In the confusion the Forty-Five'd freed itself from the band of her underwear at her back and she gave herself half a second to catch her breath before moving to the window and sliding it open after finding the clasp to the interior louver treatment.

It was as simple as opening a cabinet door.

The not so simple part followed.

"Ladies f...first..." Morell offered, sucking in the fresh purple-black oxygen as if the window were a respirator mask sealed around his muzzle.

The cold night was shockingly refreshing, and to inhale its crisp clarity was to awake from a nightmare.

Quick, quick, quick...the other side of the house is still burning.

The Fire Department ain't coming to this one.

Lucy stared down at the three stories and kicked herself out to hang from the ledge.

"Looks good all the way down..." She said, spotting three windows. The bottom two'd been blown out and she didn't want to cut her feet.

"Go…" Morell leaned on the window. "Go get the car. You can't help me. If I make it I make it but there's no other way."

Morell handed her the keys, the clink of which sounded like a pitiful wind chime.

Lucy's face was grim in lieu of his proposition and she looked back to him, framed in sickly darkness in the small, insignificant window against the pale eminence of mansion's exterior.

"Get your ass down here double time soldier." Lucy ordered, and touched her tiptoes on the crown of the second story window to begin her precarious descent. Chancing a drop to the damp turf on the first floor, she landed with bunched knees as they'd trained her, back in the Academy, even though they'd stipulated the technique was for jumping fences.

Fundamentals had a way of staying in Lucy's mind.

The chilly moistness of the spongy grass immediately began to soak into her nylons to make her steps slippery and sloshy and Lucy threw a glance to Morell's nearly timid exit from the window.

She didn't want to leave him, but saw he was making his way out, tentatively, at the behest of his own physical pain. The black smoke of the kitchen fire and the fallen-tree limb-like crackling of its slow consumption of the capacious structure provoked a series of hawking coughs from the CPD Lieutenant and she rushed on, steering clear of the blazing heat, trying to ignore the madness that had so quickly plunged Crescent into its Atlantis spiral.

After all, she was a public servant and a crime-fighter, a life-long citizen of the city whose undue false responsibility for its safety had lead to a steady diet of unfulfilled nights returning home from *work* and the dread of the morning after.

She was a slave, and no matter what she did, it would never change. People would come and go, but *it* would never change, the great mound of steel and glass, the corporate coffin ensconced in the trophies of its many conquests. And Crescent, well, Crescent was dark now, off in the distance, but it was dark to its core and always had been, its very cornerstones had been avarice, ambition, and the bludgeoning cadence of a salesman's pitch.

She didn't belong anymore.

Lucy slipped into the GTO and fired it, glancing behind her at the ugly effects of the fire and put the car in gear as her eyes panned to the burning wreckage of the car lot to her left.

Her bottom lip sucked itself in past her top as she thought about the wealth of riches that had died of cowardice in the basement and how, no matter what, they were beyond savable.

Like the citizens of Crescent they were take-charge go getters, full of the bristling pride of life when the tides were good and the status was quo but when the bough broke and chaos cracked the air like a lion tamer's whip, the long-buried fears of self-preservation's interminable loss of control worked its silent assassination within the fragile scrambled eggs of their minds and left them hollow in their moment of decision.

Lucy's flicked on the headlights and nudged her shivering foot into the gas.

The GTO slapped clods of damp turf behind it as Lucy urged the car around the side of the mansion with dangerous speed where she half expected to find Henry Morell precariously dangling from a window, unable to reach the ground.

Instead, she found him *on the ground*.

Fallen.

From just one story? All three?

Muttering curses under her breath, Lucy threw herself from the idling shake of the muscle car and grabbed him by the shoulders, stirring him from a half-moaning state of frozen shock.

Morell's face was charred black with soot and the whites of his eyes danced left and right as if he'd been shocked awake from a fitfully gruesome sleep.

"I'm okay." He said with the growl of pushing himself up, but she knew he was not. Noxious fumes and toxic gasses stole clean breath from both of them and Lucy winced, slashing her hand in front of her face like a windshield wiper.

Henry Morell was near death and she pushed him in the GTO.

"Come on," She said, her voice barely audible over the sickening cracks and snapping pops of the mansion's digestion to the intensely greedy and all-consuming properties of flame. "Let's get you to a hospital."

And after strapping their shivering bodies into the leather seats, Lucy Radzewicz geared up the GTO and sped from the scorching hellhole of fire and death; this night, the gaping maw of the Underworld, leaving its scarring dance of bristling orange fire and face-melting heat in the ghostly darkness of the rear-view mirror.

ACKNOWLEDGMENTS

All thanks goes to God Almighty for His great and wonderful blessings and for His wise and eternal love and His perfect plan. So much can happen in the course of writing one book, all things work together!

Many thanks to my family for encouragement, faith, love, and support. God knows I need it!

Thank you Laura Gordon for such excellent cover artwork. You are a pleasure to work with and really outdid yourself with *Shatterpoint Alpha*!

Thank you proofreaders and pre-screeners for your much-needed help and valuable opinions and contributions. You saw this story built from the ground up and I hope you are as blessed with holding the final product in your hands as I am!

Thank you to all those real, living, everyday people who provided me with so much inspiration. There is no story without characters, and there would be no *Shatterpoint Alpha*, or any other book, without all of you!

And thank *you* very much for reading!

The tale continues in *Shatterpoint Bravo*.